I0772733

Transcend
Book Two of The Celestial Wars

A.N. Fox

To my parents who would brave the Hinterlands for their children

This book is considered 18+. For full list of trigger warnings please consult my author webpage or Instagram for more details.

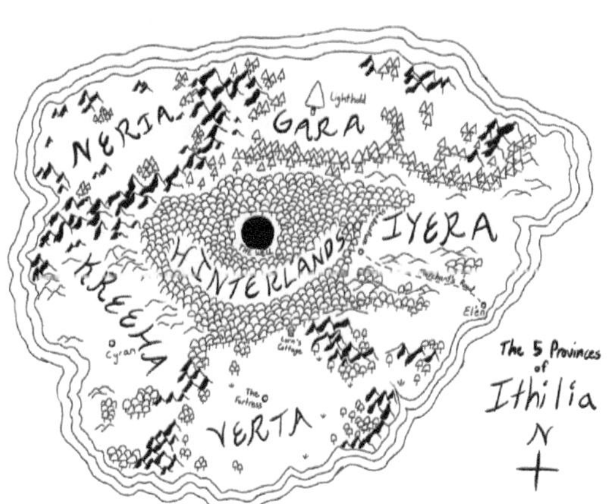
NERIA
GARA
Lighthold
IYERA
KREEHA
HINTERLANDS
The Well
Tradesman's Road
Elen
Cyran
Lara's Cottage
The Fortress
VERTA
The 5 Provinces
of
Ithilia
N

Prologue

In the beginning, the Goddesses and Gods ran rampant with their power. Their magic flowed through the world, and they reveled in it. Over time, they grew bored with one another; their magic grew dull, their power brought little joy to their lives. One of the Goddesses, Cretia, dug a fathomless depth in the center of the world. She searched within herself and found her divinity sparkling. She gripped it, enticing it forward, coaxing it with soft words until it formed within her hands. It was brilliant, the color a mixture none had seen before. She cradled it close to her body and with a toss of faith, threw a pebble of her essence within the chasm.

It fell.

The light dropped and dropped, never hitting the bottom. Cretia peered over the edge. The light eventually came to a stop. It was alone at the bottom of the chasm, the faint light swallowed up by the commanding darkness. The magical light needed more. Cretia showed her brothers and sisters her creation and persuaded them to step forward to donate their own kernels of magic. They lined up, each excited for the results that brewed beneath the earth. The Goddesses and Gods who grew tired of their immortality, bored with each other, gave a part of themselves. The chasm of magic grew and swelled. As its depths filled, the colors eddied, swirled, and shifted, the magic conjoining with each new gift. The magic multiplied and grew in abundance, the amorphous kaleidoscope filling the enormous cavity.

The Goddesses and Gods stood around the edge silently observing their power.

Satisfied, Cretia strode forward. She walked on top of the chasm, her graceful footsteps causing small ripples throughout the pool of magic. At the center of the Well she reached a tanned arm down and grasped the magic below. It writhed in her grip. She molded it, pushing and pulling the magical substance. Her keen eyes narrowed in concentration, and she splayed her arms up to the crystal blue sky above. The magic burst forth and erupted. Tendrils of light punctured the sky and rippled below—a firework display of magic, in brilliant hues.

The magic left a mark like residual paint splatters. From each spray of magic, a faint stream of light wove together, an intricate pattern. The patterns grew and altered, the light wove back and forth until no darkness and no gaps showed through. It glowed, sealing itself together. The glow subsided and out of each block of light, a person filled the space. The Gods and Goddesses twisted their heads, looking at each person that spawned from their magic. Small grins overtook their faces, their thoughts of boredom drifting away with the setting sun.

1

"We have done it. We captured her, but I do not like what I see. She has been enthralled by Cruvo."

Nivet's private journal.

Aza was unbound, unchained. They did not fear her anymore. Her magic—gone. Not gone, but like a full bottle topped with a stopper preventing its release. They dosed her with an unknown herb mixture once a day at a scheduled time to prevent her magic from rising in retribution. They would rue the day it did. She already imagined her magic swelling and overcoming them, their quaint ship capsizing. Why bother keeping her chained when they were known to be the strongest and fiercest warriors? Aza had only received weapons training over the last few months; her skills were like that of a toddler compared to a Nerian warrior.

Despite the Nerians' polite disposition, she never let herself forget that she was surrounded by battle-hardened warriors. Instead, she cultivated her anger, keeping it fueled like a well-kept fire, the embers burning deep within her—an errant, stray spark could escape, one that could light everything up and devour them all.

How dare they kidnap her?

The taste of regret was bitter in her mouth as she reflected on Lilit's words, replaying on a constant loop when the ocean waves did nothing to quell her madness. *Do not trust anyone.*

Aza should have known better. If only she had not followed Anwin down that hallway. If only she held an ounce of mistrust in her body and listened to the warning bells that should have stopped her in her tracks. Warning bells muted because of her curiosity. Muted because she had misplaced her trust in Anwin.

Aza heaved a sigh and pushed herself away from the prow of the ship. She felt herself slowly going insane. Watching the relentless autumn waves smash in protest against their ship while diving into the free-fall of her mind wasn't helping the situation.

By her estimate, they had been at sea for three days. Three days and no sign of Cruvo. Aza didn't know what she expected. She thought he would upend the entire world to come looking for her. Their magics and their beings were in complete harmony, and now instead of having this aching emptiness it was...hollow.

Unable to contact him, Aza searched for him, but he was missing in her dreams. She didn't know if it was the distance between them, or her magic being tampered with, but she had not heard from him. Disappointment flooded through her, and she could only quell the overflow of emotion with what was familiar and easier to handle, her anger. Her fists clenched against the splintered railing.

With the Wyra ocean to her back, she turned and faced the rest of the meager crew—Xira, Anwin, the tall thin man who she learned was Reed, and Rune. Rune, the leader of Neria, who was inhabited by the god Nivet.

She needed to direct her anger at someone and Nivet stood on the opposite end of the ship, his face scanning the ocean. She stalked up to him. Aza didn't bother with the pretense of calling him Rune, she knew the god who dwelt within was called Nivet. Even though they danced this particular routine many times, she went through the motions, the predictability a soothing balm for her chaotic situation. The ability to argue with him helped to diminish her rising anger. She needed an outlet, and he was an easy target.

"How long will you keep me captive?"

Nivet sighed as he usually did when Aza demanded the same information. "As I have told you before, until you learn." Nivet didn't even bother to look at her, his eyes locked onto the churning ocean, searching for some unknown danger.

She pushed his shoulder, forcing him to turn and address her properly. He furrowed his brows at her and readjusted his stance to face her, a fire within his eyes. "Learn what?" Aza barked at him.

Usually, he would drop the topic and ignore her, unwilling to give into her unceasing demands, but this time a spark was lit and he decided to join her in their game of verbal battering. "You know nothing, Aza." He stepped closer. Aza damned herself as she yielded a step. The power flowed off him like the pounding of a waterfall and Aza was getting crushed beneath it. Was this how other people felt in proximity to her? Her deep-seated instinct wanted to roar and fight him—to battle with their magic together and see who would be left standing. However, with her magic stanched, she needed to be careful.

Aza saw his jaw clench. "You do not even know, what you don't know." Nivet scoffed and gestured carelessly at the distant province of Iyera. "Anwin and Xira told me."

Aza stood firm, not wanting to back down from the fight she craved. The fight she needed. "Told you what exactly? Told you to kidnap me?" she seethed. Her fingers curled in anger, wanting action, wanting to grab her dagger and plunge it into his self-righteous heart.

Nivet barked a dry laugh, his vicious smile cutting into her. "Do you even know what Cruvo is? Who he is? What he has done?"

Aza bared her teeth at him. "I know enough." Hadn't Aza already had those same doubts? They threatened to creep in, wrap around her, and pull her down into a spiral. She *did* want answers, but not like this, kidnapped and forced into a foreign province against her will.

Nivet's eyes hardened, and he shook his head slowly. "You have no idea who the God of the Hunt truly is." He turned back to the ocean, dismissing her.

Aza stormed away and faintly heard Nivet add, his voice drifting by her on the stormy autumn breeze. "And so you will learn."

Xira, Anwin, and Reed were perched around the ship, nosily listening to their conversation and rushed to busy themselves as Aza stomped their way. She glared at them and shouted, "What are you looking at?" The edge of the boat beckoned her, and Aza resigned herself to staring out listlessly at the endless Wyra ocean.

"Aza." Xira's voice cracked like a whip through the air.

Aza huffed a breath, content to stare at the ocean and ignore all these pesky Nerians, but she conceded and glanced over her shoulder to see what Xira had to say.

Xira expertly descended the ropes from the mast and leaped into an elegant crouch near Aza. "Let's fight."

Aza turned her back on Xira and responded with a brief, "No thanks."

"You have anger, rightfully so. And nothing better to do. Come spar with me."

Aza ignored her and let herself be hypnotized by the cresting waves. She wondered if a storm would plague their ship. The clouds gathered ominously, their purple and deep blue hues were cause for concern. The distinct sound of boots on wooden planks clanked behind her as Xira stood next to her shoulder to shoulder.

"Would you want to spar with this?" Aza stifled a gasp. Xira held out Aza's sword. The sword she thought was lost and left to gather dust. Unable to adorn it during the masquerade ball, she left her beloved, gifted sword in her room, naive to believe she would be returning to it shortly. The blade glistened from the small tendrils of light overhead, the iron and steel artfully intertwined, two pieces forming one.

Her prior experience sparring with Xira had gone poorly. The Nerian had expertly disarmed her and highlighted Aza's constant reliance on her magic. Her eyes flicked from the sword to Xira, her honey-colored eyes not a sweet entreaty, but a trap. They drew a person in believing there only to be kindness, and instead was swallowed alive.

Aza grunted her assent. She curled her fingers around the hilt of the sword and took her place among the only spacious area on board, the center of the ship. Up till now, she had only practiced within the safety of the El'en castle with stable ground beneath her feet and a trustworthy opponent. So much had changed. The ship rocked atop the tumultuous waves like some writhing creature underneath was displeased with the Nerians' escape.

Although Anwin, Reed, and Nivet didn't gather around, she could feel their prying eyes on her back. She squared off with Xira, the warrior's raven black hair, reminiscent of Lorn's, was swept back, her narrowed eyes coolly assessing Aza.

Pangs of regret struck Aza like physical blows, images of Lorn as they practiced their swordplay together flashed in her memories. The familiar comfort of her rage rose within. She should be with him, not with these foreign interlopers. Yet, her anger was hollow and empty. There was no magic for her to draw upon, but she still yearned for it.

Blinded by hope, she desperately tried to draw upon her magic and found it lacking.

Xira held her sword at the ready. Aza didn't bother waiting, instead she allowed her anger to fuel her. Xira met her stroke for stroke, easily deflecting Aza's attacks. The clang of metal rang out, providing the only sound besides the tearing of waves. They circled and slashed. Aza wanted to shout, both from exertion and emotion. She was fighting sloppily. Her side was exposed as she hauled her sword down in a giant arc to cleave Xira. The warrior dodged easily, parried, circled, a look of concentration and a trace of boredom lined her elegant features. Aza attempted another wild, undisciplined attack and Xira disarmed her.

The sword clattered on the deck, but the defeat did not slow Aza. No, she wasn't done yet. Xira wanted her to let off some steam, release some of her pent-up anger. She was the whistling scream of a tempestuous wind. She harnessed the anger to drive her forward and not let the humiliation of defeat stop her. Aza brought her fists up. Xira noted the hungry edge in Aza—the urge to fight and gave a nod in assent. She obliged and tossed her sword to the side, mirroring Aza, her fists raised and ready to brawl.

Reed discreetly grabbed the discarded swords and hauled them out of their makeshift sparring ring. Aza and Xira circled each other, assessing, waiting. The storm around them grew, as if in anticipation of the fight about to erupt. The unforgiving wind whipped around their faces. Xira's cloying honey colored eyes did not falter for one second, and Aza realized the begrudging respect she held for her. Xira would not hold back, would not treat her differently than so many others would. She would respect her as a proper opponent.

Aza steadied herself. She did not fear the Nerian warrior, rather she was hesitant over her own disappointing combat skills. For a moment, Aza was aware of Anwin, Reed and Nivet watching, their eyes transfixed to the duel. The very ocean itself seemed to hold its waves content to watch what unfolded on top of its waters.

Xira unleashed herself. She was fast and agile. Too fast. Aza was unable to keep up. The Nerian's movements were rapid, her feet following some internal dance only Xira understood. Aza could only block the incoming assault. She was unable to strike with any of her own hits. The blows were softened, but still struck true, and Aza faltered under the onslaught. Her body cried out in response, but Aza's pride would not let her yield. Not yet.

She was so damn fast. Too fast. Too agile. And she was still being pummeled with her lethal attacks, her fists pounded into Aza's face, chest, back, stomach.

From a distance she heard Nivet growl a warning, "Xira...enough."

But Xira did not yield. She saw the spark within Aza, the spark of the fight to keep going, and Aza would have been disappointed if she stopped now. No, Xira would not stop until Aza herself yelled yield.

She never realized how much she relied on her magic. Even when she trained with Lorn and didn't use her magic, knowing the powerful ability was there if she needed it had been enough of a crutch to not let her truly excel. She would always be held back by the untapped potential writhing inside her begging to be used. Although she would not deem being kidnapped and sapped of her magic as a fortuitous turn of events, she couldn't help but acknowledge how it forced her perspective to change on how much she relied on it.

If she could only land one punch on Xira, she would be content.

Aza focused her mind. She forgot about the metallic tang of blood in her mouth and the drips of blood running down her face. She pushed those thoughts aside, only allowing herself to be consumed with making contact with Xira.

Aza saw her opportunity and seized it. Xira left a brief opening on the left side of her face and Aza swung. Aza reverberated with the impact as her knuckles met flesh and bone. She was able to glance a brief flash of surprise on Xira's face, before Xira grabbed Aza's over-extended arm, used her hips as a fulcrum, and flipped Aza over her shoulder, and onto the hard, wooden deck. The air was knocked out of Aza in one swift blow, her eyes taking in the expansive sky above. Swirls of purple and cobalt were pulled around in violent streaks.

Aza tried to suck in a breath, but it came to her in wheezes. Xira's face popped into view. "Yield?" her unassumingly sweet voice asked.

Aza felt a flurry of emotions, she wanted to smack her, embrace her, beg for tutelage, yet she decided on nodding her head.

A sly grin crooked the corner of Xira's mouth as she extended her hand to help Aza to her feet.

Her breath came back to her in gasps. Aza begrudgingly took the proffered hand, her feet a bit wobbly. She couldn't help but give a responding grin, despite the blood dripping from her face and the bruises that smarted as she took a breath.

"Solid hit, Aza." Xira clapped her on the back. "You have potential. You just need more time and training."

"*Actual* training from a Nerian warrior," Reed interjected, shouting from the side of the ship, a good-natured chuckle following his proclamation.

Aza rolled her eyes and a flicker of approval flashed in Xira's. Anwin appeared beside Aza. "Let me clean you up a bit, I don't need your blood coating the whole ship because Xira is trying to prove a point."

Aza let Anwin lead, mulling over what she said. What point was Xira trying to prove? Anwin sat Aza down and pulled out a tiny chest. She rifled through it and faced her with bandages and small glass vials. She pushed her long red braid behind her back and situated Aza so she could properly treat her. Aza watched as Anwin wiped off the trail of blood on her face, from a cut on her brow. Anwin opened one of the tiny glass vials and poured some of the concoction onto a washcloth, dabbing the mixture onto Aza's wounds. It stung and Aza fought cringing from it.

"Why don't you..." Aza's question trailed off, unsure how to phrase her question without coming across as ungrateful.

While tending to another wound, Anwin finished the question for her. "Why don't I use magic to heal it?"

Aza nodded, curious to hear her response. Maybe they didn't have any healing powers?

Anwin paused from her ministrations and pulled back from Aza, her green eyes locking onto Aza's silver. She pursed her lips and responded, "Magic is power. It is strong and glorious. The problem with magic is people, Ithilieans, become reliant." She gestured to Aza, "Even you can see the proof in that statement." She added more of the mixture onto a cloth and softly wiped it on Aza's face, putting some on the myriad of bruises starting to form. "We Nerians are trained from birth to not rely on it. We are not against the use of our magic, but we know what it is. It is a force. It is a power. One you can't wholly control or believe you have the right to. Who knows? Maybe tomorrow we all wake up and our magic is gone. Our people need to learn how to survive with it and without it. The magic was never truly ours to begin with."

The sincerity in Anwin's tone caught Aza from responding with an acerbic remark. Her magic was hers and it belonged to her. Why bother with rejecting your magic or not utilizing it all the time?

Anwin paused waiting for a response. When Aza remained silent, Anwin brushed her hands against her pants and gave a sigh. "This is not the time to get philosophical. My point is, we believe in being well-rounded. Having other items in our arsenal to use. These tonics and medicines we crafted from the plants in the mountains surrounding Neria. We have studied their properties, and these can heal you as well, without being exhausted or depleting your magic." Anwin stood and gathered her supplies back into the tiny wooden chest. With her back to Aza, she looked over her shoulder adding, "Plus we pride ourselves on fighting. We believe you don't truly learn from your mistakes, your wounds," her eyes gently roved Aza's body taking in the multitude of wounds she just endured, "if you heal it. You must live with those errors and improve upon them next time." Anwin left to help Reed with another task on the ship.

With the bitter autumn storm approaching, the ship was taking the brunt of the waves. Aza couldn't help but admire the teachings Anwin described, but thoughts of Lorn being abandoned in El'en swooped in. Her admiration turned sour in her mouth like eating a fruit one thought was ripe, but it turned out to be rotten instead.

Aza instantly wiped off the unconscious smile that had crept into her face. She sat up and marched over to her discarded sword and clenched the hilt, cursing herself at her guard being let down so easily. These Nerians wormed their way around her heart. Their words were misleading, often causing her to have hope in what they offered. False. Everything they said was false. Their actions belied their words. Aza hated how she was lulled into a false sense of security.

A scream of frustration died in her throat. She had a sword in her hand. She could have attempted to stab them, threaten them, take them hostage. Her lack of effort at escaping weighed on her, her shoulders sagged in defeat. She had only been at sea for a handful of days and she was already cracking a smile with the enemy.

Restless anger at herself and those around her caused Aza to rise onto her feet and storm away to the edge of the boat. The waves tested her balance and footing, but she didn't care. Better to be swallowed up by this wild ocean than to have camaraderie with her captors. She reached for her magic, like an item of comfort meant for a child and found it still missing. Instead an aching hollowness rose up to greet her and she fought the tears that threatened to break. Better to embrace the warm heat of anger, than the bitter taste of her tears.

Her thoughts of retribution quickly changed to thoughts of Lorn. She knew the grizzled hunter would fare well without her, but she missed his company all the same; his steadfast guidance and loyalty. Beyond that, he was someone to share her musings with. It was something she sorely needed and missed. At least Lorn was safe back in El'en.

The night she was captured flashed before her in rough-cut snippets. Her following Anwin down the hall. Instinct telling her to do otherwise. The pitch-black room. Reed bursting into the room and a confused looking Lorn accompanying him. Her on the floor pinned by Xira. Lilit refusing to help. The faint prick from Anwin's hand to hers, the intrusion which caused her magic to fail her.

Since her capture she replayed the thoughts one by one, like reading a storybook page by page. She flipped through them, trying to dissect what happened. What went wrong. This was not a time for emotions, rather a cold detached viewing. One she would learn from and one she would pay back in kind. One image she couldn't erase from her mind was Lorn rushing forward in a panic to help her. His thoughts were focused solely on her. He failed to use his years of training to protect himself. For someone with his skill to be caught unaware due to her poor judgment caused Aza's teeth to grind together, her jaw near locking from the pressure she exerted.

She replayed the memories again and again, but she couldn't let herself stray to Cruvo. The god who inhabited Lord Aldrich's body. If her mind veered to him, she would crumble. While her magic was muted, so was her connection to him. No more dreams with him in it. Her body ached at the sudden isolation. She had grown accustomed to meeting him at night. Their dream meetings forced her to hone her magic and were a general outlet for stress she gathered throughout the day. Aza couldn't dwell on his possible reactions to her capture. A thread of hope wrapped itself around her heart and pulled tight; he would stop at nothing to get her back. Without her magic she felt useless, unable to find a way back to him, unable to banish the

Hinterlands and free him, returning him to his body.

She tempered the inferno of her anger. She would hone the fire, like a blacksmith using the heat to forge a sword from the iron. Aza would do the same. She would exact her vengeance, return to Lorn and return to Cruvo. The battle-hardened Nerians wouldn't stand a chance against her wrath. She would feign complicity for now—it wouldn't be hard—and work towards her freedom.

Forcing herself to uproot her feet from the scuffed, wooden boards beneath her, she headed back to her small cabin below deck and climbed into her net bedding. With how small the ship was, she doubted anyone had an actual bed on board. Everyone was too practical to want something of comfort on their rough journey. The swaying motion did nothing to soothe her as she attempted to sleep. Only the banked embers of her anger kept her warm against the onslaught of the autumnal storms. The ship rocked violently like her thinly veiled emotions.

~

The seemingly perpetual storm clouds did not relent the following day. Aza helplessly paced the deck like a caged mountain lion. She refused to offer a hand to her kidnappers and instead stood by, her anger rolling off her in waves. No one bothered to make conversation, too busy keeping their ship operating with only the four of them. They were constantly running back and forth scurrying to the next task needed. When the Nerians had a moment of brief respite, they would have conversations in hushed tones, deliberately keeping Aza out of the talks. She felt the pointed stares and discreet glances.

Near evening Aza had a hard time discerning the time based on the dark clouds obscuring the skies. The clouds finally broke, bringing heavy rain down upon them. The water droplets were thick and weighed her down, drenching her cloak and clothes. Aza was thankful she wasn't stuck in the gown she wore to the masquerade. The Nerians had supplied her with clothing upon her capture. She ignored the irritation of wet clothes against her skin and let her head loll back, her arms outstretched welcoming the deluge. The storm was an echo to the torrent of emotions roiling within her and she welcomed the chaos of nature. She reached for her power again, a vain attempt, yielding a fruitless result. She fought back the curse that rose, her spirit wanting to manipulate the water around her and use it to play and form. A part of her was silenced, restrained. She vowed she would spend every second to unchain it, unleash it. In this moment, she felt a small pull to her origins. The chaotic nature that swirled around her was calling to her and she was returning to its comforting embrace. Completely lost to the storm, Aza was not aware of her body, nor of the wave that caught the ship. Carelessly standing near the edge of the boat, her balance faltered, and she tumbled down into the frothy water below.

Aza struggled to breathe. The water slammed into her; her body collided with the side of the ship. She sputtered as another wave hit her. Salty water filled her mouth. Aza tried coughing, but another wave crashed into her. Her body was being pummeled as wave after wave overtook her. Her arms floundered briefly above the surface. Aza sucked in a ragged gasp of air, and she was sucked underneath. She needed air. Her lungs burned. Disoriented, she had no idea where the ship had gone, and she imagined hearing distant voices shouting somewhere around her.

Pushed under. She was being pushed under.

With no grip for her legs, she kicked and helplessly moved her arms. It was too much. Everything was too much. The weight of her clothes, the sudden tiredness of her body. Her cuts and bruises from sparring with Xira. Fatigue set in, and a faint inkling spread through her body.

A whisper to give up. She couldn't. There was so much to do, and she needed to return to Lorn.

Before she could kick above the water, another wave crashed into her. Blackness filled her vision as she succumbed to the demanding ocean. It wanted her. Who was she to fight such a request? With only a shred of consciousness remaining, she sank under water. It was not peaceful, the water beneath as raging and chaotic as the waves above. Her mind dimmed as the heaviness dragged her down to the depths. Then a voice, one both ancient and slippery wrapped itself around her. Panic flared through her numb body. Not them. She couldn't let them have her.

"Daughter of the night, I have searched for you. All are searching for you." Eonas' voice was like the cold tendrils of seaweed that brushed against her legs. She recoiled from it. Despite her fear, she could not get her body to respond, the impending blackness overtaking her. "Curious to find you here. You are difficult to trace. Where is your magic, Daughter of the Night? Why is it shrouded and hidden like the fish that cower in the depths of my darkness?" The voice paused, like they were thinking about Aza's capture. "No matter. You are here now in my ocean, and it is time for you to belong to me."

Unbridled anger flared throughout her body. Aza fought the inevitability of unconsciousness a moment longer. She belonged to no one. Eonas, the Nerians, even Cruvo thought they owned her. She belonged to herself and would not be used. Only Lorn supported her and did not use her for his own ill-gains. He was her true friend. Aza didn't know how far she had sunk into the ocean, her eyes closed in defeat, but with this sudden declaration her eyes flashed open in rage. She wanted to speak, to yell, to fight against the Eonas' words. Her lungs burned with the lack of air, her vision tunneling to a single speck of water.

Suddenly, strong hands gripped around her, and she was yanked up. Her eyes could barely remain open with how fast they jolted up through the dark water. The purple storm clouds greeted her as she broke the surface. A wracking cough sent spurts of ocean water from her mouth. Her savior's arm around her remained firm. Her eyes stung from salt water, and the heavy rain obscured her vision. Even the wind whipped around them, blurring Aza's sight further. Shouts dragged away by the wind were lost to her ears. Her shoulders drooped from the weight, but those steady arms only gripped her tighter.

Aza was swiftly lifted, and other arms clasped onto her, dragging her on board. She flopped onto the deck, grasping the rough wooden planks underneath her fingers. More coughs wracked her body, her body rejecting the ocean water she inhaled. Eyes stinging, she tried to peel them open and see what was happening around her.

Nivet crouched beside her, his steady head a warm weighted reassurance on her back. He was soaked, rivulets of water dripped from his clothes and puddled onto the deck of the ship. His eyes were narrowed in concern, the color changing, flickering between warm brown and bright gold. The familiar boots of Xira, Anwin, and Reed circled her. She spewed more sea water. Silver coils of hair flopped in her face. Her body throbbed in pain.

"Daughter of Night, you will not escape me so easily." Eonas' voice was a soft whisper cutting through the torrent of wind and downpour circling her. "I will take care of your captors and then you will finally come to me."

All of the icy water and depths of the Wyra Ocean she had experienced so far did not chill her bones until now. Aza felt the sincerity of the threat. Her throat was raspy as she attempted to warn the Nerians around her. Her captors, yes but right now they had a common enemy, and she would not go defenseless to this God of the Sea.

"Watch...out." Aza's voice was rough and only one person caught what she was trying to say. Reed crouched down, his lips slightly downturned.

"What did you say?"

Before Aza could utter her warning again, all four of the Nerians stood to attention. Something in the distance caused them to grip their weapons.

"Say goodbye to your captors, Daughter of Night. They will not live to see the next day," Eonas confidently proclaimed.

Nivet reached his arm down to assist Aza as she scrambled to her feet to witness what everyone else was watching. The ocean parted effortlessly. A large wave cleaved the ocean in two. It wasn't the wave that made Aza gasp but the giant fins that followed the curve of it.

"Darkness below, what is that?" Aza rasped.

"It's a fucking sea serpent," Xira answered.

2

"Aza is gone. I cannot feel her anymore."
  Cruvo's private journal

Lorn paced in his opulent room for the fifth time that day. He needed to do something, to go somewhere, to put his restless energy into action.

They hadn't found her. No clues to her whereabouts. No clues as to where those backstabbing Nerians had taken her. His fists clenched, the nails embedding into his palm. He never should have trusted them. Guilt and anger fought for supremacy within Lorn's mind. The prior week he had torn himself apart from the guilt that bombarded him.

Flashes of that night knifed through him, lancing apart any shred of self-control he had. Blindly following Reed, trusting him because he had saved him from Brafter. No, Reed had only silenced Brafter to save himself and aid in his own malicious plan. He should have questioned it, questioned the timing, but he was so lost in the moment to think clearly. Seeing Aza pinned beneath Xira, her surprise as Lorn sprinted into the room. Where was her magic? She could have easily disarmed and destroyed all of them in the blink of an eye. He had seen it before. Why couldn't she use her magic?

The days following the masquerade ball and Aza's capture, were a combination of sheer luck and people wanting to return to their own respective courts. Everyone failed to notice the absence of Aza and the Nerians, most too self-absorbed in their own return trip to pay it any heed. Cruvo swore his advisors and Lorn to secrecy. If word got out of

Aza's disappearance, the province's leaders would immediately begin conspiring, potentially jeopardizing Cruvo's secret rescue mission.

Most visitors packed up immediately and left the following day, but a few stragglers lingered trying to reap any remaining benefits of the Iyerian castle. He couldn't speak freely about Aza's capture with other people occupying the castle. Through Cruvo's smooth talking, he was able to usher the remaining people out, preventing Lorn from throwing them out himself.

During that dreaded night, the marble floor was cold upon his cheek as he woke to find himself with a splitting headache. The chill of the floor was nothing compared to the ice in his veins when he realized his friend was stolen. Only thoughts of vengeance and violence filled him as he imagined Aza's capture.

However, a small sliver of reason had pierced through. Lord Aldrich was actually Cruvo. A god's power was at his disposal to find his friend. He couldn't dismiss that advantage. The Nerians must have had some sort of foul power on their side to nullify Aza's own magic.

When he found the Nerians, he would restrain them while Aza stripped them bare with her restored power. Although he had an aversion to the death and killing of people, for *her* vengeance he would turn a blind eye and allow her this retribution.

Lorn loosened a string of curses and picked up a glass vase, his arm cocked to throw it. Only a moment of clarity forced him to return the vase to its table. His anger was fruitless. It needed an outlet.

After her capture, he had trailed Lord Aldrich, relentlessly questioning him, urging him to utilize him, to send him out to hunt for Aza. Lord Aldrich had refused, instead requesting Lorn to be patient. Lord Aldrich, who Lorn had to remind himself was the god Cruvo, was as unrestrained as Lorn. Although he cautioned patience, Lorn doubted Cruvo followed his own advice—his face failed to mask the anger roiling beneath. Lorn knew Cruvo was as eager to find Aza and save her from the clutches of the Nerians.

After finding Lorn in the abandoned room the following morning, Cruvo had escorted Lorn to his private study. With an ironclad demonstration of self-restraint Cruvo ordered Lorn to go over everything that transpired that night. His face betrayed nothing, but Lorn was skilled at reading people. Just like any beast, people had their tells. He didn't fail to notice the white-knuckled grip Cruvo had on his chair, the tic in his jaw, the cold icy stare—a stare promising revenge. Unbridled fury brewed beneath the surface and one small touch could unleash it upon the world. But Lorn couldn't heed his instincts to let it lie. Instead Lorn riled him up by asking questions, demanding answers, demanding action.

In a night of desperation, he sought Cruvo in private, unsure of who knew of the god hiding in the guise of Lord Aldrich. Not bothering with pretense, Lorn demanded, "I know you have a connection with her. In her dreams you can see her. How have you not received answers? Help her!" he pleaded. Begged

Cruvo hissed through clenched teeth, "I can't. My connection with her is gone, like it has been tampered with." He clutched at his forehead, roughly brushing through his waves of brown hair. "I will let you know if I need help. Direct your energy elsewhere. I don't need it right now." Cruvo dismissed him and Lorn had paced the extent of the El'en castle.

Why was he even here? What was the point? He did not require approval for where he went. He needed to get her back—his friend who trusted him, believed in him. The image seared in his head of Aza pinned to the ground like some common thief. He shook his head, trying to rid himself of it. Even countless hours in the archery range and the training room left him wanting. What was the use if he wasn't actually accomplishing anything?

A knock at the door brought Lorn racing to it. There might be answers. He wrenched it open. A servant handed him a slip of paper and scurried off. Lorn opened the folded paper and broke the seal, a gold embossed ocean with the sun overhead.

After reading the note, he crumpled it, and hurried to meet Cruvo in one of his countless studies. Ever since the revelation of Cruvo within Lord Aldrich's body, he stopped calling him Lord Aldrich in his head and instead used Cruvo. It was confusing at times, but he pushed on, refusing to call a man who wasn't anything other than what they were.

Abandoning discretion, Lorn yanked the door open only to find Cruvo hunched over a table scanning a map of Ithilia, eerily similar to his first encounter meeting Lord Aldrich and his advisors. "Any news?"

Cruvo barely raised his head in acknowledgment. "No. Nothing."

Lorn couldn't help the slump of his shoulders, acknowledging the defeat. Each day Aza was farther away, held within the thrall of her captors, and here they were chasing their own tail, achieving nothing.

Cruvo held up his hand, pausing what was about to be Lorn's long-winded tirade about their lack of effort. "I will explain this once. Do not interrupt."

Lorn bristled at the command, his mouth opening to argue.

"I keep you here in courtesy due to your valiant efforts in retrieving Aza from the Well. Do not mistake this for kindness." His eyes flashed with a hint of green and Lorn fought the instinct to take a step back, to retreat from this powerful being. He was not dealing with a MagicBlessed man. No, he was dealing with a god of old.

"We have not found Aza. Nor will we." His fingers traced the delicate boundary lines of each province. "Our strategy is weak. They could be hiding and traveling anywhere within the five provinces. However, I believe their end goal is to enter Neria." His fingers drifted over to Neria on the detailed map, his fingers tracing the mountain range protecting the isolated province. "We would waste our efforts trying to track a wisp of smoke on the wind. Instead, we could find the source of the fire." His hand clawed as if he could pluck Neria from the map and crush it within his grasp. "My guards will be stationed around the key entry points of Neria, waiting for their moment to strike."

Lorn nodded, it was a solid plan even though it chafed at him to play the waiting game instead of striking and hunting them down. "When can you send me to the Nerian border?"

"I won't be."

Lorn's fingers instinctively clenched around the hilt of his sword. He couldn't help himself as his venomous words spewed out each word clearly enunciated, "What do you mean? I won't be?" A challenge. A threat.

"I need you elsewhere."

"I am not your hired soldier, nor do I even belong in the province of Iyera. You do not command me."

Cruvo advanced to Lorn, stalking him like a predator. "You are very bold considering you speak to a god.

"Psh, some god *you* are, inhabiting someone else's body."

Cruvo scanned Lorn up and down as if finally finding a worthy opponent. He smirked, "You have the backbone I am seeking. Where I am sending you will provide information to help Aza."

Lorn fought the urge to leave the room, but planted his feet on the floor and drew his shoulders back regaining his self-control. "Where?"

"I need you to go to Gara and spy for me."

He withheld any snide retort, shock getting the better of him. He never expected Cruvo to mention that province. "To Gara? I am no spy." His mind went to Brafter, his body left in the storage room where they had fought. In the chaos after Aza's disappearance, it went unnoticed. No one stepped up to claim the errant spy and Cruvo barely cared about the revelatory information. He simply shrugged his shoulders and ordered his men to clean up the mess.

"You will be attending as a guest in their court—an ambassador."

"Why Gara? I would be more help searching for Aza on the Nerian border."

"You met Lady Rasmina. I have suspicions."

"Suspicions?"

"Yes, something nefarious is happening and I need you to find out what it is and report back to me."

"Then send someone else." Lorn turned and stormed back to the door, intending to leave this city once and for all.

"This will help Aza." Cruvo's words were like stones dropped in Lorn's stomach. They caused him to pause, his hand hovered on the doorknob.

Without turning, Lorn barked out one word, "How?"

"The information you uncover could save Aza. Knowledge is power. We need the knowledge of what whispers I have heard."

Reluctantly, Lorn turned back to Cruvo. "What do you mean save Aza? She is in the clutches of those Nerian swine. How could traveling to Gara save her?"

"When we save her, she will still need to destroy the Hinterlands. Gara might be doing something to inhibit it."

Lorn marched back up to Cruvo, his face right next to his, fingers itching to clasp the hilt of his sword and run him through with it. "The last time she tried to destroy the Hinterlands, she nearly died and so did we. And you want to subject her to that again?"

Cruvo didn't flinch, completely unbothered by Lorn's closeness and the rage brewing beneath.

"We are more prepared. We can banish it."

"Fuck. You." Lorn was done with this conversation, he needed to leave and find Aza on his own. A blast of wind sent him sprawling against the opposite wall. The fierce wind clasped around his throat and tightened. Cruvo took his time, strolling up to Lorn while he hung suspended against the opposite wall. His eyes hardened and another flash of green passed through, the god hiding underneath this fake exterior. "Are you done with your little tantrum?"

Struggling to form words, Lorn gasped out, "No." His legs kicked against the wall behind him, struggling to hold himself upright, the power holding him both strange and foreign. "Aza is not a tool for you." The words were thick and clunky as he choked them out, the air tightening on his windpipe.

"Do not mistake me. I care for her and will not let her come to harm. We need to be prepared. We need the Hinterlands banished so I can return to my physical form. Protect her." Cruvo's voice firmed, his eyes locked onto Lorn's with a grim announcement. "War is coming."

3

"I do not understand how, given her history, she has fallen for Cruvo. He does not deserve her desire. He deserves her unbridled rage."

Nivet's private journal.

Everyone scattered on deck, ropes pulled, weapons gathered, and Nivet took his place at the helm of the ship. The storm raged on, the wind whipping Aza's silver hair in her face as she watched, frozen to her spot. Only the sea serpent's fins appeared above the water, while the body was hidden beneath the dark, tumultuous waves. It was still only a blip on the horizon, but it gained speed, aiming right for the boat. Aza didn't know where to focus her attention, on the giant creature swimming towards them or the flurry of activity on deck. These Nerians would die a gruesome death. It was inevitable.

"Nivet, we need to face the sea serpent head on. Steer the ship over here," Xira shouted against the raging tempest of the storm. Her face was overcome with a fierce resilience. The face of a captain facing an insurmountable battle.

"Anwin, take your position on the crow's nest." Anwin didn't wait for further instructions. She grabbed her bow and arrows, her balanced footsteps ran effortlessly over the rocking and tilting of the ship.

"Reed, you and I will fight up close. Grab your axes," Xira barked out her commands and everyone fell into place, including Nivet. Aza was surprised that he listened and deferred to her. Reed's once jovial face was changed with one of grim determination. He disappeared below deck and returned with two battle-worn axes in each hand.

Reed and Xira stood side by side in the middle of the ship each keeping an eye on the sea serpent as it converged toward the boat.

"Nivet, be ready. We will need you to shadow us."

Jolted by Xira's declaration, Aza found herself sprinting to Nivet's side, sloppily climbing the few steps to the helm. She didn't understand how the rest of the Nerians navigated the boat so gracefully during this storm. Her body protested every move, her lungs burned, her bruises smarted, but she needed to place those pains aside. Right now, she needed to survive this encounter.

"Nivet!" The god barely looked at her, but Aza spotted a hint of gold flash across his eyes. "Use your shadows."

Nivet gripped the helm and steered through the turbulent waters. Aza thought he would ignore her command until he finally answered, "I will be using them."

Her eyebrows furrowed and her heart began to beat erratically. "You used your shadows to get me out of the castle in Iyera. Use it now to get us out of this place." Aza's voice cracked hysterically. She could not go to Eonas and be used, not with her magic dulled.

Despite the storm and the sea serpent heading their way, Nivet turned to face her, his face a mixture of emotions. "Don't you think if I could have transported us all the way to Neria, I would have done so by now?"

Aza clenched her teeth, anger thrumming through her. "I don't try to understand the thoughts of my captors."

He shook his head in disbelief and a hint of defeat, "It does not work that way. Also, we are Nerians," he added. His voice was level, unconcerned with the impending threat of the sea serpent headed their way. "We do not run from a fight." Nivet saw the shock on her face and his eyes hardened into resolution. "We will fight. Either way, we will either live or die." His head swiveled back to the sea, a silent dismissal.

Aza couldn't believe what Nivet said. They were fighting an impossible battle. *Stubborn Nerians.*

Xira shouted up to them, "Aza, we could use a hand if you want to make yourself useful."

Her fingers curled in on her palms, the nails embedding in her skin. A small slickness coated her palms. Blood. She would help if she had her magic, but no they stole that from her.

As if anticipating her retort Xira added, "There are other ways to fight without your magic."

Abandoning her spot next to Nivet she ran over to Xira. Xira took in her seething disposition but didn't allow Aza to speak. "Tell us what you know," she demanded quietly. Her head inclined towards the impending sea serpent. "Why is that attacking us?"

Aza pursed her lips, trying to figure out how to best condense the information and simplify it for them. If it came down to a choice between Eonas or the Nerians, Aza would rather take her chances with them instead of being sucked into the watery depths of Eonas' lair. "The god Eonas wants me. When I fell into the water they were able to sense me again. They seek to destroy you with that sea serpent."

Xira nodded, her features unflinching in the face of such terror. The warrior addressed her with respect. "They will try not to hurt you." A grim smile crept over her face. "You will be both our bait and our shield." It was an order, but a thinly veiled question lay hidden beneath in the lilt of her voice. If Aza chose to help, that's how she would be utilized.

"Why would I help you?" Aza needed to voice the question, and not let them think she was at their beck and call.

Xira shrugged, her attention focused solely on Aza. "My Lady, I know the fury that roils beneath your skin. You *should* be angry at us. But would you rather be subject to the fickle god Eonas, or join your fellow Nerians in a battle to the death?"

Aza bristled at the words.

Xira's hand reached out to grasp Aza's upper arm, a firm squeeze of solidarity. "You are more than just your magic."

Time was up. There was no more talking, no more time to strategize. The beast was here, and Aza was unsure how the Nerians were not quaking in pure terror.

The sea serpent emerged from the water rising to survey its next victims. Its body was sleek and blended in with the rest of the ocean, a wash of blues and whites swirled together to allow it to mimic its surroundings. Like all beasts, it was a unique mixture of pure strength and raw beauty. Giant, needle-like teeth filled its cavernous mouth, and it snapped its jaws as a warning to the ship and its crew. A fin protruding along its entire back was a near transparent blue with a sheen similar to other fish and sea creatures. Its giant body was coated in scales, each one shimmering, each the size of Aza's body. Two luminescent-blue eyes took in the meager ship and Aza's eyes trailed to the back of its head where two horn-like features crested the top of its head.

The crew scrutinized the creature while the sea serpent stared sightlessly. It was a moment of brief calm despite the torrential downpour occurring, along with the black clouds blotting out any semblance of daylight.

"Last chance, Daughter of Night. Come with me and let me kill your captors." Eonas wasn't physically present but their voice magnified around the boat. Everyone heard it.

The sea serpent made no move, waiting on unspoken orders from Eonas.

Struggling to find her voice amongst the creature in front of her, she finally shouted back, "I am not something to be used."

Reed and Xira looked at Aza with a flicker of pride on their faces.

"So be it."

Free of its restraints the sea serpent plunged under water disappearing from view.

"I will have you one way or another, Daughter of the Night Sky."

Xira looked to Aza giving her one final command before racing off to the edge of the boat with Reed. "Try to stay near us. The sea serpent will hopefully be hesitant to attack us if you are near." Aza couldn't help but glance up at Anwin in the crow's nest, and Nivet at the helm of the ship. "Do not worry about them. The beast will be too distracted to get Anwin, and Nivet can protect himself." With those last words of guidance, Xira and Reed ran to opposite ends of the boat searching for the sea serpent hidden beneath the water.

In a tangle of supplies, ropes and barrels Aza found her longsword and gripped the hilt as if it were a lifeline. This was the first time in her life she had fought without magic, and secretly it terrified her. She relied on it. It was who she was to her core and it provided comfort to her, a presence that was always with her. Not today. Today she was alone and would have to help defeat this beast without it.

The sea serpent remained under the water, viciously circling the ship. Nivet gripped the wheel attempting to steer the ship out of the cyclone the beast was causing.

"Don't get trapped in the whirlpool it's creating, or we will all be dead," Xira warned from her side position on the boat.

"Understood, Captain," Nivet gritted out. His hands tightened on the wheel straining to maneuver the ship into a desirable position.

"Anwin, when that serpent reveals its head, you go."

Aza's eyes followed the giant mast of the ship with Anwin perched in the crow's nest, her bow readied with an arrow. Gone was the friendly redhead and in her place was a focused warrior with only one goal. To survive.

Once Nivet cleared the encircling body of the serpent, the serpent's head pierced through the water, eyes enraged. It released a guttural cry searching for the elusive ship. The boat shook from the feral roar and Aza tried to steady her feet. The ocean was in a fury, the waves hitting the ship sideways, the wind and rain continuing to rip her skin apart. She forced herself to tune out the chaos and allowed herself one steadying breath. Everything began to dim. Not a dimming of disconnection, but rather of awareness. Of connecting every piece of her body together with her mind, to operate as one.

Anwin wasted no time when the sea serpent's head emerged, letting arrow after arrow soar through the air. Each one embedded deep into the monster, despite the relentless wind. Aza could barely acknowledge the impressive feat, one Lorn would be proud of, because the sea serpent attacked. It searched for the thing causing it such damage and narrowed in on Anwin. Aza's stomach tightened. Anwin had no protection up in the crow's nest, she would be easily swallowed up. The sea serpent realized the same thing and its head darted forward to take down its prey. Anwin kept her focus, releasing arrow after arrow into the beast, not letting her impending doom slow down her attack. At the last minute, her hand swerved up and the sea serpent smashed its face into an invisible barrier. No, not a barrier, a thick wall of wind. It acted as a shield protecting Anwin from the attack.

The beast lay unmoving whether from being briefly stunned or from surprise Aza didn't know. She fought back a cry as she spotted Xira and then Reed jump off the side of the boat, both wielding their weapons, Reed with his dual axes and Xira with her longsword.

Sprinting to the side of the boat to check on them, Aza couldn't help but curse their stupidity. Jumping into the water with a sea serpent and the storm seemed like lunacy. But Aza couldn't find them. They were gone.

A vicious roar shook the planks beneath her feet and Aza scrambled to look up at the battle overhead. Xira and Reed were both on the back of the sea serpent their weapons embedded in the beast's body. They repeatedly hacked at it while the beasts flailed, forgetting about Anwin in the crow's nest. The serpent reared its head back, attempted to bite them and get them off its back. Before it could engulf them both, shadows swallowed them up and they were back on the ship next to Aza.

Their breathing heavy, Xira barely spared a glance. "Use your sword will you?" she admonished wryly as she and Reed raced off to the beast's exposed belly floating near the ship. They stabbed and sliced. Blood sludged onto the boat, but the beast was only briefly deterred. The damage was not enough to dispel the creature.

It retreated from the ship and reassessed its attack. It had gone in expecting an easy meal but found one that would not go down without a fight. The sea serpent's head was still exposed and Anwin let her arrows fly, not wasting any time.

"Daughter of the Night Sky. Your fight is fruitless. They will all die. Come now and I will spare them." Eonas' voice wove around the ship, enticing her.

Before she could respond, Nivet cut in, "Eonas, stop your games. She will not be going with you."

A sound similar to a hiss filled the air, "Nivet, why are you here? Have you finally left the sanctuary of your mountain?"

Nivet's voice was firm as he said, "You will not have her Eonas, and even if you did she would never bend to your will."

"While I won't be able to kill you Nivet, I can kill your mortal body. I know how much you prize your MagicBlessed people, but they are little more than chattel."

Distracted by the talking, Xira and Reed leaped off the ship again and Nivet loosened an enraged scream shadowing them to the stilled sea serpent. They landed on its head and hacked away at the beast. Xira slashed her longsword and stabbed one of the beasts' eyes. The sea serpent reared its head and opened its giant mouth, hoping to catch its victims. Xira and Reed fell off its head, falling straight down into the turbulent waters, where the beast's body sat coiled and writing. They were going to die.

Before she knew what she was doing, Aza climbed the netting bringing herself up to the crow's nest. Anwin never tired, continually shooting arrows into the beast, hopeful that one lucky shot would fell the beast.

Xira and Reed were both still in the water, not surfacing. The sea serpent lowered its head into the water, its sharp teeth snapping. In a matter of moments, it would have both of them. Between the coils and its giant mouth, they were in a desperate situation.

Without looking back Aza shouted, "Nivet!" Her feet clambered to the swaying crow's nest edge. Amazed at how Anwin was able to keep steady in this small swaying enclosure, she stood tall and leaped off hoping Nivet understood her plan. Aza fell through the air, her longsword pointed downward. The ship's wooden planks loomed closer and closer as Aza fell.

She clenched her teeth as she descended, the planks on the deck looming in her vision.

Before her bones shattered on the deck, shadows encircled her and she felt a pull in her gut. She was transported to the open sky and the ocean felt like leagues below her. The sea serpent was tall. No time for panic, Aza fell through the sky with the sea serpent's head looming just beneath her. She was free falling.

Her sword jarred in her hands and her knees buckled under the fall. She was on top of the sea serpent's head, the jutting black horns near piercing her chest. Her whole body protested in pain of the intense landing, and she fought to keep the longsword in her hand. The beast immediately rose back up to its full height, abandoning the search for Xira and Reed in the water. Aza fought the grim smile that rose to her face, at least she had saved them for now. Free from the serpent's trap, Xira and Reed were shadowed back onto the ship's deck, dripping wet still clenching their weapons.

The sea serpent writhed back and forth, and Aza could only hang on as the sea serpent battled the sword embedded in its skull. It wasn't enough, they needed to attack it more. She clung to the sword fighting the serpent's head flinging back and forth trying to get her to release her hold. Its deafening shrieks of pain almost forced Aza to cover her ear.

The sword was loosening bit by bit and Aza would be flung from the creature. Aza clutched the hilt and when the sword tip loosened from the skull, blood burst forth. Aza's footing faltered under the writhing beast, but before she could be thrown off, comforting shadows enveloped her transporting her to the ship. She tumbled next to Xira and Reed, both dripping water, their faces set in grim determination. She wanted to recoil from the fierceness in their faces. Here were the Nerian warriors of legend.

"We need to pierce the underside of it. The head was a good hit, but I think it is too protected. One last shot," Xira stated. "Anwin! Keep shooting." She gripped Reed on the shoulder beckoning him to follow her to the helm next to Nivet. Aza made to follow, but Xira stopped her. "I need you up with Anwin. She needs to be protected while shooting her arrows and I don't think her magic will hold out much longer."

The ship lurched and boards splintered. The sea serpent's body writhed in pain and each hit caused the boards to loosen. Even if they survived, Aza didn't know what would happen. Their ship was being destroyed, and if Eonas has their way, their bodies would be floating among the carnage and debris in the ocean beneath them.

Aza lost her footing as the ship tilted under from the sharp flailing of the sea serpent. Xira somehow remained calm, her footing planted to the boards beneath her. "Aza now. There is no time." Without a look back, Xira sprinted to join Reed and Nivet at the helm of the boat. Nivet's eyes were narrowed, sharpened taking in the surroundings as if searching for a sure escape that wasn't there. Aza could see the inevitability of their defeat, why couldn't everyone else? They might defeat the serpent only to be left to the wild ocean and autumnal storms.

Her legs pounded against the boards, fighting the urge to teeter over as the ship lurched underfoot. She scrambled up the netting, sword still in hand. She could protect Anwin. Anwin who had protected Aza from the depths of Eonas before. What felt like ages ago back at the castle of El'en. Anwin had tackled her, preventing Aza from swan diving off the cliffside into the beckoning sea below. Yes, they were her captors, but she could fight to the death alongside them, because at the very least they deserved that. They were fighting Eonas alongside her, they were worthy of one last fight together.

Hand and foot fought to hold on. Climb, higher, higher. The crow's nest bobbled more precariously than before. Anwin fired, her shots hitting true each time. The tiny projectiles seemed unable to make a dent in the giant monstrosity, but she still shot one after another, never faltering. Never letting her fellow warriors down.

Reaching the top, Aza heaved herself over the side and took in the sight below. Thick red blood gushed out of the sea serpent, and the ocean below was marred with it—the waves a mixture of briny salt and metallic blood. Finished with its agonizing movements, the beast was more enraged as it looked for something to maim. It scanned with only one eye, the other dripping blood down its face, the slash marks courtesy of Xira's longsword. The serpent began to recede into the water, aiming to capsize their boat.

"Anwin, do not let it retreat! We will not survive if it goes under water," Xira shouted with her remaining energy, the command of a captain.

Anwin took one steadying breath and reached for her remaining arrow. The wind howled around them, the fat raindrops splattering across Aza's vision. Her arrow nocked, Anwin aimed and fired. The storm seemed to pause, and time seemed to slow as Aza tried to follow the line of the arrow. Just before the creature's head submerged into the depths below, the arrow plunged into the serpent's good eye. In pain and panic, the sea serpent's head reared back up, blindly snapping in retaliation.

The crow's nest was minuscule and with barely any room for Aza to maneuver she pushed Anwin down. The edges of the crow's nest provided a weak level of protection from the beast's snapping jaws. Anwin's knees hit the ground hard, breath whooshing from her chest as Aza stood her ground, feet planted. The sea serpent's needle-like teeth stopped barely inches from her face, held frozen by an invisible tether. Aza wanted to cower, her head so close to the beast's mouth. It couldn't hurt her. Xira was right. Eonas didn't want her harmed. Aza stepped forward to protect Anwin.

The beast strained against the invisible leash. Its serpentine tongue swerved around Aza and went to scoop up Anwin. The tongue looped around her and before it could snap its head back up to gulp down Anwin, Aza raised her longsword and swiped down hard and fast against the creature's tongue.

While Aza dealt with the sea serpent, Xira knelt along the prow of the ship next to Nivet. Reed took a running jump off of Xira's folded hands as she vaulted him into the air. Shadows transported him to the underside of the serpent, now fully exposed. The shadows released Reed parallel to the soft underbelly of the serpent, his momentum pulled him forward and down as his twin axes ripped into the serpent. Down dragged the axes, ripping apart the soft flesh. The beast tried to pull away from the ship, but Xira had other plans.

Following Reed, she launched herself off the prow of the ship, shadows transporting her alongside Reed. Her arm pulled back, the longsword primed, she stabbed the sword through the beast's chest. The sea serpent was composed of more blood than sea water and roared a last defeated wail, its body unwinding back into the torrential sea from where it came.

Before the creature's final breath, it did not go calmly. Its body smashed and convulsed in one last attempt to kill the inhabitants onboard. The ship cracked and splintered, wood burst, and water seeped onboard. There was no time for rest, no time for victory as the body sank into the deep, turbulent ocean. The ship gave a final groan, the battle was too much. The water rushed in, and Aza couldn't focus on what was going on below. They needed to get down from the crow's nest.

Frantic shouting and hurried commands carried on the wind from the deck below.

"We need to go," Xira ordered while running to grab Reed alongside her.

Nivet worked the wheel of the ship, one last futile attempt to get the ship to safety free of the writhing sea serpent's body smashing into them. It was no use, they had taken on too much water. Its writhing subsided as the last of its life finally drained from it. The water covered its body like soil on a grave. But the damage was done. The ship was breaking apart. Aza could barely see what was going around her as the wind whipped the tiny pricks of rain into her skin and her face. Below her Anwin scrambled to her feet, her breathing labored.

"Used too much magic," she groaned. The Nerian warrior was fading fast, and Aza was the only one up there with her in the crow's nest. Her eyes fluttered shut, a gash of blood marring her pale skin. A wound had opened alongside her eyebrow. "My Lady, you need to escape. Eonas can't get you. None of the gods deserve you."

Aza gripped underneath Anwin's armpits and hauled her heavy body up. Each second Anwin grew more slackened, the energy leaving her as she succumbed to the enticing thought of unconsciousness. Aza tightened her grip on Anwin's upper arm, hoping the brief pain would keep her awake a moment longer. "Anwin, you need to stay with me for a moment longer."

The ship would not hold any more, Xira, Reed and Nivet were preparing to jump off the side of the ship, finding more safety in the intense thralls of the ocean rather than the impending doom of their wrecked ship.

"We need to jump Anwin. But I can't support you alone. You need to help." Fear gripped her stomach in a vise, Aza would not lose Anwin when they had finally beat the sea serpent. Eonas wouldn't be able to claim her as a victim. She would not grant them that victory. Gritting her teeth, she hauled Anwin to her feet. The woman's eyes barely lifted. "Are you not a famed Nerian warrior! Darkness below, wake up!" Aza hoped her anger could fuel Anwin to open her eyes. She only needed her to jump. "Your shooting isn't even that good. I bet I could outshoot you."

A flicker of movement and Anwin's eyes cracked open, a slight tilt of the lips. "Bullshit. You can't outshoot me." Her voice came out gravelly, like she refused to be present for this conversation.

"Prove it to me later. I need you to jump," urged Aza.

Anwin clumsily clutched to Aza, their feet on the edge of the crow's nest. Anxiousness roiled in the pit of her stomach like the waves below. This was pure madness. The fall alone might injure them.

The ship gave one final protest, and everything tilted. "Jump!"

The women clutched each other as they fell through the air. Down, down, down they went. Before they hit the water, Anwin's body slackened completely, finally losing her battle to unconsciousness. Aza tightened her grip, afraid to lose her amongst the chaotic waves. One final gasp of air, before they both plunged into the water, their descent like a knife cutting through the thick waves. Aza opened her eyes beneath the water, the salt stinging them. She still had a grip on Anwin and a scream died in her throat. The water fought its way in, causing her to struggle against it. The thick coiled body of the sea serpent still lay in front of her. The bloodied eyes and vacant face floating towards her in a strange illusion of life.

Aza furiously kicked her legs to gain any sort of distance from the entombed monster. Everything was heavy and the current pushed her down. She needed a breath of air. Anwin needed a breath of air. Push a little further.

They were both so heavy.

A final surge of strength screamed on her lips as she broke the water. Air gasped in and out. She gulped down the air and scanned the waves for their companions. No her captors. They were simply a means to an end. She needed them to survive and for nothing else.

Before she could find anyone, a wave slapped her in the face, causing her and Anwin to sink back under the water. It was too much. She couldn't last much longer.

A hand grabbed onto Aza and pulled her forward. She emerged from the water. Nivet yanked her to their mock raft, crudely shackled together with bits of rope and broken planks of wood, Nivet, Xira, and Reed held onto the round pieces of lumber, their combined weight too much for them to properly sit above the water. Reed reached to take Anwin from Aza and held on to her while the raft tossed and turned in the waves.

"Can you do it?" Xira asked Nivet.

"We have no other choice," he answered, his tone flat and resolute. "Reed, I will send you and Anwin. Then Xira and Aza. I will come last."

Before a wave crashed into them, Reed and Anwin disappeared in shadows. Aza bit back a gasp, the rough ocean wave crashing into them. Water spluttered from her mouth, coughs wracked her body. Only Aza, Xira and Nivet remained on their makeshift raft. Three lone bodies aimlessly being thrashed around the wild ocean.

Nivet's face was lined with exhaustion. The extreme use of his magic was draining him. He was reaching his limit. Only a little longer and they would be able to escape.

"Woman of Night, do not think to elude me. My sea serpent is dead, but your companions are weak. Come with me and they may yet live."

Too weak to offer a retort, Aza floated on the eddying waves, her stomach tightening in nervous anticipation. They were all exposed, they needed to escape the Wyra Ocean, Eonas' lair.

A strange quiet befell them, like the water had sucked in a deep breath. The winds and thick rain even seemed to pause in anticipation of what would happen next.

Xira's eyes widened, and Aza summoned the last resolve of her strength to look over her shoulder. She immediately regretted the action.

"Fates above," Xira whispered with a tone one would take at a sacred temple when one is faced with their sudden mortality.

A wave twice the size of their capsized ship was building and crested over them. Before Aza could think, Nivet's head whipped to Xira with a final command. "Make sure she learns."

Aza wanted to cry out, to protest, to scream, but her words were silenced as shadows swallowed up Xira and Aza, the darkness enveloping them like a cold plunge in the lake. Before she was transported, she thought she heard one last bellow from Nivet, a final war cry as he met his demise under Eonas' brutal wave.

4

"Those Nerian scum will pay. How dare they take what is mine?"
Cruvo's private journal

Galloping at a heightened speed, Lorn raced through the undulating foothills of Iyera nearing the edge of the border. Grumbling atop his horse, his heart pulled him in the opposite direction. He needed to get to the edge of Neria and find Aza, free her from her captors, not follow some speculative trail of deceit in Gara. Cruvo had sent him forth like some errand boy, but somehow Lorn found himself agreeing to the plan. He was not bound to Cruvo, but curiosity and a touch of persuasion led him on this path.

Over the last few years of hunting beasts, he had never ventured into Gara. He often skirted the provinces of Iyera and Verta, occasionally venturing into the arid climate of Kreeha. But he had never traveled so far north. Learning about their province's climate—one always plagued with rain and darkened skies, was shocking.

Lorn sent a brief flare of healing magic throughout his body. The months spent in El'en did him a disservice, his body already sore from his rough horse riding. There was no reason for his speed, besides the skewed reasoning that if he finished his business in Gara he would be that much closer to helping Aza.

Traveling at this time of year only added strain to his journey. The brutal autumn winds hinted at more devastating weather to come. The northern reaches of Iyera were preparing their crops for the winter. Signs of it were evident as he rode past horse carts and wheelbarrows laden with vegetables and fruit. Everyone was winding down for a peaceful winter inside the sanctuary of their homes.

Potentially not. With Cruvo's warning of impending war, Lorn scanned each of the homes, wondering if the people inside sensed it. The disturbance, the shift of something to come. Or were they completely oblivious to the machinations of greater entities at play?

Cruvo had sent a note ahead to Lady Rasmina alerting her court of Lorn's immediate arrival. Lorn fought the revulsion and shudder that crept up his spine at the thought of Lady Rasmina. Her presence was like the hypnotic draw of an adder. Aware of the dangers, she still drew people in to her and then without warning she would strike, her fangs hitting true. Lorn's hands tightened on the horse's reins as he remembered Aza's defeated expression, the amount of distrust dripping from people's faces as Lady Rasmina spun her words to lure people in.

Now he was unceremoniously thrust within the dangers of her court, set to find...something. Cruvo had been unclear in his exact intentions only that Lorn was there to learn, find out any pertinent information, and inform him of it.

An eerie silence descended as Lorn swept through town after town, his thoughts turning inward. It was reminiscent of traveling from town-to-town slaughtering errant beasts. Except then, his mind was solely consumed with his unfulfilled rage, the memory of his wife being slaughtered replayed in his mind.

Now the memory stung, and his heart wrenched at the thought of Lakesh, but it was bearable. His life with Aza had changed everything. His jaw clenched as he thought of the deep betrayal by the Nerians. Torn. That was the feeling that consumed him now. Every step away from Neria felt like his own personal betrayal to her, like he had given up on searching for her. Lorn released a breath. He knew Cruvo would never stop searching for Aza. That adamant, unrelenting, and borderline obsession would see Aza safe, and when word of her rescue reached Lorn he would ride to meet her and be reunited with his friend.

~

Lorn settled down for the night on the outskirts of a town, unwilling to bed down for the night indoors. His spirit was growing more and more restless and staring up a wooden plank ceiling would have him going out of his mind. When he reached Gara, his life would be scrutinized in their court, his every move and step watched. Even if the nightly chill scoured through him, he preferred sleeping under the endless night sky above. With his fire burning bright he curled up until sleep pulled him under.

A piercing cry and the familiar clop of hooves had him sitting upright scanning the surroundings.

"It is moving." The voice was tired and strained, like a repeated phrase that had been worn out on its travels.

"No one left," they murmured.

Lorn's fire had banked to mere embers, the night offering little light. Scrambling to his feet, he checked his weapons and searched for the source. An aimless horse clopped past him, its gait off and burdened.

Not wanting to startle the person, Lorn announced his presence, "Over here." He waved his hands and began jogging over to the horse, hoping the loud sounds would alert them to his presence without startling them.

Lacking any energy, the horse and rider didn't shy away from him, allowing him to grip the loose reins of the horse and steer them towards his burned out fire. The small sparks offered little light for him to assess their condition, so Lorn conjured his own magical light. He fought the appalling gasp in his throat. It was not a single rider, but two. A woman held a small, bundled child close to her as if death itself could not pry them apart. The horse was coated in blood, streaks of it running down the deep brown coat, and interspersed dried sweat coated it.

The woman's hand drifted up vacantly to shield the oppressive light from her glassy eyes. Her lips moved soundlessly, like she was speaking only to herself.

"It is moving."

"Excuse me, miss."

"It is moving."

Lorn fought the urge to reach out and comfort the two of them. The woman was not mentally present and who knew how she might respond to his touch. Keeping his light bloomed around them, he saw the woman was even younger than he was, estimating her age to be only eighteen. Without a light source, Lorn would have assumed she lacked injuries and only carried with her a mental exhaustion of running from whatever danger befell them, but upon closer inspection her dark brown skin failed to hide the streaks of blood slashed across her body. Wounds of varying degrees were hidden beneath the blanket wrapped around herself and the other child. What had happened to them? The question plagued Lorn, but he didn't not want to press this young woman into reliving the tragedy she had just endured. He needed to get them to safety. The woman's close-cropped hair heightened her round doe eyes as she turned to him. Lorn fought the shiver crawling up his back as she stared at him sightlessly.

"It's moving."

"What is?"

A child's head poked out, with a face similar to the woman behind him. A boy, possibly about ten years old stared at Lorn, his breathing ragged. "The forest."

Broken out of her intense reverie, the child's voice caused the woman to take a steadying look at Lorn, as if readjusting to where she was. "Creatures and beasts attacked." The woman's hand tightened around the young boy and the horse shifted slightly, its own injuries too grave to hold out any longer.

Lorn was caught in the story, but his need to help these two find safety was greater than hearing the story of what happened.

"Miss, let me escort you back to town where you can be safe."

"No, you must listen! It warped. Changed." Her eyes reverted to their glassy state, tears threatening to spill. "The Hinterlands, swallowed my town, devoured it. My brother and I barely escaped with the others."

"Where are they? The others?" Lorn looked past the girl to see if there were more villagers joining her, maybe they were only a small distance away.

A mournful sob broke through her defense and the girl began to wail on the horse. The horse teetered, the wounds too much for it to bear any longer. Lorn yanked the girl and boy off the horse as soon as the horse collapsed to the ground, its breathing heavy. Shocked out of her tears, she spoke in shaky gasps, "Creatures of shadow and darkness hunted us. Tore through us." Her body stilled as she recalled what happened to her. "I have never seen anything like it. Formed from pure darkness, they hunted us down like mere cattle. We are the only survivors."

5

"The reports from Xira, Anwin, and Reed indicate her ability to fight, echoes of Nerian training apparent in her form."

Nivet's private journal.

Sand molded underneath her knees as she was slammed onto the ground. On all fours, she heaved any remaining water from her throat. Xira lay beside her, her back against the ground, her face aimlessly staring up at the sky above. It was clear. The distant rainclouds that wreaked havoc on their ship were a faint smear of purple and blue on the horizon.

Aza shivered from the remnants of the icy water. The adrenaline from the aftermath of the intense fight drained slowly like a poison being leached from her body.

Chills and shock set in. She had faced a sea serpent without her powers. She had defied Eonas without her powers. Nivet. Nivet was taken underneath Eonas's brutal waves, claimed by the God of the Ocean and their capricious nature.

Even though she was kidnapped, and they were her captors, she was overwhelmed with conflicting emotions. Her anger had fizzled out, a fire without any fuel. These Nerians had risked their life for her —they didn't give her up to Eonas. Whether from purely selfish gain, or some other reason, they still would have died to protect her, and she could not ignore it.

Aza raised her head to see Reed cradling Anwin. Her eyes remained closed, but there was a faint rise and fall of her chest. Although they had lost Nivet, they still had Anwin. The group was battered, blood smeared their clothes, gashes dotted their bodies.

"Where's Nivet?" Water sluiced down Reed's face, his eyes swiveling between Xira and Aza.

"Eonas got him." Xira's voice was level, distant. She remained flat on her back staring up at the unmoving sky.

Reed's eyes shuttered closed. "Rune?" His voice was a soft question, one asked when you already knew the answer to it.

"Presumed dead." Xira's voice was hollow, lifeless.

"What about Lady Sola, Lord Mika?" he trailed off in shock. "Hakim, he will never be able to forgive what has been done."

Xira bolted upright. "I know!" Her chest heaved. She sat back on her heels, her face crumpled, and her head fell into her hands. "I know," she repeated softly. Her answer came out only in a single breath.

Aza nearly forgot that Nivet couldn't truly die, but his mortal body could—Rune who had a life back in Nerian, loved ones. These people they spoke of so fondly, they had lost him, because of her. To kidnap her and get her to learn. Learn what?

All of this death and for what?

Reed gracefully lifted Anwin's head from the cradle of his lap and stood. "May the light guide..." he began.

Xira jerked to her feet and rushed over to him. He paused what he was saying and pulled his arms up to block her. She violently pushed him, and he staggered to the side.

"Don't do it. Don't you fucking do it," she breathed.

Concern and pity crossed Reed's face. "If he is dead, we need to read the rites. It is tradition."

"Nothing is confirmed." Xira stepped away from Reed and maintained her composure. "We will wait until it is confirmed."

Reed's lips pushed into a thin line, his only sign of disagreement before giving her a quick nod.

They were all stretched thin. They traveled quickly forgoing sleep and precious supplies in order to make decent time in their journey.

Aza shakily crawled over to Anwin, inspecting her the best she could. Reed caught her movement and joined her. He crouched down and glanced from Anwin back to Aza. "She will be fine," he reassured her. "She only needs rest. She hit her limit with her magic usage."

Trusting his assessment, Aza pushed shakily to her feet. "Where are we?"

"The edges of Verta. We won't need to search far to find shelter." Reed nodded his head at a pair of rundown buildings in the distance.

Broken from her trance, Aza looked around at their surroundings. They were in a tributary, the rivers snaking together to flow into the ocean. Smooth mounds of sand interrupted each river snaking to meet the larger body of water. In the distance a faint outline of buildings hinted at a more built-up city. Abandoned wood buildings dotted the tributary, whether from disuse or old age. They were thankfully alone without any prying eyes. However, they were vulnerable. All of them were exhausted. Their battle with Eonas had drained them and they needed to recover.

Xira locked away her emotions, her face becoming the neutral mask Aza was used to. Gone was the brief moment of utter defeat. With a resolute determination, she scanned the horizon and released a heavy sigh. Sand coated Xira's entire back. All of them were dripping wet. They needed to find shelter and soon. The storm clouds over the ocean were creeping their way, threatening to burst forth overhead.

The winds picked up, whipping Aza's silver hair into her eyes. She brushed it away, tucking it behind her ear.

"Reed, are you able to lift her?"

He nodded and bent down to lift half of Anwin's body over his shoulder. His feet faltered for a moment in the uneven sand. Aza rushed over to help steady him before Anwin could slip from his grasp.

"Thanks." Reed offered Aza a worn smile and they turned towards Xira following her footprints in the sand. She set a brutal pace despite the tiredness that Aza knew affected them all. Her shoulders did not bow, her head did not droop. She stood erect, protecting the rest of them.

The storm moved in quickly overhead, and the group reached the worn building before the first raindrop could fall. Xira gestured for them to wait, her sword gripped in her hand, and checked the building for any danger first. Giving them the all clear they burst in, seeking refuge from the elements. Aza's teeth chattered, the cold from the ocean, storm, battle, and water-soaked clothes finally getting to her. She yearned for her magic to send a brief flash of warmth through her body.

Upon entering she hadn't thought to look around at the small building that housed them, her exhaustion had dulled her senses. She squinted at the darkness of the tiny building. It was more like a storage closet. It held a random assortment of fishing equipment, nets, and lines, discarded remnants and tools that the local town didn't use any more. Xira sheathed her sword and rifled through the leftover belongings. They had to take care when maneuvering around each other, the room almost full to bursting with the four of them inside.

Reed gently laid Anwin on the ground. He ripped apart dry, rotten wood to use as kindling. A crackle of magic appeared from Reed's hand as a small, but welcome fire filled the dank room. The warmth made Aza's chill even more apparent, and her body shook as she gathered more wood for the fire.

Xira held up some discarded clothes, overalls, and long linen shirts. "It isn't the best, but at least we can take off our clothes and dry them by the fire."

Aza grabbed the proffered clothes, and everyone turned around in the small room granting each other a meager amount of privacy. The room filled with the sound of clothes being shucked off, discarded, wet clothes sticking to skin. A rush of biting wind flew in from outside and chills erupted over Aza's naked body. She hurriedly pulled the long linen shirt over her head and the small pair of overalls. Although the new clothes weren't warm, anything was better than the wet clothes she had worn.

Aza and Xira clumsily removed most of Anwin's wet clothing and covered her in some over-sized fishing gear. Aza tried to be respectful of Anwin's exposed body, but she couldn't help but notice the tattoo covering Anwin's left ribcage. Before she could ask about it, Xira yanked a new shirt down covering the intricate design.

Aza's stomach grumbled loudly. Now that they were out of danger, Aza realized how hunger clawed at her and how dry her throat was. They had no food or water. Xira grabbed a sharp looking spear off the wall and tossed it to Reed.

"We need some fish and water." Without a word, Reed turned to leave the shed.

"Wait, I can go with and help him," Aza offered, following in his footsteps.

Xira placed a consoling hand on Aza's shoulder. "We cannot risk you going. We don't know what type of awareness Eonas has of you. It would be for nothing if they found you here."

Reed saw the mutinous expression on Aza and added, "Do not worry Aza. I will be quick." Before Aza could interject, Reed slipped out the doorway, the spear clutched in his hand.

Aza crossed her hands in front of her chest and glared at Xira. "So, I cannot do anything? Am I too much of a liability?"

Xira abandoned her task of scrounging the room for useful supplies and marched over to her in two small steps. They stood eye to eye.

Aza was bristling for a fight. The lack of her power, the encounter with Eonas, the loss of Rune and Nivet, everything was worn out and used and she needed to set a spark going again. Was all of this worth it for her?

"First off, Reed's magic is related to water, so he will fish faster without anyone interfering." Xira's tone remained level, not giving in to Aza's heat and anger. "Second, even with your magic dulled, any MagicBlessed that spots you will report back to your beloved Cruvo or any other god or goddess that wants you."

Aza wanted to interrupt, to deny the facts Xira listed, but her tone brooked no argument.

"Third, you are *never* a liability. If that is all you see yourself as, then we have more work cut out ahead of us than I realized. Do you not see?" Xira waved her hand out into the distant horizon where the ocean waves crashed against the sandy shore. "Nivet risked his life and the life of Rune to save you." She pointed at Aza's chest. Her eyes were not accusing, more beseeching, as if wanting Aza to see something plain laid out in front of her, but Aza was in no mood to listen to this speech.

"I did not ask for his sacrifice! I did not ask for any of this." Aza's hand swept out to the room, gesturing to Xira and the unconscious Anwin on the floor. She jabbed her finger back at Xira, her teeth bared. "*You* kidnapped me. *You* took away my choice. Even if what you plan to do will truly help me, it will always be tainted." Chastised by Aza's words, Xira for the first time appeared unsure of herself, stepping shakily away, her eyes casting about the room like she was searching for the right words to assuage her guilt.

"Even if this was for some greater good or purpose, then you are just as bad as who you believe Cruvo to be." Her rant ended with an angry huff of air between her lips. Aza's new words came out in a defeated sigh, "At least Cruvo offered me a choice." She forced Xira to meet her gaze, "You say you are better than him, but you took away *my* right to choose. So, no. You are not." Aza retreated to a corner of the tiny shed and kneeled to inspect Anwin.

Only depleted, not dead. She did not wish death on her captors. Sure, her righteous anger on the boat had burned a hole in her and ignited her, but the fight with Eonas and the sea serpent only made her weary. Weary of all the intrigue, secrets, and lies. Yearning for her steadfast friend Lorn, she sat in the corner, her feet planted and arms dangling over her knees.

Xira sat down on the ground cross-legged her fingers tracing errant shapes on the dusty floor. Without looking at her, Xira muttered, "You are right."

Aza's head snapped towards Xira.

Xira raised her face to Aza, her mouth pressed into a thin line. "You are right," she repeated firmly. "If you can believe me, we all argued over this multiple times. We thought it was wrong, but in the end we thought it was a necessary evil." Xira's honeyed eyes hardened a decision forming. "Before we return to Neria, we will show you why you should return with us. But it will be your choice. However, I ask you to make your choice at the end...once we have shown you everything. Should you return to Neria at the end or return to Iyera and back to Cruvo," Xira released a heavy sigh, the flames flickering from her breath. "Then it will be your choice."

A choice. Aza would have her choices back again. But one question lingered, "And my magic?"

"Your magic's return is fickle. It could be a day, or a week. Potentially longer."

"Why?"

"We didn't know how much to dose you with. Your magic is something we had no idea how to handle. I'm sorry to not give an accurate timeframe of when it will return. It is an estimate."

Aza's fingernails curled into her palm. The apology and the choice were a start. But they had still willingly captured her and took away her magic. It would take time to forgive them, if ever.

Xira cocked her head at Aza. "The answers you seek will be in

Neria."

Aza didn't need to ask for clarification; she knew of what Xira hinted at, the answers she searched for in Iyera. Who she was, why she had such power, her blurred memories, everything. How could she trust these people who had kidnapped her? Aza didn't doubt that Xira thought she was correct, but sincere belief had led other people astray too.

Loud footsteps approached, jarring Aza from her thoughts. Before she tore her focus away from Xira, Aza gave a firm nod, a tentative agreement to their shaky truce.

Aza fought the chuckle at Reed's ridiculous outfit. Given their limited clothing options they had to make do with what was found. Rain dripped off his forehead onto his too tight waders, the overalls clinging to his willowy form. His locs were tied back with a leather throng, keeping it out of his face while he obtained their fish. His eyes darted between Xira and Aza clearly absorbing the tension that lingered in the air.

Taking the safe route, he held up his spear showcasing his bounty. Two medium-sized fish were speared on the end. A discarded cast-iron pan was found among the refuse, and they began cooking the fish. Without any spices, it was still one of the best meals Aza had eaten. Her hunger gnawed on her and she needed to satiate it.

With their discarded clothes, the unused supplies and their four bodies, the shed was extremely tight. Aza sat next to Anwin. If she had to be near anyone in the group of Nerians, at least let it be the person who was unconscious.

After their furious conversation everything was stilted, like either person didn't know where to lead or tread next in case of unknown pitfalls in the conversation.

Xira broke the silence as she turned to Reed and announced, "Slight change in the plans."

Without faltering, Reed responded, "Where are we going?"

"To Verta. Let us pay a visit to their court."

6

"I'm assuming Aza is being brought back to the Nerian capital, El'theren. I have sent forces to retrieve her. However, I'm curious as to what is happening in Gara. I will send Lorn to investigate." Cruvo's private journal

Lorn ushered the two survivors onto his own horse that shied away from the stench of blood. Whispering a few words of encouragement Lorn coaxed them onto the horse, and he gently led them to the nearest town. It was late, the town eerily quiet. Only the heavy gasps from the young woman pierced the night. The young boy sat silently wrapped within the confines of his sister's arms. Lorn couldn't fathom the deep sorrow and fear that must have embedded itself around the two. A panic of having evaded their sure demise.

The forest they mentioned must have been the Hinterlands. From the young woman's fragmented sentences, Lorn was able to piece together a horrifying picture. The Hinterlands was growing unstable. It was getting worse and the beasts that emerged from it—they weren't like anything Lorn had fought before. Not something based in reality, their forms reminiscent of animals, instead beings of pure darkness.

Not wanting to stir up any trouble, or frighten the villagers, Lorn kept quiet, leading the two back to an inn he spotted earlier. The inn was quiet except for an old woman behind the desk propped on a stool immersed in a faded book. He gave a summarized and brief recount of the people behind him, paid for their rooms, and instructed the innkeeper to have the town look after them.

The woman sincerely listened to Lorn and promised to look after them with a small persuasion of gold. Lorn didn't want to cause a panic, but he needed to warn the town of the impending danger looming over them like the end of a sword. The innkeeper nodded, taking his words to heart and kindly led the children to their room.

Lorn bit back a stifled gasp when the children walked within the faint glow of the inn. Blood and grime coated them, their eyes now filled with a haunting look of the dead. Crouching beside them, his eyes traveled between the two. "I am entrusting you to this town. They will care for you." He nodded towards the innkeeper who returned her own affirming agreement.

"Where will you go?" The young woman's tone was lifeless, devoid of anything but a hollow curiosity.

"I'm headed back to your town." He hesitated to tell her more. "To see these creatures of darkness."

Unbridled fear blanketed her eyes as she clutched at Lorn, gripping his shirt tightly. "You will die."

"I might, but it is worth it if I can stop any of the creatures or warn any other towns so they might not befall the same fate." He pried himself from her grip and stood, sending a final nod towards the innkeeper. As he walked away, he heard a faint whisper repeat from the young woman, "You will die."

Lorn marched out of the inn without casting another glance backwards. He couldn't bear to see the empty look in their eyes.

The inn door slammed shut.

Forgoing any further attempt at sleep, Lorn readied his horse and left in search of the destroyed village. Based on their brief ramblings, he needed to head west of his camp to reach it. Lorn cursed his foolhardiness. It was difficult to see in the blanket of darkness.

Praying for safe travels, he took an even-layered trail and left, trusting his horse to not stumble. Lorn didn't push his mare, allowing her to guide. Years of instinct screamed at him to ignore the ravaged town and head towards Gara, to ignore the plight of these townsfolk, but he couldn't get the image of Lakesh out of his mind. If only one person survived, he needed to be there to provide assistance. Many citizens of the Vertan and Iyerian provinces were soft, their fighting skills lacking due to the prosperity of the Well. They were never forced to fight and keep their survival skills honed. If the beasts the girl whispered about were true, damage would be wrought on these towns. Pushing aside his instincts, Lorn would not alter his path. He needed to see it, needed to understand.

The description of the creatures sent Lorn spiraling to think of what could possibly cause such destruction. The beasts of the Hinterlands were not made of shadow, but of flesh and blood. While difficult and unpleasant, they could still be killed with proper training. These presumed creatures of shadow sounded...different, more insidious.

The night began to lighten with the hint of morning, and Lorn picked up his pace, setting his horse at a steady trot. There was no time to waste; any extra delay could cost potential lives.

After two days of a punishing pace, stopping only to sleep, eat, and allow his steadfast horse a small respite, they arrived.

Lorn didn't realize what to expect. Silence greeted his arrival. Usually, his travels were surrounded with the familiar song of animals, birds, people working, but this—a void. An absence of sound.

The soft clopping of his horse's hooves was startling in the vast emptiness. He dismounted and tied her reins loosely to an overhang of trees with soft grass for her to nibble. Lorn crept closer to the infected piece of land. He was at the base of a steep hill, a cluster of trees blocking his view. Even his horse sensed the disturbance, backing away from the crest of the hill.

Lorn crept forward, using the sparse trees and tall grass to shield himself from view. The hill gave way to an open field. There were no words to explain the horror. Bringing his forearm to his mouth, hie bit down to stop the scream of rage that was building in his throat. The injustice. What looked to be a small town with a collection of houses, shops, streets, and people was all destroyed.

Lorn had expected to see houses burned, the damage evident of people fleeing, but instead nausea roiled in his gut. From afar, the houses were coated in a strange layer of black. Even from his distance Lorn recoiled from it, his instincts surging in him to run away and not look at the foulness. But as his eyes scanned the small town, he caught bodies torn apart. Families lay discarded upon the ground. He couldn't leave them here. If there was even the slightest possibility for someone to have survived, he needed to check.

Lorn secured his weapons, checked his longsword, daggers and bow, and hoped he wouldn't have to use them. The soft, spongy grass yielded to his footsteps, muffling any noise. As he crept closer, the grass changed from soft to brittle, his footsteps altering into loud crunches forcing Lorn to check for any creatures. There were no others around him. He crouched and ran his hands along the blades. There was something foul present—he couldn't place what it was, but his magic recoiled from it. Tainted. That was the word. It was tainted. Their prosperous land was tainted with something putrid and foul.

Bodies lay scattered on the ground. Each movement brought him closer to more death and destruction. He checked for pulses, for any sign of life, anything he could possibly use his magic to heal and recover but the bodies were just that... bodies. Each time Lorn muttered prayers, the words stumbled over each other as he wished them peace to continue on in the Meadow of the Undying. They had earned their peace there. The bodies had a variety of wounds. Some had brutal claw marks gouged deep into the flesh and others had only a single wound. From Lorn's inspection on the single wound, it looked to be festering like a foul putrefaction had infected their bodies causing them to shut down. Like the antithesis of life, it was malignant.

His heart sped up. Lorn couldn't abandon this destroyed town. The dirt hardened path through town cut back, houses and buildings spread apart as Lorn looked upon the border of the Hinterlands. The impenetrable forest seemed to pulse in time with the beat of his heart. How had this forest caused such destruction? The Hinterlands had never shifted since the millennia it had been established. The boundaries were terrifying, but firm and unyielding. Only the occasional random beast would escape the confines of the diseased forest and cause havoc in neighboring towns. Small destruction, but nothing of this magnitude. Nothing of such wanton destruction, the putrid reek of decay emanating from the leftover corpses.

Lorn couldn't hide his disgust. He was trying to argue in favor of the entity which ripped apart the love of his life. Something wasn't right. The bodies, the corruption, the underlying disease wasn't the same as what he felt within the Hinterlands.

Standing up straight, his feet dragged him towards the edge of the Hinterlands. The boundaries of the forest wavered like the remnants of smoke upon the air. He had entered once before—he could do it again, find if something was festering within, some monsters of shadow hidden inside. Lorn narrowed in on one single spot of the Hinterlands. His feet unbidden stepped closer and closer. His mind raced back to everything he had learned in Iyera. The prophecy only granted Lorn a brief window of time for him to enter the Hinterlands without affliction. The time had passed and if he entered now, he would be killed or go mad. But he couldn't let this destruction go without an answer, without retribution.

Before he could take another step, phantom hands restrained him.

Lorn you cannot help.

It pulled him tighter. The voice was so familiar—he had heard it twice in his life. The voice had pulled him back from his spiral of despair before he first entered the Hinterlands...and the second time in his dream, she had offered a warning, the Goddess Issi. There was no corporeal form to accompany her disembodied voice, only the faint pull of desperate hands on his shoulders, begging him to gain distance from the Hinterlands.

Snapped from his reverie, Lorn scrambled away, his heart racing. His eyes darted back and forth searching for Issi. Was she in the hollow remains of the town? Nothing. With no people left to save and refusing to linger in the town any longer, Lorn raced back to his horse, and galloped away from the desolate town, Issi's clear voice ringing through his head, warning him and pulling him away from his demise.

Only a handful of days had been delayed in his trip to Gara. Lorn used the time to try and piece together what he failed to understand. Agreeing on a few different facts such as: the Hinterlands was losing control, its borders morphing to swallow up any neighboring towns of lands; and a separate disease was spreading, a disease that killed the townspeople and plagued their buildings.

Lorn thought back to Lord Aldrich's first forum he witnessed, the two farmers presenting the withered grapevine to Lord Aldrich, like something had decimated the crop upon its touch. Was there a connection? The corruption seemed to be similar, a crippling decay, a withering. How were the Hinterlands and the decay connected? Because Lorn reasoned they were different, when he was immersed in the Hinterlands, his magic was stifled and lacking like a heavy blanket had been placed over his senses. Whereas the corruption was more of a pestilence inside his own body and the bodies of others. They were different, but somehow linked.

The journey to the border of Gara and Iyera did nothing to quell the torrential thoughts swirling through his head. He needed to send word to Cruvo and alert him. Cruvo needed to be prepared for the upcoming danger. Who knows how far the grip of corruption could spread?

He thought back to the young woman and her brother appearing outside his campfire, their clothes torn, blood covering their bodies. How had they survived? Blood.

Blowing a harsh breath out of his mouth, Lorn titled his head to look up at the endless sky above, cursing himself. He never thought to ask how they survived. But it didn't make sense. Everything he saw in the town was touched by the strange corruption, rotting people, but the two of them had blood. Blood when there was so little blood in the town itself. Had they faced beasts from the Hinterlands? Lorn fought the urge to return to the town and question them until everything started to make sense.

Shaking his head, he dismissed the thought. The horrors they saw were etched on their faces, not easily erased. They didn't want him to inspect the town. They had begged him to stay. No, something else was amiss. Frustrated with his limited choices, Lorn plunged ahead, towards Gara hoping to unravel further mysteries.

7

"I must set aside the past, set aside any personal feelings. She has every right to hate us. She should hate everybody."

Nivet's private journal.

They remained at the abandoned shack on the edge of the tributary, healing and planning. Reed was tasked with fishing and always returned with a bounty for them to enjoy. The risk of moving Anwin without the use of a horse was too great. So they waited and Aza tentatively asked questions of her captors hoping to find information. They never disclosed much. Instead, they offered weak excuses about wanting Aza to learn the information in time. But after the upended chaos of the last few weeks, sitting around a weak fire in an abandoned shack was beginning to chafe at her.

Time was wasting. The Hinterlands was unstable and Aza dreaded hearing anymore stories about the nearby towns being consumed. Eonas attacked them and was likely still hunting them. Mysteries still surrounded Aza and she yearned to learn the information the Nerians wanted to share with her.

Frustrated with their lack of action and needing a change of clothes, Aza offered to go scouting in town and haggle with them. Xira outright refused. She was too recognizable—even with her magic dimmed, she wouldn't be able to hide her appearance.

Instead, Xira went in her place. Somehow with her hidden charm she can easily cast on and off like a winter cloak Xira returned with outfits for all of them. The conspicuous Nerian leathers were something they needed to discard or keep hidden.

By the second day, Anwin stirred from her slumber. Each of them bore the brunt of the attack. Gouges, scrapes, and bruises adorned their bodies like badges of honor. Reed and Xira didn't use their magic for healing. They informed Aza of their preference to store their magic for a time when its use was more necessary than for a few scrapes.

Aza bit her tongue to avoid yelling at them. Did they not view their near-death encounter with a sea serpent as necessary for magical intervention? If her magic wasn't tampered with she could easily heal all of them without the theatrics.

By the third day, Anwin was fully recovered, sitting upright, laughing and joking with her friends. The bruises coating Xira and Reed had gone down to soft mottled colors of purples and blues, most hidden underneath the cover of clothes to disguise their true warrior origins.

Ready to depart on the fourth day, they ate another filling meal of fish and left. Scouring the shack, Xira found a threadbare pack to hold their Nerian clothing. They each wore trousers and linen tunics commonplace amongst the farming regions of Verta, and a cloak.

The biting winds were building each day. The coldness seeped into Aza's bones like a chill she couldn't escape. The Nerians did not seem as affected by the turn in weather as she was. Considering they were forged from the coldness of the mountains they resided on, Aza expected nothing less.

A defeated sigh escaped her lips as Xira handed her a cloak, a hardened look in her eye.

"You are expected to wear this everywhere." Her tone offered no debate.

Aza reached for the cloak, hastily ripping it from Xira's offered hands.

Xira's mouth thinned and said, "I know it is not ideal. I wish it were otherwise, but if word got out of your whereabouts, Cruvo would send the entirety of his army after you."

Aza nodded, her heart giving an extra pang in her chest at the mention of Cruvo. Over the last week of capture she was simultaneously overwhelmed with the thoughts of him and wanted to ignore it—the pain too deep. But by Xira's admission, he was desperately searching for her. She was torn, her mind often conflicted when he was brought up. The lust he inspired in her, the way he trained her and honed her magic, the secrets he kept, the use of herself to banish the Hinterlands. There was no straightforward answer to her feelings. Jagged and brutal their relationship was anything but simple. Yet she yearned for him. Missed him. She hoped he would be searching for her, thinking of her as she often did as she lay down to sleep at night. Over the last few months in El'en, her dreams had been only of him. Going to sleep without that consistent comfort was a chasm too big for her to cross. Sleep was little reprieve, only a reminder—a hollow aching of where he wasn't. This strange bond they seemed to have, one of passion and raw energy was too difficult to ignore.

Yet, she wanted answers. Her goal before being captured was to find answers and these Nerians would be able to provide them. So, for now, she would follow them.

Restless and not wanting to provide any room for argument, Aza took the cloak pulling the hood up to obscure her features. A habit born out of security, Aza tugged at the familiarity of her magic and found it empty. Xira had warned her that her magic would return eventually and gave no firm timeframe. But Aza couldn't dampen the hope that began to flame in her chest.

They abandoned the forlorn shack, Aza sneaking one final look at their brief salvation. It offered them a moment of respite and for Aza a firm resolution. She would see what the Nerians offered her, what answers she would uncover and see if it aligned with her beliefs.

Xira marched away while Anwin bent down to adjust her boots. Reed froze outside the building, his jaw locked.

"Xira—"Reed called.

Stopping her incessant steps, she turned around impatiently, thinning her lips. "What?"

"We need to perform the funeral prayers." His locs swayed in front of his face as he shifted to look out across the distant ocean.

Aza's chest tightened. For Rune. For Nivet. His sacrifice granted their safety. Although he was her captor, he still valued her safety. However misguided the Nerians believed themselves to be, she couldn't fault them for that act. The host of Nivet's body surely met his demise under the torrential onslaught of those fierce ocean waves. She had no idea where the god would go without his mortal host.

"No." Xira resumed marching towards Verta, her back stiff and unyielding.

Reed fingers curled into his palms. "It is what is right."

"No. It isn't right." Xira did not stop, but Aza heard the implication. Rune should never have died, should never have sacrificed himself.

Finished with adjusting her boot, Anwin stood shoulder to shoulder with Reed, a hand placed consolingly on his back. "We will when we return home."

Reed stiffly nodded and they joined Xira, following her imprinted footsteps in the sand.

Home.

A word she knew little of. How Aza longed to speak with such confidence of where she belonged and who she belonged to, a family and friends who welcomed her home.

For her, there was only political intrigue, and unanswered riddles. No one to provide sanctuary for her. No one for her to be vulnerable with, to release her fears. The only person who treated her as an equal was miles away ignorant to her location. Her lips downturned thinking of Lorn, and how he was handling her absence.

Returning to the capital of Lorn's home province left her with an emptiness. After their months of conversation Aza discovered Lorn had never reached the capital of Verta, preferring to stay on the outskirts of his province and only traveling to distant rural cities that were overrun with errant monsters from the Hinterlands. He deserved to be here with her.

Crossing the sand bar, the wind whipped through their heavy cloaks. They didn't have much time to travel with winter descending. It would be too dangerous trekking across the land without any form of protection. Their meager clothes and supplies wouldn't last them.

They stumbled upon a makeshift trail, the smooth impacted dense sand easier to navigate than the loose powder of the sand bar. The trail skirted the edge of the town, the Nerians hesitant to parade Aza in front of other people, keeping her instead to the shadows.

When the sun waned in the sky, they made camp off to the side of the road, no hidden refuge in sight. The sand and coastal environment shifted into one of open farmland and freshly tilled soil. They passed countless workers toiling in their field rushing to get the harvest in before winter crushed any remaining vestiges of life. Out in the open they camped, no trees or dense wilderness to hide them. Unconcerned with remaining hidden, they only appeared like weary travelers and conjured a fire to keep the biting chill at bay. Aza's body shook with the consistent autumn cold, but the Nerians did not convey even a bit of discomfort. Xira commanded them to rest with her taking the first watch.

The days blurred together with the group making little conversation. They stayed on the outskirts of towns with only one of the Nerians going in to barter for supplies. Aza couldn't fathom how they returned with the items. They didn't have any coin with them. Everything had sunk in their attack with the sea serpent. But regardless of their lack of money, they were still well-fed, and their clothes shielded them from the cold that cloaked the valley. When there were no nearby towns, they hunted in the meadows and hidden pockets of woods where rabbits, quails, and wild chickens lay in hiding. Xira, Reed, and Anwin kept their guard up, constantly surveying for incoming guards of Iyera, but they came across no one.

Did Cruvo forget about her that quickly? There was no active search, people didn't care whether she disappeared or not and Aza's shoulders slumped further every day under the realization that nobody cared. Her anger turned into a taut string which snapped into an endless barrage of bitterness.

Four days and nights had passed traveling to the capital of Verta. Although they didn't speak of it, Aza began to notice things that were off during her travels through Verta. The people worked hard, tilling the land and harvesting their food, but a disquiet seemed to embed itself in their work. Keeping the musings to herself, she walked and kept looking, trying to spot what was unsettling her. With her magic dampened, she was unable to easily feel out the anomaly and had to resort to her other senses. There was nothing she could pinpoint exactly, only an instinctual stab in her gut every time she passed by a farm or a small town. Like an unseen infection was lingering underneath the ground itself waiting to swallow the province. Lacking any camaraderie with her travel companions, she didn't feel comfortable sharing her thoughts. Worried they would dismiss her — pride built a wall within never letting her thoughts and emotions leak out.

Closer and closer they drew to the capital of Verta and the

tightening in her gut grew, a warning to escape now. One night, with the campfire crackling, instead of everyone falling down to sleep, Reed motioned for Aza to scoot closer. Everyone sat encircling the fire as Reed's smooth voice filled the air.

"I know we haven't spoken lately," Reed began, his eyes searching Aza's. "Do you feel it?"

Aza gulped and scanned everyone's faces. There were no mocking faces, all were completely serious awaiting her response.

Slowly, she nodded. Her voice a mere whisper, she asked, "What is it?"

"Corruption."

Her brows furrowed. How could anything be corrupted with the prosperity of the Well? It was supposed to combat anything ill happening across the lands.

Interpreting the question in her face Reed explained, "It lies in wait. Hidden beneath the surface, ready to attack. It has already begun. The only thing holding it back is the Hinterlands."

Aza shifted uncomfortably. If she banished the Hinterlands this corruption would spread throughout the five provinces.

"Yet, you know the Hinterlands is spreading out of control, it is...unhinged." Reed looked away from Aza and at the fire instead, his hands folded around each other. "If it is ever gone, the corruption will spread everywhere, taking everything we know, any prosperity, our food, our health, potentially even our magic."

Xira and Anwin sat across from Aza, their faces stoic listening to Reed's explanation, yet Aza sensed an underlying tension thrumming through them. There was more they weren't telling her.

A clear memory shot through her, of two farmers, the two women who presented their withered grapes to Lord Aldrich. This corruption was one and the same.

Bringing her palms to her thighs, Aza leaned back to take in the clear night sky above. She always found herself drawn to it, even in Lord Aldrich's castle she wandered to the balcony, yearning for whatever her existence consisted of prior, like her mind knew she did not truly belong down here and craved to return to the solace of the stars.

"You do not want me to banish the Hinterlands? That's what you are fighting for. Why did you kidnap me?"

Reed paused and looked to Xira for confirmation. She leaned forward, taking charge of the conversation. "No, not exactly Aza. We need you to learn and see every side of the story. Then you are free to make your choice."

"Then why kidnap me?"

Anwin interrupted, "We know it was not the ideal choice. We wanted you to come with us in your own time...but Lord Aldrich—Cruvo, he was moving too quickly, and we couldn't risk you staying there any longer."

Aza fingers curled into her palms, the nails biting the edge of her skin. She scoffed, "You say I am free to make choices, yet you robbed me of them. How do I know you won't go back on your word after this is done and drug me again to take away my magic?" The banked anger swirled and sparked. She stood needing to release her pent up energy. She paced back and forth in front of the fire, looking like an enraged demon from the shadows it cast on her. "These are easy claims to make when you have maimed me! You have taken away my magic, my strength, and yet act like you give me choices. How could I make a choice to banish the Hinterlands, when you say I'm dooming everyone to death?" Aza couldn't help but have her voice rise, the sound echoing out into the meadow.

Anwin stood and strode over to Aza, her eyes beseeching. "My Lady, we want you to banish the Hinterlands." Worrying her lips between her teeth, she continued, "We agree with Cruvo. It needs to be banished."

Aza clenched her jaw and ground her teeth. "Then why kidnap me?" she demanded.

Xira stood up and joined them, their proximity a balm, instead of an intrusion. "If you tried to banish the Hinterlands, you would have died."

Their unblinking stares and resolute expressions confirmed their honesty. "No, Cruvo wouldn't have let that happen."

Xira snorted, "He is too power hungry and blind. He went about it with strength, when you do not have all the answers." Xira gestured to Anwin and Reed. "We will provide the answers, and you can make the choice when we are done."

"My Lady, there is more we can tell you, but only after we reach the safety of Neria." Anwin searched the enclosing darkness and her head snapped back to Aza. "We are never truly alone, and we dare not give names to those that hunt us."

Her statement rattled Aza and reminded her of her dreams with Cruvo. At the beginning when she didn't know who he was, he didn't want what was hunting him to find him.

Reed joined, the three Nerians providing a small support for Aza, encircling her not in fear, but in camaraderie.

"Capturing you was a mistake, and we apologize for it. I cannot begin to understand your anger. When your magic returns, we will not dose you again. You will have your full strength and have an arsenal of choices at your disposal." Xira placed a reassuring hand on Aza's shoulder and felt the truth ring between them, like a bright light for her to follow. "Nivet's final words were for you to learn, and you will."

After their unsettling conversation, Aza forced herself to lay on the cold ground and rest. The knowledge of the corruption wore at her, like it was seeping beneath and lying in wait. Throughout the night she imagined it, like the darkened color of blood spreading over her body and binding her to the ground. Aza was covered, the blood trickling into her eyes, her mouth, her hair. How the province weeped, its disease-ridden land and the blood pooled around her. So much death. The blood began to shift colors, the burgundy red changing into a pitch black. Black was usually a color of comfort reminding Aza of the night and her shadows. This was a black of disease, of death. It spread over the pool of blood, infecting it. Aza could only lay back and watch as the corruption spread over her immobilized body.

Paralyzed, she lay helplessly unable to move, unable to do anything, but watch the blood sour. A scream of rage and fear built in her throat threatening to erupt.

Jolting upright, Aza's eyes flashed open. Her hands blindingly patted her body checking for the heavy slickness of the blood that coated her. It was gone. It was only a dream. Her breath rattled out, as she forced herself to close her eyes and slow her breathing down, to control it. With the overwhelming feeling of paralysis dissipating, she opened her eyes and found Reed's gaze upon her.

His head inclined slightly, a brief acknowledgment of what she felt to be true. He could feel it too.

The corruption had reached her in her dreams. She could still feel the phantom blood coating her skin, the pool spreading below her, covering her and spreading, its darkness, one of complete absence threatening to swallow her whole.

Tilting her head back, Aza sought the comfort of the stars, her constant companions. But the clouds obscured any clarity and with it her moment of peace. Left to comfort herself, Aza laid back on the ground, her arms entwined around herself, hoping to not feel the filthy grips of the corruption threatening to pull her under.

~

Aza felt the threat build as she neared the capital of Verta, like the crackle before an impending lightning strike. The people they passed were too busy to notice their small traveling group, but Aza kept her hood down covering her distinctive features. A kernel of guilt began to grow within her. If she wanted to be found by Cruvo wouldn't she go racing through the streets announcing who she was in hopes of the information reaching Cruvo? Aza pushed aside those consuming thoughts and unclenched her jaw. She belonged to no one. The Nerians promised answers. Intrigued Aza wanted to know, learn and discover what was so important that they had kidnapped her. Why go through such great lengths to kidnap her in an enemy's castle, fight off a sea serpent and sacrifice their own Nerian lord to teach her?

During their travel, the conversation would dance around the topic of Nivet. Before they were shadowed away, Rune was swallowed whole by the wave of Eonas. She could not imagine him surviving such an encounter. Rune's mortal body would be crushed. However, the god inhabiting Rune, Nivet, would have survived.

Aza tried to broach the subject, but Xira was resolute, unwilling to discuss the possibility of Rune's death. He was her leader, and as his guard she had failed. The stiff set of her shoulders when Aza tried to bring up the subject was a clear enough indicator of Xira's frustration. Reed and Anwin offered small consolations. They would figure out what happened to him and if need be, recover the body, a false hope.

"Why is Nivet involved with the Nerians?" Aza asked, unsure of why the gods and goddesses even bothered involving themselves in the MagicBlessed affairs.

"Nivet can explain his own story to you," Xira answered curtly.

Fighting the urge to roll her eyes, Aza rephrased her question. "I guess my overarching question is, why do the gods and goddesses even bother? Why do they involve themselves in our world?"

Anwin turned around, her eyebrows furrowed. "Why do you involve yourself?"

Aza halted her head, jerking back at the question. "Excuse me?"

"Why do *you* involve yourself?" She waved her hand at Aza.

"What do you mean?"

Breathing a sigh, Reed answered for Anwin, "You are partly made from the gods and goddesses. Your origins, how you came from the Well. You are not fully them, but there is a tiny shred embedded in you."

Without giving Aza time to respond, Anwin added, "Do not worry, you are not fully a goddess."

Aza's fingers curled. She had a small essence of the gods in her. It would explain her otherness, and some part of her origins, but there were still too many questions unanswered.

Reed's hair brushed together softly as he turned to face Aza, errantly pushing the long locs out of his face.

"How do you know all of this? I don't know anything about myself."

"Years of research and Nivet. The Nerians know the true history of Ithilia and that is what we are going to show to you." Reed held up a hand, halting Aza's next question, "I'm sure you have thousands of questions." Reed gestured to himself, Anwin and Xira. "We know only the surface and cannot give you the information you seek. You must be patient when Nivet reunites with us. He can explain more."

Xira chimed in without turning around, "Our reason for entering the capital of Verta is for you to trust us and side with us. The questions of your origins and who and what you are will come in time, especially if you join us back in Neria."

Aza huffed a frustrated breath. They all knew important information about her. Why not answer her questions to at least appease her curiosity? Instead, they were baiting her, stringing her along so she felt obligated to go to Neria, because they knew her quest to find what she was overrode any other desire. Giving a curt nod,

Reed and Anwin followed in Xira's footsteps with Aza trailing behind, ready to learn more about who she was. As she walked Aza tried to search for that fragment of divinity—instead, only emptiness glared back.

~

After days of travel the vestiges of a sprawling city and a fortified castle graced the horizon. Xira pulled Aza aside warning her to lay low. "Most people do not know who we are." The statement confirmed Aza's suspicions. How would they be able to freely travel without notice? The discretion and secrecy the Nerian province sowed from the beginning was an advantage in their hands.

"Only those at the gathering in Iyera would be able to spot who we are. We cannot afford to be seen. You are to follow my every command. Understand?" Aza nodded, her stomach tightening into knots. "Not everyone has your best interests at heart. Many would use you in an instant." Xira's eyes flickered to Aza's body and ended along her hands. "It is especially concerning since your magic has not returned yet." Her lips thinned at the admission. "You are decent with your sword, but still vastly unskilled. You cannot rely on your magic anymore. Do not let anyone of the Vertan court catch who you are." Xira turned to walk away. Aza kept pace with her while Xira rattled off a list of warnings and instructions.

Comparing the castle of Iyera with that of Verta was night and day. Aza experienced little of El'en, but what she did see reeked of beauty, dripping with decadence of items of comfort. The people's pride in the city radiated. Everything was kept pristine, the marble castle a beacon of decadence. When the light from the ocean hit the jewel of El'en, it sparkled and shined like a gem all of the facets shone beautifully.

The capital of Verta, Rijal, was spread out over the soft hills and plains of Verta, taking up enormous amounts of space uncaring what it impacted. Verta being rural farmland could afford to expand needlessly. The capital city was provided small sanctuary among the convenient low hills, their barracks and crenelations of the castle walls utilizing the height to provide them an advantage of seeing any outsiders stepping foot within their province. From outside Aza could spot the brief pinnacle of the castle its peak attempting to pierce the sky above. The castle was not forged of white marble like the exuberance of El'en. Instead it displayed the rugged qualities of Verta, those that toiled by working the soil and the land. The stones were cracked embedded with years of dust and dirt. Aza pictured the people that helped to build this place, their rough, calloused hands forming each stone and placing them in intricate patterns.

They had yet to approach the fortress, instead only viewing it from the safety of a small grove of trees. Hands on her hips, Aza turned to face the group, "How am I supposed to get in there undetected?"

"Don't worry yourself, my Lady. We have a plan," Anwin answered.

"We have traveled throughout the five provinces without much incident. People tend not to recognize us or choose not to focus on anything other than their own lives." Reed tied his locs back with a leather throng.

"Yes, but I look different, feel different." Aza gestured to her body.

Reed winked at her. "We never would have guessed."

Before Aza's indignation caused her to lash out, Anwin interrupted, "We have a plan. Trust us. When Xira returns all will be explained."

Trust. What a fickle concept. The ones who tricked her, captured her. They asked for trust. Aza replayed the conversation Xira started —she wanted a fresh start with them. She craved it. But there was too much to forgive. At least for right now. Maybe over time Aza could ease off and forgive them for the transgressions, but with the fresh wound opening and bleeding it was a constant reminder of their betrayal of trust.

Aza huffed in response and turned back to examine the castle. Lorn had mentioned he had never been to Rijal before, always prone to stay at his own land. He only ventured out after Lakesh's death, typically to local towns bordering the Hinterlands, helping with any errant creatures seeking to wreak havoc. Aza wondered what he would say now, seeing her here at the capital, sneaking in to discover some secrets and knowledge of her own.

"Xira's returned."

8

"There are bigger stirrings than just the creatures of the Hinterlands. The hunter needs to keep his wits about him." Cruvo's private journal

Lorn searched for other possible survivors—a whisper of calamity on the wind. The Hinterlands was unmoving, and the monsters of shadow did not appear. Such an anomaly of destruction puzzled him.

Lorn couldn't shake the feeling of what Cruvo had warned him in his study back in El'en. *War is coming.* At the time Lorn doubted the validity of the statement, yet standing amongst the wreckage, he began to doubt himself. Here was the proof. Cruvo had devised specific plans for his trip to Gara, and Lorn would play his part. For now.

The winding trails led him to the border of Iyera and Gara, the ominous forest looming before him. These trees were rumored to be the very start in the creation of Ithilia, their thick roots embedded deep into the ground. Craning his neck back, the trees stretched high into the overcast sky, Lorn was unable to see even the tops of them. The trunks were massive, big enough to hide ten people behind.

Dismounting from his horse, he walked over to the trees and reverently placed his hand along the scarred bark. Deep gouges and rivets marked the tree and cascaded upwards into the skyline. It was breathtaking. He had never ventured this far north. The province of Gara was too isolated and separated for him to attempt. His beast hunting was primarily focused on the secluded towns that lined the border of the Hinterlands.

This forest was named the Silent Stretch. It held an indefinable eeriness that was dissimilar to the Hinterlands. Rather than a suffocation of magic and a stifling of life, the Silent Stretch was spooky with a fear of disturbing the preternatural silence. Lorn retreated from the Silent Stretch and made camp for the night. He would enter the forest the following day.

The Hinterlands was not the only place in Ithilia with wild, savage beasts roaming free. Small pockets of Ithilia held the dark creatures their presence kept shrouded by mystery and ignorance. Lorn heard rumors of these malignant creatures' existence. He had been dutifully trained and prepared by his parents, remembering their teachings. These creatures had slunk from existence, finding solitude within the dark, secretive pockets of this world, lying in wait. The Silent Stretch was one of those places where the foul creatures were whispered to reside.

The main road snaked through the behemoth trees, his own stature small in the sea of these vast trees. It was not surprising how Gara was kept separate from the rest of the provinces. The landscape provided a natural border for people unwilling to cross. It was a strange similarity shared between Gara and Nerian with the Nerian mountains providing their own protection. Often Iyeran, Vertan, and Kreehan citizens would roam freely between the southern provinces, their climates and geographies changing, but no natural landmarks to bar their passage. Many people preferred to brave the Northern Sea with its turbulent waves capable of capsizing a boat, rather than enter the Silent Stretch.

Leaning down to pat his brave horse, he murmured words of encouragement under his breath. Each step caused him to bristle and seize control of his magic, gripping at the ready like he would a sword. Lorn was still able to access his power and he relaxed his shoulders away from his ears. This forest was nothing like the Hinterlands where his magic was stifled.

Lorn huffed a frustrated sigh. Already he knew this journey would wear on him, but he would continue on only in hopes of helping Aza. He couldn't help but picture her unwavering focus when they trained together, or the brilliant smile that broke across her face like the sun after the storm, when she would get something correct. He needed to act as an ambassador at Gara for her—the information he discovered could assist her.

Since entering the Silent Stretch, rain had been his permanent partner. The constant deluge aided the growth of the magnificent trees, but soured Lorn's mood. Further and further, he delved into the forest, the rain unrelenting, even amongst the giant trees. The pine needles blocked some of the water, but with the unrelenting rain it still crept through. He and his horse were miserable. He feared for the mare's safety with the chill that seeped into their skin. Lorn was unable to build a fire due to the dampness and in an effort to conserve his magic. Instead, he sat bitterly under the cover of the giant trees with his soaking clothes.

Multiple times Lorn questioned Cruvo's choice of sending him to Gara. He hoped he wouldn't die from exposure first. Whenever he stopped, Lorn fastidiously checked his boots and feet. He could not let his feet get wet. Rot and disease would set in if he didn't take care. Lorn replaced anything mildly soaking with a fresh pair of socks or attempted to keep his feet as dry as possible. Because he had never traveled throughout Gara, Lorn was unsure of the travel time required for him to get through the Silent Stretch. Unwilling to run his horse ragged, he kept a moderate pace, the rain and muddy ground causing the mares hooves to stick and slosh in the mud. He would not risk her health to hurry through this forest. Cruvo had estimated that Lorn's journey on horseback would take roughly a week or two.

Lorn tried not to waver on his decision to go to Gara, but with the persistent rainfall and his grumpy state of mind, he couldn't help but picture himself anywhere else. However, images of the destroyed town, torn apart from death and disease, rippled through his mind each night. Helpless to do anything, he would fall asleep always questioning whether he made the right decision to head to Gara instead of finding Aza. He did not trust Cruvo, but he knew Cruvo had an insatiable desire to find Aza and would stop at nothing to get her. He needed to trust in that. Replaying that night in his head, Lorn found himself shaking his head. Why wasn't Aza using her magic against the Nerians? What had happened for her to have been pinned on the floor. His hand clenched the horse reins and he forced himself to loosen his grip. When he was done with Gara, he would tear those Nerians apart. Aza was too trusting, and they exploited that to her detriment. Dismounting from his horse, Lorn had a meager meal of dried rations, the soft drizzle of rain coating his skin in a light sheen so thin he didn't see it, only felt the thin coating on his skin like gossamer.

Every night he was troubled and restless, and he struggled to fall asleep. The looming feeling of ever watchful eyes followed him on his journey.

He missed dreaming. He yearned to see Lakesh again. His dreams satiated him, buoying his spirits with the positive memories that he clung to like a lifeline. When Aza helped cure some of the darkness plaguing his soul, his dreams of Lakesh came to him in a rush like a spigot of water that was unblocked, giving him pure unfiltered recollections of his treasured memories. But the dreams dried up, whether from his restless sleep or his lack of proximity to Aza, he was unsure.

Tonight, he dreamed.

Instead of the comforting familiarity of his wife and their farm and woods near his homestead, he stood on the edge of a jagged cliff. The waves smashed below in anger, lapping at the cliff in demand of his sacrifice. He fought the faltering of his feet as he stepped away from the edge. Even though he knew this was a a dream, his stomach rose in his throat at the dizzying height. Lorn couldn't fight the basic instinct to retreat from the sheer cliff-face and save himself from the plummet down.

A familiar voice jarred him out of his fear, causing him to stumble to the rough ground underfoot. His hands sliced against the unforgiving rock.

"Lorn, what are you doing?"

There before him stood Issi. Her blonde-white hair whipped in the wind, her stature unyielding.

Gritting his teeth, he stood brushing his errant black hair away from his eyes. "What do you mean, *goddess*?" The title was spewed as an insult. If she meant to help Lorn, Aza would not have been taken, Aza would not have to endure banishing the Hinterlands, she would not have been under the thrall of Cruvo. They wouldn't be in this position trying to untangle the twisted web of riddles and half-truths everyone in the blasted five provinces loved to deal in.

This was the first time in the last few weeks he had been able to dream, and it wasn't even of his beloved wife, only this goddess who had no business being here.

Her slow blink was the only indication she heard him. She left his question unanswered like Lorn was a petulant child. Probably to an eternal goddess, he did seem that way.

Lorn pushed himself back up to standing, wiping the blood from his hands on his pants.

"Why are you working with Cruvo?" Her voice was like the melody of a song, sweet and harmonic. Everything about the gods and goddesses was meant to draw in the MagicBlessed. Their very creation was a weapon. Who would be able to withstand the lure of such creatures? Cruvo's name fell from her lips like the soft whisper of a lover. In the fables, Issie and Cruvo were lovers. Why were they opposed now? Were the stories false?

Issi waited for his response, stoic, her limbs eerily motionless. Taking a steadying breath, Lorn cast a glance at the isolated cliff, debating his options of telling her. She did not deserve answers from him, but he was willing to in the hopes of some mutual exchange of information.

"I am not working *with* him. We share similar goals and I want to see Aza returned."

Although the wind pulled at Issi's hair, it never covered her face, like she could direct even the course of nature itself. Lorn expectantly waited for a response, but Issi remained silent, studying him. Her unnatural blue eyes worked their way up and down his body like she could see through to the core of his very being. Lorn kept his head high, unwilling to balk under such scrutiny.

"That makes sense. Considering who you are."

Furrowing his brows, Lorn fought the urge to shout, his frustration rising with the veiled conversation. "You are supposed to be clear, not give me more vague hints to follow. Why *goddess*, shouldn't I be working with Cruvo?" An exasperated sigh left his lips. He was done with the whims of gods and goddesses.

Her stoic facade had the hint of a crack, with the slight purse of her lips. "I cannot tell you. You must figure it out on your own. All your history is skewed, the time before the Hinterlands, violent and filled with war." Issi's head tilted to the side considering Lorn. "Be alert. Be vigilant. Trust only Aza."

Fighting the urge to storm up to her and demand a better response, Issi's head snapped upright her eyes widening in horror. "Lorn, wake up now!"

Confused he took an unsteady step forward to reach her, forgetting he was in a dream.

"Lorn wake up now! You cannot die! You need to fight!" Issi screamed. She cut the distance between them and slammed into his shoulders. Lorn stumbled off the cliff, falling down, down, down. Fear stuck in his throat, he eyed the water below. His body hit with a violent crash and his eyes flashed open taking in the utter darkness around him.

Lorn was still within the Silent Stretch, his horse resting beside him. They found small solace in the cover of the trees away from the consistent rain. Remembering Issi's message Lorn rubbed the sleep from his eyes and scanned the thick trees trying to discern anything amongst the darkness. His longsword within reach, he clutched it, the hilt providing a small comfort.

Issi's concern flashed through his mind. Whatever was hunting him, she was truly worried about. Lorn rose to his feet and kept the tree to his back as an extra layer of protection, his sword brandished in front of him. Fighting the temptation to strain his eyes to peer into the darkness, he stilled his erratic breath, listening, waiting, his heart pounding in his chest. He swiveled his head back and forth wanting whatever was hidden to reveal itself. Let the fight begin.

He deepened his stance, and his boots scuffed the thick layer of pine needles underfoot. Lorn's hair on the back of his neck raised unbidden.

Lorn was hesitant to use his light magic, worried the glare of the light would cause him to lose his precious vision. But he could not bear it any longer, the uncertainty, the waiting. Something was out there. Something Issi feared. He needed to face it head on. He exhaled slowly, and a soft touch of his magic flared illuminating the dense forest. Lorn saw nothing.

Easing himself forward away from the safety of the massive tree, Lorn cautiously progressed. He swiveled his head, searching for a sign of anything. Maybe Issi was mistaken?

The faint touch of skeletal fingertips coasted along his back. Lorn whipped around. His jaw dropped open. This was not some rogue creature from the Hinterlands. It floated over the forest floor, dressed in black rags, the ends torn in slits. Lorn could not discern anything within the hood. The creature floated over to him, and the magic of

Lorn's light winked out like the flame of a candle fighting a torrential wind. His light flickered, fighting against the dark entity. It cast strange harsh shadows.

Lorn's feet were locked to the ground, the grip on his sword loosening. The sword clattered to the ground. Lorn could only stare at the creature. A strange temptation persuaded him to come closer to the creature. Revulsion crept up his spine, but Lorn could not tear his sight away. Sensing a disturbance, his horse arose from her sleep, gave a nervous whinny, pawed the ground, and sprinted away. The noise drew the creature's attention, and it released an ear-splitting screech. The horse's distress broke whatever spell had come over Lorn. Awareness flooded him. Without hesitation Lorn rolled, grabbing his discarded sword.

Another foul creature leaped over him, its sharpened teeth barely missing Lorn's exposed back. Lorn scrambled to his feet clutching the sword loosely in his hand, unsure of what to target first. He struggled to put a word to the eerie ghost-like creature. Memories flashed before him from old stories told around his house late at night, stories he believed were myths. Yet it stood in front of him now and he had no idea how to defeat it. Would a sword even penetrate its translucent body?

With the eerie cloaked figure distracted by his runaway horse, he focused on his new opponent. It was a struggle to see in the darkness. His light magic struggled to illuminate. He faltered. It had the same twisted look as those from the Hinterlands. A mountain lion, but more feral. Its jaws dripping with saliva, its eyes widened in anger. It reminded him of the Howler, its body mangled and twisted from perpetual hunger.

The mountain lion leaped at Lorn, its outline blending in with the darkness of the forest. Lorn quickly sidestepped and slashed his sword up into its side. A fierce bellow echoed throughout the misty forest. Its paws swept out in a frantic rage, the long nails ripping away the flesh of Lorn's arm. Fighting the urge to release his sword, Lorn clenched harder. Lorn's head whipped back to the other creature—a wraith. He latched onto the word, small memories popping up. Wraith was the one that fit. It wasn't from his parent's stories, but rather a lonely night he had spent within the only bar in a town he had defended. The patrons were discussing creatures they had experienced before, typically citing the familiar ones from the Hinterlands. One patron spoke of the grisly tales of wraiths commonly told in Gara and during a trip through the Silent Stretch. Many scoffed at such an absurd story, calling the man someone who dabbled in fairy tales, but Lorn listened knowing that a kernel of truth usually lay embedded in the nighttime stories they all partook in.

The wraith abandoned its pursuit of the horse and turned back towards Lorn, the tattered remains of its cloak floating in the absent breeze. Lorn's light magic was fading with the effort of keeping it on. The wraith choked his magic, the light around him flickering as he looked. Cold. Bleak. His light wavered, the magic throughout his body was being doused like an errant flame.

The mountain lion pounced.

The breath rushed out of him, and his sword clattered to the forest floor. The corrupted mountain lion's heavy body pinned Lorn to the ground, its claws piercing his skin. He barely had the energy to scream as the mountain lion's jaw and teeth reared open.

He closed his eyes in resignation, his last wish that Aza would find safety amongst enemies and find happiness in this world.

Before the jaws could close onto his tender neck, a giant weight was pushed off his body. The claws of the mountain lion gouged out his skin, but he was still alive. Air came back to him in giant gasps.

"Fucking hunter! Get up! Fight!"

That voice. His eyebrows narrowed in confusion as he rolled over to find his sword. Lorn pushed himself to his feet and fought to understand the image in front of him. Lilit grappled with the mountain lion, her olive skin and darkened hair difficult to discern in the darkness, but it was her. Why was she here? Lorn made his way to help her, when she shouted at him, "Go after the wraith! We won't survive if it stays here." Another grunt and Lilit rolled away from the mountain lion pushing her tiny frame away from the intimidating bulk of the twisted mountain lion.

Sensing Lorn's reservations, Lilit's eyes flashed over to him. "Do I have to tell you everything? Steel your mind. It is afraid of light and fire. Use it!" The mountain lion jumped at Lilit cutting off her speech. Her sword arced in a vicious swing, aiming to cut down her foe.

Snapping back to the wraith, he focused on its approach. The weathered cloak, the shapeless face, it floated to him and reached out a decayed hand, wanting him to join it in death. It would be so easy to accept. It would be a welcome reprieve. Everything has been so difficult. So much work all the time. Lorn's sword lowered, the tip touching the ground. His head tilted, enchanted and numb.

"Steel your mind, hunter!" Lilit roared, locked in her own fierce battle.

Her voice jarred Lorn from his reverie. The wraith was luring Lorn in, using a disturbing sense of calm to placate him. How could he defeat this nonphysical being?

Lorn magic flared. He instinctively pressed his magic against the edge of his sword. He didn't have time to question his actions—only following the urge to meld his magic with his weapon. It was strange; he could feel his magic overwhelming the sword, yet it resisted his call like a stubborn latch refusing to open. A mutual respect was needed. The sword had its own nature and did not want to be altered, did not want to be changed. Lorn had to coax it, convince it to let go to give in.

The wraith loomed closer. Its transparent, decayed hand hovered wishing to claim Lorn. It would be so easy to give in, to let the call of the dead wash over him.

His magic faltered. Gritting his teeth, Lorn steeled his mind, unwilling to let his potential death distract him. Against his better judgment, Lorn closed his eyes. He needed to focus on his magic combining with the sword if he was going to succeed. Death was only the next stop. He need not fear it but embrace it fully if he was going to succeed.

A clear voice wove into Lorn's mind, *"One so wise, to understand what many avoid. I'm excited to see what you do."*

The latch in his mind lifted, and Lorn was free. He was unhindered. Without effort, Lorn's magic flowed through him like the sustaining rays of summer. He was light, power, and heat. Lorn funneled the impressive power into his sword. The blade glowed and the light brightened, it's magnitude surprising even Lorn. The magic felt endless.

The wraith pulled back, wary of the ever-growing light. The blade glowed even brighter with a pure and radiant light pulsing from it. It was the purest form he had ever seen, but Lorn did not need to look away. It was his own light, and he would not balk. The sword was a radiant beacon within the shadows of the Silent Stretch. It was like the hottest flames of the forge his sword was crafted in. It was pure energy. There was a pulling force around the sword like it forced everything into its own vortex.

Mesmerized, Lorn struggled to look away from his own creation. Before the wraith could escape from the blinding light, Lorn tightened his grip on the sword, and sprinted at the wraith. He swung the sword and its clear light cleaved the wraith. The wraith released a sheer screech and withered in amongst itself, the light treating it like an infection in a wound, burning it out until nothing remained.

After the wraith disappeared, Lorn stood frozen in place staring at his sword. The light flickered once, twice before resuming its dull hue, the magical light extinguished.

A soft grunt sounded next to him. Lilit had bested the twisted mountain lion, her breathing heavy. His eyes trailed over the carnage wondering why a creature of the Hinterlands was so far away from its borders.

A ragged breath escaped Lorn's lips. "Thanks."

"For someone who survived the Hinterlands, you are shit at surviving." Lilit walked away to gather Lorn's horse. She calmed her down and brought her back to the sanctuary of their spot. The horse was skittish, wary of the dead, twisted mountain lion and refused to come closer. They traveled farther and set up a ramshackle camp for the rest of the night. "I'll take first watch," Lilit offered.

The soft, morning light pierced through the thick treetops, Lorn noticed a faint redness and puffiness around Lilit's eyes. He dismissed it and fell asleep weariness weighing him down. When he woke up a few hours later, he realized he forgot to question what Lilit was even doing here in the first place.

9

"I should have come down from my mountain long ago. I could have mitigated this current disaster. Maybe I am merely hopeful—or naive."

Nivet's private journal.

Aza closed her eyes against the dust. The wheels bumped along the road. She held her tongue to prevent herself from cursing. The trap door in the wagon hid her from view and she could only hear the muffled sounds of her companions on either side.

This was one of the few ways she could enter the city unnoticed by guards. The castle in the capital city Rijal was often monikered, The Fortress. Despite the city's expansiveness, guards were stationed along every wall. Everyone who traveled in and out were routinely checked and accounted for.

They traveled in a crew of other farmers who came to the city to sell their wares. Farm animals, fruits, vegetables, crafted pottery all clanked above her. A small hole in the wooden plank to her left allowed Aza a brief look out at the obscured countryside colors washing by. She prayed it would be enough. It was a vulnerable position for her, especially when she currently lacked her magic. Xira confiscated her weapons and expertly hid them in the wagon. The wagon and goods were lent to her by a sympathetic farmer. Her ability to charm anyone was astounding—to watch her go from a hardened Nerian warrior to someone that everyone fawned over was both ridiculous and fascinating.

The villagers they passed and traveled amongst carried about life like normal. There was no disturbance or talk of the Hinterlands, no discussion of the strange corruption underlying their land. It was like they had a mask over their eyes blinded to their current reality.

Aza strained to hear the muffled sound of discussion, anything indicating how close they were to the castle gates. But there was too much extraneous noise, and the wooden planks of her hiding spot dulled the noise. Piled on top of her hiding spot were thick coats of sheep's wool their weapons hidden amongst the soft fluff. It dampened the sounds and Aza yearned to know what was happening. She hated lying in wait instead of taking action. It made her skin itch and reminded her of her time in Iyera, trying to figure out what was happening and all the pieces of the puzzle that lay before her. Without her weapons she felt truly defenseless, except for the Nerians who escorted her. Already they had proved they would protect her with their lives. Fighting a sea serpent, evading Eonas, all of it to protect her. But for what reason? This trip to Verta would hopefully provide the answers she sought.

The wagon came to a halt and Aza's heart hammered in her chest.

Before entering the cart, Xira, Anwin, and Reed expertly draped farmer's clothing over themselves, changed their posture, altered their stances, all to transform and appear as non-threatening as possible. They were skilled actors and it explained how they were able to traverse so much of the five provinces and remain undetected for what they were—Nerians. Based on Oron's lessons, the MagicBlessed people assumed the Nerians rarely came down from their mountain, when in actuality they may have been more dispersed among the people than they realized, hiding, acting, changing, shrouded.

With minimal room and her size, she struggled, wanting to toss and turn to gain a peek of what was happening. She steadied her breath, using her restlessness to tap each of her fingers together one after the other. So slow. Too slow. Something felt wrong. Rather than reveal her position, Aza remained unmoving.

Believe in them. They have done this countless times before. You have nothing to fear. If anything, they should fear you.

Raised voices alerted Aza and her breath hitched. Not daring to move, not daring to bring any attention to the underside of the wagon, she stilled herself.

Rustling above her, the sheep's wool being cast aside, then stillness.

Voices talked around her, but she had no idea what was being said.

She clenched her fist, ready to attack if she was revealed. Then a double pat on the cart and it moved forward. Aza let out a slow breath. It was too hot within the wagon, despite the chill of recent days.

She needed to get out, she needed out now. The cart needed to stop, let her out, let her out. Her eyes shut tight. The space was too small all of a sudden. She needed to get out!

The lid of the trap door opened revealing the cloudy sky overhead and Anwin's broad face staring back. Concern etched across her face as she scanned Aza.

"My Lady, you have nothing to fear." Aza smashed her eyes closed and reopened them, forcing the tears away, forcing her lungs to take great rasping breaths. Anwin checked over her shoulder and leaned down to hoist Aza up, somehow sensing Aza needed the support right now. Anwin crouched before Aza and pulled her cloak over Aza's hair and face covering her from view. Protecting her. Always protecting her. Sitting upright, Aza tried to steady her breathing but failed, the panic sweeping in and removing any of her remaining sanity. She couldn't think straight. Why was she so rattled? Why couldn't she stop this senseless fear? She had faced worse before, why now?

As if reading her thoughts, Anwin answered, "It doesn't ever make sense. But I am here with you. And I will sit with you and breathe." Anwin's hand clasped over her own chest, the hand rising and falling in time. She gently took Aza's hand and placed it on Anwin's chest encouraging Aza to mimic her. Anwin's vibrant green eyes, so different from the wildness of Cruvo's, held hers. The ragged breaths hurt her, tore at her, but Anwin was there. Her gaze unwavering, never giving false platitudes, only her presence. Breath after breath until Aza's own returned, the fear vanquished.

Realizing where they were, Aza scrambled to hide herself and jump off the cart. Anwin pulled her back to stop her. "Do not rush yourself. If we are found, we will fight. But do not ignore what happened. You are not less because of it."

Aza couldn't handle the intense gaze of Anwin and looked away.

"Mold your fear. Use it. Manipulate it."

"You do not believe me, but we all struggle. It hits us in different ways. Even us." Anwin gestured to Xira and Reed who stood nearby taking watch, making sure no wandering eyes roved over their precarious positions.

A sharp whistle from Anwin brought Xira and Reed over.

"We are inside Rijal, but we need to be cautious. It is still early. We need to wait for our moment. You must keep yourself hidden at all times. We can't risk anyone seeing you." Xira pulled Aza's hood down, covering more of her vibrant silver hair, gently pulling one of the strands between her fingers. "Fuck, I forget what a beacon you are for everyone."

Aza rolled her eyes the moment of panic gone and in its place irritation. "Like I can help what I look like."

Xira's lips thinned like she was considering the idea. "Yeah it can't be helped."

Anwin fought a chuckle as she added, "Yeah being a heart-stopping beauty is such a travesty." Her gentle mockery of Xira's criticism had Aza fighting her own smile.

How are your acting skills?" Xira questioned.

"Appalling."

Aza's head whipped to Anwin who answered for her. She shrugged holding up her hands in defense, "What? You have a glass face."

"What is that supposed to mean?"

Reed interjected, "Nothing bad, my Lady. Only that you show every emotion clearly on your face."

"Nothing to be done about that." Xira scrutinized Aza, checking her cloak and errantly brushing off any remaining debris. "Try not to talk or draw attention to yourself. There are too many vipers in this nest."

Jumping down from the wagon, Aza nodded keeping herself covered and trying to alter her stance. She commanded a presence, her height and broadness making her an easy target for curious eyes.

Reed, Xira and Anwin circled her keeping Aza hidden from the public. Stepping out of the alley they entered the main street where people, animals, and wagons full of goods bumped into each other. Aza was jostled as the chaos of the streets took over. Anwin kept a hand clasped on Aza's shoulder, keeping Aza between Anwin and the wagon of sheep's wool they needed to drop off.

Wooden stalls were hastily erected with vendors hawking their wares. Farmers, crafters, people advertising their inventory shouted and cajoled the group. Xira expertly navigated between them with a polite word, or a shout volleyed back. They blended in seamlessly with the massive crowd and Aza could only be swept up in it. Paranoid about someone catching any part of her features, she kept her head down, pulling the hood low. She even altered her posture stooping low to seem less threatening, less of an anomaly amongst this giant crowd. She could only peek around the edges of her hood, eager to see the chaotic sights that unfolded around her. The smell of animals, products, and people was stifling, but Aza found herself enjoying the press of people around her, like they were one being together moving and forming in the streets.

In Iyera she had been sequestered in the castle of El'en. Practicality and fear kept her there, worried about her extreme power and those that would gawk at her in the streets. She did not want to be constantly viewed as an oddity. Here she was still shrouded and covered unable to reveal who she truly was and walk freely, yet there was a small bit of freedom in moving about unawares of this crowd, partaking of this sense of normalcy. She refrained from inspecting the market stalls products. Instead, she used Anwin's firm hand to guide her through the massive crowd.

Despite her enjoyment of the market day, Aza still felt the underlying current of corruption. It had never left since they had neared the capital of Verta. It was the vague sense of putrefaction, like something was dead and rotting underneath all of this. It soured her experience. She only wanted to take a shred of this moment of being a part of the MagicBlessed. But the sobering truth of their mission overtook her. This was not some moment to enjoy the life here, this was to truly see something amiss, to the seedy underbelly of Verta.

The Nerians utilized the crowd to their advantage, weaving effortlessly in and out amongst the pulsing crowd. Aza cast aside her wishful thinking, hoping to linger among the market stalls and partake in the chaos of a true market day. They were leading her farther and farther away, the echoes of voices dying down as they went through several side alleys, the heaviness of corruption getting thicker within the abandoned alleys.

Amongst the Vertans, there seemed to be a heightened influx of guards patrolling the streets. She dismissed the notion that they were there for her. How could they know where she was? They were probably there for other reasons. Whenever Xira and Reed encountered the tell-tale sight of a Vertan guard with their sickle and wheat crest, they doubled-back their smooth maneuvers flawlessly executed. She could only catch a brief glimpse of the guards as they walked away, silently thanking the skillful judgment of the Nerians who escorted her.

Sweat began to pool on her forehead. Aza's body began to cramp. The effort of concealing her identity and the tension of being found out without her magic to protect her wore down her body. The mild panic attack she suffered from earlier didn't help either. It seemed an endless loop and the day had only begun. Her skin even seemed weighed down, like it was absentmindedly absorbing the strange corruption prevalent in this city. Rounding another corner, Aza pulled on Anwin's hand signaling her need to stop. Gasps raked out of her as Aza tilted her head back against the rundown wall. The filth of the building soaked into her cloak, but Aza couldn't muster the energy to care.

She was being covered. She struggled to breathe.

Her hood slipped revealing a sliver of her silver strands. Anwin delicately grasped the edges of the hood and pulled it down to cover Aza's face. She couldn't do it anymore, her body felt constricted—tight. She needed air. She needed to glimpse the uninterrupted sky above.

Xira caught the group delayed against the wall and came back. She kept her voice low as she asked, "What is going on?"

Anwin shifted trying to form a wall around Aza to protect her. "I'm not sure. This is different than what happened earlier."

Reed reached out and clasped Aza's shoulder, firmly squeezing. His brown eyes searched hers, fruitlessly scanning her body for any signal or injury—something he could try to help with. "Aza try to look at me."

So far away—they seemed so far away. She only wanted the bright blue sky above her—a clear expanse where she could escape to, not this endless torment where her breath struggled to come.

"Aza, we are here. Look at me."

Aza fought and struggled to bring her silver eyes back to Reed's own. Everything felt heavy, like if she did not escape this city she would succumb to the darkness. This city was poison, and it was poisoning her.

"Fuck. We need to get her somewhere safe." Reed reached out his hand clasping Aza's face trying to provide a buoy, something, anything for her to clasp to.

"There is nowhere safe in Rijal—not for her." Xira clenched her fist and scanned the busy main street. So far a wandering eye hadn't glanced the curious group off to the side, but it would only be a matter of time before someone did.

Reed's eyes did not leave Aza as he said, "This is our fault. Her magic is staunched and because of that she is struggling."

Anwin ran a rushed hand over her hidden blades, a rushed breath forced between her lips. "We unknowingly brought her to a trap." Anwin turned to Reed and Xira. "Is it the corruption?"

A swift nod in response from Reed confirmed Anwin's question.

"The corruption is prevalent here. That is what we wanted to show you Aza," Xira said, her head flicking back and forth between Aza and the main street, looking for any possible threats.

Reed's hand returned to Aza's shoulder squeezing, not hard enough to hurt, but enough to ground Aza in her current reality.

"Since your magic is stifled, the corruption is trying to take hold. Do not let it. Fight it. You are more than your magic. Your magic is a part of you, but is not the *only* part of you." Reed's eyes searched hers, his other hand coming up to clasp both her shoulders. He fully faced her, walking her through the steps to break the corruption's hold on her.

"Your magic is only one small piece of who you are. There is so much more, Aza. Use those other pieces and fight the hold."

"We are here, my Lady," Anwin added. Her hand grasped Aza on the shoulder alongside Reed's hand.

Xira turned away from the busy market street and her honey brown eyes pierced into Aza's not looking away. "We will always be here, my lady." Xira added her hand clasping Aza's other shoulder.

The three Nerians did not let go of Aza. They stood there vulnerable and exposed in a toxic city, their unwavering loyalty trying to beckon Aza out of the consuming darkness.

Aza's breath rasped out. Tears formed in her eyes. She could not do it.

The corruption was like a thick coat of mud covering her, coating her, burying deep beneath her skin and poisoning her body, the poison spreading numbing her, trying to take her down. She could not fight it. Frustrated tears welled to the surface, the Nerians' words barely breaking through the roaring in her ears.

What was she beyond her magic? Her magic, her power, it was everything she was—who she was. A brief spark of anger flared up at the injustice. They were the ones who took that away from her, they rendered her weak. How dare they?

Reed sadly shook his head. "We did Aza. We did take your magic away and you have every right to be mad about that."

Did she say that out loud?

"But you are so much more than that. If you do not see it, we do." His voice remained calm, grounding her, steadying her.

"Find the pieces of who you are—outside of your magic—and fight it."

Aza swallowed her anger. Reed, Xira and Anwin were here risking themselves to help her, to have her understand.

Her skin felt thick, her body turning numb to the surroundings. What was she beyond her magic?

This corruption, this filth wanted her to succumb. She would not, could not let it. Here was her family. She needed to protect them.

Family. The word rose unbidden in her mind, but she latched onto it, using the sentiment to strengthen her resolve to fight back the impending darkness.

For the first time, instead of using Reed's steadfast gaze to anchor her, Aza closed her eyes and let herself fall into the endless pit of corruption.

10

"The Silent Stretch is an arduous journey. We will see if they survive."
  Cruvo's private journal

Lorn tossed and turned in his sleep, despite the utter exhaustion that threatened to tear him down. He wanted to crumple with the weight of knowledge, with responsibility, yet sleep eluded him. Bleary eyed, he jolted awake and patted his body to double-check he was unharmed. His strange dreams with Issi left him disoriented along with the random appearance of Lilit, and the creatures within the Silent Stretch. To top it off, he couldn't even begin to scratch the surface of the way he was able to manipulate his magic and imbue his sword with light energy—or the voice that spoke to him. As he lay looking back at the canopy of trees, his mind jolted between each thought. Lorn shifted to his side and huffed a breath. He simply wanted to be left in peace.

Lorn pushed himself up onto his forearms and searched for Lilit. Her lithe form and snide face was nestled far away, curled against the base of a tree. He quickly breathed a sigh of relief and collapsed back onto his side. He didn't want to deal with her right now. A shred of guilt cut through his harsh thoughts. Last night, Lilit had most likely saved his life, the least he could show was a little gratitude. Even though she was unbearable, Lorn could discern small glimmers of who Lilit truly was. She was difficult, frustrating, abrasive, and rude, but Lorn couldn't help but see an animal stuck in a trap. In pain, she lashed out at those around her, instead of directing her ire at the reason she was there.

A neigh from his horse broke the silence. He wouldn't get any more sleep, he might as well travel and gain ground towards Gara. He was ready to be out of the Silent Stretch. Lorn scrambled to his feet in search of his trusty mare. She had done admirably the prior night, only running away when immediate danger threatened her life. He patted the side of her head and pulled his forehead to hers with a quick thanks.

"About time you woke up."

Lorn fought the grimace that rose to his face and gently broke off his contact with his horse and turned on his heel to find Lilit with her own horse saddled, ready to depart.

Without any further discussion, she climbed into the saddle and veered her horse to the vague path muddled through the Silent Stretch.

Not wanting to grumble to Lilit, he quickly saddled his horse, grabbed a piece of dried jerky from his satchel and clambered on, setting his horse on a slow pace after Lilit's mare. The heavy rain had eased. The darkness of the forest still descended around them, but Lorn would catch small snatches of sunlight. It forced its way through the trees, like a needle piercing fabric, small and forceful.

Hours had passed with no conversation. A light mist dusted them as they rode through the forest. Instead of attempting a conversation with Lilit, Lorn tried to process what happened last night. A beast from the Hinterlands and a wraith had attacked him. The mountain lion had that similar gaunt form and bloodlust crazed eyes, but there was something different about it. Like some sort of disease had overtaken its body, a new blend of creature instead of the ones Lorn was used to fighting. Why was the creature so far from the Hinterlands? They never ventured this far. Also, for it to find him in the Silent Stretch was improbable. What were the chances that he had encountered a mutated creature from the Hinterlands and a wraith? And when he fought, his sword was imbued with an impossible amount of light magic, magic that would incapacitate a typical MagicBlessed person. Yet, here he was, not even fatigued by the actions. He would never have been able to accomplish such a feat of magic.

There were countless times throughout his journey he wished to see Aza again, but right now he wanted her back not only for her safety, but to discuss what happened. She could provide more knowledge on the situation and guide him through the feelings he had as he imbued the sword. It was unlike anything he had ever experienced.

Lorn tried to steer his mind away from this tricky slope of endless questions. It resulted in him being exhausted, buried underneath the avalanche of uncertainty, but he couldn't help but wonder what she was doing right now. Was she being treated well? What had happened to her magic that night? Why couldn't she defend herself? Lorn fought the pointless circles his mind wanted to trace. His hands clutched the reins of his horse a little too tightly. The leather dug into his calloused hands.

Lorn watched Lilit plodding ahead through the dense wilderness. What was she doing here and how did she know to find him? The strange silence between the two of them suited him just fine, but right now he demanded answers.

Skillfully maneuvering his horse through the thick trees, Lorn pulled up as closely to Lilit as he could. "What are you doing here?"

Only the clopping of their horses' hooves sounded as Lorn waited for an answer.

A few moments trickled past in silence. Maybe she hadn't heard his question.

"What are you doing here?"

An exasperated sigh left her lips as Lilit answered, "I heard you the first time."

"Then why didn't you—"

Before Lorn could finish his question Lilit cut him off, "That is not how you say thank you."

Lorn reared back in his saddle, trying to hold back his own tongue from saying something regrettable. "Excuse me?"

"You could at least thank me for saving you last night."

Lorn brushed a hand through his hair, the slick mist coating each strand. Lilit had helped him. He couldn't deny that, but her audacity to claim she saved him was inexcusable. "I-"

Lilit held up a hand silencing him. "You were about to resign yourself to death. Once again I'm surprised you have lasted this long. How you made it through the Hinterlands alive is anyone's guess." She finally turned around to glare at Lorn her cold gray eyes hardening like the toughest gems mined deep within Gara. "Yes I saved you, because I reminded you to fight." She adjusted herself in the saddle and faced forward. "How you forget such a basic concept as a hunter is beyond me."

Lorn would not suffer her abuse any longer. He forced his horse next to hers on the tiny path so he could stare back at her. "You know nothing of my life." Lorn held back the shout he wanted to use and only seethed at her.

"No, you are right. I do not. However —," Lilit's head whipped to his, her voice sharp and unyielding, "I do know you do not give up in a fight. Ever." Her nostrils flared in anger.

Lorn barked out through clenched teeth, "I was not giving up."

"You keep searching for ways to end your life. It will catch up to you. Stop searching for an end, Lorn. Your wife will still be in the Meadow of the Undying with or without you."

Lilit cantered forward giving themselves a welcome reprieve from each other. Lorn could barely think straight due to the anger which blinded him. But as they traveled further through the Silent Stretch, though her words were tough, Lorn started to realize—she had a point.

~

Through the Silent Stretch they rode. The days stretched and blurred together and Lorn found an unlikely routine with Lilit. They did not bother with small talk and focused on their journey and surviving the Silent Stretch. Although Lilit was a silent companion, she was resourceful. Lorn noted it in the way she carried herself, her head on a constant swivel searching for enemies, intruders, anything amiss. She did not tire or if she did, she did not show it. It was strangely uplifting. It pushed Lorn to his limits. His spirits were dampened as he trudged through the Silent Stretch, his mind occupied with thoughts of Aza and the always prevalent doubts about being an ambassador in Gara.

When Lakesh died his purpose and reason for being had splintered. The fractured pieces drifted away, and he assumed he had them lost forever. But upon meeting Aza, those pieces revealed themselves not completely lost only buried underneath insurmountable levels of depression and anger. Finding her, accompanying her, had renewed his sense of purpose and his sense of belonging. It was not the same connection he had with Lakesh. That connection could never be brought back or found again. However, Aza brought a different sense of purpose to his life, one he was able to inspect and evaluate during their trip through the Silent Stretch. Was it wrong for him to not pursue Aza, find her captors, and bring her back to safety? Following Cruvo's orders strained Lorn in an unfamiliar way. He did not mind listening or following directions, but something about Cruvo did not sit right within him, like reaching the safety of a cave only to realize it was home to a wolf within.

Lilit and Lorn rarely had a need to talk, except about the basics of survival and when to set up camp. She was a quick, sharp-tongued woman and he had no desire to strike up any further conversation with her, yet he couldn't help but question why she was here? Did Cruvo send her here to assist Lorn? If so, why wasn't Lilit sent with him initially?

Lorn studied her. At moments her shoulders would curve under an enormous burden, or her eyes would tire, tinged with a sadness he couldn't understand. Lilit was always fearsome and unfeeling, but in those rare moments when he spotted a moment of fragility, Lorn lost any nerve to ask her what was happening. But each night when he was safe within the confines of darkness and the torrent of his own thoughts, those ideas would not leave him.

One day of travel remained. Lorn blew out a long-held sigh. Through sheer luck or pure coincidence Lorn and Lilit didn't encounter any other foul creatures within the Silent Stretch. With half a day remaining they trudged on horseback through the dreary trees, their silent ominous presence leering over them. He wondered if Lilit felt the same about this forest. Lorn couldn't help the shivers down his spine.

This dense forest was something out of legend. He pictured a reserve of vicious mythical creatures lying in wait amongst the pine giants. There was a reason many didn't travel freely to Gara—or even Neria. The natural geography between Iyera, Verta, and Kreeha allowed for easy traveling between the provinces. The natural barriers between Gara and Neria tended to leave them blocked off from the other provinces their secluded natures both mysterious and stigmatized. The seas encircling Ithilia were treacherous in most seasons only leaving the most skilled sailors to traverse and trade over the stormy seas. Lorn had never traveled on the ocean himself and wondered what the experience would be like, with the vast emptiness stretched out in front of you, land only a distant reminder of what awaited you. However, from the stories he heard in the taverns he frequented people typically complained about the vicious Northern seas. This added another layer of difficulty to access Gara. They were an isolated province and from what Lorn remembered of Lady Rasmina and their contingent, they seemed to prefer the isolation.

He was ready for action and to cease his endless thoughts. His mind felt blurry and achy. It was a painful reminder of how he used to operate after Lakesh's death and before. He was alone, an outsider amongst towns and people. However Aza had kindled a kinship with him again. With these questions that they both had they were able to share freely without judgment. He wished for her easygoing, optimistic nature, and listening ear. He needed it and was curious to see what theories she would come up with to alleviate the confusion.

Instead of Aza he had Lilit's ramrod, straightened back in front of him. Despite her tiny stature, she held a powerful will to fight. Despite their immensely rocky start, Lorn argued with himself to keep an open mind. She had helped him realize one of his deepest flaws—he was always looking for an out, an expiration date on his life. If there was an opportunity to rush into danger and his life would be forfeit Lorn took it, and Lilit had seen right through him. They needed to talk.

Based on the thinning trees, and pacing he estimated, they had little time left before they entered the true boundaries of Gara.

Due to their limited conversation, Lorn awkwardly directed his horse alongside Lilit's and cleared his throat. He turned to look at her and wasn't shocked to find her staring straight ahead ignoring him entirely. Her cool undertone skin was dusted in a sparkling, misting of rain and her ash brown hair was braided and tucked underneath her hood. The rain clung to the tip of her razor-sharp nose, like her bloodline already knew she would be a fierce fighter and gave her features to match.

"Lilit."

With barely a flicker of her gray eyes, she gave a barely audible *hmm* in response.

"We are approaching Gara. Lord Aldrich —,"

Lilit's head whipped to him and pulled her horse to a complete stop. The mare whinnied at the abrupt shift. Lorn was forced to stop his as well.

"Lord Aldrich did nothing. Cruvo did." This was the first time Lorn heard Lilit or anyone besides Aza mention the name Cruvo. Inwardly cursing himself at the slip up, he backtracked.

"I did not mean to offend. It was an accident nothing more."

Mollified, Lilit gave a sharp nod of her head, yet her eyes belied what she truly felt — pure rage.

Unwilling to start a fight, Lorn monitored his own words. "Cruvo sent me here to the court of Gara. I'm not exactly sure why, or what I'm doing here." He thought back to how Cruvo phrased his assignment, spying on Gara and acting as an ambassador. Lilit remained silent her body stiff.

"Why are you here? What is our story?"

Without hesitation Lilit answered, "I'm your personal bodyguard."

Gripping the reins of her horse, she made a soft noise in her throat to get the horse going again. He couldn't piece together why Iyera's Captain of the Guard would be sent here. Why wouldn't she oversee Iyera or lead the search for Aza? Gravers could have easily been sent in her place, why was it Lilit? Something didn't make sense and Lorn persisted.

"That's why you were sent here? That makes no sense. Why wouldn't you have traveled with me from the beginning? Why didn't Cruvo mention this to me?" He couldn't stop all of the questions from bubbling out of him like the start of a tiny wound, one of little consequence yet the blood never stopped leaking out.

Lilit stopped her horse and pulled sharply on the reins. "You think you deserve all the answers," she seethed. "You deserve nothing. I am here to assist you and if necessary protect you. So shut your mouth. Your questions will not be answered. Least of all by me."

Lorn would not be cowed by her anger. He had finally reached his breaking point with her. Ever since they met she had been insufferable, taunting him, goading him, chastising him, no longer. She could not go around and speak however she wanted without retribution. Lorn skillfully navigated the dense foliage and urged his horse to jump in front of Lilit's blocking her path. This pairing would never work. Why did Cruvo send her this way? They were two blazing infernos threatening to swallow each other whole.

"What is wrong with you?" Lorn shouted. He rarely took such a tone with anyone. He was shocked that now was the moment he allowed himself this unfiltered fury. His hands shook on the reins of his horse, his thighs tightening, he could barely contain himself.
"I am trying to work together. I don't know what in the Darkness below happened to you and I am trying to figure it out. So we can get back to Iyera and back to figuring out where Aza is." He could feel his magic pulse wildly searching for an outlet. Yet if he succumbed, he would never work with Lilit, they would always be at odds. He fought back the itch and forced a steady gaze at Lilit.

Lilit's shoulders drooped slightly before she shrugged it off and rose to meet his anger. Lilit volleyed back, "You need to know nothing! I'm here. I'm fucking here with you instead of back in Iyera." Lorn's eyebrows furrowed at the slight catch in her voice. "I could care less about you and Aza. But I am tasked with coming here with you and I follow orders." Her tone flattened, her fury tightly wound back with the confines of her body.

Lorn wouldn't let her back down so easily. She wasn't able to say such things and get away with it, not if they would spend weeks if not months together at the unknown court in Gara. He could barely control the shaking in his body. Aza had been captured right underneath Lilit. She should care about their welfare, but she didn't. As Captain of the Guard, she should take some pride in her job, but she didn't care about anyone but herself.

Keeping his voice level and controlled Lorn asked, "How dare you?"

Bored, Lilit looked beyond Lorn aiming to steer her horse away from the conversation, but Lorn cut her off, catching her eyes again.

"Do you know how much Aza tried to help you?"

Lilit shrugged, dismissing the sentiment, but Lorn pressed further. "Do you know she overheard Lord Aldrich speaking with you, and she wanted to protect you. *You*." Lorn pointed his finger at Lilit. Fighting the urge to spit in disgust, Lorn continued, "She thought you were in danger and wanted to help. And this is how you speak about her? Like she doesn't matter to you at all?"

Lorn shook his head trying to dispel the heaviness and anger that was taking over his body. He fought the cynical laughter creeping out. With a disheartened chuckle, Lilit pulled back to look at him, confusion warring over her features. "You broke her hand, shattered her bones, and she still wanted to help you. I might not deserve your respect and compassion Lilit, but she fucking does."

With one last glance, Lorn turned his horse back towards Gara leaving Lilit behind. He couldn't stand to look at her face, one of resignation and regret.

11

"I should not be surprised Cruvo has not shared any information with Aza. She does not understand why she feels the way she does around other gods and goddesses. If I see Cruvo again, I mean to throttle him."

Nivet's private journal.

Aza blinked rapidly, taking in her surroundings. Her Nerian companions were nowhere to be seen. She stood upon formless ground with a vast emptiness stretched out before her.

The sickening sense of corruption and disease plagued the air, an intolerable heaviness. Her breath was stifled. Aza stepped forward tentatively, the eerie feeling of sludge coated and weighed down her bare feet.

Aza cringed against the unwanted sensation and glanced down at her body. She was completely bare except for a thin white dress which skimmed her thighs. Where were her weapons, her proper clothes? She was completely vulnerable and in unsuitable clothing. She took a steadying breath and stepped forward, searching. Reed's words played back to her. *"Find the pieces of who you are—outside of your magic—and fight it."*

She had so many aspects beyond her magic. How could she find those essential pieces? In this strange dreamscape, Aza was unable to call her magic. It was still muffled and locked away. She wasn't sure what to do. Biting her lip, Aza blew out a breath. To fight this, she needed to figure out the other pieces of her. Who was she beyond her magic?

She was naive. Aza shook her head thinking of how many times she had been duped and manipulated by the people around her.

Not naive, a small voice whispered. She was steadfast. Loyal. Strong. Powerful. Someone with hope who believes the best in people. Someone who wishes to heal the land and to heal those troubled around her.

With each positive affirmation, Aza revolted against the strange sickness around her. The air she breathed was lighter. The positive thoughts warded the corruption away, and Aza stormed ahead, her confident steps rippling in the dreamscape.

She needed to save herself. With or without her magic she could do this.

Aza was uncertain of what she was searching for. Sludge and sickness lapped at her heels like impatient dogs begging for scraps. Whenever the corruption stuck to her, threatening to pull her under, she would remind herself of who she was. Her positivity acted as a sword, cutting the corruption away, staving off the assault. The setting remained murky as she tried to formulate a plan. The corruption was merely held back, but not banished.

A vague outline formed in front of her. Aza halted her steps. The sudden intrusion was startling. The foul and wicked feel of corruption tightened its hold as the outline solidified into a person.

Unconsciously, Aza's steps receded. She furrowed her brows and tightened her fists. A severe tension thrummed through her body, like the overwhelming collection of ether before a lightning strike.

It was a woman.

Her deep auburn hair was swept back into a regal updo highlighting her glass-sharpened cheekbones. The woman's white skin glowed in the dark. Aza noticed faint streaks of black pulsing along her forearms and coursing along her neck. The veins slipped away from Aza's view, obscured by her clothing. The woman's dress mimicked Aza's own, a mere slip that fell to her knees, except the woman's was a deep black. It blended in with the emptiness and heightened the woman's eerie glow. She watched Aza, unblinking, her large blue eyes unsettling Aza.

Neither of them moved, both stuck in stasis. Aza finally took the plunge and stepped forward. The woman did not move, merely stared. Each step was excruciatingly tough like Aza was trudging through mud or a swamp. When she finally crossed the distance between them Aza stopped. The woman appraised her like a dragon with its treasure.

Aza fought back her rasping breath. She could not reveal any weakness.

Her predatory gaze slid over Aza's limbs, the woman's eyes trailing each and every part of her—analyzing her, testing her. With each look, each prolonged moment, the woman's rotted veins pulsed, like the corruption could not be contained beneath her skin. Aza bristled under the strange inspection feeling vulnerable and exposed to this woman's wandering eyes.

Aza could wait no longer and asked, "Who are you?" Her voice sounded strange in this dimension. It echoed and rebounded back to her.

The woman's eyes flashed to her, the hint of a smile playing about her lips. Aza fought the urge to fidget and opened her mouth to ask again when the woman interrupted.

"You dare ask my name?" Her voice slinked around Aza, enveloping her. The voice was both sensuous and sinister. Sharp tingles shot down her spine. The woman stepped forward, the tips of her toes gracefully padding against the darkness underfoot without any disturbance. Each move from the woman was calculated. With each step, Aza's throat closed from her cloying smell, the odd scent of decay, of death.

A clear thought penetrated Aza's mind. It was the woman. She was the corruption.

The woman leisurely walked behind Aza, an errant hand drifting along Aza's shoulder, almost playfully.

"I have waited for you. You who are crafted from starlight." The woman's hands softly danced along Aza's exposed back. "We could be magnificent together." Aza's breath was ragged. Each touch and twinge from the woman lulled Aza into a deeper state of relaxation, her mind being placated by the stray hand, something within her submitting to this woman, submitting to who she was.

Finished with her perusal, the woman stepped in front of Aza and the cloying scent came back stronger. Aza couldn't let go this easily, be tempted this easily.

Aza batted her hand away, and stepped back enraged at herself.

The choking, cloying scent left her nose and Aza was able to get a full gasp of fresh air, without the interference of this woman.

"Get away from me. I would never work with you."

The woman's auburn eyelashes hid her brilliant blue eyes, coy and abashed. They flashed back up in anger. "You say that—yet you do not even know who I am. What I am. What we could be together."

"You are the corruption, the sickness underneath the land of Verta." Aza shook her head violently. "I do not need to know more than that."

The woman paused, her smile widening revealing her bright white teeth—a predator ready to devour her prey. "My name is Astaroth." She stepped forward straight to Aza and stopped only inches from her face. "The offer is here, Daughter of the Night. The Darkness resides in you. We would make a great pair. You will release me." Astaroth held Aza's stare and without any further words turned on her heel and walked away. Aza could not help but admire the sway of Astraoth's hips, the alluring pull of her charisma, the delicate way her footsteps touched the ground. Aza bit the inside of her cheek hard, and blood filled her mouth. She needed to stop this. She bent over and placed her hands on her knees, shaking her head.

With a giant gasp, Aza was transported back to the streets of Verta with Reed, Xira, and Anwin encircling her.

Their worried and expectant faces filled her vision. Her legs wobbled searching for purchase on the ground below her.

Xira's commanding voice broke through the confusion. The burst of colors from the sky and street threatened to overwhelm Aza with its sensory overload. "What did you see?"

~

Xira, Reed, and Anwin quickly escorted Aza to the safety of a nearby inn. They were lucky to find the inn empty from the early morning frenzy of the market. Xira rented a vacant room and once they got the keys Anwin and Reed ushered her back, keeping the nosy innkeeper away from her.

They stumbled into the room and Aza leaned against the bed. They looked expectantly at her and waited for Aza to begin. She drew a steadying breath and launched into the story. When Aza finished her explanation, a stilted silence descended the room. Aza noticed the weighty glances cast about, her confidence wavering under each one.

The Nerians knew much more than they were telling her. Aza sat on the quaint bed, her hands running aimlessly over the quilted comforter. Dusty rays of light filtered into the room. Ever since her interaction with Astaroth the heavy weight burdening her had lifted, but for how long? Was she eventually going to meet the same Fate. All heads snapped back to Aza intently staring at her.

"What?"

Reed's tall narrow frame loomed over her, his face etched with concern. "You mentioned her name."

"I did?"

Anwin approached Aza, her hand raised to comfort her, but then it fell slack against her side. "Yes, you whispered it."

Xira remained in the far corner of the room, her back leaning against the wooden panels on the wall. "What happened in there?" Her question was poised as sharp as the sword at her hip.

Aza shot to her feet, unwilling to be blamed or manipulated. "You know everything. I have already explained everything that happened. I was transparent."

Xira only raised her eyebrows at Aza, her honeyed eyes assessing. "Yes. You did."

Aza fought the urge to bristle at the comment. "Spit out what you mean."

Xira was propped against the wall. She slid her leg that propped herself against the wall and stared. "Fine. You explained what happened. You—" she brandished the dagger end at Aza, the iron winking at her, "—failed to mention how you felt."

Disbelief riddled her tone as Aza sputtered, "How I felt?"

"Yes." Xira flipped her dagger to place it back into its sheath and approached Aza. "You explained everything perfectly. From a separated lens. Detached. Yet there are glaring gaps. How did you feel? Because *that* is a giant gap in your perspective."

Rage flared up in Aza. How dare Xira use her feelings against her?

"Xira..." Anwin whispered. "Let off."

"No I won't. She needs to be aware of her faults." Xira stared at Aza, each word a condemnation. "Her lack of information puts us all in danger."

Aza didn't even realize how tight her fists were clenched or the red that clouded her vision. If she had any of her magic, Xira would have been fearing for her life.

Aza took one step forward and before she realized it, she barreled into Xira and slammed her into the wall. The room shook from her strength.

Xira was unshaken. Aza realized that Xira purposely let her do this. Xira could have blocked or dodged. She didn't, letting Aza do this and it only enraged her further. Xira didn't even view her as a threat.

Aza seethed, "What do you know of feelings?" Her forearm pressed into Xira's throat restricting her movement and air.

Xira shifted under Aza's grip and took a breath before answering, "I am not saying your feelings are bad. But you do not see clearly. They cloud your vision. You are only hindering yourself."

"How would you know?" Aza couldn't handle it anymore. Xira had crossed a line.

"Answer the question Aza. How did Astaroth make you feel? What aren't you saying?"

Anwin interjected, "Xira enough!" Anwin went to stop Xira, but Reed yanked her back.

"No Anwin! She needs to answer," Xira shouted through Aza's forearm pressed to her throat.

Aza knew of what Xira alluded to—her strange blind spot when it came to the gods and goddesses. How she always bent to their will. How she always felt like they were perfect matches for her. How something within her seemed to preen and prance whenever she was within their presence.

Defeated and disgusted, Aza pushed off of Xira, releasing her. She gripped the silver coils of her hair and yanked down, the pain bringing her a strange sense of clarity.

She brought her face up to look at everyone in the room. "She tempted me! Is that what you want to hear? And a strange part of me, one I don't even want to acknowledge or accept—wanted to say yes." She looked at each of their faces' expecting anger, or disgust. Instead, she was met with cool, collected stares.

Reed softly said, "That is what we assumed."

"Why?" Aza asked. "Why do I feel this pull, this need for all of them?" Finally breaking, Aza collapsed into the bed, hiding her face from her companions. She was embarrassed and frustrated by her admission.

The scraping of chair legs caused Aza to look up. Xira, Reed and Anwin pulled the rickety chairs from the small dining table and sat encircling Aza. They did not judge merely offering their companionship.

Anwin leaned forward, placed her forearms on her thighs, and clasped her hands together. "We have a theory. Since you are something both new and old, made of this world and without, you are this enigma that attracts the gods and goddesses." A stray strand of red hair fell in front of Anwin's face, and she tucked it behind her ear, heaving a soft sigh. "It is complicated, and our historians have tried to study and speculate about it, but essentially there will always be this strong affinity you have towards the gods and goddesses."

Reed chimed in, "Like a kinship, or meeting of powers." His finger tapped his chin while he thought, and he snapped his fingers together when he reached his conclusion. "Melding! They used the term melding in their historical texts."

Everything they said resonated with Aza, even the terms they used were similar to what Aza felt in regard to Cruvo, but she was stubborn and prone to denial. "You are all going to believe some old historian's texts? How could I have this "affinity" for other gods and goddesses, it makes no sense."

Anwin shifted in her seat, her expression sincere. "Doesn't it make sense? Or are you afraid to admit it all makes too much sense."

Before Anwin could explain further Xira interjected, "We need you to come to terms with this." She held her fingers up ticking them off one by one as she listed each person. "It explains Cruvo, Eonas, Astaroth, Darkness below, even Nivet—it explains this strange connection you have with them."

"You are made—crafted—from what they are and something else. This strange combination, for some reason, draws them to you. It doesn't help that they all want to use you right now, plus your startling beauty. It creates this inexplicable pull towards each other."

Aza shook her head in denial. If she admitted what they said to be true, then her entire relationship with Cruvo was built upon this facade. Was he aware of it?

"So now I can't even trust myself?" Aza scoffed. "This is ridiculous." Craving action, Aza abruptly stood and abandoned her companions to find sanctuary in a corner of the room. She clutched her arms around herself, trying to find solace in even the smallest of reassurances.

Reed answered, "You can trust yourself, Aza." He paused before adding, "Your judgment might be clouded when it comes to the gods or goddesses. Do not think it is one-sided. They are equally blind when it comes to you."

Xira cut in, "Do you not see how they flock to you? Swarm you? Want you? They are equally affected, which makes you a target." Her hands flashed in anger, "We are not saying to not trust yourself, actually the opposite. You need to look at everything with discerning eyes. Darkness below! How you can even look at everything with such an innocent perspective after everything you have been through is ridiculous."

Anwin's broad and sincere face cut to Xira, silencing her. Xira stopped, pursing her lips together.

Xira's words would not let her be. She unwrapped her arms from around herself and turned, tracking each person in the room. Her words trickled out slowly like water emerging from small holes in a dam, a rampage of water still held back. "Everything I have been through?"

For once an awkward silence descended amongst the group. The Nerians were suddenly unsure and unwilling to meet her eyes.

"Everything I have been through?" Aza repeated, her tone rising in anger. "Stop with the constant secrets! You will tell me!"

Xira marched forward, "We will. But you are not safe here. When we return to Neria we can disclose everything and have you learn. Just like Nivet wanted." Xira turned back to look at Reed and Anwin both of their heads nodding in unison.

"Here you are vulnerable. Your frustration is good. You deserve to be upset. You do," she reassured. "There is so much to handle in so little time, but for now you need to fight. Fight everyone. Fight Astaroth, fight any god or goddess trying to use you, possess you." Xira's hand clasped her shoulder the fingers squeezing tight, grounding Aza to this moment. She leaned in like a co-conspirator,

"They want you. Remember that."

Anwin stepped forward, her head glancing out the window. "We need to leave. Our chance of opportunity is closing."

Xira gave a decisive nod and looked at Aza, sizing her up. "We want you to learn, that is our goal—but there needs to be a small amount of trust."

Aza pressed her lips together, holding back any other vitriol she could spew their way.

As if reading her mind, Xira answered, "Yes I understand trust is fickle in our situation but maybe muster some."

Aza fought the urge to roll her eyes in response and instead gripped her cloak tighter and threw the hood over her head, concealing her features.

Xira made her way to the door and before throwing it open, she turned on her heels and asked, "Do you feel her? The corruption? Will there be another episode?"

Aza paused, considering her body and her mind before answering. She could feel the undercurrent of disease but nothing of the magnitude that she experienced earlier. With a shake of her head, they departed the tiny inn going out into the streets of Verta.

12

"Lilit deserves this punishment. How dare she let Aza be taken from us, in our own castle."

Cruvo's private journal

By nightfall Lorn and Lilit finally escaped from the Silent Stretch. Emerging into an open hillside, the strange feeling of watchfulness faded as they left the last cluster of trees. Oppressive clouds blocked sunlight from creeping through, the gloomy predisposition of Gara holding true to rumors. Despite the lack of light, Lorn noticed a vibrancy amongst the foliage, the greens and browns merging together to create a deep wash of color.

With the Silent Stretch behind them, Lorn was able to dismiss his concerns about hidden monsters and instead focus on his immersion in the court of Gara. Lilit was resolute in her silence, and they ignored one another. However, Lorn pushed his pride aside and admitted he needed her. Lorn was clueless on how to act as an ambassador and Lilit was accustomed to life in the Iyeran court. Although she was a captain, she had more political experience than he ever had. He was a transparent person. Secrets were an unnecessary component in his life. He set his lips into a firm line and steadied himself. Entering Gara would prove fruitful and help Aza. He could do it—he needed to protect her from whatever may happen.

Only when the Silent Stretch was a small dot on the horizon did Lorn and Lilit stop for the night. They encountered a few towns as they wound over the small foothills. The rain was persistent. He longed to be dry and protected inside a sanctuary of warmth with a steady fire blazing before him.

The province of Gara was startlingly different compared to Iyera. Throughout Iyera people thrived, their everyday routine filled with purpose. Never once had he considered that other provinces would not be faring as well as Iyera. The Silent Stretch created a natural boundary blocking Gara from wandering travelers. Few he encountered had traveled to Gara, the province discarded, a mere afterthought. Even traveling through the small towns dotting the dense woods, the people were private and not forthcoming, their demeanors a reflection of the eerie woods they were surrounded by. On occasion they stopped to ask for directions and rest their horses. Not once had people invited them inside. They roughly answered his question and shuffled back indoors away from the outsiders.

Lilit said nothing and let Lorn flounder at his weak attempts at conversation. Each time his hopes were dashed as the citizens disregarded him, acting as cold as the rain that soaked his clothes. He tried not to let it bother him, but if the citizens were an extension of the province how would the Garan court act?

As they traversed through the isolated towns and dense woods, Lorn scanned the surroundings for any disturbance. So many things had transpired since he left Iyera. The incident of the destroyed town was pushed to the back of his mind. The destruction, the needless death, the haunted look in the children's eyes. No, he should never have forgotten such a thing.

He debated on disclosing what he saw to Lilit, but she had not spoken to him since their fight. She was not the ideal confidante, but he needed to tell someone of what he saw. Were soldiers dispatched to the area to help fight? Did anyone know of the utter destruction that wrought the desolation of an entire town?

Before he left El'en, reports had poured into Iyera of the Hinterlands morphing and swallowing up neighboring towns. Yet a small part of him did not think the destruction of the town was because of the Hinterlands. The town was not destroyed by beasts, but rather a disease. The disquiet of it, the haunted look in the survivor's eyes was not something from a named creature—it was something else entirely. Despite their trauma, Lorn should have discovered more information. He needed to know what happened in that town.

* * *

~

They wound through the dense forests with rarely a flicker of sunlight to warm them. The rain fell and fell. A perpetual chill began to wrack Lorn's body. He did not think such a landscape could affect his mood so deeply. Even the beauty of blends of earthy greens and browns did not comfort him—it began to crowd him. For once he yearned to return home to his empty cottage, remnants of his prior life hastily discarded and uncared for. No, there was nothing for him to return to. He could not retreat to his prior life, not after everything he had experienced. Not until he freed Aza from her captors. Not until they received answers. Not after feeling the thrum and taste of unlimited power as he fought the wraith. His fingers instructively curled as if he could grasp at the faint threads of magic.

Before the journey could reach its breaking point on Lorn, the forests cleared to reveal their destination—Lighthold.

Despite his dampened spirits, Lorn fought back a gasp. All the provinces' capitals were beautiful in their own right, their detail and craftsmanship astounding. The palace was carved into and formed from the surrounding forest. Magnificent trees provided their sanctuary, hollowed and smoothed out to provide passageways. Smooth stone pathways cut through the city, bypassing the vast trees. He steered his horse close to the trees and reached his hand out to touch one. A slight tingle rippled up his hand. He pulled and inspected closer. A magical ward was protecting the austere trees. It was a clever barrier that prevented destruction from magic. *Fire* was Lorn's first thought. Anyone who wished to harm Gara would simply need to set their trees ablaze and all of Lighthold would burn. However, this magical ward prevented such wanton destruction. Soft white lanterns decorated every tree, illuminating the whole city in a vast warm light.

If El'en was the jewel of Ithilia, Lighthold was its moon. He could not help but be impressed by the magic laced through every tree.

He leaned towards one of the lanterns and peered inside. Instead of fire, he saw a ball of light. Light akin to his own magic, except manifested outside of his body. He had never seen magic held in such a constant state. He shook his head in disbelief and led his horse back alongside Lilit.

She arched an eyebrow at him. "First time seeing magic?"

"Not all of us are as bitter as you are Lilit." He pressed the edge of his lips together, suppressing another biting comment. She said nothing of what this city looked like, of what he should be prepared for.

Lilit sneered. "Look who has a little fight left in them. Good, you are going to need it."

Without another word, she cantered forward, forcing Lorn to keep up. They arrived late in the night and the city was empty. Only a few late-night stragglers wandered between the roads and paths that interconnected the behemoth trees. They would pause, briefly size up Lorn and Lilit, and carry on with their heads downturned. Only when they neared the epicenter of the city did guards stop them. Lorn remembered their crest, a tree with its roots snaked into the ground. They carried long spears, iron tips sharpened and pointed at their throats.

"Halt. State your business."

Lorn leaned away from the point of the spear and slowly reached into his tunic and pulled out the scroll given to him by Cruvo. He held his hand out to the side and the second guard grabbed it from him. "We have business with Lady Rasmina of Gara."

The guard looked skeptical, eyeing both Lorn and Lilit.

Lilit cut in, "A raven should have been sent ahead with word of our arrival. You should think twice before harassing Iyera's Captain of the Guard and the famous Lorn of Verta."

At the announcement of their titles, the guard paled and shoved the scroll back at Lorn.

They lowered the spears and beckoned them to follow. Lorn and Lilit dismounted from their horses and a stablehand appeared out of the hollow of the tree leading them away.

One of the guards surveyed Lorn and Lilit's weapons. "You will be allowed to keep your weapons. If you draw them within the presence of Lady Rasmina or anyone else from the court, your life will be forfeit, Ambassador or not."

Lorn gave a firm nod. "Understood."

The massive tree, the structure of Lighthold, was a breathtaking labyrinth. The outside held a commanding presence that demanded attention, and entering Lorn was greeted with hallways, staircases that veered deeper and higher into the massive tree. The smooth wood was a soft warm brown so pale it appeared white from the light of the lanterns. Ramps spiraled upward. Lorn leaned his head back. The vastness was overwhelming. He had come far since leaving his quaint farmhouse.

The capitals truly held magical qualities. They embodied what he envisioned The MagicBlessed of long ago to have lived in, a time when the gods and goddesses walked amongst them.

The tree palace acted as the center of a spoke. As the guards led Lorn and Lilit up the smooth ramps, Lorn glimpsed open doorways with pathways leading to other hollowed out trees. The trees oddly reminded him of Lady Rasmina. She was an awful person, but even he couldn't deny her austere beauty. It was like she was birthed from this very city. Even the paleness of her skin reminded him of the lanterns that decorated the trees.

Round and round they climbed. Lorn couldn't help his curiosity as they passed room after room. Most of the doors were closed, but the intricate woodcarvings on each door caught his attention. They each depicted different scenes, like pieces of art from a book. He tried to memorize it, searching for anything that stood out, anything he could report back to Cruvo or would help in his search of Aza.

The guards stopped abruptly outside of two solid doors engraved with the Gara crest. Lorn never realized how accurate the crest of Gara truly was, never gave it much merit until now standing within the safety of their gigantic hollowed out trees.

The guards opened the double doors. The room was equally as beautiful as the rest of Lighthold. The soft orbs of lights highlighted the beauty of the room, with a rich wood floor, and eclectic decor. It wasn't Lady Rasmina's private room, there was no bed, no personal touches. Rather it was a study with a desk pushed to one side underneath a rounded window. Everything was tidy, organized, a perfect echo of the Lady who presided over this study, collected and pristine. An overwhelming number of books were gathered on the desk. They were not left open, instead stacked with their spines facing the same way. Rolls of scrolls were gathered next to it, artfully rolled up, nothing revealed, nothing left exposed. Velvet armchairs were placed opposite the double doors, a small side table between them.

Lady Rasmina occupied one of the chairs, her impenetrable face looked back at Lorn, one of feigned curiosity. A cat entertaining a wayward mouse. She rose from the chair, closed the open book, and placed it on the adjacent table. Her moves were liquid, smooth, uninterrupted—calculated. Equally as calculated as everything she did back in El'en. She was dressed in a simple, loose, black dress quite unlike her usual extravagant attire. Despite the lack of formality, Lorn still felt out of place. His clothes were travel worn and stained, reeking of the hard days on horseback. He always felt out of his element around the lords and ladies of each province, their position of power at once overwhelming and diminishing. But he swallowed his insecurity and stood up straighter, staring at Lady Rasmina's unsettling, vaporous, blue eyes.

"Lorn of Verta and Lilit of Iyera, what a surprise." Lady Rasmina's voice always came as a surprise to Lorn, at once both soft and delicate. Yet he could not be fooled by such a timbre. He painfully remembered her harsh words, her terrible actions back in El'en, accusing Aza of being a whore to Lorn. It was inexcusable. His fingers tightened around the hilt of his sword and Lady Rasmina's eyes flicked down noticing the small disturbance.

Before Lorn could answer, Lilit did. "This is no surprise Lady Rasmina. Lord Aldrich alerted you of our arrival by raven. Stop the act." Lilit said this with a more restrained anger than she ever showed Lorn. She was acting as Lord Aldrich's Captain of the Guard and her tone demonstrated it.

*With a measured movement, Lady Rasmina regarded Lilit. "Always a pleasure, Lilit." She turned back to Lorn, her face unreadable. "Strange Aza isn't with you. A pity."

Lorn had to keep his anger in check. He was here on behalf of Cruvo, he needed to play the courtier and find information. He couldn't lose his composure every time some noble made a scathing remark. Lorn didn't even deign to give a response.

Lady Rasmina walked to her desk and looked out through the rounded window. The lights pulsed slightly. Her footsteps were quiet, silent, stealthy. "Though, why are you here without her, I wonder?"

Lorn's throat was dry and scratchy. Lady Rasmina was baiting him. By now Lorn assumed each court's spies knew of Aza's disappearance and like a healing wound, she picked at it.

Those words mimicked his exact thoughts as he tromped through the Silent Stretch. Each rainy night, every monster, every insufferable village he wondered why he was going north instead of going west where he believed Aza to be. It felt like a betrayal each incorrect step, each choice. Yet...although he didn't align with Cruvo, Lorn knew his desperation and frantic search would be more successful than his own. Lorn had never tracked people before, didn't even have the first clue as to where to start. Lorn didn't even know how the Nerians had captured Aza in the first place, how they had escaped a castle full of countless guards and nobles. As he journeyed, he convinced himself north was where he needed to go. Just like the internal push towards the Hinterlands, he was currently being pulled towards Gara. There were secrets here that could help with Aza and at the very least lead to more information.

Lilit interjected, "We were promised the care given to ambassadors. Are we done with this line of questioning? We have traveled far and wish to rest."

Lorn was thankful for Lilit's response. He had a strange feeling she actually did it for him.

"Very well. My guards will see you to your rooms." Lady Rasmina turned her back on them.

Lady Rasmina had planted a small seed of doubt in his mind. Now she had watered it and was going to watch it grow. He needed to leave and go find Aza. Why was he here?

The guards led them several floors down to adjacent rooms. Luckily they weren't adjoined. Lorn couldn't handle having such access to Lilit. Her biting comments, and antagonistic behavior was not something he wanted to deal with at all hours of the day.

The guards left, informing them someone would come get them in the morning. Lorn reached his hand out and hesitated over the door handle. He spared a quick glance at Lilit and was stunned to see a small measure of hesitation. Her lips were pressed firmly together, and it seemed like she was about to say something before she shook her head slightly and entered her room without another word. Lorn furrowed his brows, dismissed it, and went to his room to finally receive some rest.

After bathing, Lorn's head hit the pillow and he collapsed. The days of heavy travel had worn on him, grated him down. He did not dream.

He did not stir.

13

"From Xira's report, Verta has succumb. It was only a matter of time before Astaroth tempted a province into submission."

Nivet's private journal.

The group pulled their cloaks over their faces to disguise them amongst the bustling streets of Verta. The market was still overflowing with the voices of people bartering. The creeping hold of corruption still lingered around Aza. She could feel it threatening to press in at any time, to force her to succumb again—but with awareness and constant focus Aza was able to keep it at bay.

The group dragged her away from the massive crowds into the narrow alleys twisting and turning until they entered a neighborhood that was dingier, fouler, the buildings clustered together preventing the flow of air. Aza covered her nose and tried to breathe through her mouth. People who did not wish to be seen lurked in corners quietly discussing transactions, their bodies scurrying from corner to corner like a swarm of rats infesting and infecting one another. Shock rippled through her, but she bit back a gasp. Aza assumed all the provinces discouraged such practices. She assumed such seedy underbellies of society were stamped out by the lords and ladies. The Well provided their lands with prosperity, such areas should not exist. Aza clenched her fists instead. Was she really so blind? She truly believed Lord Aldrich's province of Iyera was without crime and corruption. It was possible these areas existed without her knowledge. She didn't even bother to tour the province, instead remaining confined to his castle like some prized pet. If she was honest with herself, it was a safety net.

She was scared. Scared of people finding out about her power. To have people look at her with fear was something she couldn't handle. She wanted to believe what was presented to her without questioning it. Did Lorn do the same? Was he equally as blinded? The two of them wanted to believe the best in people, their provinces and didn't bother to look further, to dig deeper.

A dark and cramped alleyway wound around the corner. Xira motioned for them to stay put as she strode forward, the darkness swallowing her whole. Aza kept her head down to avoid detection and squinted down the alleyway. She could only see two vague outlines of people. Xira stood a full head shorter than him, but the other person was fidgety, shooting nervous glances at the group. Xira gave a quick wave of her hand and ushered them forward. They squeezed through the alley and Xira pushed them through a narrow opening.

The group crashed through the doorway, the poor wooden door barely hanging on with its rusty hinges. The room was tiny with barely enough room to fit four of them within. The reek of mildew permeated the room with threads of mold growing along the rain sodden boards. The faint scritch scratch of rat claws scurried above as they waited for further instruction. A set of narrow stairs wound in the back of the room. Aza's eyebrows lowered in doubt at whether her and Anwin could even ascend the staircase due to its narrow structure.

After ushering the group in, the man Xira conversed with shut the door hastily causing the ramshackle hovel to groan in protest. He was dressed in drab clothes that fit the nature of this house. His particularly thin frame appeared like it could snap from a sharp glance, and his beady eyes bulged as he took in the group of Nerians.

"I promised you a meeting with him, Xira. I do not know what his price will be," the man's thin reedy voice whispered.

"Calm yourself, Noveru. It is one meeting nothing more."

"Wait here, I will let him know of your presence." The man sidled his thin body through the group, his footsteps marching up the narrow staircase.

"Oh, I don't doubt he already knows we are here," Xira called out sweetly.

Aza was always impressed by Xira and the many charismatic faces she donned. She knew how to handle each person like they were an easily read book. It made her a great captain.

Waiting until Noveru was out of sight, Xira yanked Aza towards her and whispered fiercely, "You must not reveal yourself to him. He deals in secrets. To find out who you are or what you are—you cannot."

Aza was fed up with hiding her identity. It was a constant struggle to be guarded, shielding herself from unwanted eyes. "Then why bring me here? Why didn't you leave me at the inn?"

Xira's anger was palpable. "Do you think so little of us? To leave you exposed to another potential attack? Especially since you still have not recovered your magic powers?"

At the sound of footsteps, Xira brushed away from Aza and regained her composure. It was difficult for Aza to reconcile how these Nerians valued her. Did they value who she was or was it for their own personal gain? She would not be so trusting again. It broke her to realize they had corrupted her trusting nature. They caused this. This uncertainty, this doubt.

Noveru's slim frame peeked around the corner, his eyes narrowed at Xira's unusual composure. Suspicion warred with curiosity as he eyes freely roved over Aza's covered form. The slimy feel of his gaze stuck with her, and she ached to do something about it. If she had her magic she would have taught him a lesson. Despite her warring emotions towards the Nerians, she did not want to put them in any further danger. Clearly they were involved in the seedy parts of this city and Aza did not want to ruin their contacts.

"Follow me." Without further instruction, Noveru disappeared up the narrow staircase, his bony frame easily managing the tight space. Reed led the group. Even his narrow shoulders brushed against the waterlogged walls. Anwin trailed him. If they were in a different situation, Aza would have found it comical. Anwin's broad shoulders were unable to navigate the staircase and she was required to turn sideways. Aza copied her, their bodies a similar build to one another.

The entire situation was completely bizarre, but the Nerians held an unusually serious air—similar to when Aza saw them in El'en for the first time. This was the mask they donned around other people. Their ferocity, their fight, how they held themselves— it was an unequivocal warning to those around them. Behind Aza, Xira followed, her head swiveling to check the door they entered through. Always the protector, Xira was prepared for everything and did not want to be ambushed.

The stairs made an abrupt ninety degree turn and when Aza awkwardly followed Anwin she fought back a surprised gasp. The upstairs was completely different from below, warm and welcoming. In certain spots Aza could see the water warped wood but overall, it was cozy. Bookshelves lined the rightmost wall, the shelves overflowing. Opposite a roaring fire brought warmth in the room. On the far end of the room a giant ornate desk was situated with two hazy windows behind it. The bright light of the room caused Aza to pull the folds of her cloak down to better hide her features. She couldn't let word get out of her whereabouts, not when she was finally about to get answers.

Xira brushed past Aza, a subtle formation taking place. Anwin remained next to Aza, her shoulder placed slightly in front of her as Reed surrendered his position in front to cover the rear.

Aza wanted to crane her neck to get a better view of who they were visiting but fought against the rampant curiosity.

"Sir, Xira of Neria is here requesting your help." Noveru stood to the side of the massive desk, his head bowed deferentially to the man occupying the chair.

"Thank you Noveru. You may return downstairs." Noveru edged around the group of Nerians, wary of touching them and scurried back down the staircase.

"Xira of Neria." The man's voice was velvet and smooth like he only used it in the dark sanctuary of nighttime. Such a fitting voice for someone who dealt in secrets. He rose from his ornate, leather seat, his tall frame filling the room. He took measured steps towards the group. Aza was only able to discern wisps of blonde hair that fell to his broad shoulders bringing attention to his ornately decorated coat. The golden buttons told Aza enough about this man's wealth. Frustrated at her clueless position, Aza had to imagine what the rest of the man looked like. She needed to keep her identity hidden and Anwin was blocking her view.

"Tor of Verta," Xira responded stiffly.

"Such peculiar timing of your arrival."

Xira gave a noncommittal response. With Aza's head downturned, she saw Xira's fingers dance around the hilt of her sword.

"And to have the whole group here. I am rarely blessed with such a gathering." Tor lifted his hand to his heart in mock heartfelt sentiment. "Except—" he paused. His head craned around the group trying to peer around Anwin. "There is someone new."

Aza hoped her subdued powers would not trigger this man's instincts.

Xira took a deliberate step in front of the man, deterring his path. "You deal with me."

With a flippant wave of his hand, he turned back to his desk, "Fair enough. What brings you here Xira of Neria."

"We want in."

"In?"

"The palace."

His eyes bulged slightly, and he quickly covered his surprise by retreating to his desk and aimlessly scanning the documents scattered atop it. He whispered softly, "Surely you cannot expect such results."

Aza tried to catch as many details of their conversation, but it was difficult to keep her features hidden. Xira drew her shoulders back and stared. "Yes we are."

He sat in his chair, leaned back, and steepled his fingers together. "It cannot be done."

Anwin and Reed stayed silently beside Aza. This was Xira's negotiation. "Things have changed—are changing. That is why we need to get into the palace. Now before everything changes."

This was a game, and the man was toying with Xira, a game of haggling to figure out what she would give in return forcing Xira to show her hand.

The man picked up a dagger, twiddling it in his hands, the tip playing dangerously around the pad of this thumb. "It is a death sentence."

"Not for us."

He sighed and placed the dagger on his desk. "For me. If I get caught assisting you...it would mean certain death." He looked at the window behind him. "Passage is expensive. What sort of secret will be your cost?" Although his voice never raised, it was full of venom and threats. Tor's regal appearance was a ruse, a gaudy curtain hiding what was actually underneath, someone deadly.

Xira stepped toward him, her hand gesturing to the window. He barely offered her a glance. "Do you not see what is happening? If you do not help us, all will be lost." Xira fought the passion rising in her voice and lowered it quickly. The buildings were close together, anyone could overhear their conversation. They weren't safe anywhere.

"I am not one for heroics, dear Xira. You will not get sympathy from me. I know something is happening. A deep undercurrent. I deal in secrets. I am aware of something big, like everything is aligning for one specific moment." He placed a finger on his temple, mock thinking. "I don't however know the exact reason." He tilted his chin to Xira. "Perhaps you know. For a hefty secret I will get you into the palace undetected and where you need to go." He crossed his fingers waiting expectantly for Xira's answer. "You get one attempt, otherwise I will not help you."

Xira turned around and made eye contact with Anwin, Reed and lastly Aza. It was loaded with emotion. A look of pity, but also a choice.

Aza realized she was the dangling carrot. She was the bait. If this man did not concede to their secret, she was the ace up their sleeve. For she was the greatest secret, the greatest mystery they had to offer. The Nerians were here to offer Aza answers, but they needed her consent to go forward. Xira was asking for it now. They could leave him and risk it on their own. Aza shivered, hating to offer this man information about her, but the sickening thought of Astaroth's rot and corruption stopped her. Revealing information. She could do that. The building creaked against the cold and wind building up outside. Aza gave a small, but firm nod to Xira. She returned it with a grim smile.

With a resolute look, Xira turned back to Tor her spine stiff. She marched up to his desk, her palm planted against the elegant wood. "You promise you will get us inside."

"Inside, yes."

"Without detection."

"Why else would you come to me?" His crooked smile slashed across his face, widening at Xira's demands. He was winning. Xira had nothing left to bargain with. This was it.

Xira's clenched her other hand. She whipped it forward her arm extended, awaiting their agreement. Doing nothing to hide his predatory smile, Tor rose, their hands firmly clasping. The sound was like the crack of a whip and Aza jerked her head up, her eyes widening.

Upon their agreement, Anwin and Reed parted from her leaving no space, no boundary for Aza to hide behind. Only her cloak offered some meager semblance of discretion. Faint, hesitant footsteps stepped towards her. She raised her head, gritted her teeth, and removed the cloak from her head. Tor stood beside Xira, a greedy and calculating overtook his face. He smoothly stepped in front of Aza, and reverently reached for her hand, placing a chaste kiss on the back of it. Aza fought the recoil. Without the covering of her cloak, she was able to see Tor in his entirety. He was quite handsome, with rich brown eyes, sandy blond hair which set in soft waves around his face and came down to his chin. The softness of his hair offset the hard lines of his face, the hint of stubble on his chin. His skin had the youthful glow of someone who was constantly outside in the sun. Despite the brutal fall weather descending, he was sun-kissed. Aza furrowed her brows. This man was in charge of secrets? Only his voice hinted at such an occupation.

"Do not be deceived by my looks. I do have my means to sneak about. Not everything is cloak and daggers." He released her hand and stood up straight assessing her. "Who are you?" he asked. His eyes ran over her form multiple times trying to piece together hidden information.

"Aza," she replied curtly. Aza didn't know how much information she had to give Tor to satisfy their deal. She would not be so forthcoming.

"The real question is not who are you, but what are you?" He reached out his hand, trying to get a quick touch of Aza again, but Xira stepped forward and snatched his hand away. She gripped it tightly and he barely grimaced.

"You did not quantify how much information you get." Xira dropped his wrist, discarding it like it was mere trash.

"*Tsk, tsk,* Xira of Neria. For this deal to work, I do get *some* information." He brushed his hands down his ornate cloak.

"I know who you are, Aza of the Well. Do you know you are hunted?" His tone baited her, wanting her to slip, wanting her to give in to his question to reveal more information.

"Ahh it is of no consequence, I'm sure you know this. That is why you are sneaking around with the Nerians of course." He paced the room, his fingers gracefully running along the spine of his books. He turned back to face her, his eyes alight with some hidden joy. "Do you know he seeks you?" He laced his fingers together as if he was holding himself back.

Aza ignored his gibes. "Am I enough of a secret to pay for our passage?" She kept her tone even, her words clipped. This man fought to unravel her, to get her to spill her secrets so he could use even more for bargaining, for leverage with whatever underworld he dabbled with. "Can you gain us entry?"

As she spoke, his face lit up, growing more and more enamored with her at whatever she was saying. She intrigued him.

His tongue darted out and swiped at his lip as he stepped forward. "I can see why he won't let you go."

Aza couldn't control herself any further and rose to his bait. "Who?"

"Why your dear Lord Aldrich." An errant hand ran down his face, his smile widening. "Or should I say Cruvo?"

The room seemed to dim. Aza's awareness shifted to Tor. He had her attention now. Before he was some mere pawn to be used, a tool to enter the Vertan palace. Now he was something else. Aza noticed the barely imperceptible tightening of her Nerian companions. Unwilling to be constricted further, she stepped out of their protective circle and approached Tor. She was a solid head's height above Tor, and she used every inch to look down upon him, summoning all of her haughtiness and disdain.

This man had no sense of self-preservation. He did not back down, did not appear regretful of his actions. Instead, a perverse excitement flitted across his features at Aza's approach.

"Excuse me?" She did not have her magic to threaten this man, but he did not know that. She could always disembowel him with his own dagger. That would be enough.

"You heard me, Aza of the Well." He held her stare, his soft voice slithering over her. "I know of Cruvo. I hear all of the whispers, all of the secrets. They find their way to me." Tor leaned forward, his lips brushing the outside of Aza's ear. "He will not stop. He will find you." Aza remained still and fought the urge to recoil. She didn't know how to process what he told her. She wanted to be with Cruvo again—

when this was over. After she received her answers. Yet how he phrased it, it seemed more a threat than a welcoming.

He pulled away, thoughtfully regarding her. "I'm curious what he would have to say about your current entanglement? A group of Nerians unlawfully breaking into the Vertan palace?" He turned and looked at Xira quizzically. "Very interesting, indeed."

Aza was tired of this man's ceaseless chatter, but before she could act, Xira pulled a dagger and pushed Tor against his overflowing bookshelf.

"Enough of this Tor. Stop toying with your food." The dagger pressed tighter against his throat. He was not worried, his expression merely bored, like he was used to these proceedings. "Ahh, Xira always a pleasure. Despite how much I love this position, you need me to enter the palace. So-," he shifted his weight forward, his hands coming up as a barrier and guiding the knife away from him, "no more theatrics."

Xira snorted. "The same could be said of you." She flipped the dagger pointing it's sharpened end at Tor. He froze, eying both the dagger and Xira. "There will be no word of our arrival to anyone."

A crooked smile grew on Tor's face. "You know this isn't how it works. I can do what I want with this information." Xira's dagger wavered, her hand lowered slowly with the weight of her decision to uncover Aza. He brushed the top of his coat and straightened it. "However, I will give you some assistance. Once I get you into the palace, you will have one day before I sell this information to the highest bidder." He raised his finger in front of Xira to prove his point further. "One day."

"Always generous," Xira ground out. She sheathed her dagger and positioned herself next to Aza. Aza was unsure of what came next. "Meet me at the clock tower by the second bell. Wear your cloaks. I can only bring in two of you."

Xira surged forward. "You promised to get us all in."

Tor shrugged his shoulders. "I did no such thing. I promised to get you in, not all. Be grateful I am granting such a request. It has been difficult to enter lately, despite even my skill." His mouth set in a firm line. "Aza of the Well, your appearance is Fate designed. Everything is stirring, moving, many pieces at play." His hand reached out like he was trying to caress her face but thought better of it and he lowered it.

He looked back at Xira, his face closed off. "You can take or leave the offer."

Xira gave a firm nod.

"Noveru," Tor called out.

Noveru materialized behind them, his thin frame easily maneuvering the tight space. "Escort them out. We are done here."

14

"My body shakes. I hear whispers on the wind of Aza, but I am no closer to finding her. I think I am going through some form of withdrawals. Aza's proximity was a drug I cannot rid myself of." Cruvo's private journal

The comforting, plush bed was difficult to rise from, but a faint part of him, a part of him always on alert forced him to crack his eyes open. Someone was in his room. Expecting darkness, he was surprised to find a muted light instead. What time was it? He clutched the dagger under his pillow and wrenched himself upright to face the intruder. Lilit stood in the corner of the room, leaning casually against the smooth wood walls.

She bit into an apple, the crunch resounding in the silent room. Lorn blew out an exasperated breath, fell back onto his bed, and released the dagger beside him.

"Good thing it was me and not anyone else. Another assassin and you would have been dead." Lilit released a dry chuckle and took another bite from her apple.

Lorn rubbed his hands over his eyes, trying to maintain a small shred of patience. "What are you doing in my room, Lilit?"

"Do you know what time it is?" She waited and took her time with the apple, her bites methodical.

Lorn propped himself up on his elbows and looked around the room. The light was unusual. Lorn had rarely seen such sunlight. It was hidden by the massive trees and persistent rainfall. They rarely had a sunny season. He didn't want to play Lilit's games and instead relinquished any control. "No, I don't know. Enlighten me. What time is it?"

She gave a grim self-satisfied smirk. "Late afternoon, nearing evening."

"Well that isn't shocking considering we arrived here late last night and we had a long trip. Let me rest."

Lilit made a *tsking* noise and approached Lorn's bed. She grabbed a chair from the nearby desk and flipped it around and sat in it gracefully. "You have been asleep for over a day."

Lorn rubbed a hand down his face again, thinking this was some sort of trick. "Lilit, stop playing around. I tire of it."

She leaned forward, her grip on the apple tightened. "You think I enjoy this? Enjoy having to watch over and protect you?" She scoffed and leaned back in her chair.

Lorn paused. His body was tired and sore. A fierce hunger gripped his stomach. The rigorous journey through the Silent Stretch paired with the unexplainable use of magic must have drained him. The only way to recover was by resting.

"Okay, I have been asleep for longer than a day. What has happened?" Lorn shifted until he sat upright. His chest was bare, with loose comfortable pants. He rearranged himself until he sat cross legged.

Lilit stared dispassionately at his chest, her revulsion evident.

Scars of varying sizes marred his golden skin, the white puckers evidence of his encounters with the beasts of the Hinterlands.

"Would you like to stare any longer?" Lorn asked. He was growing tired of dealing with her. He didn't know how much more he could tolerate. This mission was going to go terribly. They needed to be united.

She pushed her lips together into a thin line and answered, "I'm still curious how you have survived this long. Your scars are evidence of your inadequacy."

Lorn would not let Lilit rile him up. Instead he deflected with his prior question. "What has happened?"

"Nothing. Yet. Lady Rasmina wishes to meet us together since you are the ambassador." A flash of irritation crossed her features. "I tried to wander Lighthold, wherever the guards allowed me to, which wasn't much. Until we meet with Lady Rasmina again, it seems we won't have much freedom to explore."

"Can we meet with her tonight?"

Lilit's eyes flickered over Lorn. "If you rise and get ready in time, then she will meet with us."

"Leave me so I can get ready. I will meet you at your room."

Lilit rose from her chair and stalked out of the room. She gripped the apple in one hand, the entire thing picked clean to the core and left.

Lorn dressed quickly. He gave a cursory assessment of his body. He was sore, tired, and in need of something to eat. There was no permanent damage, only extreme exhaustion.

The rare burst of sunlight roused him. It was a welcome reprieve amongst this province of constant darkness and rainfall. His room was as beautiful and austere as the rest of the Lighthold. A delicate, wood-carved paneling opened out to a balcony where he was able to take in the expansive land of Lighthold. He marveled at the sight. The delicate, yet sturdy bridges linked the vast trees together with the soft glow of lights alongside each intersection. Yet as he looked, there was something missing. A lack of heart, of enjoyment. Lighthold embodied a solemnity Lorn had yet to encounter anywhere within the other provinces. Like the empty, quiet breaths taken after hours of grieving. It was both beautiful and hollow.

Lorn backpedaled from the balcony and walked to meet Lilit. Her room was located next to his and within one knock she appeared at the door. She didn't acknowledge him, merely shoved past him and stalked down the corridors. Lorn could only follow in her wake. She was more familiar with Lighthold than he was and he deferred to her knowledge. Despite her short stature she kept a brutal pace and Lorn found himself close to jogging to keep up. She ascended several staircases and Lorn fought to keep his face stoic, he showed his too emotions easily. The interior of Lighthold's palace was immaculate. Every surface smooth and etched with care. Oddly enough Lorn noticed there were no portraits here, like the past wasn't worth acknowledging in this grand place. He attempted to school his face into something feigning mere interest so he wouldn't appear as rural as his upbringing. There was little time for gawking as Lorn raced to catch up to Lilit. She halted suddenly in front of two white wood doors, their surface etched with Gara's crest, the deep-rooted tree.

Lilit turned to Lorn and addressed him for the first time since he knocked on her door. "Ready?"

Lilit pulled the door open, not even waiting for Lorn's response. He snapped his mouth close, unwilling to look like an idiot in front of Lady Rasmina and her court.

They were greeted by a elegant room filled by an expansive dining table. The magical lights that adorned the rest of Lighthold were placed amidst the room casting everything in an ethereal glow. Lady Rasmina sat at the head of the table outfitted in a dress of deep forest green, her long black hair swept up into a coronet of braids. She elegantly rose from her chair, the dress emitting a soft swish as the fabric moved with her.

"Welcome Lilit of Iyera and Lorn of Verta." She gestured to two empty chairs. "Please sit."

Lady Rasmina was not alone. Guards were stationed along the corners of the room and the table was occupied by her daughters. Lorn recognized Ruby, Sapphire, and Pearl. All named after the precious gems Gara is famous for mining. Ruby and Sapphire were exact replicas of Lady Rasmina with their pale visages and smooth black hair slicked back from their faces. Although they kept their faces neutral, Lorn easily imagined the sneers that could replace their blank expressions. From what he remembered of them at El'en, their wit was sharp, but so was their judgment and condemnation. Pearl was clearly cut from the same cloth, and heavily resembled her sisters, but there was a softness to her features. Her skin tone was slightly darker, her hair curly instead of straight, like her appearance fought against the strains of court life and longed to be running free amongst the woods of Gara, set exploring instead of stuck in this mundane life. She was the only one of the three sisters to greet Lilit and Lorn with a slight crook of her mouth. The ghost of a welcoming smile, along with a light shining within her eyes—hope. Two other people occupied the opposite side of the table. From what Lorn could discern, they were older than Lady Rasmina, yet not as old as the wizened Oron from Iyera. The man and woman were dressed in a similar fashion, both adorned in matching tunic and pants, the crest of Gara embroidered upon their sleeves.

Lorn felt out of his element. Doubt flooded him. He was not meant to be here, playing ambassador. He was meant to be outside amongst the freeing air and the nature which cradled him. Why did Cruvo send him? He could have sent anyone in his stead. And why did Lorn agree to go? Just like his determination to reach the Hinterlands a similar thread pulled him to Gara. Once Cruvo mentioned the idea, although Lorn fought and bristled against it, he couldn't deny the odd pull that dragged him here. Like his Fate was tied to this place. Lorn banished those feelings of doubt. They had no place here. Similar to hunting the beasts of the Hinterlands, there was no room for uncertainty. He needed to use his mind and strike true.

Lorn pulled his shoulders back and strode into the room with confidence, meeting each of their eyes. Lorn sat in a chair, Lilit beside him a stalking shadow.

"Thank you for your hospitality," Lorn said. Empty plates laid in front of each guest. Lady Rasmina motioned, and a guard left the room. Servants quietly entered their arms laden with decadent food. The smell caused Lorn's stomach to clench. He hadn't had such food since leaving El'en.

The room was silent except for the scraping of serving spoons on the glass. Cuts of lamb, a light collection of leafy greens, and a slab of bread rested on his plate.

Lorn didn't know what to say. Luckily, Lady Rasmina began the conversation before Lorn could.

"Lord Aldrich has informed me that you are now ambassador to Iyera. Congratulations. What a rise in station compared to a mere hunter." Lady Rasmina's vaporous blue eyes measured him.

This was a test, to gauge his reaction, to see if he could hold his tongue and truly act as an ambassador. But Lorn couldn't help the anger that sparked inside him, the vitriol he wanted to spew back. Lady Rasmina's barb cut true.

He took a steadying breath, surveyed the food and then addressed Lady Rasmina's comment, his voice even and devoid of anger. "Yes, it is quite the accomplishment. Lord Aldrich truly honors me with such a title and job."

Lady Rasmina lips curled slightly, and she dipped her head subtly at Lorn, a small acknowledgment of his well-formed response. He was learning. Her pale fingers toyed with the stem of her wine glass. "Why are you here, Lorn of Verta?"

The servants finished filling everyone's plates and left the room without a sound. Everyone picked up their silverware and dug in. Lorn's wineglass was filled. He reached for it and took a quick sip before answering, "I would assume Lord Aldrich informed you in his message. I merely do what he wishes." Lorn's eyes flicked between his meal and up to Lady Rasmina's. She held his stare.

"And those wishes are for you to come into my province?"

Lorn nodded. "Yes, they are."

"After we just had a meeting among the leaders of the five provinces? He then dispatches you to come into my land?" She gripped the wine glass and took a delicate sip, still regarding Lorn.

Lady Rasmina placed the wine glass back on the table with the precision of an assassin's blade. "We in Gara receive so few visitors. Of course, it would be a great honor to host the famous Lorn of Verta—hunter of the Hinterlands, and Lilit of Iyera." Her light and breathy voice was a misdirection and if one didn't know her well, they would be easily fooled by her welcoming words and tone. Lorn was accustomed to assessing deadly prey and Lady Rasmina was one he needed to study further. He felt like he was falling into an easily laid trap. The predator in her was sizing him up and creeping forward ready to pounce. He wasn't familiar with this style of battling, but he was a quick learner. Even though it had been months since the Hinterlands, it had felt like he had never left. He needed to defend himself, strike back, never falter, and remember his purpose. To use the information he learned to assist and save Aza.

Lorn tilted his head down in a slight bow. "It would be an honor to be accepted as a guest of Gara."

Lady Rasmina pressed her lips together and paused.

Lorn was ready for whatever court battle she was going to wage, every word that dripped from her mouth was poison and he needed to combat it with his wits instead of his blade.

"I will admit, I'm surprised to see Lilit of Iyera accompanying you instead of Aza." Her fingers danced along the stem of her wine glass, while her stare speared Lorn. "Where is your constant companion? You rarely left each other's company while in El'en. Did you tire of her already?"

The guests around the table snickered at the implied innuendo. Lorn fought the blush that crept up his neck. This was her game and he needed to adjust or leave. He couldn't sit here stammering like a shy boy in his youth, but he struggled with the manners of court. While Lady Rasmina held her decorum, her words were barbed, their strikes at once unassuming but deadly, leading to a slow character assassination and a constant second guessing of himself.

Failing to reply, Lady Rasmina cut in again. "Or was she unable to control her magic? I admit my surprise at the vote in El'en. Her magic should be locked up and she should be contained like the uncontrollable beast she is."

Lady Rasmina's unnerving eyes held Lorn's, waiting, seeing how he would respond. If Lorn and Lilit drew their weapons in her presence, they would be kicked out of Lighthold at the least and potentially executed at the worst. She was testing him, to see whether he was rash and hotheaded.

The table was eerily silent as everyone halted their eating. He caught a slight twitch of Lilit's fingers out of the corner of his eye. She was worried about his response, about how he would react.

Lorn held Lady Rasmina's stare like he would any other creature from the Hinterlands. This was a different battle, different terrain, but Lorn was always one to rise to a challenge.

"Aza is busy on another task she deems important. Lord Aldrich needed me to go to Gara and I viewed it as the greatest honor to accept. She is her own person, and she is able to go independently from myself and vice versa." Lorn brought the wine glass to his lips and the rich heady wine scorched down his throat. He held it loftily in his hand before bringing his attention back to Lady Rasmina. "In regard to her magic, I quite envy her skill and magical depths. Her control over it is quite magnificent and she only releases it upon those who truly deserve it." A ghost of a smile played around his lips before he took another satisfying drink of wine.

Lady Rasmina leaned back in her chair with her fingers steepled together. He had clearly surprised her, expecting a brutish hunter incapable of politics. She had held him at dagger point with her words and he had deftly switched it around, the dagger now held back at Lady Rasmina.

The rest of the table waited in silence for Lady Rasmina's reaction. She merely nodded her head and resumed eating. The rest of the table followed her lead.

Lorn tried to focus on savoring his food. It was decadent and perfectly cooked. Yet he was poised, ready and waiting for anything Lady Rasmina would throw his way. Lilit ate silently next to him the picture of decorum. She did not scrape her plate or make any undue noises. She had probably been to many courtly dinners and her manners were exemplary, but Lorn didn't fail to notice how she speared her food, her knife poised and slicing. He easily pictured a dismembered limb in its place, Lilit hacking, sawing, and inflicting her revenge. Even though she normally held herself rigidly, he thought even the slightest disturbance would cause her to snap. She was near her breaking point. He didn't think it had anything to do with this situation, or with Lorn. She didn't care about him. No, it was something else. Something else was going on and she was stewing over it.

Lady Rasmina had yet to introduce the two people next to her. Besides the guards occupying the room, they were the only people at the table besides her daughters. It was odd to not have been introduced yet.

Lorn cleared his throat and gestured to the two of them. "I'm sorry, I don't believe we have met before."

They were both dressed in ornate tunics, the silver linen embroidered in a deep green tree. The woman's head was shaved on the sides with a long flop of hair perfectly styled back away from her face. The blonde hair paired with the silver tunic gave her an effervescent quality. She had brown eyes unlined by any laugh lines and a faint spattering of freckles across her cheek and nose. She met Lorn's inquisitive and probing gaze. "I am Maline." She paused in her eating. "I am one of Lady Rasmina's advisors."

She turned to the man next to her, indicating it was his turn to speak. His black hair was tied back, braided and threaded with gray. He had a cropped, tidy beard which was prominent against his sienna skin. Unlike Maline, his black eyes crinkled with amusement as he met Lorn's gaze. It wasn't a smile one felt at ease over. Rather the smile of inconvenience, like he had better things to do rather than introduce himself to someone lower than his station. "And I am Flint." Where Maline was tall and lithe, Flint was short and stout. "I am another of Lady Rasmina's advisors." He gave a razor-sharp smile and resumed his eating.

Lady Rasmina flicked a lazy hand in their direction. "They are my two closest advisers. If you ever meet with me, they will not be far behind."

Lorn nodded. "Why were you not at the gathering?"

Maline answered, "Someone needs to run the province while Lady Rasmina is away." Maline and Flint shared a quick look. Lorn wanted to know what that was about.

"You have come at an inopportune time, Lorn of Verta. I am a very busy woman and will not be able to spare time to escort you around Lighthold." She tilted her head to her daughters. "They will be able to accompany you throughout Lighthold, if myself and my advisors are too busy." Lorn plastered on his most pleased expression as he acknowledged Lady Rasmina's daughters. It wasn't that he wasn't thankful for their time and effort, but the daughters were just like their mother—full of venom, fury. He wished for anyone else. Someone who would actually enjoy his company and not be plotting his downfall. They nodded back at him with mock humility, Ruby and Sapphire looking like cats who had downed a supper of milk. Pearl merely looked resigned to her Fate.

"Anything you need for your stay, please inform them or my guards. They will be able to assist you." Lady Rasmina rose gracefully from her chair, and everyone followed. "I do hope you enjoy your stay here in Lighthold." She left and her retinue followed. The door closed in their wake. Lorn let his fork clatter on his plate as he turned to Lilit.

"This will be fun."

She merely shook her head in disbelief. He caught the faint whisper of, "fucking hunter," under her breath.

Lorn chuckled at the absurdity of his situation.

15

The streets of Rijal were emptied at two in the morning. The clock tower was a giant amongst the small shops that circled it. Xira and Aza maneuvered to the shadows under the clock tower, their cloaks distorting their features. They shifted on their feet. Despite being hidden, Aza felt exposed, like any minute someone would come, discover their identities, and turn them into the authorities. In a vain attempt, she grasped at her power hoping for some use of it tonight. Still nothing. Instead of the usual hollowness, she was able to discern her magic lying underneath like that of a slumbering beast. She tried to rouse it, but it didn't respond. Aza gave a frustrated huff and cradled her hands together trying to gather some warmth to her exposed fingers.

Misinterpreting her impatience, Xira replied, "He will be here soon."

The clock tower was impressive, a massive structure within this city. It loomed over the other buildings, the stone smooth and built with immaculate precision. The abrupt ringing of the bells jarred Aza forward. She swung her head around expectantly.

A figure rounded the corner, dressed in a similar fashion to the two of them. He walked hurriedly and upon spotting the two of them he cast a look in either direction and crossed the road. Xira placed a hand on Aza steering her backwards, melting into the shadows. Xira gripped her sword the soft snick of the metal being pulled from its scabbard. The figure surged forward and stopped at the edge of the clock tower his hood facing their direction.

"Put your sword away," he hissed. "It is me." At hearing Tor's voice, Xira sheathed her sword and beckoned Aza forward. "There is very little time. This way." He jerked his head to the right, directed at the wall next to them. He fished his hands in his cloak and pulled out a small brass key. Double checking their privacy, he ran a hand delicately on the clock tower. He murmured to himself, skirting his hands over the wall like one would to a skittish horse. Finding what he needed, he pressed on the seamless stone and the stone pulled away to reveal a tiny keyhole. He placed the brass key inside and turned the key. A small click resounded throughout the night. Within the stone an outline of a door appeared and Tor slid it sideways, revealing a narrow pathway. Aza closed her mouth. She would never have imagined such a pathway into the palace. The seamless construction of the clock tower indicated no such hidden passages.

"Hurry," Tor said. Aza was the last one left outside, lost in her thoughts. She scrambled forward and Tor quickly closed the door. They were pitched into complete darkness. She tapped her foot against the ground and was met with more stone. She did not want to risk taking an errant step. The air inside the clock tower was stagnant and Aza fought a rising cough from the years of dust and decay. Someone reached behind Aza's back. A bright light momentarily blinded her. She shielded her eyes and when she moved her hand away, Tor was holding a torch. She was surrounded by winding staircases, one leading up and another leading down. She leaned her head back to scan the vastness of the clock tower above her. It spanned upwards, and she was unable to see the peak.

"We are not going up, Aza of the Well." He moved the torch to indicate the staircase below her. "Rather we are going down."

A rogue chill skittered down her spine. Being swallowed up by the ground with no end in sight was not a pleasant thought.

"Let us get this over with," Xira said. Without hesitation, they plunged into the darkness. Tor followed, his torch casting twisted shadows on the walls. Aza reluctantly brought up the rear, wishing for her magic to return.

This was too similar to her last descent into the ground at Lord Aldrich's castle, when she needed to banish the Hinterlands. A source of magic hidden deep underground, something calling to a time of long ago. Her steps stuttered. This was not the same. She was not at the castle of El'en anymore. This was merely a passageway into the palace of Verta. She was not banishing the Hinterlands, she was not lying on an obsidian table and screaming out in agony. She did not have her magic to banish anything.

Although the thought should have buoyed her hopes, it dashed them. The absence of her magic was keenly felt and she mourned it daily. Even though the Nerians protested the use of constant magic, it was a core part of who she was and she could not disentangle herself from it. They were one and the same. She was her magic and her magic was her. To part from either was like death.

They wound through the darkness, the passageway narrowing and widening in places, snaking through the underground. Unable to stand the silence any further Aza asked the question that gnawed away at her. "Does anyone else know about this?" Her voice carried through the empty hall. Tor glanced over his shoulder and answered, "Very few, I assume."

"You don't know for sure?"

"It would be arrogant to assume I am the only one who knows of this passage. I have yet to encounter someone else that does. But that does not mean others do not know of it." He chuckled to himself.

"What is so funny?" Aza asked.

He paused and faced Aza in the narrow passage. Xira huffed a breath and stood next to them silently. "That you would ask such questions. You, who should by all knowledge, not exist. So no, I do not presume to know everything. It is what has kept me alive so long." He peered at Xira who glared back. "Aza of the Well, you are one of the greatest mysteries of our century." He took a step forward, filling up the space between them. A strange reverence overtook him, his hand drifting up to her face like he couldn't help but touch her.

Xira pushed off the wall behind her, aiming to intervene, but Tor stopped his movement and jerked back. His body relaxed and a nonchalant expression donned on his face. "I believe you have found out your share of secrets already. Things are not as they seem within the five provinces." He quirked an eyebrow and turned, not stopping to look back to see if they followed.

Time blurred as they walked through the passageway. Sometimes they would encounter a branch in the passage and without a word Tor would lead the way. They didn't speak. Tor insisted on keeping silent. "You never know who may be listening," he said. The comment struck Aza as familiar. It took her a while to place where she had heard it before when she remembered Lorn had issued a similar sentiment. Two very different people, issuing the same warning, Tor's made from secrecy and Lorn's made from his background in hunting.

Before meeting at the clock tower, Aza tried to pry information from Xira on what she so desperately needed to see within the Vertan palace. But Xira remained tight-lipped, unwilling to share anything with her. What could be so important that they needed to go through this level of secrecy to enter the palace?

The Vertan palace was jokingly named the Fortress and Aza understood why. It was a formidable force to enter and escape from.

Farther and farther they altered between descending passages, ascending passages, twisting and twining. Eventually Tor extinguished his torch and indicated they should remain silent. Then, Aza heard it, a thin layer of voices. It was faint, but Aza could detect it through the walls above her. The three of them crept closer. The passage hit an abrupt dead end and Tor began feeling the wall. Small divots were carved into the solid earth and Tor climbed. It was impressive for Tor to navigate the wall with such skill, pitched entirely in darkness. It was evident he had done this many times before. Before the torch was extinguished Aza saw the ceiling span upwards, the exact height unknown. Aza could feel Xira's steadfast presence beside her, barely shifting her stance. Utter surety in their success.

There was a muffled scraping upwards and a small light illuminated their cavern. Tor thrust his head through the tiny gap and retreated, moving the false door back into place. She heard the soft labored breaths as he descended the wall and returned to their sides. "This is where I leave the both of you."

"Where have you led us?" Xira asked.

"The false door leads to a small unused storage room on the first floor." A small flash of light and Tor's torch was relit. His face was unusually grim as he took in both Xira and Aza. He turned to address Xira first. "Whatever it is you need to do, I hope you do it quickly. Their security has tightened since the last time I helped you enter. Like

I have said before, something is stirring. Something is beginning to awaken and I believe it has to do with her." He jerked his head towards Aza, his eyes holding Xira's.

"Don't tell me you are getting sentimental on me," Xira whispered. Although Xira was making light of the situation, Aza caught the softness. "We will be fine. I have handled countless situations like this."

His eyes hardened. "Do not be stubborn, Xira. You Nerians are so prideful and never back away from a challenge, but maybe this is one you should back away from."

"Some of us do not have such luxury." Xira's tone was a dismissal and Tor turned to Aza his expression guarded and unreadable. None of the prior vulnerability remained.

"It was a pleasure meeting you Aza of the Well." He gave a slight respectful bow of his head and walked away with one final reminder. "You have one day before this secret makes its way to people you would prefer not to know." His shadowy form and torch retreated down the passage around one of the winding corners and he was gone.

There was a brief moment of stillness before Xira burst into action.

"Follow me." Xira climbed, copying Tor's movements up the wall. Aza waited a beat before climbing behind her. She struggled against the exhaustion. They had been in town barely a day and yet so much had happened. They had walked throughout the night, in the dark and twisting passage and now they still had to explore the palace above them. Aza shook her head in disbelief at Xira. She feigned no signs of exhaustion, her energy and resolve impressive. Even scaling this wall was a difficult task, the rock smooth and difficult to maintain a strong grip on.

Xira reached the top and lent Aza a hand and yanked her up. They balanced on the thin ledge together. Xira patted her hands around the outline that Tor did, mimicking his motions. Finding the correct spot, she pushed hard and the wall slid sideways revealing a small storage room. Barrels and boxes were stacked upon each other, a small window filtering in weak daylight. Xira turned to Aza, her mouth set in a firm line. "This is less than ideal, but we need to be out of here in less than a day. Once word gets out of your whereabouts, it will be trickier to travel. I don't like slinking around the Vertan palace during the daylight, yet here we are." She shifted her weight and plucked at Aza's clothing. "I can easily hide myself, but you—you are a different matter. Luckily, Tor led us to a storage room."

Xira rummaged through the boxes. She grinned to herself and pulled out a box, and opened the lid. Inside were a pile of servant's outfits. She held up the articles of clothing , clucking her tongue in disapproval at the sizes and shapes. Finding the correct size she threw the outfit at Aza and grabbed one for herself.

"Change," she ordered. Their current clothes held no sentimental value, having been scrounged from neighboring villages. Aza easily disrobed and pulled on the brown pants and the green long-sleeved tunic. The pants were snug and the bottom cuffs rested about three quarters of the way down her leg.

Xira gave a shrug in her direction. "It was the best I could find."

While Xira changed, Aza tried to give her a semblance of privacy, yet her eyes were drawn to the jagged scars running along her torso. Her skin was decorated with them.

Xira caught Aza's disapproving look and shook her head. "Do not pity me." She gestured to the scars, and a hard glint gleamed in her eyes. "I earned them."

Aza kept her thoughts to herself and tried to busy herself with the storage room, feigning interest in the boxes and barrels, yet a hint of black caught her eye. On Xira's thigh three intertwined triangles were tattooed. Aza couldn't look away. The tattoo was intriguing and frustrating. It seemed so familiar, yet she couldn't place it. Actually all of the Nerians had some form of tattoo on their body. She remembered seeing Anwin's when they escaped from the sea serpent. She hadn't seen Reed's but she was confident he had one too.

Xira caught her looking again and sighed covering the tattoo with her new servant's pants.

"What—"

"I can explain another time, but right now we need to hurry. Every second counts." Her eyes roved over Aza's exposed hair, the silver brightening the room. She rummaged through the boxes again and found extra material. "This will have to do," she whispered under her breath. The fabric was old and looked like it might have been used as a cleaning rag at one point. Aza bent down as Xira expertly tied the makeshift headscarf over Aza's brilliant locks. Xira leaned back and gave a huff through her nose. "If no one looks too closely, we might be able to get away with this. Anyone with eyes will be able to tell you are different. Make sure to keep your eyes downcast, we don't want them to give you away either, but we can't afford you to go in blind. You need your vision." Satisfied with their disguises, Xira and Aza hid their weapons underneath the clothes. "Do as I say, every instruction, you understand?" Aza nodded her agreement.

Xira shut the hidden doorway, the stone moved noiselessly. They bundled their discarded clothes and hid them in the back of the storage room. No one was aware of their hidden entry. They doubted they would search for anything else.

Xira poked her head out of the true door. She opened it and slipped out, beckoning for Aza to do the same. Too late, Aza heard approaching footsteps. Rather than be stuck without the Xira's guidance, she emerged from the storage room and accidentally slammed the door shut. The sound echoed through the empty hall and the footsteps sped up. Xira yanked Aza forward, pushed her against the wall, and planted her hands on both sides of Xira's head. To Aza's shock, Xira leaned forward and nuzzled into her neck.

"Hey!" At the shout, Xira pushed away from Aza. Her face was bright red, and she coyly flitted her eyes between the guard and Aza.

Remembering Xira's warning Aza kept her eyes downcast.

"You aren't supposed to be down here cavorting with one another. We need all hands on-deck. The grand banquet is tonight."

Xira managed a weak curtsy and patted her clothing, smoothing out all of the edges. Aza tried to adopt a similar manner in an attempt to fool the clueless guard.

"Ahh, get on you two." He waved them forward. Xira and Aza hurried past him, careful to avoid brushing into him. Xira rounded the corner and pulled Aza with her. As they passed, Aza peeked and saw the guard's curious awe-struck daze. He shook his head and his footsteps resumed. Aza let Xira lead, but kept a brisk pace behind her.

"Idiot," Xira muttered as she walked away. "This is the perfect cover though. We need to get to the kitchens."

"What then?" Aza asked. She kept her footsteps quiet as she followed Xira's blazing trail.

"You will see. Quiet around the others." Before she could ask anymore questions, Aza heard the distinct cacophony of sounds indicated people at work, the hustle and bustle of servants, and workers getting everything ready for the big banquet tonight. People were dressed in a similar fashion to Xira and Aza, their outfits modest and unassuming. It was the perfect cover and perfect timing for them to blend in without any awareness raised. Whether through Fate or pure coincidence, they could do this. They could sneak through the Fortress, gain the information Aza needed to know and leave.

Shouts were volleyed back and forth as Aza and Xira drifted through the sea of workers. The workers exhibited a frenzied grace, easily dancing and floating around the others, food balanced on hands, dishes stacked precariously, each working individually but also part of a group. They were all focused on their own task, none of them taking note of Xira and Aza. Wafts of freshly baked bread and roasted meats filled the air. Aza's stomach grumbled its displeasure, their last few days had left little time for eating. Their walk through the secret passageway had taken the whole night and her nerves had left Aza unable to eat any sizable meal. She bit her lip and took a steadying breath, ignoring the tempting smell.

"I wish we had more for such a banquet," one of the chefs grumbled. They were furiously chopping vegetables and setting them aside to be used at a later time.

An awkward hush descended around the chef. His fellow cooks looked at him in worried glances. Their movements became more sharp and rigid, their chopping and stirring fraught with an underlying tension. Aza kept her head down and drifted over to the stack of plates behind the chef, urging herself to hear more of the conversation.

One cook abandoned her pot and reached over to grab the vegetables. They hissed, "Watch your tongue. You know what happened to Endyl." Her tone could have been misconstrued as a threat, but Aza caught the sharp movements of the fellow cook, her eyes widened in fear. It was out of safety that she warned him.

The chef grumbled and continued his chopping, but stopped his wagging tongue from condemning himself further.

Aza was familiar with castle kitchens. It was one of the few times she became truly comfortable around the MagicBlessed people. She remembered visiting the kitchens with Lorn constantly because of their training schedule and just an overall enjoyment for the decadent food. She found herself making many trips to it and enjoying the casual chaos that ensued.

She knew that workers would often filter in and grab stacks of utensils, plates, anything to set the tables and prepare for the countless meals served around the castle. No one would catch her or assume anything was amiss if she was around the plates grabbing an enormous stack. Except her mind snagged on the conversation. She was sure this is what Xira was trying to lead her to, something within the castle, something here.

"Hey! Look alive back there, we need you out preparing the banquet hall." Aza froze and realized the voice was directed at her. Keeping her face down she nodded, balanced the plates and went to leave. A stray hand delicately touched her arm.

"You don't look familiar."

Aza couldn't help but think of the last time someone grabbed her arm without permission. Igor, and his companions their bodies shattered in ice and left behind at some wayward inn. But this was not him and this hand was placed on her out of mere concern and curiosity.

The freckled hand floated back down alongside the owner's body and Aza couldn't help but raise her eyes to see who stopped her. The girl, for she seemed a mere girl perhaps in her teenage years, had auburn hair pulled back into a loose braid. The same light brown freckles that coated her arm dusted her face across the bridge of her nose. Her dark green eyes widened in shock as Aza looked at her, her mouth slightly gaped open. "Goddess...you are stunning."

"Wren, I need you over here," another cook shouted.

Aza's heart beat a wild pace. The comment so casually said, she thought the whole kitchen would overhear, but with the chopping of food, the clanking of pots and pans, the comment was swallowed by the noise of the kitchen.

She wrenched her gaze away from Aza but it trailed back to her, like a moth to the flame. "Who are you?" she questioned again, her voice going soft.

Aza froze, unable to come up with a sufficient response. Xira appeared next to her, tugging on her sleeve. She answered for her. "You know with these giant banquets, we hire staff out. She's new. C'mon new girl, let's get these plates set up." Xira left no room for discussion as she ushered Aza in front of her, plates balanced expertly in her hands.

Wren's sweet voice followed Aza as she walked into the banquet room. "Did you see her? She is blessed straight from the Well itself."

Xira released her grip and they stepped into the banquet hall. Windows filtered in soft light from above, the stained glasses arranged in artful displays. A long wooden table took up one side of the room, while the other smaller rectangular tables were placed perpendicular, long benches residing underneath each. Torches helped illuminate the softly lit room. Other workers moved about setting plates, silverware and metal goblets.

Besides the soft *tinking* of glasses, and shuffling of feet, it was filled with the quiet of studiousness. Careful of the other workers' scrutiny, Xira whispered, "Next time be quicker on your feet. We can't have people spend too much time gawking at your appearance."

"I know... I was surprised." They moved efficiently, a collective team wrapping themselves around the tables.

"Why? You should be used to it by now."

Aza thought about Xira's comment. She *should* be used to it by now. The way her presence affected those around her, how people tended to either be in complete shock or something far more sinister. Yet, the last few weeks she was only around the Nerians. They made her feel normal, instead of an oddity. The only time she needed to be aware of her appearance was when they were exposed to crowds. It became something she forgot. It wasn't only her looks. Even with her power stifled, people could sense something else within her—a uniqueness, an otherness that couldn't be hidden.

"You are right. Traveling with you caused me to forget."

Xira paused her place settings and looked at her. "Forget what?" The usual stern and austere demeanor faded away for a brief second, the question softly asked.

Aza clenched the plates as she said, "That I am different."

Xira searched Aza and turned back to her task at hand, neither of them speaking any further.

16

"They seem no closer to discovering Lady Rasmina's plans."
    Cruvo's private journal

Lorn struggled with his position as an ambassador. He didn't know what he was doing or how he should be behaving. Lilit was little help. She did not guide him. She was an angry shadow that haunted him as he strolled through Lighthold.

He thought it prudent to inform Cruvo of what was happening in Lighthold, so he recorded on parchment a succinct description of what had transpired his first night and tied it to the foot of a messenger raven. The bird flew away without further fanfare and Lorn watched its shape disappear amongst the thick canopy of trees. He hoped the letter made its way to Cruvo. That was the only task he had completed thus far that made him feel like was doing his job.

The first week he stumbled around the palace. Few people occupied Lighthold and those that did were reserved, barely offering a nod in acknowledgment. He felt like a ghost floating around the halls, aimless, with no one to talk to. It felt too similar to his time after Lakesh, as he roved from town to town without purpose. No, he had a purpose he reminded himself. He needed to find Aza and find whatever answers resided in Gara. Cruvo was adamant there was something going on here and he needed to figure it out.

On his fifth day in Lighthold, Lorn inquired where the library was. It was a solid place to start his research. A servant led him across a bridge from the main tree to another adjacent tree. The bridge was constructed like the palace of Lighthold, its wood smooth, marbled, with no edges or seams. The sides twined upwards and wound together above him to create a lattice. The magical lights were placed intermittently upon the path and Lorn had the distinct feeling of crossing the veil into the Meadows of the Undying. It was ethereal.

Outside the bridge, heavy rain poured down. He felt separate, apart from the rest of the provinces, and understood why Gara was on its own, why they were isolated. In a land like this how could they feel connected to the rest of the provinces?

The servant guided them through two large, engraved doors, the whorls etched seamlessly into the wood. The library was enormous and rivaled that of El'en's. It was the entirety of a tree hollowed out. Lorn craned his neck to take in the expansive shelves and the walkways which spiraled up. The bookshelves and staircases were carved into the tree.

He walked up to a cluster of tables and chairs and ran his hand along the wood. It was so light in color verging on white.

The servant left them without a word. Lilit pulled out a chair and sat down, taking in the library. She rarely spoke to him. Lorn was both perplexed and relieved. Their words always ended in fights, but she was his only companion here and sometimes he longed for conversation, for a sense of normalcy.

Lorn walked to the staircase, intending to explore the entire library. He rested his hand on the smooth railing and spared a glance at Lilit to see if she would join. She wasn't even looking his way, her expression disinterested.

Lorn let out a soft exhale and climbed the stairs. He didn't know what he was searching for, but he looked anyway. Ever since studying with Aza he had an undeniable thirst for knowledge. He wasn't ashamed of his upbringing, but there was a distinct lack of resources. Now that he knew such libraries existed, he needed to see the knowledge, to read it, and become acquainted with it. It helped to chip away at any mysteries that plagued him, like a sculptor revealing their work underneath the marble. Research could never hurt his chances of success.

By the time he made it to the top of the library, he was winded. The stairs were an excellent workout and he leaned his head against a well-placed window. There were gaps in the tree where glass windows were installed and Lorn leaned to look out. The world outside was awash in blurs of greens and browns. The rain came down violently with only a few people braving the streets below.

Lorn backed away from the window and retreated down the steps. He periodically grabbed books that might serve a purpose. He was clueless regarding where to start, but researching *The History of Gara* would prove a starting point. He hefted them down, his stack beginning to wobble. He was barely able to see over the top of it as he made it down the last stair and dropped them unceremoniously on the table. Lilit eyed him disdainfully.

"Making up for your provincial education?" she sneered.

Lorn rolled his eyes and nodded. "Yes, as a matter of fact I am."

Lilit huffed and leaned back in her chair, propping her legs up on an adjacent chair.

Lorn pulled a thick black tome labeled *The History of Gara* and flipped through it. The script was tiny, but the table of contents looked promising. He heaved a sigh and began his reading.

Hours had passed. Lilit bounced her leg against the table, jarring Lorn from his reading. He kept reading and said, "You can leave if you are bored."

"No, I am your personal guard. I am ordered to keep by your side at all times." She stood and began pacing the room. She followed the same steps, one, two, three, four, five, sharp turn on her heel, one two three, soft pivot.

Lorn clenched his teeth. He couldn't focus.

"Could you stop?"

The movement halted. "No." The movement began again.

The words jumbled on the page as she continued her pacing. He needed to research to find answers. The sooner he figured it out, the sooner he could return to Iyera.

Lorn took a steadying breath to calm his nerves before he asked, "Would you like to help?"

The movements paused again.

Before she could offer some snide remark he added, "If you do, we will return to Iyera quicker."

Silence, then precise footsteps made their way to him. The chair creaked as Lilit sat down. "Fine."

Lorn pushed a book towards her. She grabbed it and studied the title before opening it. "What are we looking for?"

Lorn had kept his head down, focused on the text in his book to keep his emotions in check, but with her question, he raised it. Her gray eyes were narrowed, waiting for his response.

Lorn needed to navigate this with skill. It was the first time Lilit had ever been vulnerable, admitting that she didn't know what they were looking for. He kept his voice level and tried to phrase his question as sincerely as possible. "Cruvo didn't tell you?"

Lilit stiffened and she curled her fingers inward. "I was sent here in a hurry. He failed to explain what we are doing here besides that I am here as your bodyguard."

Lorn needed to tread carefully. He could see how tightly wound she was. Something else had transpired that Lilit wasn't sharing. He tried not to pry too much, but he took this time to study Lilit. There were dark circles underneath her eyes, a permanent frown marring her face.

Lorn didn't push further and answered her question. "Cruvo didn't tell me much either. But there is something happening in Gara, something that could assist him and help find Aza. I don't know where to look, so I am researching everything."

Lorn slowly tilted his head down and regarded his book. He noticed that Lilit did the same. She flipped open the first page and began to read. After thirty minutes she broke the silence. "I don't understand how you do this."

Lorn paused and stretched in his chair. "What do you mean?"

"How do you sit here and just read when there is so much more to do?" Lilit rolled her shoulders back and got to her feet.

"What would you have me do instead?" Lorn knew how futile his effort would be if he didn't research first. Cruvo was right, knowledge is power. He needed to know everything. Their past, their history, everything was shrouded in mystery and Lorn wanted to uncover it. Yes, he agreed with Lilit. He would rather be out exploring the forest, feeling the freezing wind whip under his clothes and the soft loam underfoot as he traversed the forest. He was at home in nature. But he couldn't do that. He needed to be focused, he needed to uncover answers. He needed to get out of Gara and find Aza.

Lilit didn't answer. She bit the inside of her cheek as she thought about what he said.

"I crave action as much as you. I do not prefer to be sitting here in a library when I could be out there, trying to accomplish something." He rose out of his chair and walked over to her. "How about a compromise? I need to keep my skills honed. Would you like to spar every morning? Then we can come into the library and do research."

For the first time since journeying with Lilit, Lorn saw a sharpened gleam in her eye. She furrowed her brows and scoffed. "You won't even be a worthy sparring partner. But I guess it is better than nothing." Lorn wanted to smile in triumph. He knew Lilit was pleased with the arrangement even though she didn't let it show. It would take time, but he was getting her icy exterior to thaw.

~

The following week went marginally better. He regretted ever asking Lilit to spar. He understood now why she was Lord Aldrich's Captain of the Guard. She was fierce, ruthless, and her petite size was not a hindrance but a strength. She was able to quickly move around him. He couldn't keep track of her movements and paired with her strength of magic, she threw him around the room like he was a mere toy.

He had asked Maline and Flint for a training room and they led him to an adjacent tree, the bridge similar to the one they had used to get to the library. The main tree of Lighthold was the center of a spoke. The library resided to the west while the training room was to the east.

It was at the lowest level of the tree with weapons stored along the wall. Lorn would go limping to the library with Lilit strutting beside him, the faint hint of a smirk gracing her face. Her happiness wasn't his responsibility, but he was glad to see her usual fire back. The sparring centered her and brought her back to her true self. She was argumentative and insufferable, but it felt right. The circles under her eyes stayed, but he could slowly see the sorrow and uncertainty being washed away with the training. She was made for it.

They would alternate between different weapons, daggers, swords, fists, and spears. Lorn was only trained in the first three, but Lilit was skilled with using a spear and convinced him to try it. She was able to teach him the basics, and she kept her derision at bay. They were of equal skill with daggers and swords, but Lilit's strength and speed pushed her over the edge. She was a trained weapon. She used her magic in the most opportune times which left Lorn reeling. What little pride he had left was shattered as he was forced time and time again to say, "Yield." A blade held to his throat, positioned at his back, his back upon the floor as he lay gasping at the ceiling. During these times, Lilit merely grimaced. She was used to her victories and didn't revel in them. It was merely an outlet for her to get out her frustration. Lorn felt like her punching bag.

At night he would peel off his clothes and cringe at the mottled bruises that decorated his body. He was thankful for the automatic water that he was able to draw into a bath. At his small cottage, he would have had to draw a bath by hand, taking the time to painstakingly warm buckets and buckets of water. Every night he tenderly lowered himself into the hot water, the stings of the day fading, and his mind relaxed for once.

Over the coming days, everything was strained—his body, his mind. The books they researched in Gara were useful, but overwhelming. There was so much information. He was unsure what information would be helpful and had to look through everything with a discerning eye, even though he didn't know what to retain.

In the library Lilit was mildly helpful, offering small comments or interesting facts which Lorn noted and compartmentalized.

Maline and Flint would pop their heads in at times and give a brief hello before wandering off.

Lorn tried to use his magic to combat Lilit, but she was too skilled. It would temporarily blind her and Lorn would get a few hits in, but it never lasted. Lilit was able to predict where he was and still get him in a compromising position, with a blade near a vital organ.

Lorn had discovered an archery range near the training room and challenged Lilit to a shoot-out. This was the only area where Lorn truly surpassed her. Her skill was middling at best and for once Lorn smiled. Lilit had stalked away and demanded a different session. For his happiness, she didn't hold back a punch and gave him a black eye.

He tenderly patted the eye, grimacing while in the library. It strained him to read over the books, and he was going to call it an early day. The sharp clack of heels caused Lorn to look up. Ruby, Sapphire, and Pearl entered the library. Ruby and Sapphire let out a cruel laugh at Lorn's blackened eye while Pearl pursed her lips together in disdain. "Mother requested that we show you around the city of Lighthold." Lorn struggled to tell the two sisters apart, but he noticed that Ruby had a sharper cut to her cheeks and jaw, whereas Sapphire had a rounder face. Their thick black hair fell down their backs in a glossy curtain and their skin had the same sheen as their mother's. Pearl, while similar had thick curly hair and a slightly darker tone to her skin. If Lighthold had more sun, Lorn imagined Pearl's skin would darken in the sun, whereas her sisters would burn.

Ruby was the one to initially speak. The older sister often took the initiative.

Lorn realized he still hadn't answered. Sapphire added, "Tomorrow. We expect you to be properly attired." Her gaze raked over him, dismantling him.

He would not be cowed by these young women. While Lorn wasn't much older than them, he still had roughly ten years on them. Yet they made him feel like a little boy in his studies again, being mocked for something he couldn't control.

"We will leave early. You are to act with the decorum fitting an ambassador." Ruby looked at his black eye again before turning away. They were dressed in regal gowns, the fabric whispering against the floor as they walked away. Their long sleeves flowed over the long tapers of their arms and fit snugly around their midsection before pooling down to the floor. At the soft snick of the door being closed, Lilit laughed to herself.

Lorn froze at the sound. He had never heard Lilit laugh. He met her eyes and she stopped. "They hate you," she said.

It was so blunt that Lorn couldn't help but laugh too. It echoed in the library, and he winced from the pain. His body was sore and stiff from the sparring and the laughter only increased the unpleasantness. When it died down, he answered, "They aren't the only ones."

17

"I see an endless fire within her. A fire I wish to stoke, but I would not risk, if it resulted in her burning out with only embers left."
Nivet's private journal.

Aza and Xira performed more menial tasks and did their best to blend in with the other workers. They needed to break away from the group without raising suspicions.

The chaos and flurry of preparing for the feast prevented Aza and Xira from sneaking around the castle. Every time they tried to escape, someone would assign them another task. Aza was growing weary, her nerves on edge. The consistent demands of masking her appearance, the constant rounding of her shoulders to prevent herself from standing out wore her down. She always averted her silver eyes to avoid a disturbance. She played the dutiful, meek servant and it chafed at her, but she gritted her teeth and played the part. She was like a stallion made to wear a saddle, the bit in her mouth confining and controlling her. She wanted to be done with this place, done with hiding who she was, but the information Xira wanted to show her should be worth all of the posturing.

Aza caught the same mood emanating from Xira. She was doing better masking her emotions, but Aza caught the faint clench of her fingers, the impatient glances at the nearby doorways. Whenever they had a second together, Xira would give Aza a knowing look, with the promise of escaping their present servitude. Although it was unbearable, Aza considered themselves lucky. So far they were able to blend into their surroundings. Aza waited for Xira's signal when they would be able to escape unnoticed.

That moment presented itself when most of the workers were released for a brief break before the whirlwind of the night's event began. Aza strained to hear what the specific occasion was. The workers shared nervous glances, their movements both hurried, but rattled like they feared breaking a glass or making too much noise for fear of retribution. There were brief whisperings of soldiers making an appearance and the Lord and Lady of Verta themselves hosting a grand banquet. Aza assumed Lords and Ladies needed to host many a banquet, but for some reason this felt different, more sinister, like an underlying danger was present. It couldn't be mere coincidence that Aza and Xira infiltrated The Fortress on the day they were hosting this banquet.

When the servants were dismissed for their break, Xira pulled Aza around a corner, waving away other workers who invited them to break together. The servants cast after them with a curious gaze but lost interest quickly, ready to relax their tired feet and arms after bustling in the hot kitchen.

A thin sheen of sweat coated Xira's face, her clothes stuck slightly to her small frame. Aza imagined she was a mirror image from the heat of the kitchen and the closeness of so many people. It was a nice reprieve to be within the cool hallways.

"This way. Hurry," Xira commanded.

They walked at a brisk pace, not wanting to draw any attention to themselves now that they had finally escaped the prying eyes of so many people. Aza followed Xira as she expertly navigated the hallways. She was pushed into empty hallways when Xira heard the encroaching sound of footsteps closing in on them. Aza had no idea how Xira memorized this place. More and more guards were closing on their position. Their ability to explore undetected was quickly vanishing. Aza doubted the guards would be as lenient with the two of them if they were found far from their station. The footsteps were gaining in their direction and Aza began to panic. Xira had use of her magic and her exceptional fighting skills, but once they were found out how would they escape The Fortress again? They were too far to escape within the secret passage they entered through. She doubted that any escape would be possible, but then again, the Nerians did escape with Aza from within the castle of El'en. Maybe they were full of surprises. However, without Nivet to help shadow them out of The Fortress their chances diminished.

Nivet. Aza tried not to let her mind stray to the thought of the god who stole her away. While the god could never truly die, the anchor and life of Rune could. Nivet had sacrificed the life of Rune to save her. The life of a fellow Nerian to save someone he didn't even know about. She wondered what the process was like, when a god's anchor, their mortal tie died. What happened to them? Did their form escape to the ether waiting for another mortal body to inhabit? What about Rune's family, his friends, those who waited to hear of him back in the Nerian mountains? Upon hearing his sacrifice would they throw Aza out, their grief chewing them up inside? Aza froze. Did she truly see herself as returning to the Nerian mountains with them? She who was full of righteous fury at her capture. She did promise to listen to the Nerians' reasons, to see if the reason behind her capture was worth everything.

The footsteps drew closer and closer. She blindly followed Xira, unsure of how they would conceal themselves. An intersection of a hallway lay before them, and the footsteps were coming from both the left and right. They could only go straight and if they did, they would be spotted and questioned.

A tapestry hung on the right side of their hallway and Xira tugged her behind it, her fingers deftly touching some hidden combination. A faint click sounded and Xira heaved against the wall, Aza added her body weight to the stone wall budging slightly to the side. It was enough for them to squeeze their bodies through the tiny slip. Xira pushed Aza in, her larger, statuesque body protesting the tight squeeze of space. The footsteps grew nearer, and Aza forced herself through, squeezing and maneuvering her hips, chest, shoulders to make it work. Xira yanked at the secret stone door, and it moved a fraction more. With a whoosh of air, Aza squeezed through. Xira shimmied in after and they both sprang into action to shut the secret door. They were only hidden by a tapestry. If the guards noticed anything amiss, they would come investigate and their position would be found out.

The door heaved closed, and a mechanism locked into place. They eased out a slow breath and leaned against the false door listening for the guards on the other side. Aza was about to open her mouth and ask a question when Xira held a finger to her mouth.

Sounds were hard to distinguish, but after listening closely, Aza was able to differentiate the guards' footsteps converging on a single spot, near the tapestry. "Find anything?"

"No." A slight gruff of annoyance and more footsteps, their heavy boots echoing off the stone.

"Keep looking. We don't receive false alarms often. We don't want the Lord and Lady's night to be ruined by intruders."

"Aye, Captain."

Aza imagined the faint feeling of fingertips searching the wall for the hidden mechanism, but it was only her imagination. No one was searching for their hiding spot. There were no more disturbances.

The passageway was pitch black and Aza could barely see the faint outline of Xira's form next to her.

Xira tapped Aza's shoulder, and with a brief flare of magic, fire escaped from her fingertips illuminating the narrow corridor. She cocked her head to the side, indicating she would lead and for Aza to follow. The passageway was wide enough for only one person at a time. Xira doused the fire at her fingertips, sinking them into darkness once more. Aza knew Xira was rationing her magic, saving her energy reserve for a time when they would need it more desperately. Finding their way within a dark passageway was not one of them.

Sounds of boots scuffing, feet scrambling, and bated breaths filled the corridor. Periodically Xira would release the flame from her fingertip to ensure their safety and direction. The passage narrowed and twisted. To prevent any accidental injury in the dark, Aza positioned her hand on both walls to guide herself forward.

Neither of them spoke. Xira moved with precision, an intense energy of emanated from her like a hunting dog narrowing in on their prized kill.

Aza was tense her whole body clenched with anticipation of what they would find.

Xira stopped. There was no fire for Aza to see, but she heard quiet shuffling. Xira was climbing.

When it was quiet, Aza stepped forward and groped the wall searching for the handholds that Xira used. The wall was rough. The stone cut into her palms, but she climbed. As she rose, her head smashed into the ceiling, and she muffled a curse under her breath. Xira patted the stone next to her and Aza understood. She ducked and laid onto her stomach crawling over the jagged stone, her head pulsing with pain. She slunk next to Xira, their shoulders in line with each other. They were both positioned on their stomachs, their forearms propping themselves up. Xira's finger lit up again and she shook her head no, quelling Aza's sarcastic retort. She motioned for Aza to be quiet and watch.

Xira dimmed the light and shifted forward, her hands patting the wall in front of them. She grasped an edge and gently pried part of the wall away. A soft light sparked into their hidden nook. Xira pointed and Aza very quietly peered into the room.

It was opulent. A giant bed occupied the far end of the room the sheets decadent and made of the finest fabric. Next to the bed was a silver vanity, the edges of the mirror engraved. Beside it gowns and clothes were hung up on hooks.

Aza stretched further to try and peer down. She caught a desk with letters and books sprawled open. Xira pulled her back from the spying nook and motioned for her to wait. They did. Nothing of note happened. Lady's maids and workers walked in from time to time moving clothing, placing an item here or there, but nothing that screamed an answer to Aza's questions.

Her body became tired, the muscles fatigued from laying in such an awkward position on the unforgiving stone. Aza didn't understand how Xira did it. She heard very little shuffling from her, no rearranging of positions, but Aza's impatience gnawed at her. How much longer would they need to stay here?

The doors flung open with two guards bedecked in their finery and the crest of Verta stamped across the back of their uniforms, the scythe hovering over stalks of wheat. Aza felt herself staring at the crest and had the sudden urge to scream at the wheat for staying still when the danger of the scythe loomed overhead.

Lady Sarava walked into the room followed by Lord Ravinder. They nodded to the guards who promptly shut the door and began readying themselves for the banquet. Aza shook her head and crawled away from the nook. She didn't need to pry on their dressing. Even though she knew this was The Fortress where they both lived, she didn't expect to be prying.

Through the light provided by the removed stone, Aza was able to give Xira a look. One of confusion and disgust at why they were watching Lady Sarava and Lord Ravinder get dressed. Xira motioned for her to be patient. Occasionally Aza would lean forward and catch them in movements of getting ready. Lady's maids and other workers would walk in and ready lady Sarava, styling her hair in intricate braids, and placing flattering powder on her cheeks. Ravinder and Sarava talked about inconsequential things, their clothing, the weather, and their people. Aza grew bored waiting to hear something important. She rearranged her position so she could easily move back and forth, caught between a need to give them privacy, but not wanting to miss anything important said.

While resting away from the spying nook, Aza heard Lady Sarava order the Lady's maids out and for the guards to not let anyone enter the room. Another order was said too quietly for Aza to hear. Xira nudged Aza and she knew this was her chance to catch what Xira wanted to show her. Their chambers had high placed windows letting in the filtered light from outside, the slight cloudiness darkening their chambers. Torches were lit around the room.

Once the door was closed, Lady Sarava motioned to her husband. Lord Ravinder stood up, abruptly straightening his dress clothes for the night, his naturally ruddy complexion, reddening. Lady Sarava maintained her composure, but Aza noticed the slight trembling of her fingers, the errant brush of phantom stray hairs.

"She wants to meet with us. Now," Lady Sarava hissed.

She rushed over to the door and discreetly opened it to allow three people to enter. Two guards ushered in a scared and shackled young man. They dropped the prisoner to the ground, his knees crashing against the stone, and left. The young man's hair was a soft yellow that fell around his too big ears. He scrambled to his feet.

"Endyl, do you know why you are here?" The poor young man cowered in front of Lady Sarava and Lord Ravinder his complexion paling further, his knees shaking.

"I'm a good worker, my Lord and Lady. I don't know why I have been jailed. I haven't done anything." He furiously shook his head, avoiding eye contact.

"You have been caught conspiring and spreading malicious lies throughout our castle. You have been issued a death sentence."

Endyl's eyes widened, and he collapsed to the ground in fear.

"I don't understand. I was only gossiping. Nothing as crazy as you are presenting. Why would I die because of this?"

Lady Sarava skirted around him and bent down to whisper in his ear. "Your death will happen regardless. We can make this painless or very, very painful. We have developed methods of torture where you will lie awake for days begging for death. If you want a quick death, you will listen to what we want from you."

"And if you refuse and you drag this out further, we will go after your family," Lord Ravinder added.

Endyl finally looked at Lady Sarava and Lord Ravinder, revulsion roiling off him. The emotions on his face flitted between fear, anger, and injustice.

"You have two sweet siblings who live at home and your parents are older, unable to work because of their ailing bodies. We could capture them and make their lives more miserable."

Endyl was resigned, his tone dejected. "What must I do?"

"You will hear a voice within you. It will ask you to accept. If you do, we promise to leave your family alone."

A faint nod of the head was the only answer he gave before his scream filled the room. Endyl's body collapsed to the floor, convulsing. His eyes rolled in the back of his head.

Aza bit her tongue to prevent herself from crying out. Her fingernails embedded themselves into her hands. She was shaking with rage at herself for merely sitting here watching this horrific scene unfold. How could Xira remain so calm? How could she not fight against this? Xira placed a hand on Aza's shoulder, locked eyes with her and nodded. Xira was just as affected by this as Aza. It took control to not let herself go after these people.

Lady Sarava and Lord Ravinder stood beside Endyl's convulsing body. There was a slight apprehension in Lady Sarava's missteps and Lord Ravinder's fumbling hands. Silence descended, with only the ringing of Endyl's cries echoing in Aza's ears. She couldn't erase it, his cries of pure anguish. His body lay there, discarded while these two people in power stood over him, awaiting.

Another glance at Xira, and Aza understood, this is what Xira wanted her to see. This is what they were waiting for. An eerie scraping filled the room. Lord Ravinder kneeled quickly and unshackled Endyl's hands and feet. The iron chains were tossed aside to the corner of the room. Endyl rose, his movements unnatural and jagged, unlike the young man's from before. Something was off.

Lady Sarava and Lord Ravinder stepped back. When Endyl lifted his head to look at them, they both collapsed to the ground in worship. Their foreheads touched the ground, their arms prostrated in front of them. Endyl scowled at them, as if they were mere bugs to be dealt with, something to tolerate.

"You may rise." Endyl waved a hand up. His hands ran up and down his body. "This body is worse than the last one."

"I apologize, Astaroth. This is the best we could do in the time allotted." Lady Sarava bowed her head in supplication.

Aza bit back her gasp. A hand squeezed hers tightly. Aza could not look away from the tiny nook. She couldn't ignore how Astaroth inhabited a host body similar to what Cruvo did to Lord Aldrich—Astaroth, the cause of the corruption who plagued the land. Confined to Endyl's body, Aza could spot Astaroth in the faint traces of Endyl's body, her subtle lift of the head, the arrogance, the strength. This was not the same young man who cowered before the Lord and Lady of Verta. This was a god-inhabited body.

A slight huff of breath came from Astaroth. "This will do for now. Is everything prepared for tonight?"

Lord Ravinder avoided Astaroth's scrutinizing gaze and answered, "We have done everything you have asked. Our guards, our military, everyone will be on board. If they aren't, we will deal with them."

"You are confident in your abilities, yet you can't even look at me mortal." Astaroth circled Lord Ravinder, and Aza caught a brief flash of black coil through her veins.

"I am merely h-humbled by your presence," he stammered.

"Such pretty lies and flattery. I do not fall so easily for courtly pretenses. Yet both of you have been useful." She plucked at Lord Ravinder's clothing with distaste on her face and returned to stand in front of them. "Follow my instructions and you will be granted all of Ithilia alongside me."

The room seemed to darken, the torch lights flickered, and Lord Ravinder paled further, his body beginning to shake slightly. Her corruption spread, black veins of rot creeping over Lord Ravinder's hand like a lover's touch. He looked at it in disbelief, fear silencing anything further from his mouth. He accepted what was bestowed on him. Lady Sarava looked upon her husband with a faint pinch of concern around her mouth.

Astaroth watched in fascination as her corruption bleeding through Lord Ravinder's arms, the veins rotting. A smell of putrid decay spread throughout the chamber.

"My honored Astaroth," Lady Sarava finally spoke, interrupting whatever bizarre experiment was taking hold of her husband.

Astaroth tore her gaze from Lord Ravinder and took a deep satisfying breath. Her eyes closed and a faint glimmer of a smile played upon her lips. "My powers," she murmured.

The purification nauseated Aza. Her stomach roiled. Everything was too much. The sharp feel of stones underneath her, her awkward position in this cave, her hunger, her tiredness, the proximity of Astaroth. Her use of power unleashed something in Aza, a pounding headache and an intense chill swept over her body. She didn't know how much longer she could last here. But she couldn't leave, not yet. She needed to see and hear more. They risked too much to get to this point, and this was only the beginning. She could not abandon it now.

Aza gritted her teeth and pushed through, the pulsing headache and chills overtaking her body, but she fought it. Even now, in her state of turmoil, she couldn't deny the sheer magnitude of Astaroth's presence. Both revolted and drawn towards her aura like a creature surrounded by a wildfire. Instead of running for safety, she was mesmerized by the beauty of the flames rushing to consume her. Bile rose in her throat. It was a similar feeling to how she felt about Cruvo. She thought it was something separate, something special, but it wasn't. Yet during their times together he had helped train and hone her skills. *Was that a benefit for him or for you?* a small voice asked. She pushed those thoughts away. Now was not the time for her own self-pity and loathing.

Astaroth stood still, the faint smile still lingering on her face. Lady Sarava and Lord Ravinder stood casting curious and nervous glances at one another, but they were rooted to the spot too scared to move.

"Yes." Astaroth smiled large now, the once genuine smile on Endyl's face now a twisted mockery. It was a predator about to capture their prey. "Tell me," Astaroth opened their eyes and cocked her head at both Lady Sarava and Lord Ravinder. "Have you found her yet?"

"F-found who?" Lord Ravinder stammered. He took an uneasy step back, the arm laced with corruption, clutched to his chest.

Astaroth noticed the step back and she advanced and grabbed Lord Ravinder by his tunic lifting him into the air. Endyl was slim in comparison to Lord Ravinder's more robust stature, but by some inhuman strength provided by Astaroth Lord Ravinder was as light as a child.

"Do not play coy with me. You know who I speak of." Astaroth closed her eyes and took a long inhalation through her nose. Her power pulsed. Dark veins and rot crept up Lord Ravinder's arms up and neck—choking him. He sputtered helplessly in her arm, his legs kicking uselessly beneath him. Lady Sarava stood her ground, her eyes hardened and pose rigid.

Aza squeezed forward, craning to get a better view, to listen to every word Astaroth spoke.

"We heard rumors of an intruder. Our guards are searching tirelessly," Lady Sarava answered through tight lips.

Astaroth released Lord Ravinder and he crumpled to the floor. The prominent black rotted veins now fading as he lay upon the floor, the sickness disappearing as if it never existed in the first place. He coughed violently. His wracking heaves filled the otherwise quiet room. Lady Sarava did not comfort her husband, but merely stood next to him unsure of whether to aid him or stand still, unwilling to draw Astaroth's wrathful gaze.

"If you had paid attention at all, you would realize my powers are strong right now. Normally I would be unable to do that to your husband." Astaroth said the word 'husband' with a sneer on her face. "She is here, within your castle, probably spying. So close to us."

Aza froze. They were talking about her and Xira. Astaroth was able to use her powers due to Aza's proximity. She made to move, but Xira motioned for her to stay. Aza ducked out of the spying nook, unwilling to have her face be seen, even in the smallest of spaces.

Aza heard footsteps pace the room. "Oh, little fox. I know you are hiding." The footsteps stopped and Aza held her breath. Even Xira ducked lower, her body stilled. "Little fox, safe in her hole. We will find you, little fox, and smoke you out of there."

Still, they did not move, Aza and Xira held their breaths. Xira clutched onto Aza's arm, her grip strong and sure. A clear warning to stay still, to not move.

"Get your guards now," Astaroth ordered Lady Sarava and Lord

Ravinder. "There's a little fox that needs to be found."

18

Cruvo's private journal

Lorn and Lilit waited outside the Lighthold Palace for Ruby, Sapphire, and Pearl to escort them throughout Lighthold Proper. Lorn tugged at the tight collar of his tunic. Lilit was adorned in equal fashion, with her Captain of the Guard outfit. She wore light chain mail, gauntlet, and greaves along with her steel boots. The crest of Iyera was prominently stamped along the shoulder and her sword hung gracefully from her hip. Lorn felt bare in comparison—unarmed, with a fancy tight collared tunic and tailored pants. His usual scuffed and worn boots were discarded for ones freshly made, their leather smooth and shining. He could even see his reflection within it. The only impatience she showed was a constant tapping of her foot. Otherwise, Lilit donned her role well. She was his guard and acted as such.

Lorn dreaded the arrival of the sisters. He felt like a dull-witted boy in their presence, and he didn't have the necessary skill to navigate their torturous conversation. Every word, every glance was carefully measured, and if Lorn took the wrong step he would fall into a trap. Being an ambassador meant honeyed words and a coy presence, something he lacked. But this was necessary, this would help Aza. Information was here and he needed to gain every insight possible to succeed.

Ruby, Sapphire, and Pearl glided down the steps each in their respective colors, their dresses' bearing a similar cut. Their delicate sleeves tapered along their arms and the dresses fabric pooled low on the ground. Each of their hair was styled in a coronet of braids, their faces both eerily similar and yet dissimilar. While beautiful, he didn't understand how their dresses would be practical in the Garan weather.

Lorn took a steadying breath. He could do this. They were close to his age, younger than him even. He was not intimidated by the beasts of the Hinterlands, and he wouldn't be now.

The women led him along the northern spoke, the walkway covered from the persistent rainfall. They didn't talk and Lorn grimaced as he imagined the rest of the day together. They wound through other trees until they eventually emerged into Lighthold Proper.

He now understood the reason for their dress. Lighthold Proper was completely covered from the rain, a beautiful mixture of natural and artisan work wove the branches together to keep out any stray rainfall from covering the streets. Although he thought it would seem dreary it wasn't. Like the rest of Lighthold it held an austere quality. The same light magic was kept in orbs along streetlamps with their ethereal glow.

Their shoes clicked along the cobblestone street. Very few people were out and shopping in the early morning, but the sisters had wanted to get an early start to show Lorn everything Lighthold Proper had to offer.

It was quiet and peaceful. Any passersby gave small polite nods to the sisters and gave Lilit a wide berth. Her armor was a natural deterrent to anyone, paired alongside her stony expression.

After walking in silence, Ruby begrudgingly led the conversation, pointing out the beautiful shops. Lorn didn't miss the thinly veiled insults and barbs sent in his direction at any point in the conversation; insulting his status, his rural upbringing, his looks, his manners, anything and everything Ruby ripped apart with careful consideration. Sapphire did not miss an opportunity to pile on. It was never anything egregious, more subtle and consistent like a poison being slowly slipped into your goblet. It was just enough to cause him discomfort.

Many of the shopkeepers exuded the same mystical air as the rest of Lighthold. They were unused to travelers and did not welcome him with the same warm greeting he was used to in the countryside of Verta or even in Iyera. These people kept to themselves and their own. They visited swordsmiths, food markets, weavers. Everywhere the sisters escorted him they shared their knowledge of Lighthold Proper like misers distributing a coin of their wealth. Despite the company Lorn enjoyed it. It was fascinating to compare their craftsmanship and goods to other provinces.

One of the shops piqued his interest and Lorn found himself enthralled in a swordsmith shop. The swordsmith was a burly woman, her muscles evident underneath the loose tunic and apron she donned. A slight smear of ash crested her forehead. The woman had creases of age and her auburn hair was shot through with silver and tied back into a firm braid draped down her back. She answered Lorn's questions with a stern demeanor. The swords, daggers, even spears and staves were beautiful and unlike anything he had ever seen. Their colors richer, the steel and iron dangerously captivating. Ruby and Sapphire waited outside for Lorn, bored of his discussion with the swordsmith. Only Pearl stuck around, her face a smooth mask of indifference, but Lorn noticed how she twisted towards their conversation and stilled her movements to not miss a word. Lilit remained on guard, her eyes lazily flicking around the shop, a sort of grim satisfaction at the shopkeeper's offerings.

Lorn handled one of the daggers, a twining of branches engraved along the hilt. It was smooth, sharp, and something pulsed when he held it, like the iron it was forged from held an energy. Lorn weighed it in his hands, testing it, assessing it. He couldn't stand it any longer.

"What is different? I can't place it."

The shopkeeper joined him. "There will be nothing like that outside the province of Gara." A hint of pride laced through her voice, a war between wanting to remain taciturn and showcasing her pride in her work. She towered over Lorn and reached out, an invitation to take the blade from him. Lorn relented and handed it over. "It is from the mines of Gara." For one of her size, she delicately held the blade, and ran her fingers reverently over it, admiring her craftsmanship and skill.

"But the mines provide much of the same steel and iron for the rest of the kingdom."

She nodded her head in agreement. "Aye, but you don't get the good stuff."

Lorn couldn't help but track the movement of the blade as she held it, like it was hypnotizing him.

She twirled the dagger and offered the hilt to Lorn. He palmed it.

"What do you feel?"

Lorn didn't want to admit the weakness, the way he felt drawn into the sword. Yet her stern gaze pulled him apart and he knew to only answer honestly. "I feel drawn in. Bewitched."

The woman arched an eyebrow at his response. "Yes, that's exactly right. We are able to find and mine pockets of magic within the ore."

Lorn took an unsteady step back to fully face the swordsmith.

"Do the other provinces know?"

He tightened his grip on the dagger and finally understood the treasure that laid within. Raw magic imbued with the ore and found in its natural state. Something he had no idea existed up until this point. Magic was always a part of someone, not something separate, not something to be honed, sharpened. The only stories he could link to this was a Well-blessed item, something from myth and legend.

"The other provinces fail to look beyond their own borders. They do not know, because they do not look. The swords forged from the magic imbued ore are only slightly enhanced. They can aid a user's magic or provide small benefits." She delicately touched another sword on the wall, one that was resting next to the dagger he held. "I have worked for many years trying to shape the metal and work it into something usable. Only over the last few years have I succeeded."

Lorn walked over to the wall and tried to put the dagger back on it, but the magnetic pull was too much. "Why does it feel like this?"

"Magic yearns to be connected with more magic. It is chaotic, visceral, and aims for a vessel. We are drawn to the raw power of it, the potential. They are extremely rare and quite expensive." She yanked the dagger out of Lorn's hand and returned it to the wall.

"How is this any different from the MagicBlessed weapons of long before?"

The swordsmith returned to her counter and crossed her arms over her chest. Her muscles strained against her tunic. "Use your head, Ambassador." She listed reasons on her fingers with a bored look on her face. "A Well-blessed item would be exponentially stronger than any of the swords and daggers I craft. Although, I should thank you for considering my work at such a high level. If the scrolls prove correct, the magic in the Well is infinitely more potent and powerful. What I use from the pockets of ore are comparatively small amounts of magic. These swords have never touched the Well, therefore they cannot be Well-blessed." She blew out an exasperated breath and shook her head. "What a notion. A Well-blessed item."

Lilit approached the wall, her metal greaves clinking softly with each step. She mimicked Lorn's actions, her fingers delicately tracing and reaching for the blades.

Pearl cleared her throat.

Lorn started. He had forgotten about her. She had melted into the corner of the room, making herself small and unnoticeable. The shopkeeper's eyes darted to the daughter of Lady Rasmina, and she imperceptibly straightened.

"We must be going Lorn of Verta, there is much more to see." Pearl's voice was a strange mimicry of her mothers and Lorn muscles tightened, trying to control his anger. It was soft and delicate, but she wasn't her mother. She was softer and kinder without the sharp tongue her sisters or mother possessed. But something was off, the shopkeeper once again brusque and unable to meet his eye. Lorn reluctantly followed Pearl out the door with Lilit behind. He gripped the door frame and paused, realizing he never asked the shopkeeper's name.

He looked back and before he could ask she answered, "My name is Hibara. if you need a weapon, come back anytime." A flash of something showed in her eyes as they flicked up to Lorn. Then, she busied about her shop without another word to them.

The rest of Lighthold proper was equally beautiful. Lorn began to take note of the light magic in the streetlamps. They had learned how to harvest magic in unique ways. It was separate from what he had experienced in the other provinces. Gara was making discoveries and keeping the knowledge to themselves. He always viewed the five provinces as a homogeneous grouping, blurring and mixing together with no separations besides climate. He never thought there would be further divides with their knowledge or acquisition of knowledge. He always viewed magic as a linear experience. He summoned the magic, it completed its purpose and then it was done. But this knowledge presented magic in a different way. It was always present and just needed to be shaped and morphed to alter its state. Lorn mulled over the new research topic he wanted to read more about. His fingers itched to grab at the textbooks in the library to search for this information. This was something new, something different that could interest Cruvo and assist Aza, whether in the search for her or in banishing the Hinterlands.

Many of the shopkeepers behaved in a similar manner to Hibara, cold, taciturn, a slight wariness to everything they said. Lorn started to doubt whether it was the true nature of the Garan people or whether it was his company. The three sisters commanded respect and a small amount of fear. The people shied away from them. At the end of the street, a shop caught his eye. It was carved of the same ornate wood as the rest of the shops, two columns were stationed alongside the edges each a solid piece of ornate marble.

Lorn stopped the group and looked in through the glass window. Beautiful gems winked back at him as Lorn walked into the shop. Before entering, he paused and ran his hand over the marble columns. Small pieces were carved out into the shapes of glinting stars.

A thin, willowy person greeted them and introduced themselves as Rye. Their straight blonde hair draped down their back, with two thin braids pulled back alongside the side of their head. They were outfitted in a simple white linen dress, the design both simple and elegant with small cutouts on the back. Rye glided over to them, casting a curious glance at Lilit, but keeping their focus on Lorn.

"What may I help you with today...?"

Lorn fumbled until he realized Rye was prompting Lorn for his name. "Lorn of Verta." Rye eyed Lorn and spotted the embroidered symbol of Iyera, the ocean and sun on his shoulder. Rye pursed their lips together as Lorn scattered to add, "-acting as Ambassador to Iyera."

Rye made a small noise in their throat.

Lorn pushed his hair aside and dismissed his awkwardness. "I couldn't help but admire your gems here."

"Thank you." Rye gave a small smile and brushed their hand down the side of their dress. "We pride ourselves on carrying the best."

Lorn spotted small clusters of stardust gems locked behind a glass case.

"Ah, very expensive and very popular. You aren't the only one whose eyes have been captured with the stardust gems."

A pang of longing spread. Lorn tried to tamp it down, but he couldn't help missing Aza. They were gifts for her, a sword and two daggers commissioned for her. Gems he thought represented who she was and her origins.

Lorn cleared his throat and moved away from the case of stardust gems. "Yes, they are beautiful."

He inspected the other gems, some of their sizes comically and surprisingly large. After a time, Ruby, Sapphire, and Pearl entered the shop.

Rye straightened their stance and gave a slight bow to each of them. "An auspicious day when all three daughters of Lady Rasmina have entered my shop." Their blonde hair fell like a waterfall over their shoulders, soft and silky.

The sisters gave a slight smirk in response, except for Pearl who bowed back in deference. Sapphire rolled her eyes as she saw Pearl's bowed head and nudged her to straighten up.

"I have beautiful gems in each of your namesakes back here." Rye retreated to the back of their shop and returned with three separate wooden boxes. Very different from the wood of Lighthold and Lighthold Proper, the wood was polished mahogany deep in color.

With the first one they gestured for Ruby to step forward. A gold necklace with a giant inlaid ruby was pulled from the box. Lorn couldn't imagine the fortune such a gem would fetch. It was the size of a dove's egg. They reverently placed it upon Ruby's neck while she fawned over the attention.

Lorn used this moment to pursue the rest of the shop. Everything was immaculate, beautiful, pristine. He imagined Lakesh here in the shop with him. She would have marveled at each of the gems, but he couldn't picture her in any of them. Any extra adornment on her felt like too much. Her beauty was savage, one that belonged within the thralls of nature, the cutting eye of a storm, or the brutal slash of a throat. She wasn't a fair beauty, but one of strength, at once both compelling and unique. None of these gems would have done her justice, but they were pretty none the less.

Rye continued on to impress Sapphire. A similar ring was pulled out. The massive brilliant blue sapphire twinkled and was slipped onto her finger. Lorn kept an eye on the transaction while checking out the other items.

Pearl was next. He was shocked when Rye opened the box and removed a delicate necklace. Three simple pearls chained together formed a drop necklace which laid delicately against Pearl's breastbone. It was quite the opposite of her sisters, a more understated and regal piece, something more suited for her. Rye knew their customers well.

Lorn fought back the grin on his face as he saw Lilit bored out of her mind. She stood stock-still next to the doorframe looking out on the proceedings.

"You have outdone yourself Rye," Ruby commented, her fingers tracing the outline of her necklace. The ruby seemed to pulse at her throat like an open wound. "You know where to send the bill." Ruby and Sapphire left the shop without another word. Lorn trailed them. Before leaving, he caught Pearl hugging Rye and some quick whispered words between them. Lorn strained to hear and caught vague whisperings.

"—find it yet?"

Rye gave a smile that didn't reach their eyes and gave a firm shake of their head. Pearl hurried after their group, her head kept down, but Lorn didn't miss the look of guilt and relief in her eyes.

19

Nivet's private journal.

Aza and Xira scrambled back through the passageway, their boots hitting hard stone, their hands fumbling against the walls. They tried to hurry with a mixture of speed and stealth, but every so often there would be a scraping sound, a heavy footfall, or breath that seemed too loud for this quiet space. How would they get out of here? This was a single passageway. There were no branches in the path for them to take instead. This was it. All of this work and effort, only to result in their capture. They dared not speak, but Aza could feel the fierce determination radiate off of Xira. She would not bring Aza this far into the castle to result in failure. They escaped the clutches of Eonas. They would not fail today.

Time seemed to warp and standstill as they navigated the passageway. Before Aza even realized it, they had made it to the exit. In the darkness, Aza caught the faint silhouette of Xira bent down pressing an ear to the fake stone wall, listening for guards. Xira moved away from the wall and sent a spark to her finger, illuminating the surroundings.

Xira pulled Aza's dagger from the safety of Aza's clothing and planted it firmly into her grasp. "Do not hesitate. They will not hesitate to hurt you. If they capture you, I fear even we wouldn't be

164

able to rescue you without Nivet's help. If you are unable to kill, stun. If you cannot fight, run. Right now, I am your Captain and you listen to my orders, understand?"

Aza noted the grim determination on her face, the firm set of her body primed to run and fight. Aza pocketed the dagger, hiding it within the sleeve of her shirt. They couldn't appear suspicious, not yet.

Xira leaned against the wall and looked over her shoulder, whispering, "I do not think we can go down. We must go up. Ready?"

Aza's throat was thick, the words unable to come out. But she felt the grip of her dagger hidden and gave a firm nod. Xira pushed open the trap door. The stone groaned. They froze, waiting to hear approaching guards. When no one came, Xira slid the false door farther open in one giant heave, and they both clambered out. Xira carefully returned the door.

They were vulnerable in the hallway. Aza felt exposed. Xira yanked Aza forward, leading them deeper into the castle. Not towards the safety and familiarity of the kitchens but away.

At an intersection, they veered left and climbed a staircase. They emerged from the staircase and saw the backs of guards walking away from them. Aza froze, but Xira did not. She careened forward, unwilling to let a pair of guards stop her. Xira drew her sword and slammed the pommel onto the head of one guard, while the other turned around with a gasp on his lips, before Xira silenced him too. Their bodies slammed to the floor their armor rattling louder than Aza thought possible. Sneaking around was no longer an option.

Xira kept her sword drawn. A rogue shout came from somewhere to their right and guards everywhere shouted, alerting The Fortress to their position.

Xira and Aza broke into a sprint and climbed up to higher levels. Aza could barely keep up. She trailed Xira as she made sharp turns, her eyes scanning windows readjusting her position and changing their route. She had a plan and Aza could only hang on.

Guards were closing in behind them. "We found them. Close the gates. They are heading to the west side of The Fortress. Get your guards on the battlement now!"

Somehow Xira sprinted faster, her movements more determined, sharper, and Aza followed. Her arms pumped back and forth, her legs surged forwards. Xira bashed into a rounded wooden door and they were met with an autumn sunset obscured by heavy clouds. Aza nearly stumbled from the marked contrast of the brightness that assaulted her as they left the dark passageway.

A fierce wind on the battlement ripped Aza's scarf from her head, revealing her bright, silver coils of hair. She turned as guards filed in behind. They were trapped, pinned on both sides with nowhere to go.

A guard stepped forward. A metal helmet obscured his face. "Stand down. If you surrender, you will not come to harm."

Xira nodded and sheathed her sword.

Aza fought back a gasp. The Nerians never ran, never willingly surrendered. But Aza saw what Xira did. There was no possible way to fight out of here, nothing for them to do. Guards filled every extra bit of space on the battlements, their swords drawn, and shields raised.

Lady Sarava and Lord Ravinder wove through the crowd. Their guards stepped aside to let them pass.

"I never knew a Nerian to give up so easily," Lady Sarava said. The guards around her chuckled. Their distance was roughly twenty feet. Aza did not shield her meager dagger, instead she wielded it in front of her and gave both Sarava and Ravinder cold looks. Unbridled anger and disgust surged forth. They willingly sacrificed their people for Astaroth to inhabit. They were cowards seeking power and it would be their downfall. Xira might see the futility of fighting, but Aza did not—not now.

Sarava turned to Aza, her eyes hungrily scanning her body. "Aza of the Well."

The guards murmured, their whispers held a touch of reverence. Aza looked at the guards and saw suspicion, hostility, curiosity, and hunger. She firmed her stance and gripped the small dagger. She would not turn herself over.

"Come on, Aza," Xira whispered. "Let us be done."

Aza was nearly blinded by anger. This was not Xira. She would not willingly turn herself in. She would fight to the death. No, Xira had another plan. Xira locked her fingers around Aza's wrist and gently pulled her to the edge of the battlement. She briefly glanced over her shoulder. They were very high up, too high to leap.

"Drop your dagger," Xira persuaded. She guided Aza closer to the edge of the battlement, inching her away from the guards, away from Sarava and Ravinder.

"Listen to her Aza," Ravinder said. "You are surrounded. Let go of your dagger. No one needs to be hurt."

Aza's calves hit the stone wall behind her, her back left with nothing to support her.

"Wait!" Xira shouted while stepping in front of Aza. "You must promise mercy to her."

Lady Sarava and Lord Ravinder shared a glance and nodded their heads. "We promise." Aza didn't disguise the sneer that rose to her face from the utter lies they spewed. One day she would return for them and get her vengeance for all of the innocent lives they so carelessly took.

Xira turned and motioned for Aza to drop the dagger. It clattered to the ground, the sound like the final hammering of a nail, sealing her fate. But a small trust blossomed inside of her. Trust for Xira. The Nerians were always protecting her. She could try and trust her now.

Xira gave Aza the ghost of a smile and with a wink turned back to address Lady Sarava and Lord Ravinder with her arms outstretched. Her voice once soft and honeyed, hardened instantly.

"Like I would trust the word of a pair of snakes."

Xira pivoted and sprinted at Aza with her arms outstretched.

"Guards, stop them!" Lady Sarava shouted. The shrillness of her voice pierced the tense shuffling of guards moving into action. But they were too far away to stop what was already in motion.

Aza braced herself and trusted Xira. Xira barreled into her, tackling her over the edge of the battlement and down they fell.

Endyl pushed through the crowd, his face twisted into something worse by Astaroth, the faint hint of black rot veined along his face, a jagged slow smile.

Aza fought the urge to scream, the wind and cold rushing alongside them. They plummeted through the air.

They were going to die. They were not slowing, and the ground was rising up to meet them. Aza clung to Xira.

Halfway through their descent, Aza felt a faint tugging. Something was slowing their descent.

They slammed into the back of a cart and all the air whooshed out of her. She gasped for breath, her chest tight and constricted. Aza stared at Xira who was in a similar state.

The cart jolted forward. Aza couldn't think about who had them, what they were doing, or where they were going. All she could think about was her consuming pain. The bruises that would be covering her body. The struggle to find air. Like emerging from beneath a swell of water, Aza was finally able to take in a giant gasp of breath. Xira followed right after.

They laid there, focusing on breathing in and out while their cart jostled and took sharp turns. Their bodies rolled into each other from the force.

"Welcome back you two. You had a very eventful time in there." A familiar face popped into view, his locs dangling over Aza and Xira. Aza couldn't even smile at the quip, instead a sad grimace took its place. He maneuvered himself gracefully while the horse cart moved, and helped Xira and Aza sit upright, their breaths coming in smoother bursts.

Aza caught Anwin steering the horses, skillfully pulling them. They were in a quieter section of the city, but people still screamed and jumped out of the way of their cart. Aza hoped this would be enough.

The clouds broke overhead. Heavy rain obscured Aza's vision. It was both a blessing and a curse. They were shielded from others, but it also impeded Anwin's steering ability. Aza couldn't fathom how Anwin handled their cart. They tilted and swerved, but considering the obstacles in front of them, it was the best they could hope for.

The cart lurched to the side as one of the wheels caught a divot in the road. The horses did not falter as the cart tilted to the side. Aza and Xira smashed into the side of the cart, but Reed's footing wasn't secure. He tilted forward, losing his balance.

Aza summoned any remaining energy, darted forward, and yanked him by the arm. Aza braced her feet, loosened a curse, and heaved Reed back into the cart. He tumbled into the cart, his limbs askew. Reed scrambled to his hands and knees and shot Aza a quick glance. "Thanks," he breathed.

The cart was falling apart. The wheels were barely hanging on, their axles cracking from the slick mud and holes in the ground. It wasn't the sturdiest item to begin with and now with their constant battering, it was breaking.

"We need to move from here. It's falling apart," Xira shouted. She grabbed Reed and Aza. The cart shuddered violently below their feet. They struggled to move forward and reach Anwin.

Aza pushed her damp hair out of her eyes, barely able to discern what was around her. Anwin was glued to the front of the cart, her hands white knuckled on the horses' reins. Blood ran freely from her nose.

Xira leaned towards Anwin, "Now is the time, Anwin. Let go!" Xira reached for Anwin's hands and forced her hands to drop from the reins. Anwin's hand opened, the calloused skin marred with deep burns from the leather.

"This is the spot, right?" Xira twisted back to receive confirmation from Reed. He nodded his head and grabbed Aza. They both scrambled to their feet, the cart twisting and bucking underneath their feet.

"We need to jump," Reed shouted over the increasingly heavy rain, the sound nearly drowning out his words.

Holding Reed's hand, they clambered to the edge of the cart. Aza sprang out of the careening cart and tumbled into the muddy path. Her body screamed in protest. She rolled forward, aiming to protect her head and neck. She vaguely heard and felt Reed's body plop next to her, but she had no time to think and look at anything else. They needed to escape here. She could not be caught in Astaroth's clutches. Not without her magic. She didn't look to see if Xira and Anwin were with them, but Reed dragged her forward. They were cornered. The looming stone walls of the city pinned them in place. Why did they jump out here? She risked a quick look over her shoulder. The horses and cart had disappeared in the chaos.

"Help me look!" Reed frantically called. He scanned the ground and wall, searching for something, but Aza was clueless to what held their escape.

"Look for what?"

He shot her a surprised look and answered, "A grate."

Aza now understood his frantic searching. The ground was covered with mud, obscuring any sort of path on the ground. And they had little time before the guards knew where they had disappeared to. Hopefully they had followed the decoy of the horses and cart.

They were losing precious time. They needed to get away. Her senses were dull. She could barely hear, barely see, but her persistence grew. She would not give up. Aza fell to her knees and scuttled on the ground, swishing her hand over the puddles of water and mud, trying to clear them, trying to feel for any sort of grate. She clasped metal. Her fingers barely fit through the tight inner working of metal.

"Reed! Here!" He joined her on his knees and they both cleared the area as best they could, revealing a small human-sized grate. They grasped the sides and heaved. It was heavy—so heavy and Aza was so tired. The fatigue was wearing down her body, her mind. Even being here in The Fortress, near the toxic presence of Astaroth weighed on her soul. It was all encompassing, and she had endured it the entire time. The subtle signs of infection gnawed at her, cloying and insidious, but ever-present. It had never left. She gritted her teeth and fought the urge to sleep, the urge to lie down here in this downpour and accept her fate. But she was never one to lie down in a challenge. The Nerians had not abandoned her. They had not lost their faith, their hope. They were here for her. Aza released a growl and shifted the grate with Reed, their combined strength enough to finally reveal an empty chasm below.

"You first, Aza."

Aza bit back her dissent. There wasn't time. Aza had no idea where Xira and Anwin were, but she braced herself and fell down the empty black hole.

She landed unceremoniously with a splash and fought the urge to throw up. Her feet and legs were coated in thick sludge, it swirled around her, and the smell assaulted her. She cursed herself for not thinking clearly. This was a sewer. Their only escape, the only non-guarded exit. Aza tried her best to not breath in through her nose and stepped forward to allow Reed space to fall. He followed behind her. Aza could barely make anything out among the darkness, but she thought she saw Xira try her best to lower Anwin down. Her body dropped and Reed clumsily caught her, before Anwin's body would be submerged in the nasty sewage water. Xira soon followed and the four of them stood amongst the darkness of the sewers, their breathing heavy. The sewers echoed with the crashing of rain outside.

"The grate—"Aza tried to say before a harsh clinking of the iron interrupted her sentence.

"Done," Xira replied. She sealed the gate using her manipulation of earth magic, the iron in the grate responding to her. "We need to keep moving."

They walked in silence. Aza's eyes adjusted to the darkness. Luckily, there was only one path, so Aza simply trudged ahead. Anwin was conscious, but she stumbled easily. Reed and Xira took turns to help support her. Aza wanted to ask what was wrong with her, but a past memory of Lorn surfaced. One of him reminding Aza of the burnout they faced. Her nose was bleeding. Her body was shutting down. She had used too much magic in such a small time. She was the one who slowed their fall. Anwin was the reason Xira and Aza survived. The strength of her wind magic slowed their descent, so they didn't end up as two corpses splattered on the ground.

Aza tried to organize her flurry of thoughts, while they trekked through the bleary and stench ridden sewer. The Nerians had captured her against her will in El'en. However, they fought against Eonas to keep her alive. They brought her to The Fortress to reveal the secrets hidden there. They did not have to go to such extents to demonstrate their trust. Nivet sacrificed his mortal's body for her. The Lord and Lady of Verta were not to be trusted. They were working with Astaroth. The corruption throughout the land was spreading. The Hinterlands was still out of control.

Aza stumbled on a loose, hidden stone and almost fell into the sewage before Reed grabbed her by the shirt and yanked her upright.

"Thank you," she whispered.

"I could say the same. You did not have to save me in the horse cart, but you did."

"Why?"

Aza couldn't see Reed's face in the dimness, but she felt him falter beside him.

"Why, what?" His voice was soft, inquisitive.

"Why all of this?" Aza stretched her hands out wide. "Why the destruction? Why does this matter? Why do I matter?" She dropped her hands and they clapped against her sides in defeat. She yearned for the creature comforts of the castle in El'en, the lush bed, and warm baths. It was quite the opposite here in the sewers, where her stomach threatened to empty itself at every step. But at El'en she was clueless, left in the dark, unaware of what was happening, of the pieces set in motion. Of who Cruvo truly was.

Reed let out a soft chuckle.

Exhausted, Aza grew defensive. "Why is my suffering funny?"

"I apologize, Aza. It isn't that. Your questions are valid. Your frustration is valid. We do not have all the answers either. We are all operating on whispers, rumors, and prophecies. Yes, we know more information than you, but we do not know it all."

Aza released a soft exhale.

"We do have more answers. Answers that we can provide when you are back in the safety of Neria. It is impenetrable and the secrets from long ago need to be revealed to you there. But please trust me. We wish there wasn't this suffering, that the corruption wasn't spreading, that we didn't have to steal you from under Cruvo, that we were all here together under completely different circumstances. I wish for all of this, Aza. We all do. But that is not our lot in life and protecting you is worth far more than anything else now. You are worth it. Not because of your power, your magic. Just you."

Aza mulled over his words. It was one of the first times, besides Lorn, that someone wanted her for just her. With these people, her power was a part of her, but she was more than that. Xira and Anwin's jagged footsteps sounded behind her. They didn't interject.

They walked through the thick sludge, the water level rising due to the intake of rain. She had to lift her arms above the water, the level had risen to her abdomen. By the time she felt like she was about to collapse, they spotted a small light gleaming through an iron grate. Their exit had finally arrived. Aza and Reed yanked on it, but it didn't budge, the metal welded together on the outside.

Reed reached his hand forward and ice hardened at each connection of metal. He yanked his hand back and the metal grate burst from its enclosure. Aza's stomach turned as she had to get on her hands and knees and crawl out of the hole. Questionable liquid rushed past her. She held her breath and climbed out. Reed followed and helped assist Anwin. Xira came out last. She had grown used to the dim, near sightless darkness they had walked in and the brightness of the night nearly seemed too much. The clouds parted and a full moon greeted them.

Aza took a deep breath, her smell only partly assaulted by the sewers. She turned to survey the rest of the group and imagined she looked just as terrible as them. Filth covered their bodies. Their clothes were plastered to them, and they smelled awful. But they were alive. They had escaped from The Fortress and Astaroth.

20

"I have debated whether it was prudent to send Lorn to Gara. His desire to track Aza could lead to success, however the two of them together would only prove disastrous."

Cruvo's private journal

Lady Rasmina's daughters unceremoniously dropped them off at the palace and departed with barely a word. Lorn's body ached from Lilit's strict training regimen. His body was bruised and stiff, but he couldn't retire to his room. He needed to research the manifestation of magic from the ore in the swordsmith's shop. It was a potential lead. Lilit shadowed Lorn and there was a stuttering of steps as he went to the west corridor leading to the library.

"Why are we heading to the library, when we could be resting away from *them*?" Lilit jerked her head toward the fading silhouettes of the sisters.

"I have a potential lead."

She gave a sigh and Lorn heard the clink of her metal armor stop.

"I can go alone to the library, if you are unwilling to go."

"No, I am your personal guard. But—" she ground her teeth together and continued,"I need to change first. This isn't exactly comfortable."

Lorn didn't know what to think. Even this slight admission from her was shocking. She never mentioned any form of weakness, including lack of comfort. He knew she felt things other than anger and disdain, but her emotions were carefully curated and held behind a stone veneer.

"Oh, of course." He glanced down at his own rigid attire and added, "I should change as well."

Lilit gave a slight nod in relief, and they trekked up the spiral staircase until they reached their floor.

Once finished, Lorn met Lilit outside her room, both taking a step back in surprise. They were matching in a comfortable pair of black pants and a loose white tunic. Lilit pursed her lips together, but Lorn let out a full laugh. It echoed down the hall. Lilit's usually grave expression faltered, and a slight redness crept up her neck.

"Fucking hunter," she muttered under her breath. "Let's go to the library." Without waiting to see if he would join, she tromped off.

That was the first time Lorn had laughed like that in a while. It felt good. It was satisfying to break down Lilit's hard exterior.

In the library Lorn found very few books mentioning mining in magical ore. There was nothing of consequence and Lorn scratched his head in frustration. The light magic in the library pulsed at the edge of his vision. He rubbed his eyes and the lights blurred. Lilit stifled a yawn and pushed the heavy tome away from her. "We need to call it."

Lorn heaved a sigh and agreed. They hadn't found anything. But there were many books in this library, and they only had a few hours to search. It could be found with more time. He couldn't give up.

Their chairs scraped against the wood floor, and they sluggishly joined one another back through the hallway to the main palace. They had stayed later than usual in the library and the palace was empty. Stray sounds echoed from corridors as they ascended the staircase.

Before entering his room, Lorn rested his head against the door. He was tired. Yet it was a different tired than when he encountered monsters. That was purely physical, but this was a mental strain from balancing and organizing information from Iyera and comparing it and compiling it with what he learned in Gara. On top of that mental strain, Lorn couldn't stop his other thoughts from piling on top—his worry over Aza, his frustration at working with Lilit, and the vile vitriol spewed from Lady Rasmina and her court. It all converged, and his brain felt like it would deflate from the pressure.

His black eye was tender against the door, and he hissed out a breath. Not to mention the wounds he suffered from Lilit's sparring. He needed a break. Not yet, not until he could help Aza, rescue her from her captors, and understand how magic was being manipulated.

He couldn't stay in this empty hallway any longer. He craved a warm bath and a dreamless sleep. His bedroom was dark, with only a small magic light illuminating the far end of the room. The torches were out, which wasn't unusual, and he walked over to light them. He pulled a long wooden stick and lit the end with his magic. Fire burst from the tip, and he used his makeshift match to light the torches. He methodically moved to each one. His eyes caught on the dancing flames. It helped soothe his tangled mind. Lorn loosened a breath and placed the rest of the burnt stick into one of the torches.

His neck prickled in awareness. Lorn wasn't alone. He wasn't foolish enough to walk within the palace of Gara without weapons. He discreetly palmed a dagger strapped to his thigh. Whoever it was could have attacked when he entered.

Lorn relaxed his body feigning nonchalance. He pulled his shoulders away from his ears and kept his arm loose and flexible, easily able to throw the dagger if necessary. The air around him seemed to ripple. Lorn pivoted and wielded the dagger in front of him, slashing upward. A hand resisted him and pushed his dagger away. Lorn faltered and stopped his attack. He couldn't believe who was here.

She pushed him against the wall, her forearm braced against his throat and her other arm preventing his dagger from coming down.

"Lorn stop!" she breathed.

He traced the familiar curly hair, pulled back and plaited tightly against her head. He followed the tight black tunic and pants, everything screaming discreet and stealth.

"Why are you here, Pearl?" Lorn choked out. Her pressure wasn't threatening, more of a light weight to hold him in place, like he was a skittish animal, and she didn't want to frighten him away. It wasn't meant to injure.

"I will loosen my hold, if you promise to hear me out."

Lorn nodded and Pearl backed away. She smoothed her hand down her clothes and took a quick breath. Lorn's hand fell limply by his side with the dagger.

"I am being watched. This was one of my only chances to talk to you without anyone overhearing." Pearl shuffled her weight back and forth, looked at the bed and the chairs before deciding to stay where she was. "You need to leave Gara."

"Why?"

She sucked in a breath. "I cannot answer that, but you need to trust me."

Lorn was tired and didn't want to deal with more secrets, treachery, and conspiracies, he wanted a warm bath.

"I cannot leave."

It was Pearl's turn to ask. "Why?"

Lorn weighed telling her the truth. According to Cruvo, few people knew of Aza's disappearance, but he assumed most people suspected. While it wasn't common knowledge, anyone with a shred of intelligence would be able to piece together her disappearance and the increased deployment of Iyera's troops. Would spilling this one secret put her in danger? Put him in danger? Pearl was being stubborn and wasn't revealing what she knew. He would do the same.

"I can't say."

Pearl gave an exasperated sigh and started to pace. "Stop being so stubborn!"

"Me being stubborn? You just attacked me in my own room and told me to leave Gara with no other reason besides trusting you. You, who I have only met a handful of times."

"Lower your voice!" Pearl hissed.

Lorn hadn't realized he was getting louder. The whole situation was absurd. Her young age was showing. Lorn felt ancient in comparison even though she was roughly ten years his junior.

She firmed her stance, and Lorn saw a hint of boldness and determination. "You and Lilit are not safe in Gara. You need to return."

"You have not given me a valid reason to trust you, so I'm sorry if you don't like my answer but I don't just pack up and leave when strangers tell me I should. I have my own reasons for being here and if you haven't noticed I am always in danger. Whether I stay or go, it will not matter." Lorn walked over to his bed, discarded his dagger, and walked to the bathroom. He turned the tap on, and water poured into the giant tub. He found a bottle and opened the cork. A rush of earthy rosemary spiraled out and he dumped the contents into the warm water. The scent grounded him.

"What are you doing?"

"What does it look like? I have had a long day. I need a bath." Lorn gestured to his clothing and bruises. "It helps" He returned to his bedroom with Pearl on his heels. "Are there any more parting words and ill omens you wish to tell me?" Lorn regretted his hash words and dismissive behavior, but he was tired and losing his patience.

Pearl worried her lip for a moment before saying, "My mother is..."

"A joy," he finished.

"Unhinged."

His eyes widened at the admission. Lady Rasmina's own daughter claimed she was reckless. He pushed aside the tiredness and fatigue and gave Pearl his full attention.

"Explain."

"I do not have time. I was only able to sneak out for a short time without being watched. In three days' time, you will suggest a hike out to the Crossroads and I will guide you. It must look like your idea."

Lorn slowly nodded.

Pearl let out a relieved breath and backtracked to the door. "Thank you. I promise to tell you more next time." She fumbled with the handle.

"Pearl—" Lorn said.

She paused and waited for him to continue.

"Next time, no more surprises in my room."

He saw a flash of her white smile in the shadows as the door softly nickcd closed.

Lorn locked the door, shucked off his clothes, and submerged himself in the warm bliss of his bath. His mind was already in tangles, and he tried not to think too much about why Pearl would warn him against her own mother. He dunked himself underwater, letting his thoughts melt away, and the deep earthy grounding scent of rosemary replace his worries.

21

"I look at her and I wonder if she knows. At night I lie awake and try not to dwell on it."

Nivet's private journal.

Even though the group had escaped The Fortress, they were not completely safe. The sewers led them a fair distance from Rijal, but it was still close enough to be discovered. Despite the fear of capture, Aza was relieved. The thick clutches of Astaroth had been dulled by distance and Aza felt like she could finally breathe without the rot reaching out to consume her.

They were currently covered in a different sort of rancidity. The stench of the sewers stuck to them, their clothing reeked. The chill of the late autumn night did not help their predicament. They were going to get sick if they didn't find some form of shelter and wash the excrement from themselves. Reed and Anwin had the foresight to pack their supplies on the getaway cart. Reed shouldered the thick pack, which contained spare clothing, weapons, and meager amounts of food.

Luckily, Reed, Aza and Xira bore few injuries, their scrapes minor compared to Anwin. She had used too much of her magic. The magic had leeched away her life force. She was shuffled between the three of them and they helped to support her as they searched for shelter and somewhere to wash off. Anwin was tall and broad and supporting her weight became a struggle. Aza couldn't comprehend how Xira did it. Xira was a full head shorter than her, but she did not complain. She merely gritted her teeth and helped take the weight of her fellow warrior, each step painful and slow.

They debated having Reed use his water magic to wash them off, but they didn't want to unnecessarily burden another person in the group. The meager amount of magic he could use wouldn't even be worth it. The strain from the past few days made him susceptible to burnout.

After a few hours of slow trekking, they finally made it to a tiny pond of water. The animals scurried in their presence, slinking out of bushes and scampering away from the imposing and smelly group. Aza reached her fingers in, testing the water. She drew back her hand; chills coated her entire body and her teeth started shaking, but it was better to be clean.

Anwin was carefully laid on the ground and Xira and Reed laid out each of their clothes. They took turns bathing in the frigid pond. They gave each other a small semblance of privacy, standing guard with their backs to the bather. Reed provided a crude bar of soap for them to use. Aza scrubbed and scrubbed to rid herself of the prevailing scent of the sewers and then took the bar of soap and viciously scrubbed her clothes. She thought about discarding them, but decided they needed every bit of supplies they could carry. She shouldn't turn her nose up at the clothes just because they were dragged through the same filth she was.

Aza yanked on dry clothes that were provided by Reed. She couldn't help her teeth from chattering from the water that dripped down her back and the coldness of the air that pierced her skin. Instead, her clothes stuck to her wet body, and she rubbed her hands up and down her arms in hope of warming herself up.

Anwin was last to bathe after Xira forced some food down her throat. Her movements, albeit slow, were gaining strength. They all needed to rest. Aza caught the harsh drags of tiredness in their faces. Their escapades had finally hit a breaking point. They needed to stop and find shelter. They needed warmth. Aza's teeth weren't the only ones chattering after her bath.

But a fire wouldn't be wise, not with them being hunted. They weren't far enough away from The Fortress and Aza didn't know what tricks Astaroth could use to capture them. What magic did she hold? To what ends would Astaroth go to capture her? Instead, Aza gritted her teeth and fought the chattering and shivering that wracked her body. If the Nerians fought it, she could too.

"Are we staying here?" Aza asked Xira.

Xira took a breath and scanned the horizon the dim moonlight providing limited vision. "No, I believe there is shelter nearby." Aza fought the defeated look that came to her face.

"It is not much farther," Xira added. "We do not have the energy to go any longer."

Aza gave a firm nod and retreated to help carry the supplies and Anwin. She was able to stand on her own and function, however she clearly needed to rest. Anwin's weight shifted to Aza. They took meager steps following Xira's path until they came upon a small cave.

Xira went in and explored checking for any errant animals that may have made a home inside. Giving them the all clear signal, they stumbled into the cave. Aza's skin felt icy, and she yearned for any sort of warmth. The cave wasn't deep, but it was enough for them to shuffle to the back and find some solace from the chilly night and the winds.

Protected by the cave walls and prying, they decided to take the risk and light a fire. Reed left to gather sticks and tinder to help sustain it throughout the night. Xira was the least fatigued and used whatever energy she had left to magic the fire. It was tiny, but they scooted close embracing the warmth. It was much needed.

Aza did not scoff at their minimal ability of magic. She did not complain. She sat between her companions listening to their steady breathing. They did not discuss what happened in The Fortress; there would be time during the rest of their journey to revisit the horrors Aza had seen, but for now they were only people in need of warmth and rest.

Xira leaned her back against the harsh edges of the cave and took the first watch. Aza laid down sandwiched in between Reed and Anwin, their body heat a welcome reprieve after such coldness throughout their journey. Before falling asleep, Aza cast one questionable look at Xira. She gave a faint nod in return, an encouragement for Aza to sleep. Who was she to fight the orders of her Captain? She obliged.

When Aza awoke in the morning, Xira had replaced Reed's position. Aza found herself marveling at her situation. Mere weeks ago, she could not have imagined herself snug in-between her captors, and only now did she realize she did not view them as such anymore.

Lilit's disapproving face flashed through her thoughts. Her sneering tone at how easily Aza trusted, how easily she could be manipulated. Her gray down-turned eyes turned into daggers, but Aza discovered she couldn't summon the energy to care. She felt comfortable and safe nestled between these people. There would be time enough to figure out who she was and what she believed. Aza did not want to spend additional time analyzing her allegiances. She could not forgive Lilit for letting her writhe on the floor pinned under Xira. She had left her, abandoned her, wished pain and cruelty on her. If she was ever to see Iyera's Captain of the Guard again, Aza wasn't sure how she would greet her. Would she greet Lilit with blood and ice, forged by the cold and battle-hardened Nerians who now shaped her? Aza shook her head and readjusted on the cave floor. Lilit did not deserve her thoughts. She needed to focus on what was coming next. Astaroth, Sarava and Ravinder would still be searching for them. They wouldn't let them escape without pursuit.

Aza slowly opened her eyes and was greeted with the smell of roasted meat. Someone had already gone hunting. It was a meager amount of food, a pitiful roasted squirrel, but it was better than the ache in her stomach. After everyone stirred and had eaten their portion, they discussed what to do next.

"Are we going to Neria?" Aza asked and moved herself into a cross-legged position.

Xira shot an assessing look at Reed and Anwin. Reed's thin frame seemed a little tighter, the hunger pains and the rough travel wore on his body. Then she shifted over to Anwin. The extreme magic use had drained her. She was able to move and was coherent, but the dark circles under her eyes indicated otherwise. They needed sanctuary. They needed rest. Xira's lips thinned. "No, we have one more stop." She looked at Reed and Anwin waiting for confirmation. They each nodded in return, their postures straightened, confident.

"Where to?" Aza was curious what more they could uncover. What more did they need to show her? The news of Astaroth was already overwhelming.

"To Kreeha." Xira rose to her feet and dusted her pants off.

~

***

After their night of recovery in the cave, they left and skirted through copses of trees, and fields of wheat. They moved slowly, painfully aware of any onlookers, or anyone suspicious. They avoided the main roads, sticking to the small rabbit trails and less populated areas. Out of precaution they did not enter any towns or cities. Lord Ravinder, Lady Sarava, and Astaroth were looking for them; they would stop at nothing to find them.

Xira, Anwin, or Reed would scout ahead and find troops of soldiers, bearing the Vertan crest patrolling the roads. In the towns they passed posters with loose descriptions of their persons were hung up. None of them mentioned Aza's likeness, only of the Nerians that traveled with her.

Xira explained how Astaroth would be hesitant to give any information to her whereabouts, which would alert Cruvo to her presence. If he found out where she was, he would send a battalion of his guards to combat Astaroths'.

Xira smiled grimly. "It isn't ideal, but better for our likeness to be posted than yours. We need to keep you a secret for as long as possible. We still have more to do."

Aza's stomach had fluttered at the casual mention of Cruvo, but she pushed it aside. She still had not determined how she felt in regard to him. Their distance had given her clarity and she wanted to retain that fortitude.

The group made slow progress. They traveled on foot, through thick tangles of bushes and densely wooded areas. The Nerians hunted the local area for any game, and they feasted on that throughout the night. Reed's rations were running low, and they only utilized them during the day. Luckily they stayed near small streams and their waterskins never grew empty.

Aza's body became leaner and stronger from the grueling pace. She no longer reached for her magic, instead content to rely on her strength. She welcomed the soreness every night. Xira did not relent on her training. After countless hours scrambling through dense bracken, Xira still forced Aza to train each night. Although she grumbled under her breath, Aza was grateful the skilled Captain wished to train her. They sparred ruthlessly and just like on the ship, she did not hold back. Aza often went to bed accompanied with a bloody nose, a split lip, or some rough bruising, the skin purpling. It was a blessing they did not travel through towns. Her ragged and beaten appearance would raise questions.

After each sparring, Anwin would tend to her without magic, instead utilizing herbs and plants scavenged from the area, basic bandages, and cleaning the wounds with warm water. And Aza grew accustomed to the ache of her body, to the pain that radiated with each step, the tenderness of her face. As the trip wore on, her mistakes lessened along with her injuries. She remembered each misstep, each slip of her foot, each flare of her anger and she tempered it, honed it into something useful.

There was no mastering Xira—she was a skilled Nerian warrior, probably their best, but there were days when Aza landed hits or took her by surprise and those moments Aza treasured. She was getting better. Brick by brick Lorn had laid the foundation of her skill and Xira mortared it together with precision and care. There were nights when Xira handed off the sparring to Anwin or Reed, and she learned to readjust her fighting style. They each had their own strengths. Anwin was equal to Aza's size and reach with a sword, while Reed had an uncanny agility. But each night Aza went to sleep, nestled between her Nerian captors and a faint hum of contentment sang throughout her body. A familiarity, a clicking of pieces seemed to align at these moments. When they slept underneath the night sky, Aza would search the stars above, scanning for something—an echoing wave back and for the briefest of moments she felt it.

The group skirted from Verta into Kreeha without any fanfare. A guard garrison was stationed miles away from where they crossed. Aza breathed an unencumbered breath, her spirit no longer plagued by Astaroth. She smiled to herself and kept walking. Astaroth's clutches were only limited to Verta.

The dense farmlands and woods lessened as the climate and landscape shifted into something else entirely. The ground became looser underfoot as they traveled through piles of sand. The sun scorched during the day and the group shielded their skin from the harsh rays. But as night descended, a pervasive cold swept through, wracking Aza's body with chills. The extreme temperatures caused Aza to be irritable during the day, her eyes growing fuzzy from the brightness cast off the sand. Her tongue grew thick in her mouth; the need for water was too much. They had decided as a group to conserve it. The rivers and streams they had grown accustomed to had diverted south instead of traveling west with them.

Aza's body ached as she collapsed to the ground for the night. With limited cover in the sand dunes of Kreeha, they didn't dare light a fire. Aza yanked the edges of her cloak closer, thankful for the hood blocking any piercing winds from the backside of her neck. She huddled in between Reed and Anwin grateful for their body heat. There were no more reservations between them. They had struggled together, survived together. Each day as they trudged alongside her, she noticed her bitterness had been siphoned out of her.

Their companionship was a medicine that was being dispensed daily. She had no room for anger anymore. They were trying to make amends and it was clear by their actions, they meant it. She couldn't sense any deceit, but she tried not to play the naive girl again, thinking back to that fatal night where she blindly followed Anwin down an empty hallway. They were proving themselves every day. They did not allow Aza to be captured by Astaroth or by Eonas.

She shuddered. If she had been captured by Astaroth without her magic, she could not imagine the consequences, or what excruciating torture she would have undergone. They had made it out. They were beyond the Vertan borders. They were beyond the grips of Astaroth—for now.

Still wary of any guards on patrol, they set a guard at night. Xira stood hovering over them as Aza squeezed in between Anwin and Reed. They always gave her the middle position, the warmest one. The Nerians did not seem as affected by the cold weather. They did not shake or stir or shiver. They merely endured like the mountains under a storm, solid and unyielding. She wondered if they experienced the same exhaustion she did. If they did, they barely showed it. Their faces betrayed little of the difficult journey they had faced so far.

Without any prompting Xira spoke, "Our next stop is outside the capital of Kreeha, Cyran."

Aza remained silent. It was rare that the Nerians offered any information willingly. They had yet to share where they were going in Kreeha.

"We will be entering the Hall of Prophecies."

Aza's lips pushed together in contemplation. She hoped this

wouldn't be as traumatizing as The Fortress.

Xira did not divulge further, but Aza pressed.

"What is the Hall of Prophecies?" Aza braced herself for Xira's mocking answer. The name was clear enough, but Aza needed more.

Instead of a biting remark, Xira furrowed her brows and took a deep sigh. "The Hall of Prophecies is a place of record keeping. Prophets are extremely rare and treasured. They are kept in extreme isolation and trained to interpret their vague dreams and riddles. They try to put them down on paper for the rest of us to decipher. Many dismiss the prophecies. They are confusing and vague. Oftentimes people have resorted to madness assuming one thing, when the prophecy was referring to another. The Hall of Prophecies is not the resident of the prophets, but rather their records. All of their journals, scrolls, bits of information jotted down are duplicated and stored there."

Xira's eyes cut down to Aza and she swore she saw a brief flash of pity and sadness cross before it was wiped away. A drawing in the sand easily covered and obscured.

"But it is necessary. You need to see what is in there."

Aza shifted in between Reed and Anwin. "If you already know the prophecies in there, why not tell me it now without the additional risk?"

"We have never read the prophecies, but we know Nivet would have wanted you to see and discover them for yourself."

Aza hummed in curiosity, her head bobbing in thought. "How are we going to enter?"

"Reed will be the one to escort you."

Aza raised an eyebrow at him.

Reed answered her unasked question, "I am the only one who knows the language of the scribes."

This was only getting more interesting and the tiredness which forced Aza to collapse to the ground ebbed away. her insatiable curiosity taking over instead.

Before Aza could ask another question Xira silenced her. "No more questions for tonight. You need your sleep."

Aza let out an angry huff and Reed chuckled beside her. Anwin was already splayed beside her, listening. Aza and Reed joined her, their bodies collapsing, careful not to disrupt Anwin. The three of them stared up at the sky. The moon was nowhere to be seen, but the stars glistened even brighter in its absence.

~

Aza closed her eyes. Her body stirred, tingled. It felt familiar, like a welcoming. Before her were welcoming shadows. They flitted around her body and raced ahead. She followed the darkened trail. It felt like joy. It felt like happiness. It was an awakening. She couldn't resist. The shadows playfully zigged and zagged and darted to the right. She giggled like a child and tried to catch it.

The darkness led her around like a maze. It twisted and turned around corners, disappearing from view before coming back to her. Instead of being frustrated, she felt elation, a wistfulness she had not been exposed to in a month. She was buoyant. Her footsteps weightless. Where they met the ground, it rippled, like water slightly disrupted by the fall of leaves upon its surface. She laughed and sprinted after the playful shadows like it was a puppy. It was a game and it brought back the sweet memory of her and Lorn racing through the Hinterlands to reach salvation.

Although she raced after the darkness with what felt like hours, she didn't tire. She reached it, could feel it. The shadows twisted away until finally, it was cornered.

Aza paused and stilled her steps. The darkness hovered, waiting for her—with sure steps Aza moved forward, her arms outstretched. The darkness welcomed her and surged forward. It became a part of Aza and she glowed, every part of her on fire—not one of burning, but one of power. Aza's body was alive for the first time in months. She grinned.

Aza woke to hushed arguments and fierce whispers.

"We need to cover her. She is a beacon."

"How do you propose that?"

"Let's wake her up. She will be able to stop it if she is awake."

"Fuck, this isn't good."

Aza barely heard her name being repeated. It was like she was underwater, and they were trying to speak with her. She couldn't understand what their problem was or their concern. Why are they so angry and serious all the time?

Determined to help, Aza struggled to open her eyes. Her eyelids were heavy, and she convinced herself she just needed to sleep more, but those Nerians wouldn't let her, burrowing into her head, repeating her name. They were so frustrating.

She could try again. For them. Like the lifting of a heavy boulder, she pried her eyes opened. Reed and Anwin weren't next to her, she realized with disappointment. Where were they? She could barely see. A harsh glow obscured the darkness, creating shadows and spots in her vision. Xira wasn't nearby either. Where were they?

Her hearing barreled back to her, and she heard their shouts and relieved sighs as Aza sat upright.

"Aza!"

She covered her ears. Why were they shouting? Why was it so bright? It hurt. Everything hurt. Her senses were heightened. She could feel, hear, see, touch—it was too much. It overwhelmed her and the light flared brighter.

"Stop shouting!" Aza screamed back. She was being assaulted by her senses and couldn't understand what was happening, only that she was being overwhelmed.

A softer voice whispered on her right, "Aza." It was Anwin. Aza knew her, remembered her, but Aza couldn't look. She screwed her eyes tight, trying to block out everything. She wanted to return to her dreamstate and follow that comforting darkness.

"Aza, can you please stop?" Anwin asked. Aza didn't like her tone, like she was talking to a skittish horse.

The light flared brighter, and Aza saw the veins behind her closed eyes, the delicate skin sheer and thin before such a brilliant light. "Don't talk to me like that."

"Like what?"

"Like I am something to be feared." Aza heard shuffling in the sand —they were in the sand dunes she reminded herself. Aza tried to rationalize her surroundings.

"We do not fear you, Aza," Reed's steady voice reassured her. "But we do not understand what is happening to you. You need to stop."

Stop. Stop what?

"No, you are the ones who need to stop!"

"The light, the fire is coming from you. *We* cannot come near you for fear of being burned."

Aza didn't understand, she couldn't conjure fire, not anymore. She didn't have her magic. How could she?

"Aza control yourself. If you do not, Astaroth's spies will find us and we will be returned to her. You are in control. Wield it," Xira commanded.

Xira's order was what Aza needed. She found the uncontrollable well of her magic within her and tempered it. She could see it, use it again. The magic seemed to sense its withdrawal, of it being put to heel and it resisted. She couldn't help but smile.

She missed it and the magic missed her. They would not be parted. It was a retaliation to having herself be numbed and dosed, lacking a fundamental part of herself. Like a soft pat of a hand, she reassured the magic that it would never leave her again. It calmed under her reassuring touch and quieted itself. Like reaching for a phantom limb Aza pushed the fire down quelling it. The light faded slowly until Aza was able to open her eyes. She was greeted by relieved faces before she collapsed to the ground.

22

"There is still no news of Aza. I have heard whispers of her whereabouts escaping the Verta palace. Why were they there? I dwell on the possibilities but come up empty-handed."

Cruvo's private journal

Lorn chose not to disclose the new information to Lilit. Pearl's paranoia was evident. He needed to be careful of what he discussed and who could overhear.

As he returned from sparring with Lilit, he came upon Maline and Flint. This would be a perfect opportunity to inquire about the Crossroads. Lorn stopped them and mentioned his curiosity about visiting the Crossroads. He focused on expressing his interest in returning to nature and being stifled indoors all the time, so they would not grow suspicious.

Maline ran an appraising eye over him, crossed her arms, and looked to Flint. "We are spread thin, Ambassador. Unfortunately, we have no one to spare to escort you to the Crossroads. You need an experienced navigator amongst the rain, slick boulders, and woods. One could get easily lost."

Lorn had expected resistance. He feigned disappointment and let them walk away. He couldn't appear too eager, or it would look planned. With Maline and Flint's back to him and their footsteps receding, he exclaimed. "Wait, what about one of the sisters? I would gladly take one of them to escort me."

Maline and Flint shared a dubious look and Lorn cursed himself.

The charm was excessive. 'Gladly' wasn't a word one would use when referring to Lady Rasmina's daughters. "I have read about the Crossroads and heard about it when I visited Lighthold Proper. Such a marvel. I need to look upon it myself."

Maline ran a hand through her short-cropped hair. "It is an idea Lorn, but Ruby and Sapphire are not one to make that journey." They turned to leave.

"What about Pearl?" Lorn tried not to squirm from the silence. Lilit lingered behind him in the hall, and he could feel her eyes studying his back, trying to solve the puzzle that was unfolding before her.

Flint nodded slowly. "Yes, she is capable of leading you there. She is very busy too. I believe she can escort you two days from now."

Lorn let out a rare smile. "Thank you both. I appreciate the effort."

Maline and Flint stared at Lorn, but he would not crack. He could play this game. With a slight bow of his head, he turned on his heels. "Lorn, do be careful with Lady Rasmina's daughter. If something happened to her..." Maline trailed off. Lorn looked back at her. "Well let's just say nothing had better happen to her."

Lorn gave a firm nod and retreated to Lilit, his heart pounding. The look in Maline's eyes was unwavering. Ambassador or not, if something happened to Pearl, Lorn believed he would be executed.

Lilit had enough sense to wait to accost him until after they returned to his room. Lorn gestured for her to join him and placed a finger to his mouth. She pursed her lips and he saw the slight twinge of her fingers. He ushered Lilit to the bathroom and turned on the water to the bath to drown out any sound of their conversation. Lilit stood with an arched brow, casually assessing him, her gray eyes flicking back and forth patiently waiting for him to explain.

"That should be good."

"Do I even want to know what this is about?"

Lorn dove into the story of how Pearl had hidden in his room and explained their need to leave. Lilit remained calm, her expression bored.

"So, the Crossroads is where Pearl can talk to you safely without fear of being overheard or spied on." Lilit walked to the corner of the room, spun a chair around, sat on it backwards, and leaned against the frame. "Have the two of you ever thought that you could still be followed? They know where you are going. They know it will be the three of us, private, alone. Why go through all of this effort?"

Lorn shrugged his shoulders. "Yes, I considered that. But she was adamant, and something is going on and I want answers."

Lilit shook her head and scoffed. He heard the faint whispering under her breath, "Fucking the same."

Lorn bristled at the tone. "Care to share your thoughts?"

"Have you ever thought to consider that this is a trap, that they want you isolated and far away from Lighthold?"

"Yes, I have. But there is always a threat of danger. I don't trust Pearl, but she is not the same as her sisters or mother."

"Oh, come on!" Lilit pulled her dagger out of her sheath and began playing with it. "Just because she isn't as outwardly vicious, does not mean she is innocent. It's called pretending. Just because a cat purrs doesn't mean it's kind. She can still pull out her claws and scratch you."

"You were not there!" Lorn would not be made the fool. He understood the very best and very worst of human nature.

"Just because she bats her eyelashes and asks you to leave does not make her trustworthy."

"I didn't say she was." Lorn huffed a breath and turned off the water. He braced his hands on the edge of the bathtub and took a breath. He didn't understand how Lilit could rile him so. "You don't have to go with me or even agree with me. But for right now I want to see what information she has. I'm going."

Lorn heard the scraping of a chair and the soft tap of her boots on the floor. "You are wrong. I have been tasked to be your personal guard. I will go with you."

Lorn didn't turn to look at her. He didn't need her approval. As she was leaving he heard the faint mutter under her breath, "Just the same."

He didn't understand what or who she was referencing and ignored her. She was bitter being here and wanted to leave, just like him. She didn't have to agree with what he did. Cruvo sent him here to make decisions, to uncover what was going on. Lilit was only here for her strength, right?

~

* * *

Lorn woke early and put on his hunting outfit. His leather boots were worn and snug as they slipped on. He equipped himself fully with sword and daggers and he even took his hunting bow. He didn't know what to expect and after Maline's and Flint's hesitation, but it only solidified the fact that he should be armed. Lilit met him in the hall in similar attire, her fury from their prior conversation carefully contained and locked away beneath her cool expression. He could see it in the slight tick of her eyebrow, and the firm set of her shoulders.

Pearl waited for them at the base of the palace with a pack slung on her shoulders and an additional one for each of them. "You will need this." She opened each pack and handed them a cloak. Each was beautifully crafted and tailored to fit them. He furrowed his brows and rubbed the material between his fingers.

"It's water resistant. Necessary if you are going to be traversing all over Gara." She pulled out her own and draped it over her shoulders, pulling the hood up to obscure her face. "It will take us a full day to get there and back. Let's go."

Lighthold was always cloaked in darkness; the dense trees and the thick rainclouds blocked most of the light. Only the faint glow of the streetlights greeted them. It was early morning and the streets were empty with no stirrings or movement.

At the border of Lighthold, Pearl gave a nod to each of the guards who let them pass. Lorn spotted the guards' fondness for Pearl. The people liked and cared for her. He doubted the same could be said for Ruby and Sapphire.

The cloaks were a genius idea. He wished he had this when going through the Silent Stretch. It would have saved him from constant chills and changing of his clothes to retain some semblance of dryness.

While the rain provided the scenery with vibrant greens and browns, he didn't understand how the residents withstood the oppressive darkness. He craved the warmth on his skin, and Vertan soil underneath his fingers. While his homeland of Verta was not the same climate as Kreeha, where the sun never ceases to shine, it gave him what he desired—the consistency of change. There was a comfort with the knowledge the seasons would change, the brutal winters and the sun scorching summers. He imagined the warmth on his skin, bronzing the golden hue.

He slipped on a boulder as he followed Pearl on the trail. He caught himself and Lilit huffed a breath behind him. "Keep your wits, hunter" she scolded.

He didn't want to agree with her, but she was right. He couldn't risk getting distracted.

Pearl navigated the forest with an expert grace. She kept her footing and waltzed through the trails, muddy and obscured. They gained elevation, climbing over boulders, and rocks. She found notches within the stones and climbed, her clothes hiding the muscle she possessed as she easily navigated the forest. Multiple times Lorn thought Pearl would trip over her cloak, but it remained disentangled as she climbed. She remained silent and Lorn didn't pry her with nosy questions, but they could fill the silence with other conversation.

"Why the Crossroads?"

Pearl glanced back her eyes focused and determined. It seemed like she had forgotten they were following her. "What?"

"Why the Crossroads? Why there?"

She paused and grabbed a water skin from her pack. It was time for a break. She chewed on some dried fruit and considered his question. Lorn leaned against the trunk of a tree and took a bite of jerky.

"Do you know the geography of Gara?"

Lorn shook his head. Images from maps in Iyera flashed through his mind. He never paid much attention to Gara, understanding it was perpetually rainy, forested, and had mines rich in ore.

She grabbed a broken twig from a nearby tree and traced it in the muddy path. "Lighthold is actually located in a valley. To the southeast where you came from is the Silent Stretch and small foothills. To the northeast and northwest, we are surrounded by two mountains. Carved down each mountain is a river. They are fierce things we don't bother to cross— too wild, too strong. With our constant rain, the rivers never run dry and only grow stronger, more chaotic in the fall and winter." She drew a pointed tip for each mountain and pointed the stick at the left side. "Our legends reference these mountains as the Twins, separated and longing to be reunited. The only way they can connect is through their rivers." Pearl delicately traced a river down the left mountain and one down the right until they converged in the middle forming an x. "Just like the Twins rage to be reunited, so do their rivers. They cut through rock and stone, breaking down everything in their paths to be united until they are for a brief moment." She circled the x and looked up to Lorn, locking eyes with him.

"The Crossroads," he answered.

"Exactly. Only in that moment do the rivers connect, then run parallel to each other until they run out to sea." Her stick made two meager lines and pulled north into the ocean "The ocean is no reprieve its seas just as destructive and wanting as the twins, but at least they are together."

Lilit had held her tongue throughout the journey, but Lorn tensed as he heard her familiar scoff. "A touching story, but it doesn't explain why we are headed there."

Pearl's eyes flashed to Lilit sizing her up, before answering, "It is a tough journey. Secluded." She shrugged and put her pack back on. "It is a beauty few outside of Gara have seen. Why not show you something like that? You have chosen to stay in Lighthold. You might as well see something beautiful before your deaths." Pearl marched up the path.

Lorn fought the self-satisfying smirk he wanted to direct at Lilit. While Pearl was younger than he, he had to give her recognition for holding her own against Lilit.

At midday, they stopped for a quick lunch before continuing.

"We should be there within the hour," Pearl informed them.

Lorn was relieved. He was growing tired, wishing he insisted that he and Lilit had suspended a day of sparring. But the day before, they had practiced. His ribs still smarted at the hard hit she had dealt. Her speed and strength magic was amazing and she never held back.

They came upon an incline of wet stones that vaguely resembled a staircase. They climbed. His fingers ached and his body protested, but he pushed on using his legs to lift his tired body over the edge. Pearl spryly climbed up over the top and reached a hand out to Lorn. He gratefully took it and found his footing. Pearl offered her hand to Lilit, but she declined it pulling herself over the edge instead. Lorn caught his breath and put his hands on his knees before realizing what was before him.

They were on a massive stone platform that jutted out. The roaring of water filled his ears as the giant rivers hit and converged, sending out sprays of water on the lip of the rock. Lorn prided himself on the beauty he had experienced in life, the beautiful sunsets after a thunderstorm, the sky awash in vicious swirls of red, orange, blues and purples, Aza's appearance from the Well, the stillness of the Wyra ocean after he would awake in Iyera, the beauty of his wife on their wedding night. All of those memories and images were beautiful and treasured, but nothing could have prepared him for the pure chaotic nature of the Crossroads. It was violent, destructive, beautiful.

"Pearl, thank you for bringing us here."

A radiant smile crested her face. Pearl was right. This was private. If anyone wanted to eavesdrop they wouldn't be able to due to the roaring river and they would have no ability to be near them. The only path up to the Crossroads was the cliff they had just scaled. If anyone followed they would only be able to gather the three of them meeting but would be unable to discern any specifics from the conversation.

For once the rain had stopped. Pearl grabbed a cloth from her bag and laid it down, gesturing for Lorn and Lilit to join. She sat cross-legged and rifled through her bag, picked out an apple and a paring knife, her movements sharp and precise. She methodically cut pieces off.

Lorn rested back onto his hands and tilted his head back up to the sky. Lilit remained standing, pacing back and forth, always guarding. "Come and rest, Lilit."

She ignored his offering and remained pacing like a caged animal, on alert. They didn't have much time and needed to begin the conversation. "Why do we need to leave, Pearl?"

"My mother and her advisors are planning something. Something that will change the whole of Ithilia."

"Like what? The Hinterlands is already changing; there is something else happening that I'm not sure how to explain. What more could change?"

Pearl's eyes widened and she worried her lip. "I wasn't aware of all that. This is something else."

Lorn didn't know if he could handle another revelation.

"Or maybe it's all connected," Lilit interjected.

Lorn raised an eyebrow at her. She didn't acknowledge Lorn, merely resumed her pacing.

Pearl chewed on a piece of apple and swallowed before saying, "How was your reception upon entering Gara?"

Lorn considered her question. "The people were—cold, unwelcoming. But to be fair we are strangers."

Pearl brushed a curl behind her ear and sucked in a breath. "People are being taken and forced to work in the mines." She mentioned it in one full breath. "They are being driven deep underground with little food, little water, and no word to their families. Any dissension is immediately crushed. The people in Lighthold Proper either know or suspect, but they do nothing against it. Otherwise, their families and friends will be taken next."

Lorn couldn't process what he heard. Families, people, being taken and forced to work. Why? The prosperity of the Well fueled their land, there was no need to cause people to work like animals. They would be provided for. Lorn caught a stillness out of the corner of his eye. Lilit froze at the edge of the blanket. She leaned down until she was eye to eye with Pearl. "You will tell me what you know," she demanded.

~

Lilit abandoned her guard duty and sat, forcing Pearl to repeat herself. Pearl took her orders with grace, repeating herself and going over every detail she deemed important. Besides what Pearl already explained, her knowledge was minimal. Much of what she provided was speculation.

Lilit grilled her with questions. "Why are they being taken to the mountains? What is so important there? What does your mother want?"

Pearl's answer was the same, a repeated chorus of "I don't know." With each unanswered question, Lilit's frustration grew. Eventually, she reached a boiling point and stood up from her cross-legged position and paced to the end of the rock, looking out on the Crossroads below.

"What was the point of this hike? What was the point of coming out here if you don't know anything?" she shouted. Lilit retraced her steps back to Pearl and pointed a finger in her face. "We are not going anywhere. We need to figure out what your mother is up to." A rare look of panic crossed Lilit's face.

Pearl gracefully untwined her legs and brushed her pants with measured movements. "I did not say I had all the answers. I merely wanted you to be aware of the undercurrents in Gara. I am trying, Lilit of Iyera. Are you able to say the same?" Pearl seemed older, as she sized up her opponent with an arched eyebrow. Her fortitude was inspiring and Lorn had a glimpse of someone who was beyond her years, who was truly trying to make an effort and change the sickening things happening in Gara. "We do not have forever. We need to leave. Is there anything else you want to ask me?"

Lilit was seething, her careful, controlled mask slipping.

Lorn got to his feet and joined the two of them. "I never figured you for such a humanitarian, Lilit. We need to save them. We will figure something out." Lorn looked to Pearl for reassurance. She let out a breath and nodded.

Lilit shook her head and chuckled until she spilled out into full blown laughter. Lorn furrowed his brow. He had never heard her laugh before, not like this. She was losing it.

"Fucking hunter. You think I care about these people?" Lorn jolted back as if he had been slapped. "I don't care about saving these families. I care about what Lady Rasmina is doing in those mountains." He shook his head in disgust. He couldn't stand to look at her anymore. She didn't care about Lady Rasmina kidnapping people and forcing them to work deep underground with minimal food and water. There were people dying needlessly when the Well offered prosperity and she didn't even care? One look at Pearl's face confirmed the same thing. She was disgusted with Lilit.

"Maybe summon some energy to care. You are in charge of protecting me and I am not leaving. I'm staying and getting these people out of those mines!"

"We can leave, Lorn," Pearl murmured to him. He hastily grabbed his stuff and threw it on his shoulder. He cast one more look at the Crossroads, a stab of bitterness at how this beautiful scenery was tainted by Lilit's callous behavior. He crouched down and began to descend.

Lilit only shook her head and said, "Oh Lorn. If you only knew how little I cared, you would push me off this rock into those rivers below. You would wish for my death."

He didn't deign to respond, only climbed down the rock face, his skilled fingers gripping the ledges with an expert hand.

"And I welcome the day," she whispered like a prayer.

23

"We must introduce her to the information slowly. Too quickly could overwhelm her body and her mind."

Nivet's private journal.

Aza was being carried. Harsh light pulsed against her eyelids. She groaned and tried to move, but her body was weak and was being jolted with each dip and swell. She needed to open her eyes. She was being carried—dragged. Where was she?

Last she remembered, she had awoken from a wonderful dream and her magic was finally reunited with her. Tentatively she searched for the wisp of magic, bracing herself for failure. Instead of a restraint, her magic rose up in answer. Aza gasped. It was back. It was truly here with her.

Aza tried to focus on opening her eyes; she needed to see what was going on.

"Do not strain yourself, my Lady," Anwin whispered.

Aza struggled to form words, her throat dry and parched. As she attempted to open her eyes and speak, her movement was stopped and Anwin's voice was next to her.

"Here." A hand gripped her shoulders upright and a waterskin touched her mouth. Water was gently guided to her lips, and she gulped greedily. Although Anwin poured slowly, Aza didn't care about decorum; water dripped from the sides of face.

"Where are we?" Aza breathed. "Why can't I open my eyes?"

"We are still in Kreeha. We were unable to wake you after

your...episode."

Xira's voice cut in, "We need to keep moving."

Aza felt her body being moved and Anwin's soft footsteps beside her.

"Can you tell me what happened?" Aza tried to readjust, but her muscles protested, and she leaned back, flopping against whatever she was on.

"Aza try to remain still. We are taking shifts to carry you," Reed answered. She heard a brief huff of air before the movement resumed.

Aza ran her hands over whatever device she was held on. Cloth and wood. She was in some form of a stretcher being dragged across Kreeha. "Sorry, Reed, I didn't know."

He gave a grunt in acknowledgment.

"Xira can answer best. She saw most of what happened last night."

Xira's voice came from the opposite side of Anwin. She tried to picture them, Anwin flanking Aza's right with Reed in front, Xira on the left.

"You had settled down and slept for a few hours. Then, you started to glow. A soft light at first, like the glow of the sun as it rises over the mountains in Nerian."

Aza was impatient to know what happened next, but she appreciated Xira's storytelling, her voice and cadence beautiful, the pacing perfect.

"I rushed over to wake you. The light would be noticed by anyone in the area and we couldn't risk the exposure. I tried waking you, but you only mumbled back clearly lost in whatever was happening. I pulled Anwin and Reed back. Whatever was happening to you, we needed to let you experience it. I couldn't interrupt. Your light grew and grew. It was beautiful. We stood there gawking at the power of your magic, the raw beauty of it. It was blinding. I'm surprised no one came to investigate."

Aza gulped, a brief flash of guilt over their worry. While she was enjoying the dream, her companions were panicking over something terrible happening to her.

"Then, like the strike of a match, your light ignited, the heat scorching. We had to do something, had to stop it. We didn't know what was going on. We tried the only thing we could and shouted at you. We were screaming your name." Aza just noticed the hoarseness of their voices, as if they had scraped them raw from screaming. "We were only going to try a little bit longer and then we were going to try and rescue you. Have someone go into the fire—"

Aza couldn't imagine. They would have burned immediately, her magical fire not a mere blaze but an inferno, uncontrolled and volatile.

"But then you woke up."

"My magic returned," Aza croaked.

An uncomfortable silence descended while Aza was carried on the stretcher.

Aza couldn't bear to keep her eyes closed any longer. She strained and opened one, the sun unbearable and bright. The other eye followed. She moved her arm to shield herself from the brightness. Her head lolled over to look at Xira. "Thank you."

Xira stiffened. "For what?"

"For caring." Bright red, angry welts decorated Xira's fingers.

"You wouldn't be in this position if it weren't for us. This is our fault. There is nothing to thank us for."

Aza furrowed her brows.

"We were the ones who willingly dosed you and stifled your magic. This was your retribution."

Aza bit her lip. This was what she wanted, the righteous fury and anger that she had when their journey started. But now she searched herself and found it empty. Those same feelings were valid, but they had morphed into something else. She had come to understand her Nerian companions.

"No," Aza rasped. She stumbled over her words, the exhaustion and the revelation catching in her throat. "I do not blame you. Not anymore."

It was silent with only the shuffling of feet amongst the sands.

Aza collapsed back onto the stretcher, a grin breaking across her face. "But it's back. My magic." She fell asleep, comfortable, and reassured with the Nerians protecting her. Nothing could harm her—not anymore.

~

* * *

Aza woke with a shiver. Dusk was quickly turning into night. The sand dunes were scorching during the day and unbearably cold at night. It tricked her, the fluctuating temperatures. Aza craned her head back and saw that Anwin was carrying her now.

"We will stop here for the night."

They stayed within the shelter of a high sand dune, using the terrain as a natural blockade from unwanted eyes. The stretcher was lowered to the ground. Aza groaned and sat upright her body stiff and bruised. She tried to search herself in the dim light, looking for any marks that echoed the aches and pains. She couldn't see anything except that her body was tender.

"We didn't see any wounds on you." Anwin mentioned.

"Then why do I feel like I have been beaten up by Xira?" Aza groaned, stumbling to her feet. She sucked in a sharp breath at the pain. Another burst of pain flashed through her head and she struggled to remain standing. Reed was immediately next to her, ushering her arm over his shoulder. She didn't fight the assistance, instead leaning on him, and taking the help without complaint.

"Let me propose a theory. Your physical body is coming to terms with your magical spirit. Since we overdosed you and your magic was stifled for so long, it rebounded—almost in retaliation to what we had done to you. You were never meant to be severed from it. It is an essential part of you."

Anwin pulled Aza's bedroll out and laid it on the ground. Reed gently lowered her to the ground. Aza braced herself and winced from the pain, the invisible bruises peppered over her entire body.

"Then why did you do it?" Aza asked. There was no anger in her question. If she had asked that same question weeks ago, there would have been a rage behind it. But now she was only wanting to know their answer.

Xira scoffed, and answered, "You know why. We had to get you out of El'en."

Aza shook her head and immediately regretted it. She grew woozy, her vision blurring. "No, that's not what I meant," she muttered.

Aza bent her knees, planted her feet, and braced her head in her hands. Moving, talking, interacting, it was too much. But her tight-lipped companions were finally talking, and she didn't want to lose the moment. She needed to capitalize on it. "I know why you dosed me. Why did you insist on separating me from my magic? Every lesson, the fight with sea serpent, meeting Astaroth, you encouraged me to look at myself as separated from my magic—why? Why try to teach that to me again and again, if this is the repercussion?" Aza paused, her head swimming. Each word formed was a struggle, a dull pounding. Even though she was slipping in and out of consciousness all day, she still needed rest. But this conversation was important, and she didn't want to stop now. She couldn't.

Anwin sat cross-legged across from Aza. "Ah, yes that." There was a pause and a soft shuffling. "Aza, do you remember our conversation on the ship after you practiced with Xira?"

Aza couldn't bring her head up from her hands and merely grunted.

"You were so angry. Goddess, that fire in your eyes. If you were capable, you would have scorched the entire ship at that moment." Anwin chuckled. "You were bruised and bleeding. But in that moment when you were able to connect a hit on Xira, it was victorious."

Although Aza had her eyes closed, she could hear the smile in Anwin's voice and cracked her own smile into her hands.

Xira laughed somewhere to Aza's side. "That was a solid hit. I was very proud."

Aza's heart swelled at the praise, their compliments rare.

"It was an important lesson. Yes, your magic is apart of you, but it is not the *only* part of you. You are so much more if you only let yourself see it."

A sudden touch on Aza's knees had her start. She peeked her head up and only saw the pale, thin fingers placed reassuringly on her. "When I took care of your wounds, you could not fathom *not* using magic to heal and only using bandages and herbs." Anwin smiled at the memory. "We all love our magic, but it is not the only part of us. There is so much more, so much more we have to teach you."

"You are powerful without it. You are powerful with it. Either way you are an unstoppable force and we want you to recognize that, to remember that," Xira whispered, the soft tone so unlike her strong and intense personality.

Aza tried to lift her head up. Reed had joined Anwin on the ground.

Anwin's steadfast head was still on her knee like she was providing a buoy to Aza's weightless spirit—keeping her steady and grounded.

"We understand you do not have all of the pieces to understand the puzzle, but we have learned our history. Our true history," Reed emphasized. "Nivet was a vast source of knowledge and the Nerians teach their children the truth. While magic is beautiful and a gift, it can also be a curse. The gods and goddesses wielded it, killed masses, razed lands. They were merciless."

Aza struggled to keep her head up. She couldn't help but think of Cruvo. Was he like that? His original intentions were to remake the world. Her head pulsed, like it was rejecting her thoughts and she pushed them aside into a neat box for her to view and contemplate at another time.

Reed continued, "We respect our magic, but we also acknowledge the horrors it has done. You cannot have one without the other."

Aza didn't want to think about the unspeakable damage her magic could cause. She could easily imagine the power in one who didn't care about the lives of others, causing mass destruction. War easily overtaking the provinces, gods and goddesses using the MagicBlessed citizens like mere pawns.

Reed was respectful, giving her time to process the information. He was intuitive, understanding the struggles of what she was trying to process. "Because of our knowledge of the past, that is why we were able to dose your magic. The province of Neria is the only one who has cultivated, experimented, and properly discovered the correct formula to block magic."

Aza's voice cracked as she asked, "Why are you telling me this now?"

Xira stepped closer to Anwin and Reed within Aza's field of vision. "This whole thing is only for you to understand." Xira looked sharply away and turned back to Aza. "We were told to tread slowly by Nivet and give you information piecemeal." Xira hesitated, her weight shifting from one leg to the other. "If we do too much, it could damage you."

"Damage me?" Aza arched a brow at her. "Am I not damaged enough?"

Xira's lips pressed together in a thin line. "I can't speak more of it. I'm sorry. I know you want more, but I follow my orders from Nivet. Even this could be too much."

Aza straightened her legs. The sun had dipped below the horizon and clouds rushed in overhead. Aza shivered. It was exhausting going from one extreme to the other, the hot dry days to the chilly nights. "I guess I should thank you for telling me this much already."

She collapsed back to the ground and stared at the sky. She envisioned the past. The clouds painted a neutral background for the scenes to play out in her head. She pictured their uncontrollable magic —instead of something of beauty it was destructive, violent. Fires blazed through towns, people screamed in agony as water flooded them, earth crumbling under their feet, wind being whipped into tornadoes, tsunamis, earthquakes, infernos.

She sobbed, her body wracking with pain. How could something so precious and dear to her be so terrible? How did the gods and goddesses look at the MagicBlessed people and not care? One fell swoop with their hand and a whole city was demolished. Aza laid there, tears streaming down her face, picturing the devastation, the families running, the lives cut short. Her imagination unspooled and she couldn't rein it back in.

She saw Cruvo astride a giant deer, its antlers grand and piercing. He was regal as he blended in with both forest and deer, part nature and part other. A small homestead appeared in front of him, and he crumbled it. The earth gave way beneath, a giant chasm for the house to crash through. He did not falter and merely looked upon the destruction with an uncaring eye.

"No!" Aza shouted, her hand stretched towards the clouds. She forgot herself. She was here, in Kreeha traveling across the sand dunes. This wasn't real, her imagination had taken control, guilt over her magic, her warring emotions.

"My Lady!" Xira shouted.

Aza was on her side, shaking, convulsing. Something was deeply wrong. They had told her too much information and her brain was rejecting it. Nivet was right.

"Reed, help me," Xira commanded. "Anwin, you too."

Aza's teeth clacked together. She strained to keep her body still, but whatever was happening she couldn't control it.

"Aza, I need you to trust us. We are going to try and relax your muscles. This requires us to use our magic on you," Xira explained.

Aza couldn't respond, the shaking was too much. Like an overwhelming wave of water about to submerge her, she tried to relax and ride the wave, instead of bracing for impact.

She felt the beginnings of magic tentatively exploring her body, like the feel of soft fingertips checking where to begin first. A rush of warmth spread, the immersion of a hot bath soothing her muscles. It eased and flowed over her. They were trying to calm her body, relax it and from her episode.

The magic was not a rush, rather tiny slips, given out continuously like feeding bits of food to a starving person. They did it bit by bit in fear of her body rejecting it. The clench of her muscles lessened, the uncontrollable shaking was dulled to a small shiver. They kept flowing their magic into her, controlled and steady until Aza's body ceased its shaking. When she was finished, their magic retreated. Aza wanted to cry from the loss. As if reading her mind, Anwin kept her hand on Aza's back while Reed and Xira retreated setting up their bedroll on either side of Aza. Anwin repositioned herself and cradled Aza's head in her lap with her hand rubbing small circles along Aza's back.

It was a small gesture and provided Aza with a comfort she sorely needed. She didn't know if she had parents, if that was a thing tied to her existence, but the lulling pat on her back made Aza feel like a soothed child—her nightmare banished by a parent's security and warmth, by the strength of their actions and their words.

Aza was grateful they didn't ask her to explain. She didn't have the strength to put to words what had just happened. Instead, they provided her with their companionship, something Aza needed to weigh her down. Anwin eased any tension from her scalp, her fingers brushing through her hair.

Aza focused on the motion of her hand on her back. She rubbed in a small circular motion pausing for a moment at the top before continuing.

Anwin began humming and Aza released a heavy sigh, her eyelids heavy fluttered closed.

Aza didn't focus on the words and let Anwin's soothing voice wash over her. It wasn't the sweet, honeyed voice of a beautiful singer, but the rough and heartfelt voice of someone who had lived through death and life and brought that emotion into her singing. It was achingly beautiful, and Aza let herself fall into it.

There was nothing for her to be afraid of. She was safe here.

24

"As I look at Lorn, I am confronted with a mix of emotions. He has accomplished what I could never, by entering the Hinterlands, yet he should be easy prey. However, as I stare at him, my senses prickle in awareness as if I a missing a crucial piece of him. I do not know what it could be—he seems simple enough."

Cruvo's private journal

Lorn made a weak attempt to focus as they traveled back to Lighthold. The rain became a steady downpour. The water-resistant cloak helped, but it did not prevent all of the water from seeping in, nor make the path any clearer to navigate.

He followed Pearl's expert guidance. She was clearly skilled at this trail, born in Gara, the trails were in her blood. If she was blinded, he believed she would still be as graceful. Her boots deftly climbed over hidden rocks and snaking roots.

His vision blurred as the rain came down in earnest and he blew out an exhausted breath. He was unsure which was worse, the physicality of this trail, the new information Pearl had relayed, or Lilit's erratic behavior. He didn't know how to interpret any of it. Lilit always seemed collected, her emotions a vast pool swirling beneath the surface, but sometimes, Lorn could see the faint cracks. She was held together through sheer determination, and he didn't want to know what would happen when she finally broke.

Lorn's uneasy feeling since entering Gara had been proven correct through Pearl's unsettling revelation. Something insidious was happening. Lilit's prior warnings echoed through his head. This information could be false, and Pearl could be fooling them, sending them on errant quests to misdirect them. But Lorn pushed aside those doubts, recalling the small towns they passed on the way to Lighthold. The people were reserved, fearful of strangers, a silent anger brewing beneath.

They kept a rigorous pace, each of them with an unspoken agreement to return quickly. After a quick stop under a canopy of trees Pearl informed them they had roughly an hour left before reaching Lighthold.

They each mimicked the other, resting against the back of a tree, avoiding discussion. There was already too much said. Small talk wouldn't accomplish anything; the heavy rain drowned out any potential for conversation anyway. Lorn leaned away from the tree and stretched his arms into the air. It was growing dark, near dusk. They needed to hurry back. He did not want to be out in this wild forest any more than he needed to.

The hairs on the back of Lorn's neck stood up. He stiffened, reached for his sword, unsheathed it, and stared out into the darkness. He scanned and felt Lilit join beside him.

Pearl grabbed her own sword and warily wielded it, fruitlessly looking for what they were startled by. "What is it?" she asked.

Lorn gave a small shake of his head, his eyes straining to see anything within the darkness that yawned in front of him like the maw of a great beast. "Something watches us," he whispered in reply.

There were too many years of being hunted for him to ignore such a feeling. Although he had mixed feelings for Lilit, he felt validated that she didn't scoff at his instincts. Lilit positioned herself to protect his back.

He strained to see or hear what was there. But the rain drowned out his senses—the sound too loud, the forest too murky for him to make anything out. He knew something was there, biding its time, waiting for them. Waiting to strike.

Pearl screamed.

Lorn pivoted and saw her dodge something that leaped at her. She slashed her sword out wildly.

Lilit yanked Pearl behind her and brandished her sword at the beast.

The creature was hideous, diseased. It was in the shape of a mountain lion, its coat rotted and fangs dripping with a thick black pestilence. The creature hissed at Lilit and raised a giant paw in anger, batting at her, testing her boundaries. The deadly sharp claws were a dark green of decay..

This was the same beast that had attacked Lorn and Lilit in the Silent Stretch. This couldn't be a creature from the Hinterlands. While those beasts were things of darkness they were not like this. The Hinterlands' creatures were savage, brutal; this was different—their existence so raw and disgusting that Lorn had to hold back a retch at the sight of the grotesque mockery of nature this creature represented. The putrid smell rolled off it in waves. The pupils were fully dilated. The eyes were wholly black with no remnant of what the animal was before. He did not want those claws and the putrefaction anywhere near his companions.

The beast was dangerous, and he needed to act quickly. He looked to his sword and imagined it aflame in a piercing white light. Lorn focused on channeling his magic into the sword—a river flowing in, strengthening it, emboldening, imbuing. But there was nothing. The sword hung heavy in his grip, a mere weapon. It did not feel like before—there was no spark, no connection. Lorn cursed and changed tactics.

Light burst from his body. The creature swiveled its head to Lorn and leapt. He ignored his exhaustion, stepped sideways, and slashed upwards. A spray of sickly green and black blood coated his sword and the forest floor. Lilit surged forward and hacked at the creature. Her sword cleaved between the creature's shoulder blades. The beast swiped out with its infected claws and Lilit jumped backward, pulling her sword out from the creature.

"Don't let the claws touch you!" Lorn shouted. He moved in front of Pearl, shielding her with one hand held out. Lady Rasmina's daughter could not be harmed.

The creature let out a pitiful howl, and slunk forward, its weight drooping from side to side. The infected blood dripped onto the forest floor, noxious fumes spiraling from where it made contact. For a moment a sickening clarity appeared in the creature's eyes. It seemed like a regular mountain lion, the disease forgotten. It was a look of resignation, of an animal wanting to be put out of its misery.

Lilit faltered, then spun quicker than Lorn could catch. Her sword flew down in a swift arc and beheaded the creature. Its head and body collapsed in opposite directions. The permeating sickness in its body pulsed and oozed out of the creature like a festering wound. The thick black substance seeped onto the ground, pooling underneath the creature.

Lilit's chest fell in rapid breaths, still searching for any remaining danger. She took a tentative step forward and crouched, her fingers delicately reaching out to examine the substance.

Lorn watched, hypnotized, shook his head, and came back to his senses. "Don't touch it!" he barked. He didn't know what the substance was, but if it took control of a simple mountain lion and twisted it to such ends, he didn't want to know what the infection would do to Lilit.

She snapped her head to Lorn, and realization crashed through. She yanked her hand away and sneered at him, her momentary confusion replaced by scorn and arrogance. "I'm not that stupid." Lilit unfurled from her crouch and sheathed her sword. Lorn did the same.

He stared at the creature, now resumed to its rightful state; its body was devoid of the infection, the substance seeped into the ground, like it was scurrying away. Lorn wrinkled his forehead in concentration. It was familiar. Like a rush of magic, the memory came to him. The destroyed town, the young woman and her brother, the strange putrid substance. They were one and the same.

"The destroyed town," he muttered under his breath.

"What?" Lilit demanded.

He turned his head to Lilit, then saw her eyes widen. She sprinted past him. Words caught in his throat as he turned to look at what she was rushing towards.

Pearl was on her knees, clutching her forearm. Four long claw marks raked down her skin, the wound oozing and festering. The shock of the battle must have numbed her to the damage, and she didn't recognize it until now.

She furiously scratched at the wound, tugging at skin. "Get it out of me!" Pearl screamed. "Get it out of me! Get it out of me!" Each declaration grew louder, her voice full of manic desperation. She scratched harder, her nails digging into the skin, tearing the delicate skin, the wound gaping, red, and angry. The rancid putrefaction was already taking hold, veins of black wound up her arm in a slow journey. Crazed convulsions wracked her body and Lilit braced Pearl.

With a gentleness Lorn didn't know she was capable of, Lilit lowered Pearl to the ground. Although Lilit was smaller than Pearl, she was able to use her strength magic to restrain Pearl by her shoulders.

"Get over here, Lorn," Lilit demanded.

Pearl writhed and fought Lilit's strong grasp. Her legs kicked out as she desperately sought to fight Lilit's hold. With her hands pinned to the ground, she was unable to scratch her arm.

Pearl's back curled away from the ground as she loosened a bloodcurdling scream. "Get it out! I need it out!"

Lorn scrambled next to Pearl and added his strength to Lilit's hold. He pinned the infected arm to the ground careful not to touch the spreading sickness.

"I don't have much magic left," Lilit admitted. He could see the drops of sweat accumulated on her brow, the lines of tiredness on her face. She had used it in the fight and restraining Pearl was taking every last bit of energy she could muster.

Lorn didn't know what they could do for Pearl. They were at least an hour away from Lighthold. They were drained from the day long hike and the fight from the diseased mountain lion.

"Do you have any skill at healing?" Lilit asked. He barely heard her over Pearl's screaming. She was deranged. This wasn't the steadfast woman who had led them to the Crossroads. It was like her blood was boiling her alive.

"I can do the basics," Lorn gritted out. He readjusted his grip on her forearm and dodged a violent kick from Pearl. He was uncomfortable using his weight to pin Pearl to the ground, but they were desperate. He wedged his knee over her thigh. It helped to fasten the left side of her body to the ground.

"You need to try, Lorn." That was the second time Lilit had used his proper name. This was serious. "If she dies, we will be hunted like dogs. She may not show it, but Pearl is her favorite daughter. Lady Rasmina will not accept any excuses."

"I am not a healer. I haven't trained in such things." Bile rose up his throat, he couldn't handle watching Pearl succumb to this madness. This stubborn and optimistic young woman could not die like this.

Lilit's muscles strained, her arms struggling to hold down the writhing woman. Through clenched teeth Lilit muttered, "We don't have time—but your magic, Lorn. Light is rare. Light can be purifying.

I have read in—" Pearl's right arm bucked off the ground, breaking through Lilit's grasp. Lilit wrangled it back to the ground and continued her explanation. "—in books. Those with a proclivity to light magic tend to be strong healers."

This was not the time to argue, but Lorn didn't see how such power could reside in his veins. "I—"

Lilit cut him off. "The worst you can do is try. She will die either way."

Lorn didn't understand how he would even begin to tackle something of this magnitude, but she was right, he needed to try.

"You were able to power your sword with your light magic. You were able to banish the wraith. You can do this. Now or never hunter." Lilit's words buoyed his confidence. She had never spoken so candidly to him before without a sneer or a snide remark attached. This was who she truly was, when the exterior facade was torn away.

Pearl's left arm pulsed, the veins blackened and prominent. Her arm, *she*, was rotting. The blackened veins crept up to her shoulder. If they let it go any longer they would have to amputate the arm. Better a missing arm, than the loss of her life.

Lorn steadied his rapid breathing and closed his eyes. He tried to remember what happened when he fought the wraith. At that time, he was attempting to imbue the sword with his magic. He had relied on instinct and what felt natural to him.

He laced his fingers within Pearls, her hand both dainty and small the faint hint of calluses beginning to form. She gripped back, her nails breaking the skin of his hand. Her body writhed beneath him, nearly causing him to lose his balance. But he couldn't focus on that, he needed to turn inward. Find the center of his magic. Find the source. It reminded him of when he was trying to manifest his magic as a child, the constant doubt and uncertainty of what would be revealed. He latched onto it.

His mind was splayed out before him. A quaint cottage with rolling hills, fields freshly plowed, and the hint of woods lined the edges. It was his home. His heart. The edges of the sun glimmered over the horizon, the burnt wash of dusk descending.

Find my magic, release it.

Time was running out. Thoughts of Pearl's pain and screams broke through his concentration. He shoved it aside. He couldn't let it break this illusion. He couldn't waver now. Darkness was closing in on the farm. He searched, spinning around looking for a hint of something, a trigger.

In the window of his house a small flicker of light winked through the glass like the soft flame of a candle. He raced across the fields of his mind, his boots springing off the softened ground, his hands brushing across leaves and twisting vines. The sanctuary of his mind was his home. A part of his heart broke at the realization. His feet scraped against pebbles as he ran up the path to his front door.

The light was in there. It moved away from the window and further into the small cottage. His fingers clasped onto the iron handle, and he flung the door open. This was no time for being gentle. He furiously looked to the window where the small flame appeared, but it had moved. He rounded the corner and halted. His breath was ragged.

It was the flame of a candle. He wasn't imagining it—but someone held it.

She cradled the iron base of the candle holder, its small thin tapered handle spiraling inwards. The candle appeared to be one of theirs that they crafted on the farm from animal fat and tallow. The off-white candle wax dripped steadily down the sides while Lorn caught his breath. She faced him, the light from the candle casting a beautiful and eerie glow around her face. Her hair was free, flowing softly down her back the hint of a curl playing around at the ends. She was here. This was not some fake, imagined illusion from the Hinterlands playing at his heart, or his best memories. This was her. He could tell in the well-worn smile and the lines of mirth etched around her eyes. At how she looked at him as if she could both devour him and playfully chastise. The sharp wit of her eyes, the work hardened contours of her body. A wry grin was plastered on her face as she took in Lorn's disheveled appearance.

His mouth hung open idiotically, but he couldn't muster the energy to care. Lorn was about to speak when she interrupted.

"I am so proud of you." Lakesh's grin widened. Her hands delicately sheltered the tiny flame. "There is not much time. You need to save her, Lorn."

He couldn't forget why he was here; he couldn't dissolve into this illusion. He ached to reach out and touch her. This was her. It wasn't fake. It wasn't a fabrication or a memory he held onto. It was her—her spirit greeting him.

"I wish we had more time Lorn. But know that I have never abandoned you." Her eyes shifted to the side, uneasy. "They said I could be the one to deliver this to you. Well, I demanded is more like it."

Lorn released a ragged laugh. It was thick and wet with unspent emotion. She was always feisty, not one to back down from a challenge.

Lakesh looked down at the candle and the licking flame with a small amount of reverence before offering it to Lorn. "Take it. You'll need it." The vague outlines of a shadow appeared next to Lakesh, the features muddy and distorted. Lorn couldn't focus on it, even if he tried.

"There is no time," the voice said. It was gritty, rough, and ancient. "The girl will die if he doesn't accept it now."

Lakesh nodded her head in acceptance and offered the candle to Lorn again.

Lorn gulped, his throat dry and scratchy. He reached forward, gently cupping the underside of Lakesh's hands. At the contact his eyes locked to hers as she said, "I love you Lorn. Never forget that." She smiled warmly at him.

"Never," he answered.

The candle transferred to his hands. Lakesh and the strange shadow's images disappeared in a jagged stuttering. He stared curiously at the candle. A lone bead of wax dripped down the side. It spilled over the iron holder and fell onto his thumb. It burned. More and more it burned. He opened his mouth to scream when the entire candle melted at once and flooded over the sides of the holder. It clung to his skin and burrowed underneath. Everything exploded in pain. It was like his veins were on fire. He was a shooting star launching brilliantly across the sky. He was the sun burning, burning, burning. It was unbearable. By the time he thought he would collapse from the endless pain, his mind's illusion shattered. The outdoors, the house sunk away like he was caught in a sinkhole. He fell to his knees and watched as his surroundings blurred away, until he was the only thing remaining.

He was ready.

His eyes opened slowly, and he looked around with a detached numbness. Peace and acceptance washed over him. This was not some young woman before him, it was someone he simply needed to heal. There was no rush, nothing as important as ridding the rot that overtook her arm. He looked on dispassionately and funneled the power that crackled beneath his skin. He was disembodied. He viewed himself from afar—a simple man brightening and brightening.

The blinding light consumed his body and beamed into the forest. Nothing could dampen him—not the fall of night, not the rain, not the shadows that threatened to engulf them. He simply was, with no beginning and end.

The woman restraining the person on the ground had left, her weight no longer contributed. The light was too much, but not for him. It was his duty. He was a protector. A simple clarity flashed through his mind. This was who he was, this was what magic should be. Pure unfiltered power to heal and protect.

Any sense of time dissolved as he forced the rot to run in fear. It had nowhere to go and in its cowardice vanished. The woman laid still, too still. If he was in his right mind he would have become worried over her lack of movement, but that was not him and she was simply a vessel he needed to fix. Her arm was fixed. There was no more corruption. He sneered at such a thing. How disgusting, revolting, and vile. It had no place here. A sense of shouting broke through. He couldn't make out the words. The sound—it was familiar. Something he used to be called.

"Lorn! Fucking hunter, snap out of it! You will die! She will die! Stop! Stop!" She had such a grating voice, always angry, but that name was familiar. She was like the buzzing of an angry gnat. He brushed it away, focusing on the unfiltered power. The whole forest would be cleansed. This rot, this corruption needed to be gone. He smiled in grim acceptance. Yes, corruption was the correct word. It was an echo of something long ago. Something familiar. The magic came easily, and he extended it further. Everything would be better. It had to be. All the filth would be banished. He could cleanse it all.

His eyes were unfocused, unable to make out anything in particular like he was seeing in a different dimension, one where threads of magic swirled around him and his light was not a blinding pain, but a welcoming reprieve.

Out of the brilliant light an outline appeared. It was comforting. His mind jolted. The outline solidified. This woman was beautiful. He felt like he knew her at a time, her deep copper skin limned in his glistening light with hair unbound and loose down her back. Her steps made no sound as she approached. She was not scared of him. Her smile was radiant, and he felt himself smiling back. Like the stalks of flowers blowing in the wind, she gracefully moved forward, and he had no choice but to halt his plans. She was his. Behind a closed door in his mind, there was an incessant knocking. He wanted to ignore it, but the pounding continued. Her name. What was her name? If she was his and he was hers, shouldn't he know her name? It flew away from him like a ribbon on the wind; he tried to catch it, but it eluded his grasp.

She clasped a hand to his shoulder and crouched to meet his eye-level. That wasn't right. A goddess such as her should be standing. He was made to bow before her. She should never come down to his level.

"You have done enough, Lorn." Her warm brown eyes flashed to him. Those eyes. Eyes that expressed her mirth, her wit, her shrewdness, a calm retreat for him to return to. But his name wasn't Lorn. That's not who he was. He was light. He was power.

She pressed her lips to his. It was soft, inviting. It welcomed him. It was the sanctuary after a long day. How could such a goddess kiss him so tenderly? He closed his eyes and accepted the rare gift. Too soon she pulled away.

"It is time to let go, Lorn."

Lorn? Maybe that *was* his name? The goddess flickered before him, and the illusion vanished. His heart broke and with a piercing clarity the name Lakesh shot through him. Memories of his life, of their lives together collided with his current reality. The light around him trembled.

"Lakesh," he whispered. The magic faded, the light winking out like a doused torch. Lorn sucked in a gasping breath, like he had just come up for air after almost drowning in an ocean. He collapsed next to the young woman, her name buried beneath rubble of confusion.

25

"It is a great sin to take one's magic away. Was it necessary to protect Aza, ridding her of Cruvo's claws? The condescension that I know better is grating, however correct I prove to be."

Nivet's private journal.

Aza felt triumphant. The great sand dunes of Kreeha were behind them. No more loose sand to kick up when her feet grew too heavy. No more sandstorms to shelter from. It was a bittersweet moment. While the sand dunes were both tiring and treacherous, dawn and dusk were glorious. When the sun crested the horizon the dunes were painted in an array of colors, beautiful gradients of pale yellow to burnt orange, deep umber, even rare speckles of scarlet. The ground sparkled like gems hidden underfoot.

As they trekked deeper into the Kreehan province, Aza's mind wandered to the Lord of the province. She recalled his charismatic, arrogant, mercurial mood. What would he do if he found her within his borders? It never occurred to her that Lady Sarava and Lord Ravinder of Verta would commit such treachery, siding with a demon such as Astaroth. They were power-hungry cowards. Aza replayed every interaction with them at El'en. At least Lady Rasmina had been clear in her disgust and ambitions. Lady Sarava and Lord Ravinder pretended to be witless and guileless, using their hidden ambition to get closer to her. A strange memory popped up; When Lorn had been asked to dine with them, he commented on how they were circumventing the conversation and kept trying to figure more out about her. Even then they were plotting. Aza gasped and clapped a hand over her mouth.

The Nerians paused in their walk and looked at her questioningly.

"They voted against me at the meeting," she whispered. At the conference with the Lords and Ladies they had cast a vote on whether Aza should remain free to roam or kept confined. Looking back on it now was quite silly. They could have never confined her. Her power was too great. To think that such a moment had felt so confining. But the vote had been three to two. Aza knew the vote against her would be Lady Rasmina's, but she always wondered who the other vote belonged to. The Vertan court had wanted her confined and easy to manipulate. That meant the Nerians, Kreeha and Iyera had voted for her freedom. The thought gave Aza a small measure of reassurance. Maybe Lord Sune wouldn't turn her over to the other courts if they were captured.

"Aza, what's wrong?" Reed asked.

She had not realized she was standing still and looked up at the group, their faces filled with worry.

"I've discovered the two provinces who voted for my confinement were Gara and Verta."

The Nerians broke into relaxed smiles, their worry melting away. Anwin snorted, "Yeah, we could have told you that a while ago, Aza."

Reed gave a soft laugh, and Xira smirked before turning back on the trail and continuing their walk.

Aza didn't find the situation as funny as them. She trudged alongside them but kept her silence.

Anwin nudged Aza with her shoulder. "Ah, c'mon Aza. Of course, we knew they were traitorous scum. Why do you think we hate going to court? They have dirty secrets you would be appalled to learn."

"You wouldn't find the situation very funny if you were always kept in the dark with little knowledge of any of it," she replied through clenched teeth. They could laugh about it, but Aza was embarrassed. She had easily fallen for these people, swayed by their words, and their false actions. For the Nerians to easily see their façades was frustrating. Aza felt like an idiot.

Anwin's smile and laughter sobered.

Xira's voice cut through the tense silence. "Do not feel inferior for believing their ruse. Most of the five provinces believe them, that is why they are so successful."

Xira's comment buoyed Aza's spirits. She rubbed her hand along her arm, fighting off a wayward chill. It was difficult to not chastise herself for believing their false stories, but she couldn't shake off her guilt over Cruvo—over how easily she had fallen for him and was drawn to him. Although the Nerians had reassured her, she felt like a gullible child. She wanted to see Cruvo just once more to confront him about these thoughts. The Nerians while helpful, did not understand —could not understand the feelings of the gods and goddesses. Cruvo's feelings could be true or manufactured, but either way Aza aimed to find out. The Nerians left her to her thoughts for the rest of the day without any teasing.

Over the rest of the week, they fell into a steady routine. They stayed on the trail winding through cities and towns which they gracefully skirted to avoid any further suspicions or questions. At night they would take turns keeping watch, while the rest of them bundled together to stave off the chilly nights. Layers were important. During the heat of the day, Aza struggled with her heavy cloak. They could not risk her revealing herself. Sweat dripped down her face in rivulets. By the time dusk settled, she had the freedom to remove her cloak but couldn't because of the deep chill that pervaded Kreeha.

Aza came to an agreement with the Nerians about her magic. While she could feel it crackle and writhe under her skin, they wanted her to use it sparingly until they were deep within the safety of the Nerian mountains. But for now, she could release tiny amounts to ebb the tidal wave of power. It was like she had regrown a missing limb and every moment she celebrated it. Although she had become accustomed to relying on her own strength and fortitude, the joy and happiness of having her magic back was enormous, like the reunion of a long-lost friend. At certain times of the day, it would release in happy bursts, flowers blooming abundantly underfoot, a jagged line of light erupting into the sky. She tried to keep it discreet and only after mock glares from Xira did she rein it in. But she could see the Nerians' small smiles; they were happy for her.

After another chilly night, Aza suggested shadowing the group to the Hall of Prophecies.

The group looked at her with perplexed expressions, each of their brows drawn in disbelief.

Anwin chewed the sparse meat they found for dinner and asked, "Have you attempted such a shadowing before?"

"No, but I don't see how the mechanics can be any different. If you are worried about my strength I feel fine, actually better than I have in a long time."

Xira leaned back on her hands and nodded. "Go ahead. Shadow Reed to the Hall of Prophecies."

Before closing her eyes, Aza faltered briefly, expecting an argument, but continued when there were no complaints. She centered her magic. It was like placing a blanket over Reed, her shadows and darkness leaking out of her to cover him. It had been a long time since she shadowed herself and she had never shadowed someone else, but it came to her naturally. With Reed covered, she commanded the shadows to take him away. Aza opened her eyes and found Reed across from her, the shadows still covering his body. With a simple command the shadows disappeared. Aza was disappointed, but Xira wasn't surprised.

"It was a solid attempt, Aza. There is no shame in trying," Reed said.

Aza examined her hands as if they held the answers for her failure.

"It is not your magic," Xira answered. "How much shadow magic have you attempted?"

Aza thought back to her magic sparring session with Cruvo. She had very rarely tapped into her shadow magic. "Very little."

Xira eyed her knowingly. "I figured as such. With Nivet, he was limited to areas he had been before, or at the very least, seen or been explained to in extreme detail. The first option is the most effective and the latter is the least effective. For example, when we were shadowed out of the El'en castle, Nivet had been to the castle before, but not that particular room. We had to explain in great detail where it was located and what it looked like before he could transport us out. We had to test it multiple times before he could successfully shadow us out."

Aza shifted her legs. Although she had forgiven them and had come to trust them, it was still uncomfortable discussing the night she was duped and stolen. To hear how they planned and plotted was tough.

"Also, the farther the distance, the greater the strength, power, and focus needed." Xira brushed her hands together, finished with her dinner for the night. "For now, we walk." Xira stood, preparing to take the first watch.

Aza snuggled next to Anwin and Reed. She preferred their body warmth compared to using her own magic to warm herself up. There was something solid and comforting about the two people next to her, like they were a steadying anchor amongst the vast and violent ocean.

~

Although disappointed she couldn't shadow the group to the Hall of Prophecies, Aza did not mind walking. She noticed the edges of her body had hardened with muscle and her skin basked in the warmth of the Kreeha desert. Even though they were sneaking from village to village, she still enjoyed watching the people and the unique characteristics of each town. It grounded her. How the people went about their day and conversed with one another. It forced her to realize she was not alone, her actions were not isolated, they will have lasting impacts on each of their lives. It is her duty to do right by them.

Aza grew eager the closer they gained on the Hall of Prophecies. The dry, arid desert shifted to balmy and humid. Lush trees thickened providing a comforting shade. She heeded the Nerians' knowledge on fruits and let them guide her on which to pick from the trees, the taste delicious and refreshing amid the oppressive humidity.

Aza grew curious to what Kreeha's capital, Cyran looked like. The capitals of El'en and Rijal danced through her mind, and the stark contrast between them. Each one represented the provinces perfectly; Rijal, a stone Fortress built from the laborers' hands and El'en's castle a thing of beauty like a rare seashell plucked from the ocean. She tried to imagine what Cyran would look like but felt like nothing in her mind would do it justice. She imagined Lord Sune's extravagant wardrobe and gold encrusted items and pictured Cyran to be a fountain of wealth, with fountains spilling over in gold. Unfortunately, the Hall of Prophecies wasn't located in Cyran but on the outskirts of the capital so she would have to let her imagination to do the work. One day she would return and see what splendor it held.

Aza kept probing as they traveled, searching for any signs of the lingering corruption. Ever since entering Kreeha, there was an emptiness, a lack of filth pushing at the edges of her consciousness like in Verta. The corruption—Astaroth—was only strongest in Verta and needed Aza's power to grow her borders. The tendrils of corruption were there, but faint like the weak sprout of vines as they struggle to latch on to a new hold.

Besides the stray troop of guards on patrol, they ran into no others. Reed assured Aza the Hall of Prophecies was a place for scholars and academics. It wasn't heavily guarded, because the information was readily available to those who wished to seek it. In addition, usually a person needed to accompany a mentor, because the language of the scribes was held by only a few.

At an intersection, Reed guided them to the east. If they continued west, it would take them to Cyran, the capital of Kreeha. North led to the border of Neria.

Thick leaves covered the path as they followed a rushing river on their right. The path climbed upwards, the hard-packed ground getting slippery underfoot with the flecks of water shooting up from the river and the smooth river rocks embedded in the path. Rounding a corner, they turned and the path opened into a cliff-face. Aza clung to the side, avoiding the open drop into the rushing river below. It was a steep fall. Aza's stomach was in her throat.

"My Lady?" Anwin asked.

Aza didn't know why she was fearful. Her magic had returned. If she fell she could easily use her wind to slow her fall and pull herself out of the water.

"Just need a quick breath," Aza lied. Anwin patted her shoulder knowingly.

"It happens to us all. Doesn't it make you feel better knowing you are a little more MagicBlessed than you originally thought?"

Aza smiled and huffed a breath. "Yeah, that is one way to look at it."

Aza steadied her feet and moved on. The path grew narrow, Aza had to walk one foot in front of the other. She never slipped.

At the end of the pathway a beautiful stone bridge was erected over the river below. Across from it was their destination—the Hall of Prophecies. It was like a jewel hidden amongst the foliage of the jungle. Aza's clothes clung to her in the humidity, and sweat dripped into her eyes, but she couldn't stop staring in awe at the building. It was blinding in the sun, its sandstone blocks edged in gold. Each side of the building was protected by gold statues, a raven in mid-flight and opposite sat a poised tiger, its expression proud and resolute. The building was cocooned amongst the comforting greenery with the lulling, soothing sound of the rushing river beside it.

They crossed the stone bridge and Aza pictured herself residing here, amongst the flow of nature with endless time to research topics that had nothing to do with her divinity, the corruption plaguing the land, or the Hinterlands. As they neared the end of the bridge, Reed pulled her aside with their backs to the Hall of Prophecies.

"I should have explained sooner, but only you and I will enter. While they welcome anyone within their walls, there are strict rules you must follow. This is why only the two of us will be entering while Xira and Anwin remain outside."

Aza leaned closer to hear him over the roaring of the river below.

"You must never speak. There is a long-standing tradition that the scribes uphold. I am the only one who knows the language and you must defer to my knowledge to get us through."

Aza tried to not let her confusion show. How could he communicate with the scribes if they weren't allowed to speak?

"The information in the Hall of Prophecies is available to anyone, but what we are searching for is long buried and most either don't know about it or have forgotten. We will be in there for a while, but you must keep your silence no matter what you discover."

Reed stepped back and glanced over his shoulder. He pulled out a leather throng from his pocket and loosely tied back his locs. A thin sheen of sweat coated his arms and forehead. It was unbearably humid, and the clouds gathered oppressively overhead. Xira had informed her that this area of Kreeha experienced torrential rain in the winter compared to the frigid temperatures of Verta and Neria.

"Ready?"

Aza nodded and stepped alongside Reed letting him lead. At the sight of visitors, people trickled out of the Hall of Prophecies. They differed in age, and dress; some wore airy trousers and loose-fitting tank tops while others wore dresses or shorts. But all were identified by their simple homespun linen, in varying shades of white. It was quite the juxtaposition to the ornate and beautiful building that the inhabitants wore simple and plain clothing.

Anwin and Xira lounged on a set of chairs, appearing relaxed, but she saw the alert shift of their eyes as they observed the surroundings.

A woman far along in her years approached them. The simple white linen draped her form, her sinewy arms corded with muscle. Sun rays poked through the dense clouds and limned her in a golden ray, basking her already golden skin aglow. Her wavy black hair was in the process of graying, the mixture a beautiful sweep and brush of color. It reminded Aza of the mixtures of the layers of sand at the beach, a gray intermixed with a deep black. The woman smiled in familiarity at Reed, her rivulets of wrinkles a sign of a happy and fulfilled life etched on her face.

Aza didn't know if the rule pertained to outside, so she kept her mouth shut in caution.

Reed stepped forward, an equal smile on his face. Aza was curious how this interaction would play out and she nearly bounced on her toes in anticipation.

Instead of speaking, he began to move his hands. Aza snapped her mouth closed. They were signing—the language of scribes.

A vague memory or sensation tugged at her. She knew this was a language she had experienced or seen before. It felt familiar. Reed moved his hands freely, his expression shifting and changing effortlessly with what he was signing. The woman responded in a like manner. It was a frustrating moment for Aza to be silent; she had so many questions to ask Reed.

The woman gestured to Aza, her eyes widening slightly, and Reed loosened a belly deep laugh. It startled Aza and she looked at him, worried about being dismissed from the Hall of Prophecies, but there was no one escorting them out, no guards to remove them. Reed had warned her not to speak, not that noises were unacceptable. She shook her head at her ignorance.

The woman and Reed started to walk towards the building and Aza tugged Reed back. Keeping her mouth closed, she pointed to the woman. She didn't know her name and it felt rude to be welcomed into this sanctuary without knowing it. She pointed again and tried to communicate what she wanted. Reed was fighting the smile spreading across his face.

Not wanting to play this game, Aza bent down and traced letters in the dirt. When finished, she proudly stood, her hands on her hips and a triumphant smile on her face. *Name?*

Reed gave a mock clap at her effort, bent down and wrote below hers. Aza peered over his shoulder impatiently.

In small precise lines, *Roan* was marked below her question.

Aza nodded her thanks and looked up to see Roan smiling in appreciation and bemusement. She gestured for them to follow.

Aza dusted her hands off on her pants and trailed after them. She leaned her head back to take in the sandstone building. It was beautiful and exquisitely built. She kept her hands pinned to her side, dismissing the urge to run her fingers over the craftsmanship and marvel at it. They climbed the few steps with the raven and tiger statues greeting her like stoic guards. The dark lacquered door was bordered with engravings—shapes, small animals, and organic designs she wanted to study further, but had no time for. Aza cast one more glance over her shoulder at Xira and Anwin basking in the sun, resting casually at the tables adorned outside. Anwin waved and Xira nodded.

A large mess hall greeted her. Long wooden tables paired with benches were scattered along the room with a handful of scribes cleaning up the remaining clay plates. To the far left of the room, a cut-out of the building expanded into a kitchen with the familiar sounds of knives chopping carried out to her.

Roan passed by her scribes and they each gave friendly waves and smiles and resumed their work. The questions bubbled forth, but Aza held back. She yearned to speak their language and to be able to sign her questions to Reed and Roan or the other scribes who passed by them on quiet feet.

A scribe exited out of a door in the back of the room and a glare of sun burst into the room, revealing a glimpse of a well-tended garden and the cluck of chickens. It seemed they sustained themselves out here.

Roan and Reed exchanged signs back and forth while Roan led them to a staircase. It branched with one leading up while the other led down. Roan paused and answered something from Reed. She shook her head and pointed down. The pathway was illuminated by torches. While dim and dark, it wasn't foreboding. Roan moved with precision, her footsteps sure and steady. Reed stilled his hands while they descended. Deep underground they went, level after level. At each level Aza tried to linger and take in what each level contained. Each level mirrored the others with a slew of tables and scrolls. Shelves were lined with thick tomes and organized with meticulous precision.

Deeper and deeper Roan led them, until finally they reached the bottom. The scrolls, papers, and tomes were all well cared for despite the vast depth they were held at. The floor opened up into a small study similar to the other levels Aza passed. There must have been a specific system. Possibly the more dated scrolls and prophecies were being kept deeper underground. Roan glided forward until she reached the back wall. She reached an aged hand against the smooth wall and pressed an innocuous brick aside. A tiny gold key was removed from within her linen robes, and she inserted it into the wall. With a resounding click, the wall slid sideways. Roan gestured Reed and Aza forth. From what Aza could discern Reed gestured his thanks and Roan left them, her poised back gliding up the staircase they had just descended with nary a concern on her face.

Reed took a steadying breath, locked eyes with Aza, and stepped into the room.

26

"A whisper of Aza's magic called to me. Luckily, due to our continuous exposure to one another, I can sense her from far away. I will find her."

   Cruvo's private journal

Lorn couldn't move his body. He floated through empty space, the vast darkness cut through by pools of light. The light swirled and moved as he drifted aimlessly through, searching for an anchor—to return. He was both physical and not, caught in-between these states of being. Until he wasn't.

He cracked open his eyes and the soft forms of his room solidified. His head pounded with every breath. Lorn tried to lift his arm, but it felt like he had been burned throughout his body, the pain pulsing. Even keeping his eyes open and focused was a monumental task. He gulped and tried to speak. His voice came out as a dry, rasping croak.

Before he could plead for water, a hand lifted a glass to his lips. The vague outline of their fingers seemed familiar, the pale skin tugging at his memory. But he needed the water and dismissed his uncertainty. The water was cool and refreshing and slid down his throat only to be met by an empty stomach. Lorn tried again to focus on who was handing the glass to him, his vision blurry and his head pounding; he was unable to get a clear image. They gave him small bits of water, acclimating him to the taste. Then the glass was taken away. With the small amounts of water, the pain in his skull subsided to a dull roar. Lorn put all his energy into trying to see who was here with him. The outline of his bed cleared, and he was met by the stern and disapproving stare of Lady Rasmina. If he had any strength remaining, he would have scrambled back from her deadly gaze.

There was a movement out of the corner of his eye, and he was relieved to see Lilit standing guard, her hand playing around the hilt of her sword. Lady Rasmina wouldn't dare do anything with Lilit here.

Lady Rasmina retreated and forcefully set the glass on a nearby table. If sound could cut, Lorn would have been sliced through, his heart exposed. She kept her composure, the only hint of her anger was from her sharp movements and the faint pull of her mouth and the raging fire that burned in her eyes, a fire that would have destroyed Lorn if there was any action behind it. Now that Lorn thought of it, he didn't know what Lady Rasmina's magic was. Would she burn him alive with the inferno that swirled within her eyes?

With Lady Rasmina's back turned, Lorn sent a silent plea to Lilit. She gave a minuscule shrug, he was on his own.

Lady Rasmina pivoted and clasped her hands together. "So, I hear you had an excursion with my daughter?"

"I—"

Lady Rasmina cut him off. "You take an excursion with my daughter to the CrossRoads, an already treacherous journey and then on the way back she is maimed." Her nostrils flared and the grip on her hands tightened, the white somehow paling further, her blue veins prominent. He couldn't help but think of the putrid black veins that ran up her daughter's arms. "Somehow I am led to believe you two came out unharmed, yet she was injured—near death, if I am to believe."

"Really—" Lorn pushed off the bed and sat upright.

"No," Lady Rasmina firmly stated. "You listen to me, hunter. If I didn't have my daughter begging on her knees for you, pleading for you, I would have already had you executed, consequences be damned."

Lorn opened his mouth to voice his innocence and tried to explain the situation, but Lady Rasmina advanced. She marched over, regal and commanding. She planted a hand on his headboard, scanned his exposed body, and narrowed her eyes at him. She was barely restraining her anger, but he could not shy away. He did not cower beneath her penetrating stare, her oppressive stature.

"You will never be allowed out of Lighthold with my daughter again. If a similar situation ever occurs, your deaths will be the punishment. Am I clear?"

Lorn wanted to defend himself, to explain the situation that occurred, but Lady Rasmina would never listen to the truth. She believed her own skewed story. He didn't even know if Pearl disclosed what had truly happened. Was her version of events the same as theirs? Pearl had been out of her mind, incoherent, but she had remembered enough to beg mercy for Lilit and Lorn.

He swallowed back his words and gave a stiff nod. Lady Rasmina stepped back satisfied, her hands clasped primly in front of her. Before Lady Rasmina reached the door, Lilit's voice broke through the silence. "He saved her," she barked.

Rasmina paused, her hand hovering over the door handle.

"Lorn saved Pearl. She would have died, screaming, in pain. At the very least her arm would have been amputated. You should be thanking him," she spit out.

Lorn arched a brow at Lilit's admission. She was vouching for him.

Lady Rasmina glanced over her shoulder. "I tire of this Lilit. You have already explained yourself multiple times. I do not wish to hear it further." She left the room with a swish of her gown.

"Thank you," Lorn rasped. His throat ached like he had spent hours screaming.

"You do not need to thank me," Lilit hissed. She readjusted her stance and made to follow Lady Rasmina's path.

"Regardless, I do appreciate it."

"Well, she is acting irrationally, and you did save her daughter. I only spoke the truth." Lilit left and closed the door. It was softly shut without any of Lilit's usual ire.

Based on the dim light, Lorn guessed it to be about midmorning. He wondered how long Lilit and Lady Rasmina were in his room, waiting for him to stir. Lilit had not abandoned him. It was such a strange thought that percolated in his mind. He couldn't let go of it. She had not left him—she, who wanted to return to Iyera. Leaving Lorn to his own mess with no one to vouch for him would have been a surefire way to have him executed. Would Lady Rasmina have listened to Pearl's testimony without Lilit adding her own truth, her unadorned perspective on the situation?

He needed to check on Pearl, ask how she was. The memories of that day were blurry. He had snatches of clarity, the all-consuming power he wielded.

Lorn gingerly moved his legs to the floor. He held onto the edges of the bed, stabilizing himself. There were no external wounds, no gaping holes, or surprising bruises. The soreness, exhaustion, and pain had to do with the amount of magic he had wielded, his body unable to cope with the vast magic. He hadn't paid it any attention until now, but he could feel the magic prowling underneath, slumbering like a great beast. It was there, resting waiting for him to call upon it again. He didn't want to bother testing his limits. If he did he thought his body might deteriorate from the inside out. Every subtle shift of his body left him wincing. He would need to recover first, before he attempted to wield this new power.

Lorn stood up and swayed. He clutched the wall, his breathing heavy. He rested his forehead against the wall and focused on not collapsing. His head pounded, his vision threatened to tunnel in. He focused on the sturdy floor beneath his feet, on the smooth wooden wall underneath his calloused fingers, on the feel of his breath going in and out of his lungs, on the taste of the few water droplets left on his tongue. After minutes of centering, he peeled away from the wall and cracked his eyes open. The pounding in his head subsided and his vision did not darken. A good sign. He left the comfort of the wall, his fingertips drifting away from the steadying surface. His steps were shaky, but he was able to hold himself up. He made it five steps before he was drawn to the bathroom. The bathtub beckoned him, but he had to decline. He couldn't risk drowning in the water if he passed out and was unable to support himself.

Lorn turned his eye to a distant chair. It was on the opposite side of the room. He forced one foot in front of the other and kept his body straight. When he walked the hallways of Lighthold, he couldn't appear weak, curled in on himself using the wall to steady his footsteps. No, he needed to demonstrate a commanding presence. Each step required immense focus. Whenever the pounding in his head threatened to consume him, he paused and didn't let himself succumb. The chair was within reaching distance. Instead of collapsing into it like he wanted, he forced himself to lower with restraint. Every limb ached, his blood felt like it was boiling, but he did it.

Lorn repeated the process multiple times before he was satisfied. Lunch was brought to his room. The food helped to bolster his strength.

By the afternoon, he felt competent enough to go and visit Pearl. He paused outside Lilit's door, unsure of whether to invite her along. She would be furious that he was wandering the palace without a guard, but this was a conversation he wanted to have privately with Pearl. Also, after Lilit's strange support in front of Lady Rasmina, Lorn felt like their relationship had shifted. It wasn't monumental, but like a slight redirection. She clearly was uncomfortable with it, so Lorn let her be.

He wandered for a few minutes, before he realized he didn't know where Pearl's room was located. If it was anything like her mother's, it would be at the highest peak of the palace. He released a tired breath. It would be a lot of stairs for him to tackle, but he could do it. He had to do it.

Lorn found a stray worker and inquired after Pearl's room. He indicated she was on the top floor, the third door on the left-hand side. Lorn nodded his thanks and began his arduous trek up the spiral staircase. At each level, Lorn took time to compose himself, steady his breathing and control the shakiness in his legs. Level after level, it worsened. His breathing was ragged by the time he reached the top and sweat lined his brow. Lilit would most definitely be upset about this trip he was taking. He smiled grimly. He was used to her anger and vitriol. It would be welcome after their awkwardness. Lorn found the third door on the left. Two guards were stationed outside, both gripping spears.

Lorn inclined his head in a show of respect. "May I see her?"

The guards shared a similar look, their lips thinned, their jaws clenched. The older one on the right with a full beard and a battle-hardened visage answered, "We have strict orders from Lady Rasmina to not let anyone, but family enter this room."

"I understand, but I need to talk to Pearl. It is of the utmost importance." Lorn could see the guards considering the request, but he understood the position he was putting them in. If they were caught disobeying Lady Rasmina's orders, they would be relinquished of their jobs, or even punished by more severe measures. "I promise on my life and on my magic I will not harm her."

The guard eyed Lorn up and down. "Aye, we know of what you have done for Pearl."

The guards must have sensed Lorn's confusion because the younger one on the left added, "Rumors are that your quick thinking saved the life of our Lady."

The older guard said, "We know she would be dead by now without you." He scanned the hallway and considered something before saying, "Most of the court is busy in meetings on the second level of the palace. You have five minutes. I cannot offer you any longer."

Lorn thanked them both and made to enter.

The older guard grabbed Lorn by his upper arm. "Our young Pearl is beloved by the people. We would do anything for her. Saving her life...it means everything. You are owed a debt by our people, should you ever need it." He released Lorn's arm. These typically cold and standoffish people owed him a debt. Lorn understood the significance of this admittance. He gave a firm nod, his eyes hoping to convey the gratitude his words were unable to form.

Pearl's room was as decadent as befitting her status. Heavy drapes covered the multiple windows. The one over the balcony door was pulled aside revealing a small peak of Lighthold Proper, the buildings minuscule at their great height.

She was resting in her giant bed, her small frame situated in the middle, the pillows and blankets indented. A giant shaggy dog barked at Lorn's entry. Pearl had her eyes fixed on several novels splayed out in front of her. A lap tray held one red thick tome cracked open, and a cup of tea. A swirl of steam lifted into the air. Pearl's eyes flicked up to Lorn. Despite the dog's enormous size, it did not disturb Pearl's items. It carefully dismounted from the bed and curiously trotted forward sniffing at Lorn.

Pearl let out a soft smile before calling back the dog. "Thunder, enough." The dog casually looked back at its owner and returned to her side.

Lorn was not scared of dogs; he was used to them from living in the countryside, but he had never seen one of this size. It came up to Lorn's waist, its shaggy coat both thick and wiry in shades of grays, blacks, whites, and even deep blues. It looked to be from the highlands of Gara, probably used as a deterrent against wolves and predators, and used to protect the rare highland sheep of Gara, prized for their wool.

Pearl scratched Thunder's neck and it released a contended grumble.

"He's beautiful," Lorn commented. It was true and not some courtly flattery. This beast was strong, the colors some tapestry of nature, and its presence was something else entirely.

Pearl snorted. "She is," she corrected.

Heat crept up his neck at the mistake. "My apologies."

She waved a hand at his apology. "I am used to it. Most men assume Thunder is male. it always does well to remind them otherwise." Pearl grinned at him. "I assume you are not here though to meet my dog. Why are you here?"

Lorn's legs were about to give out from his rigorous trek up the stairs. He saw a chair and gestured to it asking if he could sit. With Pearl's permission, he sat grateful for the short reprieve for his legs.

"I want to know what you remember. From that day," he added. The chair was cushioned and lined with velvet. His fingers ran absentmindedly over the soft fabric.

Pearl straightened in bed, her hair loose and chaotic, strands pointed in every direction. He thought he spotted the edge of a feather quill tucked somewhere amongst the strands.

"Of course." She readjusted and Thunder flattened against the floor, her paws stretched out leisurely in front of her, watching Lorn.

"I do not know how I can ever thank you."

"No, please. You misunderstand me, that is not why I am here. I just want to know what happened."

"Oh. Regardless, I do appreciate you saving my life. From what I heard, at best I would have an amputated arm, at worst I would have lost my life."

"You are welcome. I never would have let you or anyone die from such an affliction." A warning knock rasped against her door. They had only a handful of time left. "I do not have much time. The guards gave me five minutes."

With the warning, Pearl donned a serious expression. "I don't really remember much. It comes in waves and flashes. I remember the creature that clawed me, Lilit killing it, then nothing. Just endless pain. Such a pain. It felt like I was both inflamed and dying. Like a putrid decay was taking over my body. Like I was a rotting corpse, praying for it to end but instead I was being burned alive."

Lorn had moved to the edge of his seat. What she explained gave him further understanding of the magical process and what had occurred.

"Did you feel the burning at the beginning?"

Pearl paused and closed her eyes. She scrunched her face then stilled. "It is hard to decipher when everything happened, but I believe the burning occurred later. It was the feel of decay overtaking my body first." She opened her eyes and shivered. Thunder rose to her feet and settled in bed next to Pearl, disturbing the stack of books. Pearl caught the cup of tea before it spilled.

A quick knock on the door startled Lorn.

"You need to go," the older guard said.

Lorn used the arms of the chair to bolster himself and as quickly as he could, left the room. "Thank you," he whispered to Pearl.

She nodded and a distraught look settled over her. Lorn had no time to think about it, because Lilit stood before him, seething. It was the angriest he had ever seen her. A prominent vein bulged on her forehead and her fists were white knuckled with rage.

Luckily he wasn't sparring for the next few days, because she would have taken it out on him in their practice. "The Ambassador is needed elsewhere," Lilit said through clenched teeth. She jerked her head to the side. Lorn was smart enough not to argue and he attempted to walk casually away from Pearl's room, the shaking of his legs and his limp becoming more prominent. When he reached the end of the hall, he held onto the stair railing, leaned against it, and tried to catch his breath. Lilit waited stiffly beside him. She didn't speak, but he could feel the fury radiating from her, the faint crackling of uncontrolled magic.

It was a painstakingly long journey back to his rooms, with constant stopping. His shirt was covered in sweat and his body was screaming at him to stop. Within the safety of his room, Lorn did not mind showing weakness in front of Lilit and collapsed on his bed. His composure slipped and his limbs shook. His breathing was erratic.

With the door fully closed, Lilit finally let him have it. "This is what you deserve!" she shouted. Realizing how loud she was, she lowered her voice, but the anger remained the same. "Wandering the palace in your weakened state, ascending at least eight flights of stairs, fully exposed, no guard. Weak," she spat. With each claim of his ineptitude, Lilit's judgmental footsteps sounded like the dull thuds of fists hitting a body.

"Lady Rasmina wants you dead and you make it very easy for her to stage something and make it look like an accident. Not to mention your complete weakness. You cannot even walk without fatigue, yet you were so completely stubborn to go up eight fucking flights of stairs alone!"

Lorn listened to the tirade, too tired to argue, and honestly she made solid points. He would have been upset if the reverse happened. With his breathing under control and his limbs stilled, he was finally able to ask, "Why do you care?"

The angry footsteps stopped. "Why do I care?" she whispered. "Why do I care? Because you play right into their hands. They want you dead and you are acting exactly how they want, exactly how they predict you will act. Stop being noble. Stop being so predictable. You are a liability. You are a threat. They want you gone. Why do you think you are here?" Lorn tilted his head to the side and caught Lilit with a hand clamped over her mouth. She was never this chatty, this loose with information. The tight steel vault had cracked and with it came years of pent-up emotion.

"Who wants me gone?" Lorn stared at Lilit, his eyes trying to penetrate the stone wall of gray.

She pulled her hand away from her mouth. "Everyone, of course." Lilit attempted to mask her error with feigned bravado, but Lorn could see through it.

"List them, give me names. Who?"

"Lady Rasmina."

"I know that. She clearly threatened me in front of you. That is no surprise but who else?" Lorn pushed off from the bed and stood up facing her. "You say they, who *is* they? You know more but you won't say." He stepped towards Lilit. She was so close to revealing something, he could sense it.

Lilit only spends her time with Lord Aldrich who is under the guise of Cruvo, only he would make the most logical answer.

He answered for her. "Cruvo?"

Nothing about Lilit's appearance was meek, her features sharp and blade-like, her tone abrasive, her emotions a weapon used to flay others, but in this moment she seemed scared. Shrunken in on herself. Then it was wiped away, buried under years of her hardened training, years of schooling her thoughts and emotions.

"Yes, of course. Why do you think he sent you here? Do you think he wanted you to survive? He doesn't want you anywhere near Aza. He's hoping you will meet some unfortunate end, either by a creature or by Lady Rasmina. Stop playing into their hands. Stop acting like such an easy target." She unclenched her fingers and strode to the door.

Everything Lilit told him wasn't making sense, something wasn't adding up. "Wait."

Lilit paused before opening the door, her shoulders stiffened.

"Why send you? Why would Cruvo send someone to protect me? You saved me in the Silent Stretch."

"As punishment," she replied as she left. The door slammed shut. Questions trailed in her wake.

27

"The records from the Hall of Prophecies haunt me. I do not think I will have the strength to tell her."

Nivet's private journal.

The humid storm overhead had finally erupted as Aza and Reed reemerged from the Hall of Prophecies. Aza shakily climbed step after step, her thighs and mind tired from what she found. She was surprised she was able to hold her tongue and not break the sworn vow of silence. Her mind was reeling.

Reed shot concerned glances her way, and she could feel the brush of a stray finger as he hesitated to help her walk as if she was so frail she might collapse at any moment. No, she was not going to faint at the information. She was not going to falter. She just needed a moment. A moment of rest without looking over her shoulder every second expecting to see danger staring back at her.

When they reached the main floor, Roan appeared from kitchen and escorted them out the front door. Aza wished she could communicate her gratitude to this older woman but didn't want to make a fool of herself communicating in a language she didn't know. Instead, she merely turned to the woman and tried her best to offer a sincere smile. Roan understood what she was trying to convey and clasped her hands together and bowed her head to her fingertips. Aza mimicked the movement and when she raised her head found Roan's appreciative smile shining back. A few scribes were shuffling around, finishing up their last bites of dinner and cleaning up their plates. Aza took her time as they were escorted to the front door, watching the scribes animatedly communicate with one another their hands moving gracefully, their expressions lively. If only they had more time, Aza would have loved to stay here and study with them, to learn more about them and their language and why they chose this life.

Night had fully descended. A few stars winked through the heavy rain clouds, but otherwise there was no light to guide them. The Hall of Prophecies did not have any torches outside, but the light from within the building shone from the open door and windows provided a little light for her to see.

Anwin and Xira were not at their designated seats. Aza squinted trying to discern anything amongst the heavy rain and darkness. Odd shadows morphed and shaped from the surrounding jungle. Uncertainty clenched her stomach.

Roan stayed within the doorway and waved a goodbye. Aza saw her stiffen and her lips thinned as her eyes darted past Aza. Reed turned his head at the same time and jumped in front of her.

A ring of fire erupted around the Hall of Prophecies illuminating a squad of guards armed with bows, their arrows aimed directly at Reed and Aza. Torches behind each soldier kept their faces in shadow, like faceless monsters.

Aza's magic crackled around her, the energy building.

The storm echoed its agreement as a slash of lightning cut the sky.

Reed discreetly reached behind him and held Aza's wrist and gave a firm shake of his head. He was telling her to stand down, to hold her attack.

This entire journey had been a lesson in trust. She trusted Xira when atop The Fortress battlement, she needed to trust Reed's judgment. She pulled back her magic like an animal on a leash. It was difficult. Sweat crested her brow at the strain, but she withheld it.

A shadow stepped out of the line of soldiers, his braids creating a soft musical clinking as he approached. The soldier next to him moved the torch alongside, casting his handsome features into the light. Lord Sune gave a charismatic smile as if they were meeting over a cup of tea instead of being held at arrowpoint and threatened.

"Aza of the Well. I am deeply honored you are exploring Kreeha. I invite you to honor me by joining me at my palace in Cyran."

Reed tightened his grip on Aza, even though the magic building in her body should have pained him. "We appreciate the offer, Lord Sune, but unfortunately we have other matters to attend to," he said.

Lord Sune eyed Reed, as if he hadn't expected him to talk, a mere accessory to Aza. "Ah, Reed of Neria. It has been some time. I truly insist you join us." Lord Sune's baritone voice reverberated. He reached a sculpted arm out to one of his guards and gestured. The line of soldiers broke apart and Xira and Anwin were forced through, their hands and legs bound, and gags placed in their mouth. "I insist you join us at Cyran," he repeated. There was no mirth in his eyes, nothing remained of the charismatic, charming Lord, instead a ruthless ruler stood in his place.

Aza couldn't hold her tongue any longer. She broke free of Reed's hold and stepped in front of him. "And if I refuse?" Aza held her head up and straightened her posture. "I could destroy you and your soldiers in one swipe. So no, I believe you are at my mercy, Lord Sune."

He smirked and walked over to Anwin and Xira. "It's funny, the rumors one hears from around the five provinces. But for some reason, and I don't know why, but I am led to believe you don't have your magic any longer." Lord Sune yanked Anwin to her feet and pulled a scimitar from his sheath. He held Anwin against his chest, the scimitar against her throat. "Prove me wrong Aza. Decimate them all."

The scimitar pulled away from Anwin's throat. Lord Sune made a disapproving sound. "No magic, Xira." A guard adjacent to Lord Sune walked forward and knocked Xira in the head with the hilt of his scimitar. She collapsed to the ground in a heap.

Aza screamed and Anwin's eyes bulged, her protest muffled by her gag. Aza's magic crackled along her veins, roaring at her to release her fury. To let go. To demolish and kill everyone. But Reed for some unknown reason wanted her to hide it. She needed to trust him.

He stood silently next to her, his body tense, but his face relaxed, emotionless. It would be a tactical advantage for Aza to pretend her magic hadn't returned and discover Lord Sune's motives in Cyran.

"Time is running out Aza." The scimitar nicked the edge of Anwin's throat, the soft, white skin beading with blood. It trickled down, like a tear, cascading down her throat. Aza eye's danced between Anwin, Xira in a heap on the floor, and Reed silently standing beside her, letting her make her own choice.

"Fine, on one condition."

Lord Sune inclined his head, listening.

"You must release Xira and Anwin. We will not be bound. We will go willingly to the capital with you."

"Fair enough." Lord Sune elegantly cut the ties around Anwin's wrists and ankles. She ripped the gag from her mouth and glared.

Aza raced over to Xira and huddled over her. The guards tensed at her action but relaxed when they saw what she intended to do. Reed was next to her and helped to lift Xira. The three of them carried Xira off to the side and gently tapped the side of her face to see if she would wake.

She was unresponsive and Aza's fingers pulled away from Xira's head coated in blood. Aza was shaking in anger. Reed placed a cautious hand on Aza's shoulder. Her pulses of magic were erratic, and they couldn't lose their advantage. Everyone assumed her magic was gone, she needed to keep it hidden, locked away—for now.

"I will heal her," Reed whispered. "The damage is minor. She was only knocked out."

"Only," Aza seethed. She whipped her head over her shoulder and stared at Lord Sune who patiently waited for them to regroup.

Anwin brought Aza's focus back to their circled-up group. "It could have been worse." Anwin leaned closer in the semblance of a hug. She whispered into Aza's ear, "Lord Sune is not like Ravinder and Sarava. It is a show of strength. He is scared. Control your anger or it will control you."

Aza curled her fingers into her palms. Her eyes could not stop focusing on the trickle of blood on Anwin's throat, like a bloodied tear. Tears she did not want to shed at their expense, no more, not after what she discovered in the Hall of Prophecies. No more people needed to be sacrificed in this never-ending battle.

"There is little time," Lord Sune announced. "We must be going."

Aza schooled her features into a cool look of disdain, and carefully, painstakingly, locked away the magic which licked at her fingers, which called to her. The magic which wanted her to succumb to this rage—to succumb and finally let go. She lovingly locked it into a vault, reassuring it they would reunite again. She placed chains over the door and turned her back on it. When she had full control, she firmed her back, lifted Xira, and followed Lord Sune to the capital of Cyran.

****

~

The trip to Cyran was surprisingly uneventful. Hidden beyond the stone bridge were a retinue of guards and horses. As they descended further from the steep trail they were provided carriages. True to Aza's word, they did not try to leave. There were no threats of magic. Their weapons were confiscated, but Lord Sune promised their return upon their arrival in Cyran.

Aza stilled any emotion that threatened to break free. Anwin's whispered words ran through her head. She needed to see what he wished to discuss first, before she revealed her magic.

Although she was loath to admit it, riding in a carriage to the capital was a welcome reprieve. Lord Sune suggested she and the Nerians be separated, but Aza argued against it, claiming they would hold true to their word. If they doubted her, she offered to take an oath binding. She couldn't be separated from them, not after what she learned.

The views were beautiful. The lush, humid jungle, the greenery shrouding and cocooning them. Farther from the sand dunes, Kreeha was abundant in rivers. They sliced through the land, and she often felt the carriage bob and jolt as they crossed over makeshift bridges, some made of wood, others sandstone. The journey wasn't long. The Hall of Prophecies was located roughly a day's ride outside of Cyran.

Xira finally stirred. It was the first time Aza had seen her discomposed. She groggily sat up, assessed the situation when Reed answered her unasked question, "We are going to Cyran."

"I see," she responded in a clipped tone.

After that there was no more discussion, only cutting glances.

The time to ask Reed about the Hall of Prophecies and the scribes had passed, her questions soured, turning to ash on her lips. She longed for her optimism before they entered, before Lord Sune had captured them. But the dread in her stomach only grew, pulling her down like an anchor until she was underwater with doubt and uncertainty drowning her.

~

* * *

As they neared the capital Lord Sune aimed for discretion ordering the Nerians and Aza to remain within the carriage. Commotion of Aza's appearance would spread potentially alerting others to her presence —like Astaroth or Cruvo. Maybe Lord Sune was working independently if he didn't want Astaroth to know they were in Kreeha.

Cyran was beautiful. Aza found it challenging to compare each capital, but they each held their own beauty. The Hall of Prophecies was a small prelude to what Cyran would look like. Sandstone buildings, multiple stories tall were packed together with lush plants crawling over the buildings like they were a part of the architecture. The buildings were angular with the rooftops in flat, straight lines and gated terraces along the top. Colorful flowers and deep green, leafy plants spilled over the rooftop in greetings. Vines curled over pillars and walkways.

The capital was never quiet, along with the bustle of people and carts going to and fro, the roaring of rivers raced under them. Xira had explained the geography of Kreeha to her and Aza tried to compare it with her geography lessons with Oron back in El'en.

Kreeha was situated in a grid with small rivers separating each of the city sections. The castle was at the head of the rivers, separate from the rest of the land with the four rivers funneling alongside it. Each district ran along the length of the river with bridges connecting the four districts together. The four districts being the market, entertainment, military, and hearth. The three rivers separating the districts were the Gold, Silver, and Iron. The Gold River cuts through the middle while the Silver lays to the left of the palace and Iron to the right.

"The legend is the ruler of Kreeha should always have generosity in their left hand, but defense in their right and gold through their core." Xira rolled her eyes. It was the most Aza had heard her speak since she roused.

Although they were being forced to travel to Cyran, she wanted to get out and explore the city. To go along the terraced rooftops and amongst the three rivers and see the greenery fight to claim dominance in this beautiful city. Aza tried to feign nonchalance as they rode through the city but each time, she would sneak a look out of their carriage window and marvel at the sights.

Xira, Reed and Anwin collectively fought the smiles on their faces. Aza blew out a worried breath. She thought they would be disappointed in her excitement, but they weren't. They understood her desire to look upon the beauties of their world.

The castle of Cyran did not disappoint. The architecture of the city was mimicked in the castle, but it was like comparing the beauty of a feather to the entirety of the bird. The castle sprawled on its own, bridges at each point connecting it to the land and the rivers slicing through it. It was a model of geometric proportions with pleasing sharp angles, and crisp corners, each level stacked on top of the other, the sandstone edges dripping with greenery and lush flowers that were gilded in the setting sun. Water poured off the highest level and fell in a graceful line down the sides of the building into the rivers on each side. Traces of gold lined doorways, bridges, and Aza caught glints of it on each level.

The carriage came to a halt and the guards ushered them outside. Lord Sune greeted them and gestured to the guards. Most fell away to assist with other matters and only two stayed. Despite the days travel, Lord Sune appeared as regal and arrogant as always. His thin braids were pulled back, revealing his strong jaw, and umber skin limned in the evening sun. He was dressed in the Kreehan fashion with loose robes draped expertly over his muscular form.

"Welcome to Cyran, Aza." He smiled. It was one of pride, and glory at his home. Aza couldn't deny his cockiness. For once it was warranted.

"Follow me. We have much to discuss."

Aza startled as a guard sidled next to her. She recognized him. The tan skin and blond hair. She squinted her eyes and tried to figure out where she knew him from.

Feeling her assessing eyes, the guard quirked his head at her and furrowed his brows.

It clicked. She snapped her fingers at the revelation and shouted, "Hanu!" He was Lord Sune's guard at El'en.

He appeared uneasy at her revelation and shifted from one foot to another.

The Nerians and other guards cast a quizzical look their way before Aza waved them off.

"No bad blood. Not yet, anyway," she whispered, trying to put him at ease. Aza couldn't explain what she was feeling. When Lord Sune first captured them she was so angry she could have burned an entire village down, but the anger had turned into an almost violent giddiness. Her magic had returned, and no one could hold her back, not anymore.

Hanu gave a nervous smile and then schooled his features into something more appropriate for a guard. "Well met, Aza."

They trailed Lord Sune through the castle and Hanu lowered his voice. "I do apologize for us meeting under these circumstances."

Aza tried her best to study him out of the corner of her eyes. He seemed sincere. She couldn't sense any ulterior motives, nor sneaking suspicions. She gave a dismissive wave. "This? Ach, not your fault."

Hanu suppressed a chuckle and disguised it as a cough. The other guard working alongside Hanu widened his eyes at him. Hanu scrambled to compose himself. "I must admit, my Lady, you are not what I expected."

"And what did you expect?"

They turned a corner and Hanu paused for a moment to consider his response. "Someone terrifying."

"Who says I'm not?"

Hanu clamped his mouth shut.

They halted in front of a beautiful double door, the outside painted with gold whorls and swirls against the dark oak. A faint hint of jasmine wafted through the air.

"Let us discuss here," Lord Sune said. He opened the doors and Aza gasped. It was beautiful. Delicate colorful linens were draped over rich, plush chairs and couches.

Hanu and the other guard were left outside to guard the room.

Xira unceremoniously plopped onto one of the couches, grabbed a slice of mango from an ornate bowl and popped it in her mouth. "Delicious as always Lord Sune. No hard feelings about the head wound either." Her words were light, but Aza saw the fire in her eyes.

After Xira's entrance, everyone found a seat. Anwin and Aza shared a couch, and Reed situated himself on a teak chair with Lord Sune sitting opposite.

"Would you have accompanied me back to Cyran if I did not use force?" Lord Sune licked his lips nervously and narrowed his eyes at them.

Xira casually shrugged and grabbed another mango, chewing thoughtfully.

"What would you like to talk about? If we were in real danger you would have alerted the other five provinces to our whereabouts, and they would be here now. Which means you either want our cooperation or something we have." Xira leaned forward, placing her forearms on her thighs. "Your show of force was exactly that, a farce to make us feel desperate and trapped. But you should know better. We would never go with you willingly, unless we wanted to hear what you have to offer. So please go ahead and enlighten us."

Lord Sune moved to the edge of his chair. "Very well, Xira of Neria. You are right. I would like to work together." Lord Sune's eyes flashed to Aza. "I should be talking to you. I would like to strike a deal with you. You, *Aza,* are our salvation."

Aza looked questioningly over at Xira who gave a shrug. It was her choice whether she wanted to lead the conversation or give the reins to Xira.

Aza took a steadying breath, her fingers played over the elegant golden embroidery on the linen of the couch. She double checked her magic was locked and secured tightly within. "And would you say, *Lord Sune,*" her voice dripping with disdain over his name, "that the best way to get me to listen is through threatening my companions?" She sized him up, not backing down.

Chagrined, he lifted his hands in mock supplication. "Would you have accompanied me otherwise?"

"Yes! I would have. Not a smart way to start a positive working relationship is it? How can I trust you and why would I even assist you?" She exhaled. She was getting too heated, and her magic could slip in anger.

Sune ran a hand through his braids. "I heard rumors of a group traveling and a sort of fearsome magic. I had you tailed and when I discovered it was you, I had to act quickly. I had no idea what to expect. You had vanished from Lord Aldrich's court and now were traversing the five provinces with a group of Nerians, who have a fearsome reputation I might add. On top of that, Verta's court has spread vicious rumors of you infiltrating The Fortress and threatening

Lord Ravinder and Lady Sarava. How you managed to sneak into such a well-guarded palace is beyond me. So yes, I thought I would need to persuade you through threat of violence. I have no idea where your allegiance lies."

"Then why try to sway me? Why try to capture me and persuade me to work for you or with you? Why expose yourself to such a risk?"

"Because all of Kreeha will die if I do not."

Aza clamped her mouth shut and leaned back into the couch. She calculated his intentions. She would not be so trusting again—to fall for some simple lies.

"Explain," Xira answered for her.

Lord Sune ran a hand over his jaw. His lordly mask fell, and a hint of fear flickered over his arrogant facade.

"What do you know of the goddesses and gods?"

28

"Strange stories have emerged from Gara. Are they true or mere rumors?"
    Cruvo's private journal

It had taken a full week for Lorn to recover his strength. He did not trust himself to attempt magic again, but he could feel it there—always present. Along with his recovery, the memory of that day returned to him in pieces. He clearly remembered the day, the information Pearl disclosed at the Crossroads, and the encounter with the corrupted mountain lion, but after that it came to him in jagged bursts like a dream he couldn't quite remember. Memories of people passed through his mind, their faces blurred, voices unrecognizable. Lorn remembered the flow of power, the vague numbness to his surroundings, his only focus on healing Pearl.

Since he was confined to his room for his recovery, he didn't have to interact with Lilit often. When he did leave his room, he dutifully knocked on her door and she accompanied him for a small walk around the courtyards. They didn't dare speak about anything from the Crossroads, uncertain as to who could be listening.

He veered away from discussing sensitive topics. The rare opportunity for Lilit to be talkative was gone, the moment had passed.

Lorn was forbidden from physical exertion for two weeks by the palace physicians. Lilit was unbearable because of it. Lacking a sparring partner, she practiced alone in the mornings while Lorn rested in his room.

Instead, he frequented the library with a slew of research to do. He even snuck a few books out of the library to read in private. There were strict rules in place to prevent him from taking the books, but his boredom was reaching insurmountable heights.

One day, he persuaded Flint and Maline, who oversaw the integrity of the library among many countless duties, and they reluctantly approved. Permission for each book was required. Certain copies were limited, and he was unable to take them to the sanctuary of his room, but most were approved.

With multiple research topics to pursue, Lorn was voracious. He read late into the night and trained his body in-between. He stayed within his rooms, attempting to regain his strength. When the research became too much and his eyes strained from staring at the pages, the words blurring together, he completed small exercises.

During his trips to the library Lilit begrudgingly helped, but they did not broach the topic from before. Lorn pulled any books relating to magic mined in ore, the gods and goddesses, the strange, corrupted animal, but all the books proved fruitless, skirting around the topics. It was whispered about between the lines, hinted at and Lorn began to imagine he was making this up that there was no allusion to these topics and his addled mind was forming connections where none existed. It seemed like these topics were wiped from history.

When all else failed, he researched the nuances of magic—light magic in particular. After Pearl's explanation, he was confident that his light magic had been the burning sensation she experienced— what purified her body from the corruption. A terrifying ordeal but something that was necessary to spare her life.

Breaking his silence with Lilit, Lorn had to ask. "You mentioned in the forest that you read how light magic was connected with healing. Where did you learn that?"

She flicked her eyes up at him from the book she was reading and gave a succinct answer. "In El'en."

"Yes, but where? In most of the books I research there isn't any depth or mention of what you said."

"I read it in a book, like I said." She snapped hers closed.

"But what book, what was the title? Was it in El'en's library?" Lorn needed to know. He didn't want to spend more time sitting in a library chasing his own tail if the answer was in front of him.

Lilit leaned back in her chair and crossed her arms. "It was a book.

In El'en." She shrugged. "I don't remember much else."

Although Lorn was loathe to admit it, he had become used to Lilit's presence like a spur stuck to his foot.

"You are lying," he stated. It was plain as day. She wasn't disclosing everything she knew. While good at schooling her features into an unreadable scowl, Lorn knew that something was off.

"Leave it."

But he couldn't, Lorn couldn't leave this nagging feeling. After two weeks with no answers, he craved to unravel this mystery, like a thread he couldn't help but pull. "Why was this your punishment?" he blurted out. Lorn stilled and watched her cycle through different emotions, anger, fear, disbelief, sadness.

Instead of answering, Lilit stood up and left.

He couldn't believe it. Lilit, who valued her duty above all else, had left him alone in the library. She had just admonished him two weeks ago because of his foolishness.

He shook his head in defeat and returned to his research.

The tap of heels on wood caused him to look up.

"My, my, Ambassador. What did you say to her to rile her up so?" Lady Rasmina ran her fingers over the books on Lorn's desk. Several gold rings winked back at him. A white gown covered her lithe arm and flowed down into a tight floor length gown. Blue gems encircled her throat, sparkling as she moved.

Lorn stiffened. He had not seen her since the morning he had awoken after the incident. While the flames of her fury had been banked, they were not gone.

Lorn wanted to snap at her in response, but he knew that would prove fruitless. He was an ambassador, he needed to act as such. Politics and courtly manners were a priority. He wasn't the first person to be mocked openly with cutting words.

"To what do I owe the pleasure, Lady Rasmina?"

"My advisors encourage me to show you more of the Garan province. I have been a careless host it seems."

Lorn eyed her, calculating. "Of course. I am at your disposal."

She pushed away from Lorn's table and folded her arms in front of her chest. "And since you have such a proclivity for endangering my daughters, I will be the one to show you Gara. Be ready to depart in two days. We leave for the coast."

Before she left the library, she paused, her hand clasping the doorframe. "One more thing, I know you will ask Maline or Flint for permission, but no, you cannot bring any of these books on the trip."

Certain he was alone Lorn loosened a quiet curse. Either Lady Rasmina knew what he was researching, or she was trying to stall his efforts. Either way, he wasn't pleased. He wasn't sure how long this trip would last or how long Lady Rasmina meant to keep him indisposed. Lilit wouldn't be pleased either. His skills would be put to the test, he did not envy spending multiple days within Lady Rasmina's presence.

~

Lorn found himself journeying alongside Lady Rasmina's retinue of guards and soldiers accompanying her to her coastal retreat. Lilit remained tight-lipped. All of their camaraderie and work he accomplished gaining her trust and confidence had been extinguished like a bug crushed beneath a boot. She reverted to the sullen bodyguard without any of her biting comments. He pictured Lilit as a building, her once solid foundation now riddled with cracks. His presence and Gara was eroding her.

Lorn pushed his hair back and huffed a breath. He didn't want to corrupt Lilit's stony veneer, but he needed answers and right when he was close to discovering something she pushed away. What would he be willing to do to understand? Would it be risking her eventual breakage? To have her self-control crumble away and be left to scramble in the wake of the destruction.

The dense woods ambled past them as he tried to banish the thoughts of Lilit spiraling, a trained dog finally succumbing to madness. She was a force to reckon with and Lorn could not imagine someone of her talents in weaponry and battle being loosed with her veneer of self-control and restraint finally cracked.

They rode in nimble carriages, the construction light and ingenuous, allowing them to travel quickly over the paths while not succumbing to the muddy pockets. The road north was windy, climbing small hills and rain-soaked mountains to only descend the other side.

The carriages were small, sized to fit only two to three people. Lilit was sequestered to his, but often she preferred the torrential downpour outside to his company within the carriage. The most she could muster was only an hour or two before Lorn could see her eyes twitching around the cabin like a caged animal. She would abandon him, sit astride the carriage, and come back covered in rain, her hair lank with pieces falling aimlessly plastered to her face. Her gray eyes were no longer deadened, rather they embodied sharp, awakened liveliness like the steel of her blade.

The mountains were unlike the Nerian mountain range, their cold temperatures unbearable. The Garan mountains were wet and slick, their sides cascading into beautiful and dangerous waterfalls. Their carriages were narrow and their horses surefooted, but Lorn held his breath whenever they wound around the steep mountain peaks, the fall below vast and filled with sharpened rocks at the bottom, welcoming a wandering traveler's unfortunate demise.

Alone most of the time, Lorn kept his eyes glued to the window of his carriage, searching for any sign of what they had encountered before. Corruption is what his mind echoed to him later, the word like a familiar warning from a time long past. But nothing emerged from the woods, or the peak of the steep mountain faces they traversed. There were no threads of disease throughout the land, the diseased mountain lion a strange outlier.

On the second night of travel, Lorn fell into a familiar dream. A steep cliff face greeted him, and as he stood high above the crashing waves, soft stretches of pliant grass welcomed him in the breeze. He searched for her, the familiar presence of a goddess in his midst. The hairs on the back of his neck prickled and he turned. Issi was before him, as beautiful and radiant as last he saw her. He imagined each of the gods and goddesses exhibited such raw beauty, but something about Issi's struck him, like the somber chord on a violin or the lone star shining in a nighttime of darkness.

His anger at the goddess had dimmed. Lorn couldn't deny that she had saved him. If he hadn't woken in time in the Silent Stretch, he would have succumbed to the wraith or the corrupted mountain lion.

A cobalt dress twined down her pale skin, hitting the tops of her bare feet. Her hair hung loosely, the pale blonde strands blowing in the breeze.

"I guess I should thank you," he said.

Her lips thinned in consideration. She stared at him, the eerie blue unsettling. Even here in this dream, energy radiated off of her, pure power coming in waves like ether gathering in storm clouds.

"You did well defeating one of Astaroth's infected minions."

His eyebrows rose in question. "Astaroth?"

"Yes." She flicked her hand in a dismissive manner. "The Corruption as your people put it."

"What is it?" Lorn asked.

Issi's eyes trailed up his body, both disinterest and interest warring in her features as she took him in. "Not a what. A who. She is a," Issi heaved a sigh, "*goddess* in some twisted sense of the word."

"Is she connected to the Hinterlands?"

"In a way."

"Speak plain, Goddess. I am tired of riddles and vague answers."

While talking with him, Issi betrayed an almost bored, nonchalant demeanor. At his harsh words, she sharpened, her features turning rigid and unyielding, her eyes hardening to icy points. She marched to him, her height and aura infringing on him. "Fine, hunter." The goddess paced around Lorn, stating each warning like a stab in the air. "Be wary of Lady Rasmina. Do not trust Cruvo. Aza is alive and well. Is there more you demand to know?"

Lorn wanted to laugh at the absurdity. Most of this information was not revelatory. How could she deem herself as helpful? But he was thankful for the information regarding Aza. It brought him immense relief to know that Aza was faring well. From Lilit's prior declaration and his own suspicions, Lorn didn't trust Cruvo or Lady Rasmina. Her information was lacking.

"What is Lady Rasmina doing under the mountains? What is she searching for?"

Issi stopped her relentless circling and stopped in front of him. She pursed her lips together in thought.

"Can you give me anything helpful?" he asked.

"Even the best of intentions can be waylaid. We are each in control of our own destiny."

"Why is she stealing people? What is she trying to find in the mountains?"

"A solution," Issi answered.

"A solution?" Lorn repeated dumbly.

"A solution to a problem that has plagued her." Issi strode away from him to the rolling green hills. The wind whipped at her dress and hair, and she looked like someone born of a storm.

"How is that going to help me?" he shouted.

She glanced over her shoulder and answered, "If you are smart enough, you might discover the answer while on this trip."

Issi was leaving and Lorn blurted before she could go. "Is Aza truly okay?"

Her eyes softened for a moment, the icy veneer of the goddess melting away. "Yes. For now." Amongst the rolling hills and storm clouds Issi vanished as if she had never stepped foot in his dream. Lorn woke groggy and disgruntled.

29

Nivet's private journal.

They talked long into the night with trays of food being brought in by servants, beds of rice, ripe fruit, along with spiced chickpeas and decadent sauced chicken. The aroma nearly made Aza weep. The past weeks of travel had been tough, their food merely consisting of travel rations and whatever animals they could hunt. Their portions were small, and her body had grown lean.

They had discovered Lord Sune was working alone. When they had traveled to El'en, he and his court had uncovered information. While Aza was embroiled in her own affairs, Lord Sune discovered the treachery of Lord Ravinder and Lady Sarava and their alignment with Astaroth.

As they lounged on the plush cushions and vibrant linens, Aza pieced together the tapestry Lord Sune wove with his voice. He was operating with missing information, not fully grasping what Astaroth was, only that something malignant and dark was working with the Vertan court. Lord Sune and his court had retreated to Kreeha, and as they traveled through Verta, they could feel the undercurrent of disease present. They returned to Kreeha and studied anything they could get their hands on. When he heard rumors of the Nerians and Aza traveling into their borders, heading to the Hall of Prophecies, he had acted out of pure desperation.

"I do apologize to you all," Lord Sune professed. His hand pulled at his face as he grimaced. "Looking back, it was rash. But it was the only thing I could think of. If your lack of magic was true, it would be the only way I could persuade you to return with me to Cyran and listen."

Aza heard the frantic desperation in his tone, the urge to save his people and protect Kreeha from what was about to happen.

"So what deal do you have for us?" Xira crossed her arms over her chest and stared at Lord Sune as if trying to unveil his intentions.

"I—"

A disturbance sounded outside the doors, and they all turned their heads to look.

"Sir, you cannot enter this room."

"Hanu, I can enter any room I wish."

A muffled huff of breath sounded, and the door cracked open. A thin wisp of a man entered, with his black hair slicked back into a bun at the top of his head and stray strands ran free. He readjusted his glasses and froze when he saw who was in the room.

"Sune, I heard the rumors, but I did not want it to be true. What have you done?" Ryu, Lord Sune's consort, ran a beleaguered hand down his face in exasperation. "I deeply apologize for whatever behavior he has committed." And Ryu did something that surprised Aza, he gave a deep bow.

He remained in that position until Aza cleared her throat and spoke, "Thank you, Ryu." He straightened, shook his head, found an empty chair and sat down.

"I had no other choice, Ryu," Lord Sune explained.

Ryu pressed his lips together in doubt and gave a noncommittal noise in his throat.

Lord Sune shook his head and resumed his prior statement. "I would like for us to work together."

Reed interjected, "What would that entail?"

"I understand the Nerian province does not involve themselves in the other provinces, but we need to align ourselves. This evil will pervade everything and will reach up to you within the safety of your mountains. It will reach us. It will get us all." Lord Sune clasped Ryu's hand with affection. "You are powerful warriors, and clearly you know more than us, otherwise why would Aza of the Well be traveling with you? Call your warriors down from the mountain, announce that we are aligned together for the war to come, because war is coming."

The Nerians remained silent, each regarding the other and silently appraising Lord Sune and Ryu.

Ryu heaved a sigh. "I understand you are hesitant, especially under whatever circumstances he has brought you here. However, I have been leading the study on the ancient texts, trying to glean any information we can find. This information is obscured, destroyed, and deeply difficult to decipher with the remains left, but are you aware of the gods and goddesses' existence roughly a thousand years ago?"

Aza attempted to give nothing away and schooled her features into a bored expression, even though her heart was racing. They were sitting across from someone who was part goddess. Surely they must know this.

Ryu examined his fingers, collecting his thoughts. "I know it sounds fantastical, but the gods and goddesses are not mere myths we discuss in stories over campfires. They existed. They lived. More importantly, they destroyed." Ryu's eyes flashed to Aza. "Our power is a small fraction of theirs; imagine the strength of a raindrop compared to that of an entire storm. That is the difference between us and them. They walked and ruled Ithilia and followed their own whims. If they wanted to raze a town, they would. Most viewed MagicBlessed as mere toys to play with, toys to discard when they were bored."

Ryu squeezed Sune's hand. "Please say something. With you sitting there, staring, it is quite intimidating I will admit. It sounds like a fanciful story told to children at bedtime, but I swear it is true."

Aza looked to Xira, Reed, and Anwin and the four of them collectively nodded, echoing the same sentiment. "We know."

Ryu sighed with relief and leaned back into his couch. "Good, because I feared that would be the most difficult part to convince you of their existence." He turned to Lord Sune. "Have you told them about the Hinterlands?"

He shook his head. "Not yet." Lord Sune trailed over Aza's appearance lingering on her silver hair.

"We know what has been revealed in El'en. The Hinterlands is unstable—morphing and consuming any neighboring villages," Aza answered. She shifted uncomfortably, her fingers nervously fiddling with the beautiful embroidery.

"Yes, that's exactly right." Ryu leaned forward, his face lighting up. He was a person who consumed knowledge like water and although the situation was grim, the revelations were something amazing for him to discover. "The word you used, unstable, is exactly right. If we let it continue, it will devour Ithilia. Since your...appearance, our researchers have discovered its volatility. Like its foundation has been pulled away and it is situated on unstable ground. We have linked the Hinterlands appearance with the disappearance of the gods and goddesses."

Ryu unlinked his hand with Lord Sune and took a hearty gulp of wine. "We believe we must banish the Hinterlands. It cannot continue in its unstable form. We will all suffer, and the Well is being tainted. Our magic will drain first, then our provinces will lose their sources of food. Water will dry up. It will be a long suffering and a long death. Not to mention the foul creatures that emerge from the Hinterlands preying on any surrounding towns. We believe you are the key to banishing the Hinterlands, Aza." He nervously adjusted his glasses and continued, "However, if you banish the Hinterlands, based on our research, we believe the gods and goddesses will return."

"It is a gamble between certain death and uncertain death. Who knows what will happen when the Hinterlands is gone," Lord Sune said.

This information wasn't new for Aza or the Nerians, but they sat and patiently listened. Aza was uncertain of what she could share with them, of how trustworthy the Kreehans were. They had brought them here under threat of death, but they were desperate. Desperation made people do unspeakable acts.

Xira popped another piece of mango in her mouth and chewed. She rose to her feet, pacing over to the curved window. Coming to a decision, she turned around, leaned back, and placed her hands against the windowsill. "What if I told you, we know of all this. And we are already trying to fix it." Xira flicked her head at Aza. "Aza will banish the Hinterlands and when she does the gods and goddesses will return. We will need to be prepared."

A weight settled in her stomach. Aza knew her destiny, she knew what Fate had already written about in the Hall of Prophecies. She only needed to be strong enough to accomplish it. They needed to return to Neria.

Lord Sune let out a long whistle. "Where have you received your information?"

Xira shrugged. "We cannot divulge all of our secrets. But we can work together."

Ryu stood. "How can we help?"

Lord Sune joined him and placed a gentle hand on his shoulder. "It is late and they have not had time to rest. Let them sleep and we can discuss more tomorrow. Rooms have been arranged for each of you. We will guide you. Anything you need, feel free to reach out and ask."

They climbed flights of stairs located on the interior of the palace. The center of the palace was hollow with greenery and a small waterfall trickling into a pond below. Glimpses of gold, yellow, and white darted amongst the water with lily pads protecting the fish. Sweat dripped down Aza's back. The palace was built with a refreshing breeze, but the humidity of Cyran was weighing down on her. She eyed Lord Sune and Ryu's loosely draped fabrics, envious of their clothing. In this environment she needed something to wear that wouldn't cling to her skin.

The fresh scent of blooming flowers and vibrant greenery enlivened her invoking a feeling of safety. At the top floor Sune and Ryu guided them to their separate rooms. Aza hesitated. She did not realize the privacy of her own room would be so isolating. The past weeks she had spent nestled in between her companions. A sharp worry spiked.

"We will discuss more in the morning. Please let us or the servants know if you need anything."

Aza rested her head against the doorframe in exhaustion, but a single thought came to her. "A moment, Lord Sune." She forced herself to straighten her posture for only a moment more and slid her eyes to his. "Do you have any news on Lorn of Verta."

Sune and Ryu shared a hesitant look. "Last we heard is that he is in Gara."

"Gara?" Reed questioned.

Aza pushed the tiredness away and examined her companions' faces. They were surprised by this.

"Do you know why he is there?" Xira quickly retraced her steps and stood next to Aza.

Ryu shook his head sadly. "Unfortunately no, but he is in Lighthold."

Aza didn't know what that meant or how to decipher it. But it clearly meant something to the Nerians. Each of their faces drained of color.

Lord Sune folded his hands together. "I am sorry I do not have more information. I will try to learn more if possible."

Aza gave a grateful nod and watched as they retreated. As soon as they disappeared from the hallway, Xira, Reed and Anwin, pushed Aza into her room.

They shut the door and Aza barely had time to take in the extravagance of the room before her companions answered her unasked questions. and voiced their own.

"Why would he be in Lighthold?" Anwin voiced.

Reed paced around the room. "He could be looking for Aza. Knowing their connection, I doubt he would let her capture go."

Xira countered. "But why Gara? He saw us take Aza. He knows it was Nerians. If anything, he should be heading west towards Kreeha, not Gara."

"Unless he was tasked with something else," Anwin suggested.

"I don't want to sound arrogant, but I don't believe Lorn would refuse to come after me," Aza said and shrugged.

"No, Anwin's right." Xira's eyes sparkled as she latched onto the idea. "What if someone stressed to him the importance of going to Gara."

Aza ignored their pointed looks. She understood of whom they spoke, of who they referred to. She couldn't accept it, didn't want to accept that Cruvo would mislead her friend like that. "It could be his fault," she mumbled.

"Are you still defending him?" Xira seethed. "After what he has done? How he has tricked you."

Aza couldn't understand why Xira's words were laced with so much emotion and anger.

Aza stood toe to toe with Xira and used her height to try and intimidate the captain. She trusted them, but it was infuriating to have them withhold information even though they were doing it to protect her. She found she didn't care. "I understand he has capitalized on my 'melding' as you put it, Reed. But that is all." Aza fought to keep her words measured. "So, what else has he done?"

Xira loosened a frustrated grunt and backed away. Reed placed a consoling hand on her shoulder and reassured her. "Xira, she does not understand, she does not know of the atrocities."

Aza's glance lanced Reed. Atrocities? What atrocities?

"This is not the time," he whispered.

While Reed calmed down Xira and Anwin guided Aza away. "I do not claim to understand your connection with the God of the Hunt, but please understand Xira is trying to protect you. In time, when you discover what we have learned, we will be here for you."

Aza took a deep breath and distracted herself by looking around the elegant room. It was fashioned in the same style as the rest of the Kreehan palace, with elegant, geometric design and lush greenery. She peered through the curved doorway into a green tiled bathroom and clawfoot bath. Gold attachments, knobs, and levers glinted back at her. They all needed rest and this new discovery of Lorn's location only added to the additional stress of the journey. Aza did not want to defend Cruvo especially when it came at the expense of Lorn. But it was hard to diminish the time she spent with him, how he shaped her magic, the power that surged through her when in proximity, like her very blood sang in his presence. To dismantle that illusion and discover it was all a lie, or that he was preying on her susceptible feelings was crushing, but she could not let herself dwell on it further.

"Lorn. I care about Lorn," Aza repeated. They regrouped and Aza gave a forgiving nod to Xira who accepted. "What does it mean that Lorn is in Lighthold?"

"We are not sure, but it can't be good. Lady Rasmina has an... interesting history. I do not envy his position." Xira looked to each of her companions. "It is late. We need proper rest. All of us." Her eyes lingered on Anwin. "I know you want answers about Lorn. Hopefully we will discover more in the morning from Lord Sune and Ryu."

They departed and Aza was left by herself. It was disconcerting.

Her hands fidgeted with the edge of her pants, plucking at the dirty fabric. She undressed and enjoyed the luxury of a warm bath, taking her time scrubbing each crevice, which seemed to hold an impossible amount of dirt and grime. She emptied the water once and refilled it so she could relax in a clean bath.

When finished, she dabbed her wrists with rose oil and found a thoughtful bundle of clothes deposited on her bed. The clothes were fashioned in the Kreehan style. Aza gasped. Beside the clothes were her sword and dagger, a gift from Lorn from what felt like a lifetime ago. She reverently ran her fingers over the stardust gems and remembered what Lorn had told her, how they were mined deep within Gara, the stones prized for their ever-changing color like tiny galaxies were encapsulated within.

She placed the weapons on a nearby side table, its beautiful teak wood engraved with animals and vines.

The Kreehan robes and pants fit beautifully and were a pale cream color. It contrasted with her dark skin and made her radiant. She was thankful the weeks of dirt had been scrubbed from her body and her stomach had a filling meal. The canopy bed had soft white linen dangling from the bars up top. She brushed aside the sheer curtain and stood with the back of her knees hitting the mattress. She held her arms out at the side and let her body fall weightless against the bed. The soft mattress met her worn body and she sighed.

"Lorn, promise me you will be safe," she whispered, a prayer to an empty and lonely room.

30

"Why is Lady Rasmina bringing Lorn to Holdsfast? If I had any concern for his well-being I would advise against it. However, I wish to see what unfolds."
Cruvo's private journal

The wind whipped Lorn's hair in his face shielding his eyes from the magnificent view. Where Iyera's coastline was soft like the comfort of a pillow, Gara's was hard each edge of the beach and sand brutally assaulted from the riotous waves casting down. It was primal and beautiful like the hypnotic flames of an inferno or the devastating beauty of a storm.

Houses dotted the coast in defiance of their potential destruction. Lorn understood now why people did not sail the Northern Sea. Its capricious waves could easily capsize any ship willing to try. And those mad enough to dare test the gods and goddesses and survive told their tales well into their cups at other taverns. The wild Northern Sea was rumored to calm in other seasons, but not during winter.

The sea crashed in anger against the cliffside. Pieces of rock broke off, falling into the water. The wind pierced through the slats of the carriage, his meager clothing seeming unsubstantial against such chill. Storm clouds gathered overhead, a deep cobalt blue.

The carriages passed by the quaint houses and ambled up the road to a magnificent mansion. It dwarfed the other buildings and Lorn felt a shred of embarrassment at the excess of wealth in an otherwise moderate fishing village.

The citizens of Holdsfast appeared to be shaped and spat out by the Northern Sea—cords of muscle bulged from their varying body shapes both thin and stout. He watched them, their hair and beards plastered with sea salt, haul their catches of fish, crabs, and lobster. They eyed the passing carriages warily, their hollow faces expressing what Lorn feared—this town had experienced trauma.

Although the mansion in Holdsfast could not be farther from the grand tree in Lighthold, it held a similar austerity to it—set apart, with very little warmth. It was foreboding, a dominant blight on this small town. The behemoth marble structure was framed by dual pillars and a grand staircase leading to the interior. The carriages pulled up to the grounds, which were immaculately trimmed, the trees and flowers arranged in neat rows.

Once parked, Lady Rasmina strode inside without a backward glance to Lorn or Lilit, leaving a guard to escort them to their rooms.

The interior was as beautiful and cold as the exterior. There were beautiful pieces of ornate artwork and furniture but held little warmth, like the family gathered the collection of pieces out of duty. There were no portraits. Lorn couldn't imagine Lady Rasmina's three daughters as children playing in such a cold place. Lorn imagined the home had never experienced laughter.

Lorn paused, entering his room. It was difficult to adjust to such grandeur compared to the quaintness of his beloved cottage in Verta. A decadent oak bed frame commanded the room with the plush bed piled with pillows. A dresser sat opposite the bedwith a doorway leading into the bathroom. Lorn heaved a breath and collapsed onto the bed. Traveling in a carriage, while convenient, left him sore and stiff.

A servant had informed Lorn that they would be dining in the formal room within two hours. Lorn washed quickly and rested. The house did not welcome him.

~

Lilit remained tight-lipped as they descended to the formal dining room. She had hardly uttered a word on their journey, the sudden outburst in the Lighthold library a rare occurrence that Lorn spent too much of his idle time trying to dismantle.

His movements were stiff as he gripped the stair banister tightly. Lorn did not envy interacting with Lady Rasmina—he needed to steel himself.

Dinner was a surprisingly boring affair with Lady Rasmina distant, staring absentmindedly out the window at the storm, rain pounding against the glass. Lorn still regarded her warily and he barely remembered consuming his food. It fell to ash in his mouth. He mentally prepared himself throughout the dinner, waiting with bated breath, for her witty, barbed remarks. When a fork scraped against a plate, Lorn prevented his eyes from darting like a rabbit in a trap.

Seeming to understand she was not contributing to the conversation, Lady Rasmina began idle small talk. Lorn learned about the manor. It seemed to be a fond destination for the ruling family, the mansion often a secluded reprieve from the pressures of Lighthold. By the time the fruit compote dessert was served, Lorn was itching to race back upstairs. Even the dormant power under his skin crackled at his restless energy.

As the softened, warmed apple reached his mouth an older woman barged into the room. The sudden intrusion snapped Lady Rasmina out of her fogged state. Although wrinkles lined the woman's face and her hair was cut in a severe bob, the entirety coated in silver, there was a spryness to her. The woman pursed her lips at the sight of Lady Rasmina with two Garan guards trailing the older woman.

"My apologies, my Lady. We understood our orders, but she somehow made it past us."

The woman harrumphed in response. She cockily eyed the guard up and down and turned her nose up at him, bringing her attention back to Lady Rasmina.

"I will escort her out."

"If you know what's good for you, you will release that hand from my upper arm. Not too long ago, you soldiers had to protect me and now you are escorting me out like I am some frail woman who cannot dispatch you where you stand." Her demeanor sharpened and exhibited the same haughtiness that Lorn had become so accustomed to in Lady Rasmina.

Lady Rasmina pushed herself up from the table and only a slight pinch on her face demonstrated her displeasure. "Mother, you were not invited tonight."

Her mother waved a dismissive hand and sidestepped the guard boxing her in. "Nonsense. My daughter rarely makes trips out here anymore. I need to enjoy the time you deem to visit." She arched an eyebrow at her daughter and seated herself at the table. Bold, yet graceful, the woman seated herself across from Lorn. She was dressed quite the opposite from Lady Rasmina's austere wardrobe of formal dresses. Expensive fabric draped her in the form of a pair of well-crafted trousers and a long-sleeved tunic.

She cocked her head at Lorn. He didn't know whether to be relieved by this woman's presence or even more on edge. Two vipers were now in the pit with him, and one had decades more experience and cunning.

"And who are your guests this evening?"

Lady Rasmina pursed her lips together and introduced them. "Lorn of Verta and Lilit of Iyera, may I introduce you to Lady Avareth, former ruling Lady of Lighthold."

Avareth gave a whistle. "I am sitting across from the fabled Lorn of Verta, hunter of the Hinterlands and the famed captain Lilit of Iyera." She nodded her head in appreciation. "What brings you to Gara?"

Lady Rasmina answered for them, "They are here as ambassadors from Lord Aldrich of Iyera."

Avareth leaned back in her chair. "Are they now?" A knowing glance was cast between mother and daughter.

Lorn cleared his throat. "Yes, after emerging from the Hinterlands, Lord Aldrich promoted me as his ambassador. It was quite an honor."

She now turned her penetrative gaze to Lilit. "You are a quiet one. Nothing to say? Hm?"

Lilit speared a piece of leafy greens and angrily chewed it while returning Avareth's stare.

"Ah, no words are needed. I know much about the well-renowned Captain of Iyera. A well-trained dog at Lord Aldrich's beck and call."

The words hit their mark. Lilit stiffened beside him and swallowed her food. Her fingers danced around the hilt of her sword.

Avareth motioned for a glass of wine to be brought and filled. She sipped it deliberately. "Still no words to say?" Her eyebrows raised. "Shame." She tutted.

"Mother," Lady Rasmina interrupted. "Play your games some other time.

She gestured to the table and guests. "I am only getting to know your guests."

Lilit's teeth clacked together. "I wonder what the former Lady of Lighthold would say about the "pet" of Lord Aldrich, saving her granddaughter's life? Or would you still like to continue spewing your vitriol?"

Without missing a beat Avareth leaned forward, swirled her wine, and took a quick sip. "Last I heard it wasn't your help, but rather Lorn of Verta's quick thinking and impressive magic who saved my beloved granddaughter."

"Oh no," Lorn interrupted, "Without Lilit's strength, we would not have dispatched the infected beast so quickly." He wanted to add more to the story, of how Lilit had pulled him back from the edge of insanity and prevented him from succumbing to the immense power the overwhelmed him. How easy it would have been to destroy both himself and Pearl in the process.

Avareth folded her hands together and contemplated the two of them. "Interesting."

When dinner was finished and it was polite enough for them to excuse themselves, Lorn rushed to the exit with Lilit hot on his heels, her fury palatable. Even though Avareth's words were sharp, Lorn was grateful it achieved something—Lilit was no longer a disinterested, detached observer on their trip.

Avareth shouted, "I look forward to chatting more with the two of you."

~

The hour grew late and Lorn retired to his room. Lilit didn't join him upstairs, instead veering towards the front door of the mansion.

Out of the upper floor windows he saw Lilit's retreating silhouette descending to the raging ocean. The storm spiraled on, the rain falling in thick sheets. From what he could discern, she did nothing to shield herself from it, merely letting the rain drench her. The biting words of

Lady Avareth had hit true.

Lorn took a well-deserved and restful bath. The claw-foot tub overlooked a large, expansive window to the immaculate gardens below. Finished he dressed and lay down on the plush bed despite the energy that buzzed within his body. The hypnotic pull of magic hummed under his skin. Tomorrow he would practice. He needed to develop it. Exhaustion tugged at his limbs, but he laid there on his bed in a strange half-awake state. It was late into the night when he heard the slam of Lilit's neighboring door. After the reassurance of her return, he finally fell asleep.

~

He was not surprised to find Issi standing across from him. The dream scenery was the familiarity of a forest. The moon cast rays of light between the filtered leaves and soft pines and twigs were scattered across the ground.

"What message do you have for me this time?" Lorn asked.

She regarded him, her electric blue eyes both alluring and unsettling.

"How are you managing yourself?"

"What do you mean?"

"Your new magic. Have you tested it yet?"

Lorn shook his head. He had been too worried to test the power. With no known factor to stabilize him or anchor him in reality, he feared succumbing to the magic. Hints of that moment fed themselves to him. Moments of his detached numbness or his persistent urging to eviscerate everything in sight.

"You will need to. We will use this time to practice."

Lorn took in the goddess fully. She was dressed in clothing fit for sparring, her blonde-white hair plaited back away from her face. She was prepared for this. He tried to think of any repercussions but couldn't. He needed to figure out how to wield this magic, only a goddess could teach him such skills. The magic was equal that of a god, who else could be his teacher? Lorn couldn't help but think of the parallels between himself and Aza.

"Very well, let's begin," he answered.

Without warning, Issi lunged, and a blast of magic went straight to Lorn's chest.

31

"Her presence is overwhelming. I find myself struggling to be around her. It is intoxicating. My prescribed treatment is distance."

Nivet's private journal.

Sand slid between her toes. It was cool and dry. A Kreehan sunset greeted her, the warm hues dancing in the sky, threading through clouds, the brilliant pinks, oranges, and yellows bringing forth a bittersweet nostalgia. But she was not in the Kreehan sand dunes anymore, they had made it back to Cyran.

Aza shielded her eyes from the brilliant sun and surveyed the land. She was still dressed in the Kreehan fashion, but wore no shoes, no weapons. She flexed her toes in the sand enjoying the feel of it running between each. Aza had encountered such odd things, so far in her life, she did not consider the strangeness of this any different.

There did not seem to be any threat or underlying danger, so she plopped onto the sand bank, leaned back onto her arms, and enjoyed the Kreehan sunset. The temperate was mild for once, neither hot nor cold, and she basked in the setting sun, her breathing free and easy.

At the top of the sand dune, she noticed a shadow approaching. It was the outline of a man. A man she would recognize anywhere. She intimately knew the details of his body, his stance, his walking pace, the set of his jaw, and his magical signature. She had never realized how much of an imprint he had made on her, how much she knew him like he was another part of her body.

She hated how she scrambled to her feet, and she hated how her feet ran of their own accord to greet him.

He sprinted to her.

She hated how familiar he was and how her body ached to have him close.

They collided like two shooting stars aimed at the other. Aza wrapped her legs around his body, and they tumbled to the sand. They peppered kisses to each other, their magic rising up in greeting.

"My stars, I have missed you and searched for you." Cruvo's lips clamped on her neck, and she lost the ability to speak.

Their hips moved of their own accord as their bodies reacquainted themselves with each other. Her mind flashed to the night she was captured and the promises he had seductively whispered to her of a night together. She had not seen him, heard from him since.

"Cruvo," she moaned. His forest brown hair fell alongside his face as he pinned her beneath him and worked his hands under the smooth Kreehan robes. His luminous green eyes latched on to her, searching her eyes as his hand ran down her body.

"Where are you? I have been so worried. What has happened to your magic?"

While these questions were important, she dashed them aside. She couldn't focus properly when his hands were doing such delicious things to her body, not when she had missed him, craved him. His nearness was a drug to her magic.

Brief flashes of Xira, Reed, Anwin and lastly Lorn finally caused her to pause. "Wait." She pushed his hands away and forced herself away from his body.

He listened and sat back on his heels. The word 'melding' echoed through her head. This feeling, the way she couldn't listen to reason was because of him. Like the undertow of the current, she didn't realize the depths she was in until it pulled her under, and he *was* pulling her under. *He is using you,* replayed through her mind.

Once her breathing was under control, Aza asked, "Where's Lorn?"

Cruvo started. He cocked his head and eyed her. Aza stared back. This was her chance to receive answers. "Where's Lorn, Cruvo?"

At the mention of his name, he grimaced and ran a hand through his hair, brushing the errant strands away from his eyes. "I had to send him to Gara."

"Why?"

"I had information that could assist you, *and* he is serving as an ambassador to me in Gara."

"Is he safe?"

"My stars, I know how much he means to you. I would never place him in blatant harm." Cruvo came closer and caressed her face, bringing his forehead to hers. "Please tell me where you are."

The nearness of him was too much, but Aza paused, and worried her lip. She settled for a neutral answer. "I'm safe."

He pulled away and examined her, his face in disbelief. "I have heard worrying rumors. Verta is after you."

"Yes, well I'm not there any longer." She strove to keep her answers vague, but Cruvo pried.

"Tell me where you are, so you can return to me in Iyera, return back to El'en. You belong with me." He gripped her face and tilted her head to the side, planting well-aimed kisses along her neck. She gasped for breath. It had been too long, and their connection was too strong. She fought to keep her wits. "Tell me, my stars. You should not resist this. As I have said before, we were made for each other."

Aza's mind was overwhelmed, the sensations too great. She had missed him, missed this. But something prodded her in the back of her mind—an insistence to not let herself relax around him. Not everything was as it seemed.

She pushed him away and he stopped. "How are you here?" She hadn't been able to sense him for over a month and now he was here in her dreams?

"I assumed your magic had been tampered with and now it is back." He moved to continue his ministrations, but Aza crawled out from underneath him and stood up. She couldn't remain on the ground any longer. She needed distance. If she remained too close, she would compromise herself and curse herself later for the foolishness. She needed a clear head.

"But how are you here?" She flung her hands out at the sands. Aza filtered through her memories of Cruvo mentioning distance being an important factor to their link.

He gracefully rose to his feet. His face held a tiny bit of hurt. "I have been looking for you. I'm with Gravers now. We have been scouring every inch of the provinces to find you. He stepped towards her, his magic billowing off him in waves like the lull of the late afternoon sun causing her to doze off. She motioned for him to stop. He faltered but stayed in place. "We are still looking for you. Tell me where you are, and we will come to you. Those Nerians will regret ever taking you from me."

Xira's silent look of approval after a day of sparring, flashed through her mind, how she believed in Aza's fierce strength and fortitude, how she encouraged Aza, pushed her to her limits, how she protected her from Astaroth, risked her life to show Aza the truth.

Shades of Anwin's fire red hair played next as it danced in a Kreehan sunset, as her nose bled freely from magic usage, and her body was limp after saving her and Xira from their freefall off Verta's Fortress. The steadfast healer who mixed herbs to relieve Aza's pain and did not chastise her for any mental breakdowns.

Reed's gentle smile and quiet presence was next. How he leapt off a ship wielding two axes in hand to slash at an insurmountable foe—a sea serpent. He was the calming presence that linked them together. His deft hands as they signed to Roan at the Hall of Prophecies.

Those Nerians. Only a month ago, Aza would have spoken about them with the same derision as Cruvo. But too much had changed in the last month. They had shared the same rigorous journey, protected one another, defended one another. She was linked with them whether she wanted to admit it or not. Hearing Cruvo speak with such disdain caused her to rise.

Aza marched over to Cruvo and pushed against his chest, hard.

Caught by surprise he tumbled back into the sand, his feet tripping over one another. "Those Nerians!" she shouted. Even in this vast dreamscape, the sound echoed back at her and fueled her anger. "Those Nerians have been honest with me! They have protected me, taught me. They haven't kept me in the dark, ignorant like some pet to be gawked at and seen as a pretty adornment like some gaudy piece of jewelry!" Her chest heaved with the thoughts that had swirled in her mind over the last month. Over the potential lies, and deception, or what she feared to be true about Cruvo. He had lied to her or at least misled her. He had always known more than she had. He could have shared the information, but instead held firm to their power imbalance.

Cruvo gracefully rose to his feet and stared at her with an incredulous look. "Have I not taught you how to wield your magic? To rise up against people and not be ashamed of your magic?" he whispered.

Cruvo maintained his intense eye contact and took careful, measured steps to her. "Have I not let you stay at the castle in El'en, given free rein to go anywhere, do anything? Did I not let Lorn stay in the castle with you when I could easily have dismissed him? Do not stand there, Aza, and pretend I am a monster. The Nerians have spun a pretty web of lies for you to get caught in. They have ensnared you." Cruvo stood less than a breath away from Aza, but she did not look away.

He did not touch her, for his words were doing it, causing her to doubt. "Do you truly know these Nerian companions of yours? They captured you, and I'm assuming drugged you."

He leaned into the shell of her ear and whispered, "You have your magic back. Why don't you leave? You do not need them." His mouth danced over the thin skin of her neck, her body was electric. "You are power. You are strength. You bow down to no one."

Sensing her hesitancy, he trailed a fingertip down her exposed shoulder and followed it over the curvature of her spine. "Do not let Nivet fill your head with his nonsense. You are so much more than he wants you to be."

The words he was whispering had lulled Aza into a stupor but at the mention of Nivet, she furrowed her eyebrows and pushed away from him. "Nivet isn't here."

Cruvo's mouth fell open for a second before he clamped it shut. He quickly smoothed over his misstep. "You travel without him?"

Aza crossed her arms over her chest. "Yes." There was something she couldn't quite place, something off about Cruvo after the mention of Nivet. Like he didn't believe Aza had come to these conclusions and these ties of her own accord. Like she had been coerced or under another's spell...like Nivet. Cruvo was jealous and believed Nivet was manipulating their collusion of magic.

"I need time," Aza announced. She decided it was the safest option. She didn't know what to think and curse Cruvo, he had placed the tiniest seed of doubt.

"Time?" he repeated.

"Yes. Do not come after me. You know I am safe. You know my magic has returned. Let me have time to discover who and what I am apart from everyone without your interference. I will return to you when I am ready."

"Aza, that is not in my nature. I hunt things. I can never let you go." His eyes glinted with satisfaction. She believed him, he wouldn't let her go but she needed to try. The headiness of his proximity was too much, and she needed to discover who she was without him.

Despite the lies and treachery, she still had a tender heart when it came to him. It was a weakness she needed to work on.

"Goodbye, Cruvo." Her heart pounded and her body seemed to scream at her for her decision, but she forced herself to wake up. The beautiful Kreehan desert vanished, and Aza woke to an empty bed and an unwelcome heat between her legs. At least it wasn't regret.

32

"They have brainwashed her. She rejected me. Aza is clearly not in her right mind. The situation is more dire than I could have imagined."

Cruvo's private journal

Despite a full night of sleep, Lorn woke exhausted, his body worn and tired from his magical practice with Issi. His sympathy for Aza expanded ten-fold—she had been dealing with this every night, honing her skill, all the while dealing with the mystery of her origins. She was never granted a moment of peace.

He inspected his body in the mirror of his bathroom and found no bruises marring his body. Only his memory and his knowledge that Aza had encountered the same dream-like situations made him stop from questioning his sanity.

After gathering Lilit, he descended downstairs, had breakfast, and decided upon his course for the day. Even though they were far away from the vast library of Lighthold, he would continue his research. He scarfed down a delicious breakfast of salted fish, something in abundance on the edge of the coast, and decided to explore the small town of Holdsfast.

He did not comment on Lilit's late-night departure, preferring to keep his balls intact. Lorn knew she was one big crack away from breaking entirely. The less time spent with Lady Rasmina and Avareth the better.

They left the forlorn mansion, ambling down the pebble strewn path. A persistent drizzle sprinkled over them and Lorn pulled the hood of his cloak higher. He was thankful he packed Pearl's gifted cloak. He had no idea how he had traveled Gara without it.

Workers scoured the immaculate gardens, leaning over vibrant green bushes and colorful flowers, pruning and trimming. Arbors and trellises were covered with thick vines, the leaves choking out the others, fighting for dominance.

A unique flower caused him to stop, his fingers rubbing curiously against the petals. Most of the plants in Gara were unfamiliar to him, the climate vastly different than his home province of Verta.

The leaves were a stark white, with bleeding streaks of black marred through it. The budding flower was a beautiful obsidian color, the petals softly opened in an elegant shape.

"Have you ever seen anything like this?" Lorn looked over his shoulder and saw Lilit give a disinterested shrug.

"Am I supposed to be an herbalist now?"

He ignored the sarcastic remark, straightened up, and descended the hilltop. For some reason, he couldn't get the thought of the flower out of his head. How it appeared like the corruption veining through a person, consuming them.

The villagers of Holdfast regarded Lorn and Lilit with the same disinterest and distaste as the rest of the villagers they had met in their prior journey. They did not take kindly to strangers, despite Lorn's persistent attempts at friendly conversation. People's greetings ranged from hostile to fearful to suspicious.

Even though they were not forthcoming, Lorn did not stop. Instead, he visited the shops, let people become accustomed to his face, his demeanor.

Needing a rest he stepped outside, regarding the rugged beauty of the ferocious cliffside and Northern Sea. Lorn squinted his eyes and saw a pier with small ships bobbing on the violent waves. If he could, he would collapse back onto the ground, with the tall soft grass swaying around him and let the rain fall, but the ground was muddy, and Lilit would have some biting comment to say about his behavior.

He longed for solitude, for his prior life. It was odd to spend vast amounts of time with someone else when he had spent the last few years hunting and traveling alone. With Aza, it hadn't felt like a strain, but a natural pattern like breathing. However, Lilit was the thorn in his side, the spur on the sole of his foot. Yet just like the ocean that sprawled out in front of him, the fierce storm on the surface didn't taint what was below, a wealth of beauty and knowledge. He needed to bear her anger and help her through whatever she was struggling with.

The tall grass whipped at his legs and torso as the wind picked up. A deep boom resounded throughout the land. Lorn closed his eyes and counted the seconds. With perfect timing, he opened his eyes and saw a giant spark light up the entire sky, the jagged lightning strike down onto the ocean. It was beautiful. His magic hummed in satisfaction at the raw power. Another boom and another flash of lightning. Magic pulsed expectantly. He narrowed his vision, focusing on where sky met sea. When lightning struck down again, he loosened his magic, the relief like releasing a long-held breath.

He glistened and shone like a star shining in the night, but with each strike of lightning he glowed brighter. His eyes fell closed. Dully he was aware of the raw power of nature, his magic, and the soft beating of his heart.

A rough shaking forced his eyes open. Lilit was clenching his shoulder, her fingers digging into the muscle, the small pain bringing him back to the moment. Startled, he shook his head blearily, like a fog lifting.

A small tinge of fear had edged into the corner of her eyes, but he blinked, and it was gone. "Control yourself. What in the Darkness Below, was that?"

"Nothing," he murmured. "Just got carried away. Let's go back to the manor. Maybe tomorrow we will be successful."

Lilit stiffly nodded but as they returned to the manor at the top of the hill, Lorn didn't fail to note the tight grip Lilit had on her sword hilt and how she regarded him like a beast from the Hinterlands, something feral and rogue she needed to dispatch if necessary.

~

Over the following days, even though Lady Rasmina promised to show them Holdfast, she had made herself scarce. Lorn tried again and again to make conversation with the people in town, but they were a stonewall he could not break.

"Just give yourself time," he reminded himself daily.

On the fifth day, Lorn decided to go for a bolder approach. He didn't care anymore. He couldn't sit here being pampered while people were slaving away, being stolen, and forced to work in ruthless camps.

He was not discreet, and boldly started asking the people of Holdsfast what they knew of Lady Rasmina, if they heard the rumors, would they consider them true, what could they add, who were being taken, what could he do to help, where were they held captive. Most ignored him or shooed him away from their business. Some threatened their lives and told them to leave or else. But Lorn could not ignore the open fear they all possessed. Some spat when he said her name.

One elderly man, after threatening Lorn with the tip of his harpoon, walked away muttering to himself, "The only good thing that came from her was Pearl. A gift from the sea that one."

After the countless threats and strange comments, that one stuck with him the most. He mulled over it for the rest of the day.

Wanting a bite to eat, Lorn found himself outside of a small ramshackle wooden restaurant serving bowls of hot fish soup. He paid for two bowls and sat away from the townsfolk, their wary glances and tense bodies warning him more than any sword could. Frustrated, he did not want to deal with subterfuge any longer. He wanted straight answers.

A middle-aged man, clearly a sailor with his bulky muscles and stout frame, sat next to Lorn with a bowl of piping hot soup. Before Lorn could question him, the man stopped him.

"Keep eating, look ahead. Don't appear shocked. Her spies are everywhere."

Lorn relaxed his face and forced himself to take on an easy smile. He gulped down a bite of the soup and nodded absentmindedly.

"You are either a fool or extremely brave to be asking such questions around here. Especially in such close proximity to Lady Rasmina herself."

He clapped a meaty hand against Lorn's back and laughed loudly before pulling Lorn close and whispering in his ear, "The other townsfolk don't want to share with you in case you are a spy, but my gut says otherwise." He pulled back from Lorn and gave him a thoughtful look. The man smelled of salt and fish, his chin covered in days of stubble and black chin length hair windswept.

Lorn leaned over his bowl of soup, contemplated it, playing with the spoon in the bowl. "I am no spy. I merely need answers."

"That is what I figured. I will try my best, but to understand us, we need to gain your trust. Meet me tonight, at the pier. Come alone." He peered over Lorn's shoulder at Lilit and nodded. "She's fine too."

The man downed his bowl of soup in one mighty gulp, wiped his chin, and stood up to leave.

"Wait, what do I call you?"

"Name's Devlin." He pushed his hands into his pocket, nodded, and disappeared along the edge of the sandbar.

Lorn turned to Lilit and raised his eyebrows. "It's something."

"Sure it is hunter. Sure it is."

~

They retreated to the manor to eat dinner and would wait until Lorn could escape back down to Holdsfast to meet up with Devlin. For once, Lilit was chatty on their way up the pathway, warning him of meeting people he knows nothing about. While frustrating, it was also a reassurance she had sunk back into her prior ways. He hid a slight smile as he nodded absentmindedly to her points of danger and his overall ignorance to the seedy behaviors of people.

Lady Rasmina and Avareth joined them for dinner. Typically, their dinners were dull affairs with benign small talk consisting of the weather, their day, any small irrelevant information regarding their history or jobs. But tonight, something was different. The silverware scraped against plates in a discordant cacophony, his body buzzed with alarm. Lady Rasmina and Avareth held themselves tightly, their eyes skewering him.

He wanted to smack his head in frustration, his careless questioning about Lady Rasmina must have traveled back to her. Devlin was correct, her spies were everywhere.

"So, Lorn," Avareth began, "please enlighten me on your relationship with Lord Aldrich. I was familiar with his parents long before he came into reign. An unfortunate incident about his mother, the poor lamb. And his father sent away for his 'health' right after his rise to power. Quite curious really." Avareth spun this tale with a feigned emotion, but Lorn could tell she didn't care. Like reciting the news of something happening far away one had no interest in.

"He actually sought me out. Heard rumors of what I had accomplished and tasked me with entering the Hinterlands."

Avareth swirled her wine. "I wonder why that was. Why specifically *you*?"

Although Lorn understood why he was chosen, a theory revolving around the prophecy and him being the only one to enter the Hinterlands, he was smart enough to withhold that sensitive information. Lorn shrugged and said," Based on my skill I can assume."

"And then you were successful and returned with, what's her name again?" Avareth placed a thoughtful finger on her chin. " I have heard so many stories of her, ahh yes, Aza of the Well. The one who cannot control her power and instead lashed out and hurt my daughter." Her tone sharpened like the point of a blade.

"I believe that is in the past and has already been discussed and held to a vote at a council."

"Do you really believe someone with so much power should be allowed to freely roam? To ruin lives as easily as snapping a finger."

Lady Rasmina sat at the table silently watching the conversation whip back and forth between her mother and Lorn. Lilit had stopped eating, her fork clutched tightly in her hand.

Lorn leaned back in his chair and appraised Avareth, her silvered hair pulled back into a small coronet of braids, elegant and suitable for her age. He quelled the flames of anger that licked at him. He could defend Aza without excess emotion.

"Even the MagicBlessed range in their powers. Some hold a deeper well of magic compared to others. Some have a proclivity for more dangerous magic and can be prone to abuse power. I would say it depends on the person."

Avareth narrowed her eyes.

He continued, "Would you say the same argument about me? I was able to access a vast amount of magic to heal your granddaughter. Do you believe I should be locked up and detained?"

"That remains to be seen," Avareth replied.

Lorn decided to pursue another avenue of discussion. "What about the stories of the gods and goddesses from long ago? If you believe the stories, we have derived our power from them and the Well. Do you believe our very existence shouldn't be? People can be monsters with or without their magic."

Lady Rasmina's gaze sliced to him upon the mention of the gods and goddesses. Even Lilit seemed to halt her breathing. But Lorn couldn't stop this discussion. The magic in his body swelled at the mention of its suppression.

"Do you think, if the gods and goddesses were here today, they would be benevolent? No, they would reign down their terror on everyone. The MagicBlessed would be mere bugs to their vast power. It has been done before," Avareth said sharply.

"Done before?" Lorn asked.

Avareth fumbled for a moment and set her wineglass down, it clinked against the table sharp and unsure. "Yes—in the texts and scrolls I have read."

Skeptical Lorn questioned, "What texts? I have studied everything possible in the Lighthold library and I have never come across any information on the gods and goddesses."

"Darkness below, hunter, I have been alive much longer than you. I have been exposed to more information than you. In books, I have read about their destructive tendencies."

Lorn didn't believe her. She knew more, had firsthand experience with them. He tried not to let surprise show on his face.

"Mother, it is a pointless argument. Lorn of Verta is like an obedient dog following those in power, whoever is gracious enough to give him a shred of attention," Lady Rasmina said. "He will always defend the strength of magic."

Lorn gnashed his teeth together, restraining himself from saying truly awful to their hosts.

To his surprise Lilit cut in, "Thank you for dinner. We will retire to our rooms now."

Lorn left the room beside Lilit and could feel the judgmental eyes of

Lady Rasmina and her mother on his back like a target.

Outside their rooms Lorn swallowed his pride and thanked Lilit. She pushed him into his room and said, "They know."

"Know?"

"They know Lord Aldrich is inhabited by Cruvo."

"What makes you say that?"

Lilit blew out a breath. "How they talk about magic. Do you think Lord Aldrich is the only one who has been inhabited by a god before? The gods and goddesses have probably done this for countless years, picking who they want and choosing to use their body."

She walked over to the window and peered below. "We need to be careful. But I think they let more slip than they intended. I don't think..."

"Don't think what?"

Lilit shook her head and turned to him, her distant musings vanishing replaced with the crisp action he was used to from her. "I don't think either of them are currently inhabited with gods or goddesses. I am used to the signs. Rest up, hunter. Hopefully tonight isn't some sort of ambush." She brushed past his shoulder and left.

Not for the first time, Lorn wondered what he was doing in the province of Gara.

33

"I only felt pride as I watched Aza fight Xira on the ship deck. She was born for it."

Nivet's private journal.

The following morning, Aza woke, groggy, unrested, and disheveled. After having her first dream with Cruvo and not sleeping beside the Nerians, she was grumpy. Her mood didn't improve when they met Sune and Ryu for breakfast. They didn't have any information on Lorn, except that he wasn't alone. Lilit accompanied him.

Aza's utensil clattered against the table. The last time she saw Lilit, Aza was begging for her help, and she had abandoned her. Lilit was now with the dearest person in the world to her. The urge to abandon their breakfast and sprint to Gara was overwhelming. Only Anwin's steadying hand provided her any comfort and an unsaid reminder that nothing could be done.

Lord Sune and Ryu didn't understand her reaction. To them it was good news, someone as formidable as Lilit of Iyera was there to help defend and protect Lorn, but it couldn't have been farther from the truth. Lilit only cared about herself. Whatever happened within Gara would be for Lilit's benefit.

Conflicting emotions warred. Lilit had tried to warn Aza, tried to keep her on guard, but she had abandoned her in a time of need. Lilit couldn't have known that the Nerians would prove supportive, guiding Aza towards a new path.

Aza gently brushed aside Anwin's comforting hand. Anwin

faltered, but quickly composed her shock. Aza hadn't acted this coldly toward them since she was first captured, but Cruvo's taunting voice replayed in her mind. She trusted them — she did. But a construct built in her head about how gullible she was, hopping from one group to the other, falling for their word like it was truth. They had proved themselves time and time again, but she couldn't ignore her raw emotions.

Xira missed nothing, her eyes flitting over the quick snub.

After finishing his bite of food, Reed leaned forward and said, "Thank you for getting information on Lorn. We all appreciate it."

After breakfast, Aza retired to her room. She bounced on her feet and shook out her arms in a weak attempt to dispel the uncomfortable, pervasive feelings that took hold. Now was not the time to doubt her Nerian companions. A sharp knock on the door interrupted her exercises. Aza opened the door to Xira's sharp stare.

"Something is troubling you. Let's go spar."

It was the perfect remedy to how she was feeling. She grabbed her weapons and followed Xira to the Kreehan sparring room, the lavish walls equipped with weapons. Aza fixated on the scimitars, her hand drifting over the curved blades, and golden hilts. They glistened from the early morning sun lancing through the window. With the copious vines and ivy crawling through the palace it gave it a mystical air.

~

Breathless and sweating, Aza had to concede Xira knew how to get her mind off of her thoughts. She was forced to focus on her movements. Every jab, block, slash slid her thoughts farther from Cruvo.

After they finished, Aza hid a smile, proud of how far she has progressed. During each sparring session, Aza was able to land solid hits on Xira, the reliance on her magic gone. With her power returned, she would be even deadlier in a fight.

Before Aza could leave the room Xira stopped her. "Something set you off. Would you like to talk about it?" Although she casually cleaned her blade, Aza didn't miss the intensity of her question.

Aza hesitated. Was it worth it to share what happened? No more secrets. Trust went both ways. "I saw Cruvo last night."

Xira stiffened. "And something he said has rattled you, I assume?"

Aza rubbed a hand down the side of her face and groaned. "Yes. I hate to admit it, but yes. It did." She shifted unsteadily from one foot to the other. Discussing the gods and goddesses was always an uncomfortable subject. "Although I trust you now, it still bothers me. Cruvo mentioned how I am merely a tool for your use. It has made me doubt everyone again, especially you."

"Let me give you some advice. Trust only yourself Aza. If you stick to that, you cannot be used as someone's tool."

Her gut twisted. "What do you mean trust myself? That is the whole reason I fell for Cruvo. My fucking instincts made me feel things for him! The 'melding' as you put it makes it impossible to be around any of the gods and goddesses without feeling a shred of something." Aza blew out a breath, forcing herself to calm down. Getting angry wasn't going to solve anything. Yet it was frustrating to not feel at home or trusting of her own body.

A softness touched Xira's expression. "I'm talking about something deeper Aza. Not your base reactions to their proximity, but something within you. Trust who *you* are, Aza." She pointed her finger at Aza's chest. "Think about when you are around Lorn. We watched you with him, assessed whether he was a threat to you."

She tilted her head up to the ceiling as if searching for the exact words she needed. "Seeing you together was like the purest form of friendship. It was unencumbered. That is what you should look for. Your trust, without anything else hindering it." Xira cocked her head and patted Aza's shoulder. "C'mon. Let's go freshen up before we meet with Lord Sune and Ryu."

~

The humidity of the afternoon swelled within the palace, but well-placed windows provided proper air flow and ventilation to stifle the most troubling heat away. Kreeha was prone to violent and rapid rainstorms only to be brushed away moments later with the sun shining fiercely, their late autumn so at odds with the other provinces. Lord Sune provided them with complimentary Kreehan style clothing to help with the humidity.

Aza steeled herself as she went to meet Lord Sune and Ryu within their study. They clambered to their private study and Aza surreptitiously eyed the Nerians. Their thin and travel-hardened bodies were relaxed. The proper night's rest in a bed restored the smudges under their eyes and their faces appeared less gaunt. The rich Kreehan food and rest restored the toll of hardship that was etched on their faces.

As they walked into the room, Sune and Ryu stopped their frantic whispering and straightened up. Without any pretense, they dove into the conversation freely sharing what they could offer each other as allies.

Reed and Anwin lounged on an adjacent couch, letting Xira lead the negotiations while Aza interjected when necessary. She did not want to overstep on any information they deemed secret. Although Reed and Anwin appeared the picture of relaxation, Aza noticed their eyes darting around the room, calculating each of Lord Sune's and Ryu reactions. This was a tentative truce, formed from a need to protect their provinces, nothing more. Aza had not forgotten that Lord Sune had come to them in a threatening manner. A flash of Lord Sune's scimitar in front of Anwin clouded over her eyes and she blinked it away. He had apologized. Desperation bred mistakes.

Several times, Xira reaffirmed to Lord Sune and Ryu that Aza would banish the Hinterlands. They had no other recourse. Aza voiced her assent, her fingers clasping the side of her thigh tightly, leaving imprints through the fabric. Her chest grew tight, and breathing was difficult.

The beautiful Hall of Prophecies flashed through her mind and what she had discovered. She stiffly nodded. She needed to banish the Hinterlands. It could no longer be, this blight on their world. But with it would be the consequence of the gods and goddesses returning with their full power and the ability to inhabit their physical forms. Another slew of problems would be unleashed because of the decisions they chose today.

Xira further explained the presence of Astaroth and her foothold in the Vertan province.

Ryu looked grim, his hands interwoven with Sune's. Their worst imaginings had been confirmed.

"Ready your soldiers. Create more Goldenring armor and try to outfit everyone in Kreeha with it. Practice your magic, have your citizens be able to wield and defend, teach classes. I reckon you have a few months to prepare. We will need time in Neria to prepare Aza for her task. Use your time Lord Sune, to prepare your people. Otherwise, when the time comes they will all be slaughtered carelessly by the gods and goddesses." Xira delivered her speech with precision, a general giving orders.

Lord Sune looked lost in thought. He stood and walked over to the open cutout window. His hand clasped the lattice, edged with thick flowering vines. The vines pulsed and grew, the tendrils snaking over his arm like caresses. "Our people are not prepared for war."

"Prepare them. For it is coming whether you want it to or not," Xira declared. "This is not time for remorse or pity. We must act!" Xira rose to her feet Reed and Anwin joined her. "The Nerians will stand with the Kreehans, but you must give them a fighting chance. Either prepare them now or they will be needlessly killed later. Until the Meadows of the Undying claim us." Even with Xira, Anwin and Reed outfitted in the loose, flowy, fabric of Kreeha there was a sharpness to them, an underlying threat, a palpable force so strong you could not help but be pulled into its tide.

Lord Sune snapped out of his melancholic reverie and faced the Nerians. They bowed to Ryu and Sune with their fists over their hearts. Ryu's eyes widened and Lord Sune's mouth fell open. He clamped it closed so fast, Aza heard his teeth clank together. They repeated. "Till the Meadows of the Undying claim us."

Aza was unsure of what to do and what the significance of this declaration meant, but she scrambled to her feet and copied them. She caught Reed's slight smile out of the corner of her eye. When they straightened up, she did too. A knock at the door echoed through the silence and Lord Sune looked quizzically at Ryu. He opened the door and Hanu's sandy blonde hair popped in.

"I apologize for interrupting, Lord Sune, but there is an ambassador from Verta wanting to meet with you."

He shared a quick glance at Ryu who shrugged and said, "We should meet with them. After what we have learned, it might be good to assess their knowledge."

Lord Sune agreed and turned to Hanu. "Please escort them to my other study, the one with the false door. Place the Nerians behind the false door so they can listen in on our conversation with the ambassador." Sune looked to Xira, who nodded.

"They mustn't see the Nerians here," he added to Hanu.

"Of course, my Lord."

"Ryu, let's go greet our guest."

~

Hanu led their group down a flight of stairs into a similar looking study to the one they were just in, yet he directed them to the adjoining room that blended in with the walls. Inside was a quaint bench and a peephole. Vents were discreetly slatted on the walls to provide better listening.

"You must be absolutely silent behind this. The noise still carries easily."

They each shuffled into the minuscule room. Aza peeked through the peephole. A vine obscured the room, but she was still able to discern enough. Anwin and Reed were pushed against the wall while Xira and Aza switched. They had no time to discuss the Vertan ambassador, but it struck Aza as odd timing.

Impatiently, Aza wrung her hands. It was too much of a coincidence for this to be real. An ambassador from Verta showing up to the Kreehan court when they were in residence here. Astaroth was still looking for her. She tried to dismiss her uneasiness. Vertan ambassadors could be meeting with Lord Sune for countless other valid reasons.

Aza peered through the peephole just as the study door cracked open. Lord Sune gestured an arm forward, and a woman with close cropped curly hair walked in. She wore no armor, only a long sleeved bright yellow dress. It offered a lovely contrast to her dark skin.

Embroidery of wheat was stitched along the hem of the dress as it swished with her precise steps.

The Vertan ambassador exchanged pleasantries as Lord Sune, Ryu, and Hanu filed into the room.

Aza's breath grew heavy, and a overwhelming feeling of dread numbed her body. She felt too heavy to move and was too entranced to look away. But something was deeply wrong. Aza forced herself away from the wall.

Xira saw the fear on her face and acted quickly. She jostled Aza aside and slid the door open. Within the confines of the hidden room, Xira could not pull out her sword, but as she barrelled into the open study, she wielded it cautiously sizing up the ambassador. Aza followed right behind, her own sword in hand while Reed and Anwin fanned out behind them.

The ambassador closed her eyes and took in a deep inhalation.

"Ahh, little fox. I have finally found you." Out of the sleeve of her dress a dagger slid down and slashed out at Ryu who stood closest to her. Hanu yanked Ryu out of the steel's range and shoved him behind his body.

From the open window, vines shot out and wrapped around each part of the ambassador's body. She struggled against the binds and her sleeves shifted to expose her putrid veins.

Lord Sune shook his head at the ambassador, walking up to her. "Bold of you to infiltrate my palace. He leaned closer and inspected the rotted veins. "Astaroth."

She sneered, her smile a jagged mockery twisting the woman's face. Pity swelled as Aza thought of Endyl in Verta, who was forced to occupy Astaroth in his body, left to a similar fate as the woman before her. Although Astaroth could not inhabit her own body, she was still a threat, and the arrogant Lord Sune thought she was quelled.

"Step back, Lord Sune! Astaroth is still dangerous."

Revulsion filled her body as bile crept up her throat. Before Aza could utter another word, the vines holding Astaroth withered and died, the black rotted veins crept up her face and pulsed with power. Lord Sune sent more vines snaking at Astaroth, but at her touch they withered. Lord Sune's mouth was agape at Astaroth's powers.

"Lord Sune, your meager powers can do nothing to hold me." Astaroth darted forward with a blade in hand and swiped at him.

Shock had frozen him, but Sune quickly unsheathed the scimitar hanging from his side and blocked her strike. Astaroth hit him with a sturdy kick to the stomach and he flew backwards.

Hanu sliced at Astaroth with calculated precision as Lord Sune crumpled. With unnatural speed, Astaroth spun from the attack and with her free hand, gripped Hanu by the throat. Astaroth lifted him effortlessly in the air. As Hanu sputtered and choked, black rot poured from Astaroth's hands into Hanu's throat, creeping across his tanned skin. A smile slashed her face.

Aza took a step to race over and help, but Anwin and Reed pulled her back. Aza fought against their tight grasp, but a hand snaked over her chest constricting her. "Xira will handle it. Your proximity will only heighten her powers," Anwin rasped. Aza slackened, mollified by Anwin's answer.

The small study was ablaze with action. Xira stood in front of Aza, watching and waiting for an opening. As Hanu struggled against Astaroth's grip, she surged forward, vaulting over furniture to reach him.

Before Xira could reach Hanu, Ryu pulled out a tiny, gilded blade from within his robes, and raced forward screaming his fury.

"Ryu, no!" Lord Sune shouted.

Ryu stabbed but missed. Astaroth easily sidestepped the attack and dropped Hanu who crumpled to the floor clawing at his rotting throat.

"How precious. The Lord of Kreeha's consort come to rescue a worthless guard." Astaroth easily batted away his feeble attempts to stab her.

Lord Sune scrambled to his feet and ran to Ryu's aid.

But Ryu with his lean frame, who poured over books, was no match for Astaroth's power and strength. She casually eyed her opponent and with a swiftness Aza couldn't track, she lunged forward, her sword pierced Ryu's stomach. His eyes widened in shock, and his pitiful dagger clattered to the ground. Astaroth held her sword in Ryu savoring the moment, while her corruption spilled into him. The blood dripping from his wound, once red transformed into a putrid black and pooled at his feet.

Astaroth saw Lord Sune and Xira advance but did nothing to stop them. She only looked to Aza, a smirk on her face. "Do not go into hiding, little fox." She closed her eyes in ecstasy and pulled in a deep breath. "I do love the feel of my power around you." Lord Sune roared and slashed across with his sword. Astaroth's host's head tumbled to the floor.

Aza looked on with a shred of pity. The woman Astaroth was using didn't deserve to die like this, executed like a traitor.

The heaviness evaporated, a weight lifted off her shoulders. Anwin and Reed's tight hold loosened, and Aza raced over to Lord Sune. He was crumpled on the floor cradling Ryu's head in his lap.

"Ryu, Hanu..." he rasped. "I cannot... my magic can't heal whatever she has done to you."

Hanu's eyes bulged as he clawed at his throat, choking on the rotted magic infecting his body.

Ryu's red blood swirled with tinges of black and green. He burbled out blood, dribbling down his chin. Ryu's skin was pale, and his eyes grew glassy.

"Sune," he croaked.

"No, no, no," Sune murmured rocking back and forth. "This is not how you go, my love. You cannot leave me. We have so much to do. We cannot let her win."

Xira patted her hands over Hanu in an attempt to heal him. He was further from death, his body fighting the corruption, but there was no stab wound for him to contend with.

Aza placed a consoling hand on Sune's muscled shoulder.

"You need to move."

"Never," Sune barked out.

"Do it, Sune," Xira added. "She can heal him."

"What?" Lord Sune's eyes widened, and his mouth flopped open in disbelief. "But your magic is gone," he sputtered.

Aza did not need to explain herself, so she only repeated, "Move."

Reed knelt gently and guided Sune away.

Aza took his place kneeling beside Ryu. She eyed the growing wound on his stomach and his blanched face. What little time he had left was dwindling.

"My Lady," Ryu whispered, more blood spilling out of his mouth.

The magic that had been crackling behind her veins now was a raging inferno, growing and spiraling out of control. She let it take over.

She clasped Ryu's hand like a lifeline, his fingers entwined with hers and she felt the small hint of life. It was being diminished and stamped out like a poisoned tree, the insides rotting. She clung onto that flare of life and her magic surged through his body like a stampede of wild horses—it ran free. The magic, the lifeblood, she poured it into Ryu.

First, she needed to exterminate the infection, the corruption which altered his blood and his wounds. It clung to him like poisonous barbs, sticking to his wounds and preventing any healing. She needed to eradicate them.

Sweat collected on her brow and her breathing became tense. She imagined Lorn's light, bright, piercing, purifying. It poured through Ryu's body, both of them burning bright like the constellations above. Light filled the room, blinding everyone, but Aza only had sight for Ryu. He screamed in pain as the corruption was eradicated the tiny poisonous barbs unwilling to leave and stubbornly resisting. But they would go. They could not withstand her power. She burned brighter, not a flame of heat but of purifying light, of basking in the summer sun, her feet warming on the Kreehan dunes.

"Stop it! You are hurting him," Lord Sune bellowed. Aza heard his pleas from far away, so focused she was on Ryu.

"No, she is your only salvation," Anwin answered.

Aza heard muted screams, but she focused on the light and Ryu. His face eased, calm and relaxed. His body slumped towards unconsciousness, but Aza couldn't let him go. She had only rid him of the corruption, she had yet to close the stomach wound.

She focused on the organs, muscle, and sinew stitching them back together like a needle through thread. Piece by piece he was mended. Ryu's eyes had long since closed and his breathing had stilled.

When Aza finally finished, she had thought he was dead. But she clung to his intertwined fingers, so slim and delicate, the fingers of a scholar, not of a fighter. Beneath she felt the hint of lifeforce. She blew out a relieved breath. She had done it.

"You aren't done yet," Xira claimed.

Aza wiped the sweat from her brow and crawled over to Hanu. Then she began the painstakingly arduous task of healing his corruption.

34

"I have never liked Gara. The constant rain and dour citizens left much to be desired."

Cruvo's private journal

Lorn whittled away time in his room, impatiently looking out his window and listening for the footsteps of workers and the ladies of the house to retire for the night. Each hour scraped by, Lorn alternated between sharpening his weapons and tossing and turning in his bed.

Eventually, the moon was high and bright overhead, and the manor was silent. Lorn kept his footsteps light, grabbed Lilit, and they both escaped out of the manor. A few guards patrolled the grounds, but it was easy for them to evade their sight. Were it not for the bright, full moon, they would have stumbled multiple times over the rocky terrain, but luckily the light guided them down to the main center of Holdsfast.

Lilit voiced her misgivings only once before going silent on the matter. "You are so quick to jump at information people give you without thinking of the repercussions."

Lorn merely grunted and focused on his light steps, paranoid of noise carrying back to the manor, even though the crashing of the ocean waves likely drowned out other sounds.

They reached the town center of Holdsfast. The salty air had rusted the boards of the buildings. Lorn dipped in-between the sea-worn buildings, darting like a stray cat until they made their way to the shabby pier. During their days here, Lorn hadn't time to inspect it. A lone lighthouse provided the pier with company, the giant structure's torchlight flickering even in the consistent rain.

Lorn and Lilit crept onto the pier, the wooden boards creaking from their sudden weight. He did not see Devlin or any meeting place that would be sufficient.

"Hunter, this way." Devlin popped out from the edge of the pier, where the sand sloped to the side, curving away. He waved his hand, gesturing to them to follow.

Lorn hopped off the wooden pier and into the sand below, steadying his hand against one of the poles of the pier, the hard shells of mussels and barnacles cut into his skin. He pulled his hand away and wiped it on his pants, following Devlin. The man's stout frame easily navigated the sand that Lorn had mastered yet, trudging through without any hesitation. They walked a fair distance from the pier until the sand lessened, transforming into rocks shielding tidepools. It was difficult to navigate in the dark, but Lorn followed Devlin's sure path, attempting to place his feet in the exact same spots.

A cave bloomed into view. They entered, the waves echoed inside, slapping against the rock. Lorn paused, unable to see a thing and loosened some of his light magic. They were walking on a rocky shelf with the water brushing over the sides. The cave continued, but Lorn couldn't tell how far, the darkness swallowing up what little light he provided.

Devlin let out a snort and reached down to grab a discarded lantern. He lit it and said, "Feels like we won't need this anymore."

Lorn shook his head, "No, keep it on." He doused his own light magic. "What is this place?"

"A place to meet without being overheard or spied on. You can only enter when the tide is low. When the tide rises, this cave would be a death sentence." Devlin kept his voice low, the cave walls rebounding his voice, magnifying it.

"What information do you have to tell us?" Lorn asked.

Devlin gestured for them to sit against the rocky shelf, their feet dangling over the lapping waves.

Lilit remained guarding the entrance, her sword out and ready. But he could see her focus was split, both on the entrance and on their conversation.

"We do not have long. I understand you are staying at the manor with her and her mother."

Lorn nodded.

"First you need to understand Lady Rasmina. The manor you are staying at has history. Her parents, the former Lord and Lady, always took their summer retreats here. Lady Rasmina was a sheer terror, playing with the local children, ever much the haughty lady she was growing up to be. But we still loved it, every second." Devlin smiled fondly. "As she grew up, her parents visited less and less. When they did show up, it was often only her mother and Rasmina. Yet something was off. She did not chase after the other children who were now growing well into their teen years and a strange melancholy followed her, like the salt in the air —you know it is there, but you can't exactly see it, you know?"

Devlin ran a hand over his stubble and considered the water lapping at them. "After a time, her father died. His heart failed him. Lady Rasmina was never the same. We did not see her for roughly ten years. We questioned what became of her, only hearing fragments. None of us travel to Lighthold. We were born and bred here. The ocean is our home. We do not leave it lightly.

"So we sat here, wondering what had become of our Lady, the one who would skin her knees and haughtily order us about, every bit the shrewd leader she would grow to be. Until one day, the manor atop the hill was no longer empty. Lady Rasmina had returned with two little girls in her carriage, their wide curious eyes peering out at our little town, so different, we imagine, from the grandness of Lighthold."

Devlin wove a smooth story with his gruff voice laced with his fond memories. Lorn pictured the scene clearly.

"Of course, we had heard rumors of her marriage, something political we assumed to secure their position as Rasmina's father had just passed and her mother never wanted to lead. So, she stayed with her two squalling babes up at the manor, and we would speculate about why she was here and what caused her to show up. Then one day, like no time had passed, she had descended like a goddess from above. She was always draped in finery, and this time was no different. She met us all, the townsfolk she used to run and play around with, like no time had passed. Yet, we could still sense the same deep shard of melancholy buried deep within her. Paired with her sadness was a cold fury forged like a blade of ice. Although she tried her best to hide it, we could all see something had happened. But day after day, she would return to the town and small pieces of herself would return, moments where she was not burdened with this unknown sorrow and anger and a spark of the tenacious girl would appear."

Lorn tried to reconcile the woman he knew with the person Devlin was describing. She seemed a different person entirely, her past self like a tempered blade, honed and disciplined. He wouldn't let it blind him to her current transgressions.

"Those moments were clearest when she was around my brother." Devlin laughed, the sound echoing like a monster in the cave. "Mina and Drion were oil and water—two sides of the same coin. He was the only one who could get her out of her shell, to push the anger and sorrow aside and instead direct it at him." Fondness creased his eyes. "They were like that as children too, constantly at each other's throats. Eventually their fighting turned to fondness and even though she was still married to Lord Mathor, they began a discreet relationship."

Lorn tried to school his features, but at the disclosure, his eyebrows raised.

"Yes, I know, highly improper, but we had never seen this Lord Mathor and we don't really know what had transpired over the last ten years. And I'm not trying to excuse her actions, but something was going on in Lighthold and my brother was the only shining ray of hope she had. It is rare to see 'Mina smile, but oh, around my brother she did. After a month here, she would return to Lighthold, but she never forgot us again and whenever she could, she returned, kept Ruby and Sapphire up at the manor with some of the workers or her mother, and she would come down and be herself again, with her people, where she belonged."

Lorn looked to the entrance of the cave. They didn't have much time left, they needed to return but he couldn't tear himself away from the story and the rich tones of Devlin's storytelling.

"I understand you need to leave, so I will leave you with this knowledge and we can continue next time: "Mina's daughter, Pearl, her namesake is true. She was born of the sea. She is my brother's daughter."

Lorn inhaled sharply. It made sense how she looked so dissimilar to her sisters, how she treated other people. The people of Holdsfast had helped to raise her instead of being raised with the nobility of Lighthold. Even now, she was trying to free the people under her mother's capture.

Devlin pushed himself off the ground and clapped his hands together, rubbing the grit from them. He handed the lantern to Lilit who guided them out of the cave. Once outside she dimmed the light and the three of them used the moonlight to guide their way.

"When can we meet again?" Lorn asked. He rubbed his hands together for warmth, they had grown numb in the damp sea cave.

"Meet me in a week from today, same place. The tide should remain low."

Lorn nodded and he gave a brief goodbye. Lorn and Lilit walked in silence until Lorn couldn't stand it anymore. He needed someone to discuss this revelation. "What do you think about what you heard?"

Lilit snorted. "I think she is a bitter woman who has faced tragedy and has let it consume her."

Lorn misstepped and almost fell to the ground. He paused to regain his composure.

Lilit glanced over her shoulder and whispered, "What?"

He jogged to catch up to her and said, "Nothing, that was very astute."

Lilit rolled her eyes. "Part of my job as being a captain is being able to read people."

Lorn grunted his agreement but couldn't help but think of how quickly she had answered his question and how it mirrored what he knew of her so far.

35

"I believe she has only tapped the very surface of her power. If she truly uncovered the depths of her magic, she would be a phoenix born anew. I would bask in her glory."

Nivet's private journal.

Aza was exhausted. Her head pounded, sweat lined her brow, and dripped down her spine. The thick and cloying humidity of Kreeha paired with the depletion of her intense magic caused her vision to sway. But she gritted her teeth and forced one foot in front of the other. She could not show weakness, not now when Astaroth knew their position and had infiltrated the Kreehan palace. After curing Hanu and Ryu of their corruption, she wanted to curl up in a ball and rest for an entire week, but she couldn't, not yet.

Guards were called in to carry Hanu and Ryu to private rooms for rest. The shock that had stalled Lorn Sune had been washed away and in place was the arrogant lord ordering his guards to be on high alert and to not let anyone cross their borders.

After their orders, the guards left with an urgency to their footsteps. Lord Sune turned to Aza. His features warred between immense gratitude and something else, Aza struggled to place, perhaps regret. She knew what he had to do.

Aza blurted, "I have to leave."

Simultaneously, Lord Sune stated, "Thank you for saving their lives."

His brows pulled together in consternation, but slowly he nodded.

He didn't like sending their savior away, but it was for the good of Kreeha. They couldn't be targeted yet. They needed time to bolster their forces and prepare the Kreehan soldiers for what was to come.

"Let us grab our things and we will leave." Aza marched brusquely past him, not in anger but in understanding. They needed to ready themselves, she couldn't spare any extra emotion toiling over her love of the Kreehan palace, its serene beauty, and captivating sights. She was loathe to leave it so soon, but they could not linger any longer.

"Wait." Lord Sune grasped her arm. He let out pained breath and quickly removed it. She was still emitting magic like the spray of mist from a pounding waterfall.

"You do not need to leave immediately. We can provide you all with horses, accustomed to the terrain of Kreeha, supplies, and a few guards. You do not need to depart like thieves in the night."

Aza nodded her thanks and raced outside of the room. If she stopped moving, she would collapse. Xira, Anwin, and Reed flanked her. Despite the magic pouring from her, she felt their steadying hands along her body, preventing her collapse. When she reached the safety of her room, she crumpled onto the plush bed and didn't open her eyes for many hours.

~

Reed was the one to wake her, gently jostling her shoulder. The act of using magic was always draining, but fighting something like Astaroth's corruption in a body was something else entirely. It was like fighting a many-headed serpent. When Aza vanquished one site of infection, multiple heads sprouted in its place. It required immense focus and discipline to not despair, letting the corruption take hold of the infected body. She could not imagine having to cure someone from the corruption after it held their body more than fifteen minutes, the hold would be too intense.

She gingerly pushed herself up and asked, "Is it time?"

Reed checked outside her window, the curtain falling back into place. "You have roughly thirty minutes to wash up and prepare yourself. Here." He placed a tray of warm food on her nightstand, the tendrils of heat swirling like beckoning fingers in the air. "Lord Sune provided extra clothes and armor for traveling. We have yours packed already, but here is one for you to wear now."

Aza nodded her thanks and Reed left.

She quickly readied a bowl of warm water and used a washcloth to sponge the grime from her body. Her silver hair was growing longer with their travels. Not having time to braid to protect it properly, she used a leather throng and loosely pulled it back.

The outfit provided by Lord Sune's court was cut in the Kreehan style with practical additions for travel and the elements. It draped her body in the same criss cross pattern with a tight waist and billowing legs, but the fabric was thicker, able to withstand varying temperatures and dangers, but still breathable. It was paired with leather armor, and greaves. Lord Sune provided her with countless daggers which she slid into place on the baldric over her chest. She palmed the hilts of each, hoping she wouldn't have to use them.

For the last time, Aza rested on the plush bed and wolfed down the food brought to her. The Kreehan specialties were heartening and when finished, she looked longingly at the empty plates and bowls knowing it would be a while before she had another meal as filling as this.

Everything was happening too quickly; Astaroth's infiltration and Cruvo's sudden appearance. She had barely any time to sort through her jumbled thoughts. Aza pulled open the door and left the comforts of her Kreehan room for the last time. She did not spare a glance back. There was no room for comfort in the journey ahead.

~

Aza met everyone outside the Kreehan stables, on the outskirts of the Silver River which roared beside them, as if sensing the desperate urgency they each held. Aza wondered if it felt the magic pulsing in her veins and responded in kind.

Lord Sune's most trusted guards guided four horses from their stables, their coats gleaming and oiled. Each was a beautiful chestnut, their sand-colored tails neatly swishing patiently, awaiting their riders.

"Your supplies are already packed. I understand your need for discretion, but I hope you aim to reach the safety of the Nerian mountains?" Lord Sune raised a tentative brow at Xira who said nothing.

"Thank you," Aza said.

Sune startled and stepped forward. "No, my dear Aza of the Well. It is I who should be thanking you. You saved the life of my love and of my best guard." He tapped his fingers to the middle of his forehead and brought it to his heart in a fist, his head bowed. Lord Sune's guard followed suit.

He raised his head, his braids parting from his face, softly clinking together. "You must travel hard and fast, north. Avoid the eastern edge of Kreeha if you can. If I were Astaroth I would work to cut you off as fast as possible from their eastern front."

Xira smirked and reached out to clasp Lord Sune's forearm. They stayed that way, staring at one another until Xira said, "I will pay you back in kind for that knock to the head."

Sune chuckled under his breath. "I don't doubt it, Nerian."

Without further pretense, they each mounted a horse, the guards leading them to a gate leading along a northern road outside the city of Cyran. Panic bolted through her for a moment. She had never ridden a horse before and was worried the inexperience would slow her. But she trusted her instincts and a soft voice within. Her body took over and soon it felt natural to sit in the saddle, like she had done it her entire life. The majestic horse carried her well as they cantered through the dark city streets, quiet but for a few late-night stragglers caught in the torch light.

At the Cyran city gates, Xira bade the guards to remain and defend their city. They protested, repeating Lord Sune's orders.

"We will travel faster alone. Feel free to tell Lord Sune I threatened you."

"I'm sorry but we cannot let you go alone."

Xira sighed and looked at Aza.

She didn't like to, but she knew they would be better here,

protecting their home city from possible invaders. In one easy motion she pulled the earth up as a barrier in front of their horses.

Blocked from pursuit, Xira, Anwin, Reed, and Aza urged their horses forward and left the shouting guards behind. They could easily get out of such a thing. They only needed to get someone with earth magic to mold the wall back down into the ground.

Aza thought she heard the faint soft laughter of guards on the city walls, chuckling at their friends' predicament.

It was a lovely sound that buoyed Aza's hope as they cantered into the pitch-black night on the winding trail, to leave Kreeha and finally reach Neria.

~

They cut a brutal pace through Kreeha, winding through densely vined jungles and deserts with hints of sand dunes winking at them in the distance. Tension thrummed through her body. They needed to make it to Neria, within the safety of those cold and forlorn mountains. Astaroth would be hunting them. Every day the craggy peaks grew closer, their tops dusted with snow.

Winter had descended. Camp, sleep, ride, and repeat. The somber and urgent thread between the four of them halted any conversation. It was time to return home.

Aza's body strained, on edge, listening for a hint of a soldier or a creep of corruption like smoke on the wind. She imagined the black gripping her and choking her, climbing up her throat until that was all she was. At night she woke quickly, gasping for breath, and dismissed those fears.

Their horses were indeed great for travel. They galloped across the landscape with ease, navigating the tough dry desert along with the lush green jungles. Aza was tentative about her skill, but like putting on a well-worn dress, her body acclimated quickly, and she rode in the saddle well.

One night, Xira announced, "One more day of hard riding and we will be within the Nerian boundaries. Astaroth will not easily cross our borders."

Aza imagined the rigorous path up the mountain. Oron's words from long ago came back to her, how no one was able cross the Nerian borders—their mountains impenetrable, the mountainside too tricky to traverse skillfully. Outsiders have never been to the Nerian capital, El'theren.

"And why has no one ever been able to enter Neria?" Aza asked.

"We have our ways," Xira replied, her grim smile cutting like a knife.

They departed early the next morning, eager to be within the safety of the Nerian mountains and free from the pursuit of Astaroth. The Kreehan landscape had changed, its lush humid jungles turning into dry desert then harsh mountainous rock. The weather changed with it, and Aza's skin pebbled from the wind chill. The once humid and cloying heat of Kreeha gave way to freezing temperatures.

The horses' hooves broke through thin ice crystals forming on the small patches of grass poking through the jagged rocks.

Halfway through the day, a sudden sense of despair gripped Aza's heart. Noticing her horse had come to a stop, Anwin swung back. She did not choose coddling words and cut straight to the point. "What's wrong?"

Aza's hair fell in her face, and she brushed away a silver strand, her face pinched, and breathing rough. "I don't know. But I feel like a rabbit walking into a snare."

Anwin's eyes widened, and she immediately whistled.

Xira in the lead and Reed covering the rear, converged where Anwin and Aza were. Anwin told them what was happening.

Xira's head whipped back and forth. "Can you tell us more, Aza?"

She shook her head. "I have strong feelings all the time. Maybe I should dismiss this one."

"No, do not doubt yourself." Anwin reassured her.

Reed brought his horse next to Xira. "We could try another path, but if people are waiting to ambush us, they could be stationed elsewhere around the mountain. They know we want to retreat there and are trying to cut off our attempt."

Xira nodded, deep in thought, weighing their options. "I agree, Reed."

"We cannot sit here debating our options. We are left exposed, and every minute wasted is another minute in danger outside our borders." Strands of red hair pulled loose from Anwin's braid, tossed about in the wind.

Anwin was right. Their new terrain left them completely exposed. There were no trees, and no shelter besides the odd outcropping of rocks.

Aza found it difficult to believe her intuition. Even though they were exposed, it also meant they should be able to see if any troops trailed them or were waiting to ambush.

Xira's chin firmed with her decision. "Aza, your magic has returned, and you are turning into a respectable fighter. If there is an ambush—we fight through it. Understand? We need be deep within Neria tonight, if possible. We need sanctuary."

Despite the decadent food and day of rest at Lord Sune's palace, their months of travel wore on them, the deep hollows in each of their cheeks, the returning circles under their eyes.

Aza tried to calculate the days. She was taken from El'en around mid to late fall and now it was nearing mid-winter. Too long to be spent traveling the five provinces and defending their lives around every turn.

With each of them in agreement they rode forward, but Aza couldn't dismiss the uneasy feeling in her stomach, like they were heading towards their own demise.

~

The rocky terrain was difficult the closer they drew to the borders of Neria. Aza's magic hummed in anticipation, a thrilling song of harmony whenever her gaze lingered on the sharp peaks jutting high into the cloud-dense sky. Yet like the edge of a knife, she was balanced, and whenever she came back to reality, the slithering feel of Astaroth's corruption beckoned closer. She rolled her neck to stop the creepy feeling from gaining any ground, a weak attempt to dispel her unease.

Although the horses did their best to navigate the tricky rocks, Xira decided it best to leave them. They dismantled the saddles, bridles, and supplies dividing it between them evenly. Aza brought her head in thanks to her horse, the soft nose nuzzling against Aza's chilled skin. She hoped they would find sanctuary in whatever nearby town they could or find safety in the wilderness.

Aza gave her horse one last pat before departing, the loose shingle and rocks easily slipping beneath her feet. She suggested making a smoother path for them to cross, but the Nerians looked at her as if she had grown two heads.

"Do not waste your magic on something so trivial," Xira barked.

"You will need it, if your intuition is correct," Reed said, softening Xira's prior statement. He sent her a wink. "It usually is."

Anwin stepped past Aza and patted her on the shoulder. "I would take that bet every time."

Aza let out a soft huff of breath and fell in line next to her companions.

Aza's training had paid off. She walked with surety to her steps, unphased by the trickiness of the ever-changing terrain. They climbed steep inclines, interspersed with pine trees laden with snow.

The barren mountainside soon was covered with a thin layer of snow and Aza lost her train of thought staring at the blindingly white tracks. It was so faint, the amount of snow trivial, but she found herself bending down to pick it up and feel it between her fingers. She furrowed her brow and a flash of familiarity swept through her. She pushed it aside and stood. There was little time for delay. They were finally within the Nerian borders the clear demarcation line indicated with snowfall. With each step, her confidence and hope surged. They were finally here within Neria, now only to make it to the capital, to her Fate.

"Almost there," Anwin reassured her. Puffs of air escaped her mouth. The red-head's face softened, an apparent longing taking place. It had been a long time for her Nerian companions since they had been home, even before Lorn entered the Hinterlands. Summertime, when the Nerian mountain range was not covered in snow, when they were not putting their lives in danger at every moment.

"Once we climb this foothill, it will level out for us to rest, and then we will show you our ways up the mountain." Anwin grinned, her teeth glinting back.

Xira and Reed trekked ahead of Aza and Anwin, their strong bodies easily tackling the countless foothills they have climbed. The trees grew denser, their thick roots exposed over the ground and Aza looked down to avoid tripping. Before she could register what was happening, Anwin yanked her back, using a pine tree to shield them.

"What—"

Anwin brought a finger to her lips and rolled her eyes back towards Xira and Reed. Aza pulled her hood over her exposed hair and peered beyond their tree cover. Xira and Reed were in a similar position, finding cover from the pine trees. They stood across from one another.

Xira's sword was unsheathed and ready in her hand, while Reed was slowly pulling out both his axes. She knew he favored dual wielding axes, her practice sparring matches with him a tough match-up, the weapons unfamiliar for her to attack against.

Anwin's cheerful demeanor vanished, frost settling, and in its place was the Nerian warrior. Each of them. The easy-going, relaxed people she had grown used to had hardened like ice.

Anwin's bow was already nocked with an arrow, and she positioned herself around the tree. "Stay hidden," she ordered.

"My magic has returned. I can help," Aza reasoned. She was a woman grown, yet she felt like a petulant child asking for permission.

Anwin bit back a sigh and explained, "It is not to keep you out of the fight. But I don't know if the enemy has seen you yet. Best to stay covered until your position is revealed. You are their top target and our most precious thing to guard."

Aza understood and bit back any further argument. They had gone through this whole journey to bring her back safely to Neria.

The sun slashed through the pine trees like blades. It was beginning to set. Something wet landed on Aza's cheek. She looked up to see a soft flurry of snow descend from the clouds.

Anwin crept further from the tree, her bow readied, arrow aimed. She scanned the hilltop. Aza patiently watched and waited for a sign, a sound, something. The hillside was quiet except for the soft exhale of wind across her cheek.

A marching of footsteps echoed above them. Aza only saw Anwin's eyes widen as she pressed tighter to the trunk of the tree, her arrow aimed at a distant target.

Aza wrung her hands together. She needed to see who was up there, but she could prove to them she could listen to orders.

The marching stopped and a single set of footsteps moved forward, crunching in the snow.

"Nerians. I know you are there. You have taken someone that doesn't belong to you. Please return her."

Aza gasped. It rippled across the hillside. Her hand went to cover her mouth, but it was too late. She knew that voice. She could recognize it anywhere. Cruvo had come for her at last.

36

"The court of Gara is more insidious than Lorn realizes. He will be eaten alive."
Cruvo's private journal

The next morning Lorn was stunned that one of the servants relayed a message, requesting his presence with Avareth. Lorn informed Lilit and they both joined the prior Lady of Gara.

Avareth was resting in the gardens with a surprising amount of sun poking through the clouds.

When they neared, she rose from the wrought iron chair and said, "Good morning both of you. I understand my daughter promised a proper tour of Holdsfast and this manor as befitting an ambassador of Iyera." She pulled her white shawl tighter over her shoulders as a bitter wind swept through the garden, rustling the leaves. "Unfortunately, my daughter is taking care of other matters, so I will be your guide today."

Lorn murmured his thanks and Avareth began her tour. They wound through the carefully curated garden, as Avareth expertly narrated. Lorn couldn't deny the beauty of it. His background in farming piqued his interest and he asked many questions. Every response turned into a captivating story. Avareth clearly took pride in her family's manor and expanded on each plant that Lorn took an interest in.

He tried to reconcile the new information he had learned from Devlin as he looked at Avareth. Her husband had passed away suddenly. Heart failure was what Devlin said. People passed away all the time from unexpected illnesses and accidents, but was this one of them? Left widowed and her daughter quickly married.

The gardens sprawled over the south and west side of the property facing the entrance of the manor and crawling over to the side, where the forest bordered their property lines. At the end of the garden tour, Lorn couldn't help but search for the peculiar flower that had sparked his interest the other day — the bright white leaves with veins of black.

Noticing his hesitation, Avareth asked, "Is there something else you need?"

"Actually, I saw this striking flower the other day on my walk. Its leaves are pure white with dark veins of black creeping up, and the entire flower is black like obsidian. Do you know it?"

"An interesting eye you have there, Lorn of Verta. That is the Widow Maker. Only those with great skill can handle such a flower. Steeped into a tea just long enough, the drinker will be temporarily paralyzed. Steeped longer, they will be rendered unconscious. Steeped too long, the drinker will die."

"Why have I never seen it before?"

"It is a very temperamental flower. Tricky to grow in the right conditions and fickle when it blooms. It prefers the conditions of Gara, but typically only locations on the coast, like Holdsfast, can propagate them. I believe this manor is one of the only locations known to have cultivated them properly."

Lorn nodded his appreciation at their skill. Growing and maintaining crops was a difficult endeavor.

Avareth led him around the east and north side of the property, The north side faced the ocean. A staircase was cut into the cliff to lead them down to the sandbar. The east side of the manor was filled with complimentary and expensive outdoor furniture.

Avareth finished the tour and led them to one of the expansive wrought iron tables, its iron work latticed and designed like the crest of Gara.

Avareth motioned for a servant to bring them lunch.

By the time their lunch had ended, the paltry amount of sun they were granted was swept away by the thick clouds, threatening another rainfall.

Avareth regarded Lorn with soft blue eyes. "I hear things, hunter. I hear you have been asking questions around town."

His stomach churned. "What types of questions?"

Avareth leaned forward, her eyes narrowed at him. "Don't play coy with me. I know exactly what you are asking. You are playing a dangerous game. My daughter is not one to trifle with."

Lorn spread out his hands and said, "I only wish to understand."

"Oh, really?"

"She is the one who brought me here. I am merely talking to the locals, seeing what new information I can gather."

Avareth smoothed her hair back. "I will only say this. Don't. Don't pry. Don't ask questions. Leave things alone. There is more at play here and you cannot understand all the details." Avareth stood up and gave a curt nod to Lorn and Lilit before leaving.

After Avareth was out of sight, he asked Lilit, "What do you think?"

She fiddled with the edge of her dagger, playing around with the sharpened tip. "I think if I have to listen to you both talk about plants for another hour, I'm going to drown myself in the ocean."

~

By the time a week had crawled by, Lorn was restless. Every day in the small town amounted to little. He paced the gardens, tore through the manor, engaged in listless small talk with Lady Rasmina and Avareth, walked on the beach, explored the neighboring forests, and sparred with Lilit. Yet it didn't matter. He wanted to know more about the story Devlin had spun, and he couldn't let it go. His mind latched on to it like a fish on a hook. Even the practice of his magic with Issi in his dreams did nothing to quell his restless spirit.

It was invigorating and fantastic to practice with such skill and finesse with his magic, the well of his power seemingly unlimited compared to the minuscule amounts of magic he was able to utilize prior. He dared not practice during the day in fear of garnering attention, but at night the magic that had manifested in his body released given its freedom.

He imagined Aza feeling the same. The freedom in her dreams to be who she wanted, wield what she wanted, without any fear of repercussion. Innumerable times, he had whispered prayers for her safety. Issi had only reassured him of Aza's safety, but the goddess was mercurial and private. She did not willingly share information. It seemed Issi trained him merely out of some strange form of duty to him. He had yet to figure it out. They barely spoke, and Issi treated him like a task she was burdened with, not one she found enjoyment in.

After hearing Devlin's story and the warning from Avareth, Lorn decided to push his luck and ask Issi a question. The worst she could do would be to not answer. There was no harm in trying.

He requested a break, leaned against a tree trying to recapture his breath. "Should I fear Lady Rasmina?"

Issi stood across from him. She was smooth as polished stone, her electric blue eyes like shining gems as she slid them to Lorn. "You should fear nothing, hunter."

Lorn heaved a sigh at her ambivalent answer. "You understand what I mean, Goddess. Do not act so obtuse."

Her eyes narrowed slightly. "You should be wary of everyone. From what I understand, Lady Rasmina's history is...complicated. She hates everything about your world, especially magic and especially us."

The 'us' was said with fervor, implicating the gods and goddesses.

"Why?" Lorn wiped the sweat from his brow with his sleeve and pushed away from the tree supporting him.

"Continue meeting with the sailor at night. You will soon understand."

Frustrated, Lorn roughly ran a hand through his hair, a few strands caught on his fingers. "Why can you not speak plainly? You have answers that would solve many problems."

Issi barely shifted her stance, unruffled by Lorn's anger. "I am not all-knowing, hunter. With the gods and goddesses in a non-corporeal form, I gain insight to other people's habits and choices. Think of my spirit as being one with the air. Yet I cannot be everywhere at once, I can occupy a specific space or none. I vowed to myself long ago I would not interfere anymore."

"Yet you are interfering now?" Lorn gestured to himself. "You have spoken to me and guided me multiple times. Does that not count as interfering?"

Issi's lips thinned, and her hand trembled slightly, the one sign Lorn had ever seen of her facade cracking. "That is different." She walked away into the forest. "We are done for today. Be wary of everyone."

Lorn blew a long breath out of his lips and shrugged. He hadn't received the answers he wanted.

~

Lorn and Lilit escaped from the manor easily and met Devlin in the same seaside cave. Lorn had such an excess amount of energy, he was bouncing on his toes as he raced down to meet Devlin.

Without pretenses, Lorn launched into his next question. "So Pearl is the daughter of Lady Rasmina and your brother Drion?" Lorn feared his next line of questioning, both Drion and Lord Mathor were not around; they were either exiled or dead. He didn't know which answer he preferred for this tragic tale. "Where are they?"

Devlin nodded and said, "All in due time, hunter. Yes, Pearl was a love child between Rasmina and Drion. Every few months, she would journey back to Holdfast alone except for her now three daughters. My brother's heart broke every time she left and every time she visited. Holding his own baby, yet months would go by, and his daughter was a different version of herself.

"Even though the town didn't know of Pearl being Drion's son—they knew. They could see the love between the two of them and between Drion and Pearl. They kept their secret, having no love for Lord Mathor and having never met him. Yet they knew and loved 'Mina and with the birth of Pearl and her rekindled love with Drion, the mantle of sorrow and fury was slowly lifting from her shoulders. A couple of years passed with their love kept a secret and Drion never told me directly, but I know he treasured every moment he got to spend with them, every moment he held his daughter. Even though Pearl didn't know, she referred to him as her mama's friend, as an uncle. All of us in the town were referred to as her aunts and uncles."

Devlin paused and cleared his throat. In the darkness of the cave and the sharp light from the lantern, it was difficult to discern

Devlin's features, but Lorn caught a tear running down the sailor's face.

"Then one day, it all was ruined. Lord Mathor accompanied Rasmina to the manor, to Holdsfast, and it was the end. I'm not exactly sure what happened. Rasmina has never opened up to about it. But I was tending to my netting near my house, when 'Mina raced down. You know how she always dresses. Elegant. Regal. A lady in every sense of the word, not a hair out of place or an emotion unchecked, even as a child. But she looked like she had experienced a monster. Her hair was ripped free from any bindings. It whipped in front of her panicked eyes, true fear held behind them. Her dress was torn, and her feet were bare, with mud and blood coating them. Pearl was around two years old at the time, and she was holding tight to her mother, her eyes wide.

"I remember being shocked. How was Pearl not crying? How was she clutching her mother—her mother who was normally so composed and not crying at the sight? I wanted to break down. A fear unlike anything I had ever known crept up my spine, paralyzing me.

"'Where is he?' she screamed at me.

"I knew immediately she was talking about Drion. Lord Mathor had finally found out. But how she was acting was too much. Love affairs were not unheard of, usually the cheater was left shamed. The nobility did not execute for such transgressions. Perhaps lands or titles stripped away. Nothing like how she was acting. She was the true Lady of Gara, she could not have her title stripped away. But 'Mina looked at me with true fear in her eyes. I tried to calm her down, but she shook me off.

"*'Devlin, trust me.'*

"She shoved Pearl into my arms and made me promise to hide her until only she or Avareth came to get her. Pearl reached a chubby arm for her mom a soft cry of, *'Mama.'*

"Now Mina only showed softness around her children. And that moment was no exception. Tears ran freely down her face as her fingers delicately traced her youngest daughter's round cheeks. *'Mama will be back. Go with Uncle Devvy.'*"

Devlin's voice was choked full of emotion. He tilted his head back up to consider the cave ceiling. Lorn didn't interrupt. He would be in shambles if he had to describe the worst day of his life to a stranger, the day his wife was killed by the Howler.

"I listened and hid with Pearl, that little girl means the world to me. I would do anything for her, the joy of my brother's life. I told Rasmina that Drion was in the western forest gathering wood. She took off at a full sprint, her red dress torn, muddied, her feet bleeding from sharp rocks, and twigs piercing her delicate skin.

"Since I was hiding with Pearl, I have no idea what happened next. I hid with her in this very cave. A cave in which 'Mina would play with us when we were kids. Pearl barely cried, her eyes so like her mother's, wide, staring at the lapping waves in a trance, like someone far beyond her years. Every so often her chin would wobble with emotion. Day turned to night, and I fed Pearl small scraps of dried fish and gave her water from the waterskin I brought. I told her we were playing a game. To see how quiet we could be and surprise mommy when she returned."

Devlin cracked a small smile. "She liked that game, wanting to surprise her mommy. I was tempted to leave the cave. Pearl was falling asleep in my arms due to the long day, dark cave, and the lapping waves. But I remembered 'Mina's frantic words, and I couldn't fail her. So, I held her, my brother's daughter, through the night until the next morning, I crept out of the cave meeting the rare sunrise. The light blinded me. And a shadow appeared. I ducked back into the cave in case it was someone trying to take Pearl away.

"'Pearl,' they shouted. It was her.

"'Mina had returned. I rushed out of the cave, worried for her health and for little Pearl who had missed her mother for an entire day. 'Mina was in the same disarray as yesterday, muddy, bloodied. Her dress in small shreds barely held onto her thin frame. She swayed with each step, like she was intoxicated but that wasn't it. I knew then with all of my being; my brother was dead.

"I ran to meet her on the sand, careful not to jostle sleeping Pearl. Upon seeing me, Rasmina collapsed to the ground and a heart-wrenching wail emitted from her like the sound of a dying animal. I joined her on the sand and both of us intertwined in our grief and love of my brother. The product of their love lay nestled between us, sound asleep despite the racket we made. Somehow, we stumbled back to my house, where we slept. Someone tried to take Pearl, I think Avareth, but Rasmina howled, and Pearl rushed back to her mother's side, crawling into her like a sickle moon. Eventually I coaxed it out of her. All she said was *'They are both dead,'* and *'I buried them.'*

"After a few days of us shuttered away from the world, Rasmina led me to my brother's body, the ground freshly disturbed, amongst the giant trees. This thin slip of a woman who had no work-toughened callouses buried my brother on her own. She choked out through sobs that she stayed through the night with only the slim light of the moon to help and dug his grave by hand.

"Weeks passed and she finally returned to Lighthold. Lord Mathor had died too, but I never knew what happened between the three of them, what had transpired in that forest. I only know that Rasmina remained alive, while the other two died, whether at each other's hands or not."

Lorn tried to reconcile what he knew of Lady Rasmina with this tragic story. The woman he knew now so full of vitriol and bitterness. But that did not explain the people being kidnapped currently and forced to work in the mountains. It made him pity her, but it was not enough to wash her sins away. He needed more.

"I am deeply sorry for your loss, and for hers. I know it does nothing, these empty words of comfort. Nothing can fix it. Nothing can bring him back. But I need to understand why Lady Rasmina is capturing people and forcing them to work under the mountains. What is she searching for?"

Devlin wiped the stray tears from his face. "I do not condone what she is doing, nor do I know why. I am assuming it is like everything else—to solve whatever happened with Drion and Lord Mathor. All I know is she wants magic gone."

Lorn's eyebrows raised. "Gone?"

"Yes, she wants it gone, entirely. I believe whatever she is searching for, will put an end to it."

Lilit stirred, backtracking to them and placed a steadying hand against the cave wall. "We need to leave."

Lorn shook Devlin's hand. "I appreciate you telling this terrible story. It does help with my understanding of Lady Rasmina and might help me answer some questions and potentially save some lives."

"I do this all for her and for my brother."

Lorn emerged from the cave into the night like he was being

rebirthed into the world. He imagined Devlin holding his precious niece throughout the night, quelling her fears, her sadness, and holding onto hope only to find it ripped to shreds.

37

"I need to give Aza more credit for what she has accomplished. If the feelings I have in regard to her proximity are what she feels when with Cruvo, I have been too harsh. No wonder she has confided in him."

Nivet's private journal.

Aza was a coward. She clutched to the pine tree at her back for support and curled inward. Her emotions warred—the overwhelming urge to run to Cruvo and collapse within the safety of his arms and the urge to run past him and figure out her destiny among the looming Nerian mountains. Her magic pulsed, each one growing in power, like a beacon divulging her presence.

"My stars, I do not know what they have told you to join them. They are using you. You have been held by them for too long, too easily swayed by their opinions. Come back to me." His voice carried down the hillside like a hand caressing her face, beckoning her to him. She dug in her heels, the thin layer of snow cracking under the pressure. She would not be swayed by him. If Cruvo truly supported her, he would let her go and allow her to return when she was ready. This was not love. This was control.

Aza focused on her breath, the steady flow, reminding herself again and again. *This is not how I truly feel. It is only my body reacting to his proximity. It is not how I truly feel. This is only your body's response.*

But she wanted to cry out from pain. Proximity to the other gods and goddesses caused an undeniable pull, but with Cruvo, it was magnified, heightened. Due to their excessive time together, her body, her magic, craved him like an addict. The distance she had gained with the Nerians had helped ease the building desire, but now he was here dangling himself in front of her, begging for her to return. It was too easy to imagine them together, her body wanting the release she craved so desperately.

She dug her nails into her palms and broke skin. The brief flash of pain ebbed the craving and with frantic desperation, she clutched on to that power—thc power to resist.

"I can feel you, Aza. Your magic, your power. It is intoxicating. Return to El'en. Forces are moving. Ill-Fated events are happening."

Anwin slipped away from their shared tree and Aza reached out to grab her, but it was too late. Quiet as a panther, she ascended the hill.

Xira and Reed watched, their weapons readied. Xira motioned with her hands. Anwin crouched, watching Cruvo pace the hilltop. Aza strained to see Anwin, the subtle readjustment of her body and fingers, her breath stilted.

When the shot was clear, Anwin released the arrow. Aza held her breath. It flew straight and true, whistling through the air, aimed perfectly for his heart.

A flash of concern speared through her. If they killed him, Lord Aldrich would die, not Cruvo. The gods and goddesses couldn't die. To openly attack the leader of Iyera was an act of war. This arrow could decide everyone's fate.

Cruvo was decked in traveling clothes, with no armor to protect his body, taunting them with his vulnerability.

Aza wanted to close her eyes, but she forced herself to watch as the arrow flew closer. Before it could pierce his skin, a wall of earth burst from the ground as the arrow embedded deep into the dirt. Cruvo stepped around the barrier and brushed a few stray flecks of dirt from his tunic.

"You Nerians were always fun to fight. Bold and unafraid. But you made a vast mistake. You thought I came alone?" He motioned with his hand and a retinue of soldiers appeared on the hilltop. "Now, let's be civil and make yourselves known."

Anwin had scrambled to another position while her arrow flew through the sky. Xira and Reed climbed too, each fanning out. From her separate cover, Anwin shot off another arrow.

This time Cruvo didn't wait for dramatic effect and burned the arrow midair. "Get them," he ordered.

The soldiers spread out down the hill, their swords raised. Aza's breath came to her in strangled gasps. This isn't what she wanted. There couldn't be any more death. The Nerians easily defended themselves, but there were at least thirty soldiers with Cruvo, presumably Iyera's best fighters, combing the mountainside looking for her. Aza needed to act. She couldn't stay here while others fought for her. She could resist Cruvo and stop the fight that was about to break out.

She allowed herself a moment to close her eyes, her resolution made. She straightened her spine, firmed her legs, and stepped out from her cover. With her chin held high, she stared at Cruvo who stood so far away, and she marched resolutely up the hill. The soldiers froze in place, their eyes trailing over her as she ascended, afraid of her power.

Aza yanked the edge of her hood down, revealing the shock of silver hair.

A triumphant smile spread over Lord Aldrich's body and with each step, Aza felt his magic pulse in awareness, like two stars orbiting each other.

She couldn't bear to look at her Nerian companions, but she forced herself to. Reed's eyes widened, forlorn as he watched her go to Cruvo, his mouth forming the word, *don't*. Xira's mouth was set in a grim line, her head shaking slightly.

Aza looked to her right and saw Anwin crouched amongst the branches and snow, her bow nocked, eyebrows furrowed in consternation.

Cruvo reached a hand to her, the distance between them closing. But she couldn't touch him. She didn't trust herself. If she touched him, her magic would sing in awareness, and like the sweeping wave of the ocean, drown her within the tide of her senses.

She was Aza of the Well, a mixture of Goddess and MagicBlessed, a conduit of power, a product of the prophecy, in charge of her own destiny.

"Tell your soldiers to retreat," she commanded.

Cruvo frowned, and slowly pulled the offering of his hand away from Aza. He cocked his head and studied her.

She did not balk from the scrutiny. The hardened journey added sharp edges to her soft exterior. She was no longer the pampered resident of Lord Aldrich, safely tucked away in the El'en castle, the only struggles being gawked at and dealing with courtiers. She had battled gods and goddesses, escaped the confines of The Fortress, battled a sea serpent, had her magic stifled, and had survived and succeeded despite those challenges.

Lord Aldrich motioned for the guards to retreat, and Aza saw the familiar icy blue eyes of the man behind Aldrich. His personal guard Gravers had joined.

"Cr—," Aza stopped herself. She did not know who in Lord Aldrich's guard knew him to be Cruvo. "Lord Aldrich, surely you can see I am here of my own volition. Let me go to Neria. If I want to return to you, I will. There does not need to be a battle here. There are bigger enemies we must prepare for."

"Aza," he breathed and for a moment Aldrich's visage disappeared and Aza saw Cruvo in his place. The darkened skin framed by thick, beautiful, brown hair. The loose waves framed his strong jaw, those piercing green eyes.

"I've missed you." Aldrich stepped closer. He reached up to cup her face with his hand, but Aza stepped back. He paused, letting his hand drop. "We have searched for months for you. I am glad you are safe, but you can return home now. Come back to Iyera with me. Please." He extended his hand one more time, an invitation Aza couldn't accept.

"I need to do this. I need to go to Neria. I am not asking permission. You will let us pass." Aza clenched her jaw, her back unbowed.

He stared at her and finally said, "You do not know what they are like. You may not even return. Think, Aza. Think of how they had to steal you out of El'en and sail across the ocean just to bring you back into Neria. Why would they do such a thing? If they wanted to talk, why couldn't they do that without capturing you. They took away your magic," he seethed and stepped closer. "You think they won't do it again? Take you within Neria, where I cannot reach you, keep you sedated, and locked up."

Lord Aldrich's soldiers let out sounds of disgust. One soldier spit on the ground.

He was so close to her. One step forward and she would be within his arms, her head resting on his shoulder. But she couldn't. The Nerians would never do that to her.

"You don't know for sure, my stars," he answered.

Aza hadn't realized she said the last part out loud. Doubt wormed its way around her heart, but she fought it, thinking of every moment on their journey; every joke, every time they trained her, kept her safe from enemies and herself.

She firmed her back and said, "No they wouldn't. Now let us pass."

"I can't do that." Aldrich shook his head sadly. "They could trap you and keep you there. I'm sorry. This is for your own good."

Before she could issue a warning, his soldiers advanced.

Anwin fired an arrow. It ripped through a soldier's calf. He dropped to the ground screaming.

Xira burst from her tree, engaging with two soldiers. She handled them quickly, slicing one along the leg and knocking the other out with the butt of her sword.

Three soldiers gathered around Reed as he elegantly dispatched them.

Aza loosened a breath. Her companions were doing their best not to kill, only harm.

Aza didn't know what to do. She needed to get the soldiers to stop. Despite the Nerians' superior fighting skill, they were outnumbered, and Astaroth was still pursuing them.

Aza pulled her sword loose and held it to Aldrich's throat. "Order them to stop. Now," she hissed. She struggled to hold the sword against his soft light brown skin. Only one sharp movement and his life would end.

Cruvo smirked. "Aza, you would only kill Lord Aldrich and not myself. This threat means nothing to me." He gently steered the sword away from his throat. "You know who it would tear apart. Lilit."

Aza gasped but firmed her grip on the sword and stepped closer, the sword back to his throat.

"Yes, Lilit confessed everything to me. How she let the Nerians take you and did nothing to stop it. She was effectively punished. I almost killed her dear mortal, Lord Aldrich, in that moment. I was so mad. But sending her to Gara with Lorn was a more fitting punishment."

Cruvo yanked the sword away, his fingers wrapped around Aza possessively. "I love your ferocious edge, Aza. I see the Nerians honed more of it. It was always there in El'en, but now you are like a polished jewel, gleaming brightly, unobstructed."

Aza held his stare, their face mere inches away.

"You will not harm me, because despite Lilit's flaws, you care for her and by extension care for Lord Aldrich. Do not play with me, my stars." His hand trailed over her fingers and danced up her arm. She wanted to relax to his enticing touch. Her magic coming alive within her body, every sense burning brightly, alive in his presence. She softened her grip on the hilt of her sword as Cruvo leaned closer.

"Why are you avoiding my touch?" he whispered. Cruvo leaned closer, bringing his mouth to her cheek. She shivered.

This was what Cruvo wanted. He wanted her unnerved, the emotions and magic becoming a confusing tangle for her to weave through.

"No!" Aza screamed. She pushed hard on his chest, and he stumbled backwards. He didn't fall, but the surprise on his face gutted her.

Soldiers cried out around her, as Xira, Reed and Anwin fought them. They were getting pinned. Despite their superior fighting skills, there were too many.

Aza's body tingled, her magic aching to be used. She did not want to repeat that night at the inn, where she instantly killed the intruders without thought. She needed to paralyze the soldiers and not kill them.

She sheathed her sword and grinned at Cruvo.

He shouted, "Aza, no!"

With a skill and precision, she didn't know she was capable of, Aza enveloped every soldier and coated them in shadow like a heavy blanket of night and transported them to the bottom of the foothill. The far away cries of surprise echoed up the snow-covered hillside. It was enough to buy them time. Only Gravers and Lord Aldrich remained.

"We will continue on," Aza insisted.

"I cannot let you do that," Cruvo said.

A flare of fire burst from her left hand as a shard of ice emerged from her right hand. "It was not a request."

"You know I love our time sparring, my stars."

Aza wanted to close her eyes in pain, but this was not a dream. This fight was real. The consequences were real. She could not harm Lord

Aldrich, but she needed to incapacitate both him and Gravers.

She screamed a cry of rage and defiance, the anger fueling her action. The fire in her hand molded itself into a spear and she hurled it towards Gravers. Not enough to injure, only enough to scare. Frighten them away from this fight and allow the Nerians and herself to escape unharmed.

Gravers dodged, rolling to the side as Cruvo nullified the fire dousing it with water. She barely registered the smell of smoke as she hurtled towards Cruvo, ice flaring from her palms. But he was accustomed to fighting with magic, and the darts of ice withered from the air and splashed to the ground. Aza unsheathed her sword and swung, while her other hand worked to freeze Cruvo's feet to the ground. His eyes widened and he blocked with his own sword in time.

The delay was enough, and Aza gained ground, her sword inching towards him. He easily unstuck his feet by melting the ice and Aza saw a flash of luminescent green cross his eyes. She could easily shadow Gravers and Cruvo down to the bottom of the hill like his soldiers, but she needed him to back down of his own volition. She didn't want to force him. She wanted—no needed him to understand this was her will and she could not be taken. Not by him or by anyone.

Aza's sword clanged against his. She couldn't hurt Lord Aldrich's body, and he knew it, but she gritted her teeth and said, "Let me go."

His eyes softened as he said, "I can't."

Cries rang out down the hill. It startled Aza and she faltered, her weight shifting. She disengaged from Cruvo, pausing. Cries of pain were common from the Iyeran soldiers, but these cries sounded different. They were screams of pure fear.

Aza looked over her shoulder to see what was happening. The soldiers she had shadowed to the bottom of the hill were being hunted. They raced up the snow-covered hill as fast as they could with beasts nipping at their heels. From what Aza could see they seemed like ordinary wolves. But if they were ordinary wolves, the soldiers would have no trouble dispatching them. Her brow wrinkled in confusion, and she strained to see farther down the hill. The wolves were twisted, with black lines creeping over their thick winter coats, their trail leaving a slurry of blackened paw prints. Aza cringed from the sharp clack of gnashing teeth and the cry of soldiers as they were dragged back and ripped apart, the snow spattered with their blood.

"Save us!" they screamed.

Aza was frozen. She couldn't process what was happening, so similar and dissimilar to the creatures of the Hinterlands. Before she realized it, she was racing down the hill, and she released her magic. It burned the wolves, their pitiful cries echoing out over the mountainside. She had forgotten about Cruvo. Her feet pounded on the hard snow, with only the thought of rescuing the soldiers playing through her mind.

Before she made it another step, Xira crashed into her, and they toppled onto the hard ground. The air was knocked out of her.

She rolled to her back and gasped for air, clawing at her chest. Xira tightened her hold on her wrist and was trying to yank her back. By her side, Reed slid to a halt and grabbed Aza's other arm. They pulled her away from the soldiers. The few wolves that remained ripped the soldiers apart. Others laid on the ground in strange shreds, screaming for someone to end their life. She couldn't take it.

"No!" she shouted and thrashed against their steel-like hold. "I can help them."

"They are Astaroth's infected. We cannot risk you," Xira panted.

Aza stopped fighting them and looked further down the hill. At the bottom with a slice of a smile stood Astaroth. She was inhabiting another body, this one the sharp cut of a soldier, the heavy armor covering much of their appearance, but Aza knew it was her.

More wolves gathered behind her, their maws oozing black sickness, their coats matted and diseased. Under a sharp command, the wolves sprinted up the hill, ignoring the injured soldiers, their sole focus was on them.

Aza sent one last pitiful look at the soldiers before making her decision. She hated leaving them to a grim fate, but they needed to escape. Without a second thought, she shadowed her, Reed, and Xira to the top of the hill. Aza found Anwin running to meet them and shadowed her too.

Their fight forgotten in the face of a bigger enemy, Cruvo raced to her and demanded, "We need to leave. Now, Aza!"

"You know I won't. Leave us, so Lord Aldrich and Gravers can still survive."

"Do you understand Astaroth's powers? What she can and will do, if she unites with you?"

"I don't care. I'm leaving with them. And you must let me go." Aza's hands tightened on Xira and Reed while Anwin gripped her shoulder. They had not let go when she shadowed them.

The wolves were gaining up the hill and they had little time remaining.

"Go," Aza said, her tone sharp and clear.

A shadow fell over the group and Aza looked up in alarm. Something large was overhead. She cursed. Another beast for her to contend with.

Cruvo's eyes widened, and he swiveled his head between the large beast overhead and to the Nerians surrounding Aza.

"It cannot be," he whispered. "I thought they were all gone."

Flames burst from Aza's fingertips, ready to take on whatever beast was approaching. With the wolves to their right, the mountain to their back, and Cruvo in front, she had nowhere to go. They must fight.

Xira's jaw was slack as she reached for Aza's forearm and lowered it slowly. "It is no danger to us, Aza"

"The shadow loomed closer and closer. Cruvo and Gravers stepped back, wary.

"It cannot be," Reed breathed.

Anwin had tears shining in her eyes. "It is. He is alive."

A dragon landed, its massive body filling the hilltop clearing. Nivet sat regal atop its back. Its glistening, icy blue body seemingly formed from the Nerian snow.

"I believe the Lady said, 'go'." Nivet fixed Cruvo with a piercing stare, one of loathing, disgust, and barely restrained anger. The dragon fixed a sapphire eye on Cruvo.

It snapped its leathery wing out from its body, shielding the group.

Xira nudged Aza forward. "Climb on," she ordered.

Aza approached the creature tentatively and tried her best to scramble up the tough hide. Spikes of pure white like snow jutted from the middle of its back, and Aza situated herself between them. Aza moved gently, unwilling to inadvertently hurt the beautiful creature, its scales iridescent and shining like the reflection of the sky in the ocean. Some scales were a blinding white, while others ranged from a deep blue to a near black like the night sky.

The wolves bounded up the mountain, but the dragon was unbothered. Nivet kept his stare on Cruvo and Gravers and said, "Isarr, protect." The dragon twisted its neck to inspect the incoming wolves and released a spray of ice and frost.

Long needles of ice impaled the wolves. They gave small yelps of pain as they collapsed on the snowy mountainside, the black corruption leaking from their wounds.

"Keep out of my province, Cruvo," Nivet spit. He leaned forward and rubbed the dragon's neck. "Isarr, fly."

The dragon spread its massive wings and lifted them into the air. Aza used her thighs to clutch tightly to the dragon's massive frame, her arms wrapped around the jutting spike. A horse had been unnerving to ride, a dragon—unfathomable.

Despite her mixed feelings towards Cruvo, she couldn't help but stare down at his stubborn figure, silently urging him to leave before Astaroth could make it up the mountain. His figure grew smaller and smaller.

With each flap of the dragon's prodigious wings, they flew closer to the jagged peaks of the Nerian mountains.

She had made it at last.

38

"Lorn's fatal flaw is, despite his trauma, he chooses to believe the best in everyone. Perhaps I will cure him of such an ailment."

Cruvo's private journal

The following day a tempest raged outside, the manor windows rattling from the storm. Lorn had to remain inside, which was the worst due to his restlessness. He was accustomed to remaining indoors when the brutal winters of Verta ripped through the land, he and Lakesh whittling away the hours of the storms under blankets, in bed relearning the curves of each other's body or playing card games beside the fire. But his brain was wrapped in a persistent fog. Everywhere he looked, he relived the story Devlin had told him the night prior.

Feigning a pounding headache, Lorn declined breakfast, preferring to take it in his room. He couldn't face Lady Rasmina, not after what he had learned. He had so many questions he wanted to ask, but Devlin had been through enough and he could not pain him to ask for more details. Ghosts of Lady Rasmina's panicked form filled his room, of her shoving a young Pearl into her uncle's arms hoping to return.

The reason she wanted to banish magic entirely, to lock away an essential part of each MagicBlessed person for good couldn't only be due to a discovered love affair. What trauma had occurred for her to reach such a conclusion? Lorn debated the ideas in his head wishing to discuss it with Aza. She would provide him with fresh insight, yet he imagined she was miles and miles away from him. Safe but far. He heaved a sigh and idled his time away resharpening his already sharpened weapons.

Around midday with the rain still pounding against the manor, he decided to draw a bath. Even the biting hot water and earthy perfumes did nothing to quell his thoughts. He imagined scenario after scenario, but none of them felt like the answer.

By evening, he had remained in his room the entire day, but he was expected to join them for dinner. Due to the excess of time on his hands, he dressed well with a proper tunic, a deep forest green and trousers of rich umber. Looking in the mirror, he decided to go for a sleeker appearance and slicked his hair back. His usual golden hued skin had faded to a softer color, his countenance pale. The faint scars from his battles blended in with his paler skin. The Garan climate did no favors to his appearance, but he wouldn't be here forever. He shrugged; he had no one to dress up for or impress. Lakesh would be chuckling at Lorn's attempt to dress up for their guests, but behind that chuckle would be a flash of desire. She secretly loved him in formal attire and not covered in mud and muck from the farm work.

Luckily, he wasn't the only one dressed up when he joined the dining room. Both Lady Rasmina and Avareth were outfitted in elegant black dresses. Lady Rasmina's dress was long sleeved, clinging to her arms and her body, flaring out to the ground with a deep slit along the side exposing a pale leg and a red heel shoe. The red was carried up to her lips, painted in the same color when Lorn had first met her. Although she was gorgeous, Lorn repressed the urge to shiver, her mouth looking like she had recently feasted on fresh blood.

Her mother was dressed similarly but more subdued. Long sleeved and fitted with a high neckline. It flowed to the floor, with no leg slit and reached the heels that were replaced with black flats. Both their hair styles flowed freely. Lorn couldn't shake the image of Lady Rasmina running to Devlin with her hair unbound and messy.

Lorn, for once, felt like playing courtier. He clasped each of their hands and brushed a kiss against their knuckles. "Thank you for hosting us here. You look especially lovely tonight."

Avareth merely smirked at Lorn's pitiful attempt at flattery, but Lady Rasmina gave him a rare smile, the only sign of pleasantry she had ever directed at Lorn before. It was a smile lacking teeth, but a smile nonetheless.

Maybe time was the only thing needed to break down her hard

exterior.

Lorn was seated next to Lilit. She remained quiet, which wasn't unusual, but he still sensed something askew. He had spent enough time with her to know when she was analyzing an opponent, this time no different than any other.

Dinner was exquisite. The cooks really outdid themselves. Lady Rasmina and Avareth had a delicate chicken sliced over a bed of leaves, drizzled with a lovely vinaigrette.

Lorn and Lilit had the same dish but with freshly caught fish from the ocean. Its skin was flaky, light, and delicious.

"May I ask why we were served the fish and you chicken?"

Lady Rasmina answered politely, "I noticed how you and Lilit have loved every fish dish served lately. My mother and I have had our fill of fish for now. Sometimes different can be good."

"Thank you for such consideration, I do love it." Lorn chewed on another piece, thoughtfully trying to discern the taste. It was delicious but with Gara's different climate and food offerings he always wanted to understand what was cooked within his dish.

"Avareth, your knowledge of the plants in Gara is immense. Do you know what this fish has been cooked in? I'm trying to place the flavor, but I am struggling to do so."

"Oh, all of the typical Garan spices we use for our local fish. But this dish we figured you and Lilit would love has been steeped in one of our specialty teas."

"Really? I have never thought of doing that."

Lilit nodded her stiff agreement and said quietly, "It is delicious."

Avareth whistled. "High praise, coming from Lilit of Iyera."

Several more courses were served and as time wore on, Lorn discovered this was the most pleasant conversation he had ever had with the ladies of Gara. He was growing tired, the rich food sitting contentedly in his stomach.

The final dessert course was a rainberry custard. His spoon slid through the yellow custard in a smooth motion. He brought it to his lips. It was divine, smooth, rich, creamy with just a burst of fresh loveliness from the rainberries—a local berry with a vibrant pink exterior that bleeds red when cut open, grown in the thick bushes of Gara.

"Thank you both for planning this extraordinary dinner, and please thank your chefs. Everything was amazing. This flavor is familiar, what is it?"

Avareth leaned forward, a glint of eagerness in her eyes. "The same tea we steeped the fish in. We thought it would be a perfect finish to the evening."

Lilit went rigid beside Lorn, her hand going to her head. Lorn tried to turn his head to look at her but found his body stiff. He attempted to lift his fingers one at a time, but they were not cooperating. Even with extreme effort, he was only able to straighten his pointer finger. "Wha —" His mouth was thick and immoveable.

Across from him, Lady Rasmina and Avareth had not touched their custard, whereas his plate was half eaten, the rainberries split in half, their blood-red insides pooling on his plate. Lady Rasmina pushed herself up and slowly walked around the table.

She wrapped her fingers under Lorn's chin and forcefully yanked him to look at her.

"You should know this, Lorn of Verta. What flower can be steeped long enough to paralyze its victims? Or steeped long enough to render unconscious? Or even death?

A groan escaped Lilit. Lady Rasmina tutted, "Oh no, Lilit of Iyera. You aren't going to die. Not yet anyway. But I have a short amount of time before you are both rendered unconscious, so I will try to speak quickly. After hearing about you asking questions around town and finally receiving positive news from Lighthold and my developments there, I decided to act. Mother agreed. Now was the time. We used Widow's Maker to poison you. The very plant you took great interest in Lorn. How poetic." Her voice turned sharp, a dagger aiming to cut.

"You even thought to use my own brother, Devlin. He told you what I wanted him to tell you. I saw how you softened, how you thought I was misunderstood. How easy you are to manipulate." Lady Rasmina must have read a question in his eyes. "Yes, it was all true, but instead of wallowing, like *you* have, I decided to act. Nothing like that should ever have to happen again. But I get ahead of myself, let me fill in the gaps of that story.

"You might be familiar with the gods and goddesses, those terrible, awful things should never exist. I'm sure you know about how they love to possess the MagicBlessed for fun. They love the power or perhaps they are bored. Either way they promise the host power or riches or a changed world. Well, it happened to my father. He accepted a goddess into his body. Kerali was vindictive and bored. She didn't do anything special while she inhabited my father. She has a special affinity for Gara, loved it since the old days. Those are her words," Rasmina added.

"What the gods and goddesses don't tell their mortal victims is that they can leave any time, and when they do, the host's survival rate is only fifteen percent. A fifteen percent chance my father would survive and that is *if* the goddess decides to be gracious and leaves his body slowly and with care. But they don't care. They leave, ripping the hosts' souls to shreds. When my father died, it was because Kerali left, bored with whatever my father couldn't offer anymore. I returned to Gara, content to rule. I vowed to never let a god or goddess inhabit my body, to do right by my people.

Lilit loosened a low scream. "Yes, that's right. Your precious Lord Aldrich, whom I assume is possessed by a god, only has a fifteen percent chance at best of surviving whatever god inflicts their damage.

"I married for Gara, to a man I grew to care for, and I vowed to stay away from Holdsfast and what held my heart dear. However, I came to discover my husband made a deal with a certain goddess. Kerali had tempted him, and he had allowed that despicable goddess within his body. My husband was then dead to me. I retreated to Holdsfast to recover what little sanity remained.

"As Devlin told you, I fell in love with Drion. Besides my mother," she nodded to Avareth, "the people of Holdsfast were the only thing that kept me sane. Drion especially. Our moments were stolen and sacred. I would think of him every moment when I returned to Lighthold. I protected my two daughters, eventually three, when Pearl was born. Then, Kerali found out about my disloyalty. I had never slept with my husband since his co-habitation with Kerali. I told Kerali I never would. Only once did I break that vow. When I learned I was pregnant, I could not have Kerali suspect the child wasn't my husband's, so I played the part and she believed I merely craved Mathor for that night." Lady Rasmina's eyes hardened, her grip on the table tightening.

"She could abide my lack of marital relations, but she could not abide my infidelity. Even though the goddess did not have her full power back, she still had more than me and more than everyone of Holdsfast. She returned here with me, vowing to see who sired my bastard child. Well, Devlin told you the rest of the story, how he protected Pearl, and I ran off to find Drion. Kerali found him first, and if you know anything of the goddesses, they view us like pests."

Her voice grew soft, faraway lost in that moment. "Kerali was sadistic, torturing Drion with magic, trying to make him weep from the pain. But instead, it was me, crying on my knees. Begging her to stop. I tried to use what pitiful magic I had to stop her. But her affinity is with lightning. She scorched him alive, slowly. When he was close to his breaking point, she would stop. It became so intense, I couldn't stop hearing his wretched screams in my head. All he repeated to me was, *'I love you and I love Pearl.'* While I stood there on my knees sobbing, begging my father's murderer for mercy. But the gods know no mercy.

"She cackled, his once kind and gentle face distorted into some grotesque mockery. My beloved husband torturing my current lover. I couldn't handle it, so I did the only thing I could think of doing. Drion was going to die. but I could make it quick. While Kerali was distracted, I sprinted at Drion. She only laughed harder, thinking I was going to try to save him and burn there with him. But I pulled out my dagger and I stabbed it directly through Drion's heart. He smiled and thanked me when I did it."

A lone tear streaked down Lady Rasmina's face. She wiped it away and looked at it dispassionately.

"Blood bubbled from his mouth, his body slack against the ground. Kerali had lost her interest now that her plaything was dead. I sobbed over Drion's body and looked up at Kerali. She didn't care; she just smiled.

"'Learn from this, Rasmina. Now you will not only have one body to mourn over, but two.'

"And with that, she left my husband's body and his empty corpse collapsed on the ground. And I was left to sob over two bodies. I buried them both."

Lorn struggled to keep his eyes open, but they threatened to flutter closed.

"Any minute you will be unconscious. But I will leave you with this." She leaned forward and whispered in his ear, "I not only want to get rid of magic, I want to rid ourselves of the gods and goddesses themselves. They will all burn for what they did." Malice and vindictive righteousness swirled in the depths of those vaporous blue eyes.

She pulled away, and before Lorn succumbed to unconsciousness he saw Devlin's stout frame fill the doorway.

"Take them," Lady Rasmina ordered.

39

Nivet's private journal.

The GodsBane mountain peak was brutal and breathtaking. Aza couldn't deny the feeling of freedom that came with riding an ice dragon through the chilling skies of Neria. She was not dressed for the climate, but she found the chilling air a thrill and a desperately needed respite for her overheated and overworked body. The cold had worked its way through her exterior and was unlocking some unknown part of her.

Magic swelled in urgent release, but she couldn't let go, not with the proximity to her companions and Nivet. They needed to focus on staying on Isarr and bask in the triumph of their return home.

Aza straightened her clenched fingers from Isarr's spikes. She spread her arms out alongside her and felt the air rush past her body and the dragon's smooth shifting weight under her thighs. She tilted her head back and breathed in an crisp breath and exhaled small icicles, only the tiniest release of her magic flow.

For the first time she heard the faint chuckle of Nivet. Facing his back, she tried to imagine what his smile looked like, a slash of white across his dark, smooth skin, his tight, curly hair shorn short with tattoos swirling around the side of his head. Instead of a bitter reluctance there would be actual mirth in his eyes.

For a split second, a different image overlaid the one Aza envisioned. It was a broad man with taupe skin glowing with a gold aura, his long obsidian hair, soft and flowing like a waterfall, pulled into a loose knot at the nape of his neck. The sharp cut of his jaw lent itself to his prominent nose. The slash of a smile crinkled the edges of his swirling golden eyes.

Aza blinked fiercely against the cold air stinging her eyes and shook her head. Was that Nivet's true form?

Weariness had finally worn her down, despite the exhilaration of the dragon ride. After ascending the brutal GodsBane peaks, Aza tried to spy what the capital of Nerian was like, comparing it to her experiences of Iyera, Kreeha, and Verta. The mountains were piled in thick snow, the difference between Kreeha and Neria almost comical. How only days ago she longed to be free of the humidity that caused her hair to stick to her skin.

Aza thought she spied a city built amongst the dangerous mountain terrain and with a dropping sensation in her stomach, the dragon steered down. She could only lean forward and hang on, swallowing the joyous scream in her throat.

They landed with surprising gentleness, cutting through feet of snow. Aza tried her best to gracefully dismount and slide down from the proffered wing of Isarr without causing damage. While the rest of her companions disembarked, her feet carried her to the front of the dragon, the crunch of snow beneath her boot.

The creature loomed over her. She delicately traced her hand in the air following the thick, muscular neck, the scales alluring like the finest jewels. At her inspection, a huff of breath escaped Isarr. She paused, the giant dragon twisting its head to look at her properly. The sapphire eye pinned her in place. She couldn't help but stare at the magnificent creature.

Aza reached out her hand. Isarr stared, his teeth the size of her, but Aza was not deterred. She persisted taking careful steps forward until Isarr, like a giant dog, nuzzled her hand.

She smiled. Such a beautiful creature.

A faint voice wove into her mind, *Welcome home, my Lady.*

Aza shakily stepped back and watched as Isarr used his mighty legs to push off from the ground and fly away, the beautiful blue speck a wash of color in the slate gray sky.

Screams sounded behind Aza, not of pain but of immense joy. Anwin and Reed clasped Nivet tightly between them, while Xira observed.

It wasn't lack of emotion that kept Xira from running to the trio, but too much emotion. Aza had grown used to the tightly controlled movements of her captain, the tick of her jaw, and the clenching and unclenching of her fingers. When Anwin and Reed finished, Xira marched up to Nivet and pulled him down into a ferocious hug despite her small stature.

"Don't you pull that shit again."

His stern demeanor melted and as he pulled Xira away he said three simple words: "You did it."

Triumph gleamed in her eyes.

Reed warily hovered his hand over Nivet's body. "But how are you alive? How did you escape Eonas?"

Nivet's eyes glanced past Reed and said, "A tale for another time. Come, let us return home. You are all weary from your journey and from what I hear you have many stories to tell me."

Aza released a subtle wave of heat to warm her body against the cold, sharp wind of the mountains that settled in her bones. She enviously eyed Nivet's thick fur lined coat, pants, and boots. She would need to be outfitted in what they offered instead. She rubbed Kreeha fabric between her fingers, it was a precious gift but would not last for this brutal winter weather.

The Nerians surged forward eager to return home, while Aza cautiously lingered, giving plenty of space between the celebratory group and herself. She felt like she was standing outside a window and looking in on a joyous scene. The exhilaration from riding Isarr had dwindled, like a candle whose wax had puddled, and its wick left to drown.

Aza, uncertain, rocked from foot to foot. She had felt daunted before, but she knew once entering El'theren she would not return the same. There was no going back.

Nivet shared smiles with his Nerian companions. A drawn-out exchange of clasping hands and cheers on the back. Nivet steered them forward and they willingly obeyed, stopping their endless stream of comments. The months of their arduous journey had left her companions longing for home. She noticed in the nights around a campfire, their voices growing fond as they danced around the subject of Neria. The tough exterior would melt away leaving only blatant longing for what they sorely missed, their loved ones.

Nivet looked over his shoulder, gold swirling over dark brown.

Aza steeled herself. This was still another god within a mortal's body, another god who used others for their own purposes. A pang of sadness clattered around her heart for the mortal Rune. What kind of life had he led? Was he a truly a willing host for the god, Nivet? The mortal cut a handsome figure in his thick clothes lined with fur and the snow swirling around his imposing figure. Surely there were family, friends, lovers who missed the mortal.

Aza could not break away from his stare as she analyzed the god in front of her. Xira, Reed, Anwin—she trusted them. She had come to learn and love their idiosyncrasies. They had defended her, but Nivet —he was still a god, and she did not want to easily fall into the trap of trusting another one.

The pain of Cruvo was too raw. Her logic and emotions conflicted with one another. She couldn't deny her feelings for him, and she couldn't sort her feelings from the overwhelming urge to be near him. The melding made their proximity too much to bear. Aza tried to compare every god and goddess and how their presence felt. There was always an inexplicable draw to them like a moth to a flame. Although ashamed to admit it, Astaroth's presence was like the draw to a dangerous vice, both alluring and enticing, yet vicious. Eonas was a siren's call, their magic like an impending tide threatening to drown her; Cruvo was the pulse of an earthquake, inevitable and everywhere —but Nivet.

As she drew a breath, it came to her. His was the darkness cast off by the sun during dawn or dusk, the tempting and comforting darkness of a night spent with a lover. The darkness of closed eyes when locked in a kiss.

Altogether different.

Each god and goddess had their own unique magical signature. The desire to be within their proximity consisted of a different pull, a different weight, something Aza needed to always be aware of. She could not let herself be persuaded so easily again.

Nivet watched her scrutiny, and with careful and sure steps, he retreated to her, letting his companions rush towards home. The home that Aza wanted to witness.

"I do not know everything of your journey here, but I appreciate you coming along."

Aza held her tongue. She could not yield an inch to him, the softness in her had been erased due to Cruvo's manipulation, whether sincere or not.

"Your magic has returned."

Aza's magic coaxed itself forward at its mention. Nivet's eyes winced in a small flash of pain. Before Aza could ask about it, the moment of weakness was gone.

"No thanks to you."

"You are right and for that I apologize." He bowed his head and Aza realized she did not want to pick a fight, not yet.

"I do not wish to fight right now." Aza pursed her lips and urged her legs to move, for her to move past Nivet and walk into the Nerian capital, but she was rooted to the spot.

"As you wish," he answered. Noticing her hesitation, he offered a hand. "There is nothing to fear in my city."

She looked uneasily at the hand, the dark brown skin contrasting so beautifully with the white snow, but she was afraid to touch him, afraid to touch any of the gods and goddesses and what would transpire from that one small touch, how one small acquiesce could lead to her downfall.

"I cannot," Aza admitted.

Nivet's hand dropped like a line being cut; it smacked against his thigh. They danced around the other, like two stars unwittingly pulled into the other's orbit.

"Very well." He turned and walked away.

Aza blew out a breath, the white puff of air curling in front of her. As Nivet walked away, Aza felt a sharp cut of sadness, his retreating figure like a ship departing on the horizon never to be seen again. She thought of his last stand against Eonas and how he had protected his companions instead of leaving them to die, how he bellowed a war cry against them, protected them.

She couldn't take his hand, but she could walk beside him into the Nerian city. Finally her weighted feet unstuck and she jogged over to Nivet. "I am excited to see the province that carved the likes of Xira,

Anwin, and Reed."

His mouth pulled up slightly and he answered, "I do not think you will be disappointed in what you find."

~

They did not head directly into El'theren. Instead, Aza kept pace with Nivet as they hiked up a winding trail laden with fresh snow. They had lost sight of Anwin, Reed, and Xira, their conversation taking longer than Aza thought. The trio had slipped ahead, eager to return to their home.

They walked in surprisingly comfortable silence, except for the soft crunch of snow underfoot. Aza was busy trying to figure out Nivet, his angle, his purpose, and his intention. The incline was shrouded within the protection of mountainsides, the rock face shielding them from most of the harsh weather. Aza ran a hand over the rock. Veins of a brilliant blue streaked through it, each striation like a river. Rare bursts of flowers were interspersed along the rock and the path, breaking apart the expanse of brilliant white. It was an altogether different beauty than the other provinces. She could see this terrain shaping each of her companions. Xira like the hardened stone with streaks of beauty hidden within if one looked closely, Reed like the calm snow falling around them, easily turning fierce if needed, and Anwin the gentle, blooming flowers hidden amongst the severe climate.

Nivet let Aza soak in the scenery in silence, clearly understanding her weighty thoughts. It was a thoughtful act that Aza appreciated.

The steep incline leveled off and Aza halted.

Beautiful. Absolutely beautiful.

She thought the sparse mountain leading to the city would equally sparse and devoid of warmth or beauty, but she was utterly wrong.

El'theren was magnificent. Their trek had taken them to a vantage point allowing Aza to bask in the glory of the city. The city sprawled over the mountain. Buildings were constructed using the same stone Aza passed on her way up, each building swirled and highlighted with the blue luminescent color. The road was composed of hexagonal stones in a honeycomb pattern lovingly placed down the hill, with a low wooden fence on the perimeter of the path. Each building had a small chimney with swirls of smoke puffing out, their roofs covered in a soft blanket of snow. It was a beautiful coalescence of hard stone and delicate gems shimmering in the gray clouds.

Aza found herself gripping the wooden railing lining the mountainside and scanning El'theren. Down the mountain, Aza spotted the trio entering the city, with soldiers stopping from their duty to give their respects to the three of them. She was shocked to find the soldiers not giving a simple bow of their heads, but fully dropping to one knee, their hands making a configuration Aza couldn't discern from her distance.

A flash of familiarity rose in the back of her mind, but she dismissed it, instead trying to focus on the moment of relief and success. She had made it to El'theren. She could gain the answers she sought.

Beyond the city buildings Aza saw a structure carved into the mountain. It was imposing with dual columns lining the entrance and a giant set of stairs leading to the entry and composed of the blackest stone. A frozen waterfall decorated the south side of the mountain, the faint rushing of water heard from afar. To the east a dragon circled in the distance and dipped below the mountain peak.

She could feel Nivet's prying gaze on her back, but he maintained his distance, allowing her this moment to acquaint herself with El'theren. Aza wanted to stay here, absorbed in the city and how it flowed and moved, how it breathed with life, but she couldn't stay. There were things she needed to accomplish and learn. With a heavy heart, she pulled away from the wooden railing, her fingers aching to clench it for another moment and lean forward over the vast city and scream her excitement into the sky with the soft, gentle snow falling around her.

In another time, she would be able to do such a thing. But not now.

~

Aza and Nivet were catching up to the trio ahead, whose pace was slow and ambling as they laughed and shared hugs and celebrations with people who emerged on the streets, out of shops and houses. They were well-loved and well-known among their people. Aza could only smile in appreciation. Her companions deserved all the love they could find. The citizens were so absorbed in welcoming their soldiers home, most didn't spare another glance at Aza, and for once, it was refreshing to not be seen as a commodity that is stared and talked about.

Instead of blatant stares, Nivet received small head bows in respect, and he returned them. The people were not cowed by his power or what he was.

A scream ripped through the air and Aza tensed, her whole body on edge searching for danger. Nivet placed a reassuring hand on Aza's shoulder, leaned in close and whispered, "It is alright. Look."

She jerked away from his touch and quelled her magic, which was pooling itself within her body, searching for an outlet. She tried to see what Nivet was showing her.

Three children were ripping down the snowy hill, tearing past people, brushing them aside, and knocking into them with a casual thrown sorry in the wind. They were a clash of bright red and auburn hair sprinting.

"Mama! Mama!" The chorus of the children's shouts overlapped with endearing exclamations. Anwin pushed past her friends and sprinted, tears shining down her face, as she raced towards her children.

Aza watched with intense concentration. She realized she knew nothing of her companions' personal lives. She had never fathomed anything like a family for any of them. She belonged to no one and nothing, adrift like a piece of timber in the sea, but these people they had tethers, connections, somewhere they belonged. It wrenched Aza's heart to watch her friend collapse to the ground with sobs in her throat and tears streaking down her face holding each of her three rambunctious children while she laughed and cried. She wrapped her arms around them, chuckling over their antics and each vying for her attention.

Behind the children, a broad man walked down the same pathway with a woman who looked eerily similar to Reed and two older people. The man had a great big smile as he watched Anwin and her children.

After inspecting each of her children and commenting on their appearance and how big they had gotten and how responsible they had been while she'd been gone, she disentangled herself from her children and stood slowly locking eyes with the man. Without hesitation, she launched herself at the man. He caught her easily, her legs tangled around his midsection. The man didn't falter and clung to his wife while their kids circled around the two of them, clapping, hugging, and jumping.

The other family reunions were still precious, but without the same dramatics.

Reed marched up to the woman who looked exactly like him, and they embraced. "I'm glad you're home," she breathed and hugged Reed.

The two older people embraced Xira. "Mom. Dad. This was routine. I'm fine." Aza saw the resemblance, Xira's father with the same raven black hair and her mother with the same honey-colored eyes.

"Nonsense," her father barked out. His hair was just as long as Xira's and tied back into a loose ponytail. "We can still be worried about our daughter, despite her being the Captain of the Nerian forces." His eyes flickered to Nivet, and he stepped back from Xira. "Especially from what we have heard from Nivet."

Xira bristled at the comment and was about to defend herself when her mother interrupted.

"It is not a doubt of your skill, but rather a worry of two parents over their daughter." Her eyes, so similar to Xira's, crinkled in joy at her daughter.

Mollified, Xira gave in and gave her parents a proper embrace, letting the stiffness and responsibility melt from her shoulders in the presence of her parents.

Aza watched, unsure of her place and what to do. The only thing she could think of was to stay by Nivet's side feeling awkward and empty at having no one around to greet her like these families had done.

Anwin was back to her feet, her hand entwined with her husband's and her three children clinging to her like she would disappear from their grasp if they let go. Her husband let go and marched up to Xira. He was a giant before her and gently clasped each side of Xira's face and bent down to bring his forehead to hers. Everyone looked on in quiet respect.

"My wife was yours to protect, cherish, and honor in my absence. You have fulfilled this promise. As long as my heart beats in my chest, I will thank you." When finished with Xira, he marched with purpose to Reed and clasped each side of his face and brought his forehead to Reed's. The same sentiment was repeated with everyone looking on in silence.

After he was finished with Xira and Reed, she could see a pleased determination in her companions' eyes like they were granted the greatest gift.

He was not done. Her husband made his way to Aza, his steps sure and steady, his blue eyes gazing into her own and before Aza realized it, Anwin's husband gently placed his calloused, work-toughened hands on either side of her face. He only had to bow slightly to bring his forehead to hers. It was tender and intense as he repeated himself again. Even Anwin's chaotic children were quiet as they watched their father partake of this ritual. "My wife was yours to protect, cherish, and honor in my absence. You have fulfilled this promise. As long as my heart beats in my chest, I will thank you."

Unexpected tears dripped down her face when Anwin's husband departed, his steadfast presence and reassurance causing her to drift once more. She thought of the times she had tried to protect and save Anwin: the sea monster; Astaroth; the ambush by Lord Sune. These Nerian companions, these friends, were her sisters and brother. They were bound by more than mere duty—a strong cord connected each of them.

A sharpness sliced through this moment, and she wished for Lorn to be here; to witness El'theren and their people, to see these mountains that forged these hardened warriors, intimidating, but also filled with an unending love.

When Anwin's husband returned to her side, the silence broke. Each group and family talked over one another inquiring about where they needed to go next, what would be happening.

Nivet assured them all. "We will be staying here for the winter. Right now, you can return home. I will be showing Lady Aza to her house." At the mention of Aza, the children's eyes widened in wonder, openly scanning her and grinning at her silver hair and her equal appraisal back.

"Rest and enjoy your family. Tomorrow we will have a giant feast and celebration."

The children cheered, Xira's parents smiled, and Reed's sister gave a giant whoop. Each group departed to their own homes.

The oldest daughter of Anwin, her hair a deep auburn, a mixture of both her mother and father's, patted Anwin's belly. "Mama, mama. How's the baby?"

Anwin smiled and brushed wild hair from her daughter's face. "I'm going to see the healers today, but I think the baby is doing well."

Aza's mouth hung open and she couldn't move. Anwin was pregnant the whole time? Every dangerous scenario, every moment where her life could have ended flashed before her. White hot anger blasted through her. She wanted to go to her friend and yell at her to never do something this stupid again. Before she could step forward, Nivet grabbed her arm and anchored her.

Anwin must have seen Aza's shock, and she sent a sly wink over her shoulder before joining her family up the mountain. Reed and Xira were not surprised. They did not falter under this new revelation and merely smiled at Anwin's good news and the charm of her children.

Nivet leaned in and whispered, "She knew what she was getting into. She is an adult and she had other priorities."

"What? Like getting herself killed?" Aza hissed back.

"Like bringing you home." Nivet changed his grip to allow Aza to interlace her arm through his, and he steered her in a different direction from everyone else. Shocked at his proximity and touch, Aza's anger fizzled out like a campfire doused with water. She could handle it; she would handle it.

As she walked through El'theren, the only thing she dwelt on was that this wasn't the first time someone welcomed her home.

40

"They do not deserve Aza. How dare she do this to me?!"
    Cruvo's private journal

Swirls of darkness licked at his feet and engulfed him. It did not concern him. It was a comforting embrace, like a friend lulling him to sleep. He pictured Aza's concerned face looming over him, a pinched brow, her silver eyes sparkling.

Hunter, a voice called to him. But it was not hers. Familiar, but not his friend. The persistent fog of his brain couldn't let him place the voice. It floated away, like music that has died on the wind.

What was he thinking about?

It didn't matter.

Only the darkness mattered.

~

The strange in between of sleep and reality cracked. The dull roar of his pounding headache was too severe to ignore, the leaden feel of his muscles. He moaned in pain like a wounded animal caught in a trap.

Lorn attempted to open his eyes, leaving the sweet comforting bliss of sleep only to find himself in actual darkness. He patted the ground warily. It was uneven, cold stone. His head lolled to the side, with no energy to push himself up into a seated position. This was no building.

It was a prison.

He strained to hear any voices or sounds, but the pounding in his head made it difficult to discern whether the faint sounds and echoes he heard were real or imaginary. He groaned and clumsily patted his body searching for injuries. There seemed to be no open wounds, but he still felt the residual effects of the drug that had addled his body and mind.

The night came back to him in small bursts, a jumbled, distorted mess that he tried to sort out through his groggy thoughts. Although the flower tea paralyzed and rendered him unconscious, it also altered his perception. Trying to remember his memories was strange; colors were heightened, face shapes warped.

He hated to admit it, but Lilit was right. He should have been more suspicious. Devlin was the brother of Lady Rasmina's deceased lover. Of course he was working with her. The information fed to him was a carefully crafted story for Lorn to let down his guard.

Lilit was not here. Despite her abrasive personality, he found he missed her. Her biting remarks would prompt quick action from him and get him out of this fugue so they could come up with a plan.

"Lilit," he breathed. With enormous effort he rolled onto his side and nearly blacked out from the exertion. His body felt weak and malnourished. Sleep swept over him, swift and sudden.

~

Lorn sputtered awake. A pure note of clarity rang through him. The voice that whispered to him was Issi trying to reach him, but it was like she was speaking through a veil.

The pounding of his head receded enough for him to painstakingly push himself up into a seated position. He focused on his breath and through slitted eyes noticed something was different. Light. The flickering light of a torch crept into his cell like a wayward child. It highlighted a prison of jagged stone and rock with a wooden bucket in the corner, a scattered pile of straw, and a threadbare blanket bunched on the opposite wall.

If Lady Rasmina wanted him dead, he would be. They needed him for some purpose he reasoned.

Through the iron bars of his cell door, a plate with a single potato and crust of bread was discarded. Lorn didn't have the energy to stand, but he crawled, wondering when the effects of the poison would finally leave his body.

The potato was cooked, but cold. The crust of bread was rock hard, but he didn't care. His stomach growled and he wolfed it down, the food tasted and felt like leather.

The effort from crawling and eating was all he could manage for now. He collapsed next to the discarded plate and closed his eyes.

~

He woke, heaving. He retched up the pitiful dinner on the ground.

"Widow's Maker often leaves the victim unable to eat for a few days. Among other symptoms."

Lorn looked blearily over his shoulder, searching for the voice. He would never be able to forget Lady Rasmina's falsely innocent voice, light and airy belying her vicious intent. Tragic history aside, she could not get away with what she was doing.

"You will not die yet, hunter."

Lorn's mouth filled with cotton, thick and unable to form words, but he couldn't let the opportunity to talk pass. Meager meals were placed before him, but the workers were shrouded in darkness and left without a word.

"L-Lilit," he rasped. Every part of him ached. Moving his jaw was painful, but he fought through it. The combination of the jail cell, the bitter cold, ragged meals, and effects of the Widow's Maker left him a husk of his former self.

The torch behind Lady Rasmina left her face covered in darkness. A pause and then she answered, "I am not one to waste and discard lives needlessly. She remains alive only if she can prove her use to me. However, if her fight continues," she paused, a slow intake of breath to gather her thoughts, "then we will have to put her down like the animal she is."

Lorn reached a hand forward, clawed his hand, and pulled his body toward the cell door. "Leave her." His breath came is gasps and his throat ached. "Let her go." He strained against every muscle in his body. She couldn't be here because of his mistake, his folly. Lilit had warned him. She deserved to be free.

"Getting sentimental, are we?" She brushed her hands on her dress, smoothing out the fabric. "We are close to finding what we need, and dear hunter you are part of that equation. Lilit will rot here with you until I tire of her." She turned and departed, her footsteps echoing in the empty cavern.

Lorn's tiredness won out and he collapsed, the hard ground crashing into his worn cheek.

~

The days blurred together, and it was difficult for Lorn to keep track. The faceless and silent servants left his food without a word, and he ate the tasteless hard bread, his teeth hurting with each bite.

Eventually he gained enough sense to test the edges of his magic, the once powerful well, dried up and withered inside of him. They must be giving him micro doses of some herbs to stifle his magic.

Time was cruel, an unending and drawn-out suffering where his body would tire, but his mind would not allow himself the same reprieve. It filtered through what had transpired and how foolish he had been. Often Aza occupied his thoughts. He hoped and prayed to whoever would listen that she was safe. It became difficult to remember why he was here. What was his original purpose of being in Gara? Cruvo clearly wanted him dead and Lady Rasmina, despite abhorring the gods and their practices, didn't mind torturing him.

When his mind cleared and he no longer wallowed in self-pity, he latched onto Lilit, hoping she was still alive, that Lady Rasmina had not seen fit to kill her. Although as prickly as a thornbush, she had not abandoned him. Time and time again she had saved his skin, and he could repay her in kind. This was not the time to give up.

Delirious, he called out to Issi, shouting with his raw voice. "Goddess, where have you gone? What was it all for?"

He would shout and scream despite the toll it would take on his throat, despite the consequences. Lorn received only a cup of water a day. Squandering it by screaming was never a wise choice, but he was often left with nothing to do, and his mind was cracking.

In the stasis between dreams and reality he imagined Issi's voice, like that of a current of water flowing towards him. But when he desperately reached for it, it slipped through his fingers.

Another voice and image tried to penetrate his dreams, but he could not bear to dream of his beloved in this state. Weak and borderline deranged was not how he wanted the phantom image of Lakesh to see him. But his mind was a cruel master and wherever he looked, images of her taunted him.

At times like these, he curled into the corner like a beaten dog. He whimpered to himself, "Not real. Not real. She's dead." It was a newfound torture, reaffirming his loved one's death. His once sure and steady mind was slowly deadening in isolation in the darkness, from the flicker of the torch on the wall and the bars in his cell.

Other times, horrific images of Howlers and other beasts from the Hinterlands played in the shadows. Some days the torches went out and no one bothered to return for hours or days, or weeks.

He knew each divot and crevasse. Every sound called to him. His body thinned and his once hardened muscles were emaciated. Some days they fed him a potato or a scrap of meat, and he savored those treasured moments.

This was his life.

~

Surprise visitors were a blessed reprieve when his mind fought for a foothold away from insanity.

A vision from a lifetime ago, Lady Rasmina's advisors Maline and Flint observed his pitiful state in his cell—ragged, and broken, muttering to himself about an absent goddess and the ghost of his wife.

Although they were the enemy, he couldn't help but rush to greet them for any semblance of a sane conversation.

"Is Lilit free?" His voice sounded foreign; it had descended into chaos. Lorn's strength had returned only enough for him to stumble around in his cell, but his muscles had atrophied, and the drugs in his body addled both his balance and his mind.

Beside the sparse lighting of torches, Flint provided his own and for once Lorn could see their faces clearly. Starved for the sight of another person, his eyes traced each corner and facet clinging to familiarity.

Unexpectedly, his mind held a brief clarity that would soon be sabotaged. He needed to capitalize on it.

Maline and Flint shared a heavy, disapproving look. "She is not," Maline answered with a finality.

"You should never have come here. You would have been safer far from Gara. But," Flint released a long sigh, "your suffering will be soon ended."

Lorn rested his head on the iron bars and methodically started banging his head, the clang resounding down the cavern. "Let her go," he cried. "It is me you need. For Darkness Below knows why. She is not necessary."

"That would never be possible, Lorn of Verta. She is a liability. As are you," she added. "It will all be worth it. All your suffering—the gods and goddesses will be punished, magic halted. Soon." Maline turned on her heel and left.

Flint lingered a moment and stroked his beard taking in Lorn's disheveled physical and mental state. He leaned in and whispered, "I should not say anything, but I bear a message from Lilit. *'Don't you fucking give up, hunter.'*"

Lorn smiled. A rare, genuine smile. The first time since he had been down here in this despairing hole.

Flint pulled back and joined Maline, walking out of the tunnel. Lorn discerned Maline's hushed reprimand of Flint. "You shouldn't have given him hope." Their shadows receded.

If Lilit was still fighting, so could he. The isolation and drugs had punished him. He needed to figure out a plan to stop this and to rise from this.

~

On a particularly hard day, a servant dropped food outside his cell. Lorn had become accustomed to letting them leave, without prying information from them. It was a futile task. Rather than the receding footsteps, there was a stillness.

He had found peace in a corner of his cell with his head in his hands, trying to ignore the beasts that prowled across his vision. But the stillness caused him to stir, and he cast a curious glance at the servant. The haze of his imaginary beasts diminished, and he was able to focus on the servant. The tray had its usual crust of bread, meager stew, and water. The servant, their face shrouded in shadow and hooded, pointed to the cup of water and quickly shook their head. Looking left and right, they grabbed the water, obscuring it in their robes and swapped it with an identical cup.

Lorn shakily moved to his feet, using the wall to steady himself. He wanted to shout, but the servant put a finger to their lips and shook their head. Before he could get too close, the servant scurried away. Lorn scrambled to the tray and inspected the water, sniffing it. Before, the water always had a slight floral scent and taste, but now it smelled crisp and fresh.

He tentatively took a sip and closed his eyes in bliss. It wasn't tainted. He had a chance.

~

As the days passed, Lorn learned to only trust the servant who swapped the water. Typically, he received the trustworthy servant on alternating days, but other times, the days stretched together, and he needed to conserve the clean water. It was difficult.

The drugged water tempted him, to quench his thirst and the perverse need to addle his mind. He had become dependent on it with their constant drugging. As a preventative measure, he would toss the drugged water in the corner making sure the other nosy servants wouldn't notice what he was doing.

Eventually the images which haunted him began to dissipate like smoke on the wind. He no longer saw images of Howlers and their bloody welcoming, nor his deceased wife talking to him. With his sanity returning, he tried his best to keep his mind sharp and worked on regaining his strength, which had been whittled away after his inactivity and lack of nourishment. He needed to escape, but the iron door was locked. Yet with the drug leaving his body, he could feel the pulse of steady magic thrumming through his body. He tracked the servants, who came when, keeping a list of days in his cell. He broke a piece of rock from the wall and used it to track time the best he could.

Lorn planned. He would save himself. He would save Lilit. They would both get out of this prison alive.

41

"Aza has formed a friendship with Xira, Reed, and Anwin. Yet, she is wary of me. I understand—they thought me dead. However, I find I am jealous. How I long for her to look at me as she does them."

    Nivet's private journal

Nivet had guided her to a quaint cottage a short distance from the center of town. The inside was as lustrous as the rest of town with the familiar, vibrant vein of blue running through the stone. The inside was insulated with wooden timbers, decadent tapestries, and layered rugs, in shades of bright whites and rich, deep blues, purples and reds. An elaborate stone fireplace was the focal point with a small couch and chairs placed around it. The inside was warm, and toasty compared to the cold outside and Aza eagerly entered, kicking off her thick boots on the entry way, rushing to run her feet over the thick rugs. Over the last few months Aza had experienced a range of living conditions, from sleeping on the ground outside under the stars, to the opulent rooms of Cyran. This room welcomed her. It was the comfort of a warm hug on a cold night. Conflict warred within, unsure of whether to keep her emotions tightly guarded or let them free. Would Nivet use her emotions against her, manipulating her? Aza's caution was discarded, crushed like frost underfoot. There was no time to second-guess her choice in entering Neria. She trusted her companions and they trusted Nivet.

She didn't bother to hide her radiant smile and sighed in relief as her toes wiggled in the soft furs.

Nivet cleared his throat and gestured around the cottage. "I know it is small, but we do not have many extra housing options here in Neria. I figured you wanted privacy, and this has a secluded outdoor space." He tilted his head to the left. "Over here is the kitchen. The bedroom is on the other side with a washroom attached to it. The bathtub has running water, so you won't need to fill it with buckets."

Aza had closed her eyes in bliss and relaxation, but something in Nivet's tone caused her to open them. A thread of nervousness or uncertainty, something that didn't suit him.

"I love it. Thank you."

The uncertainty that Aza thought was there vanished, and he hardened under her gaze, his hand clenched at his side.

"I will leave you to it. Rest. You are free to explore the city. No one will harm you here."

He turned and went to open the door when Aza blurted out. "Wait, I don't know where everyone else lives."

"Rest for today, Aza." His eyes softened. "Your journey has been arduous. We will come and get you tomorrow and give you a proper tour of the city."

Aza gave a nod and Nivet left through the aged, wooden door, its hinges creaking slightly as he exited.

She stretched her arms over her head and breathed a giant sigh of relief. This small cottage would be perfect, the stress and worry already melting away from her shoulders. But first a bath. The rigorous traveling on horseback from Krccha had left a layer of grime and dust stuck to her skin.

~

Washed and smelling like the fresh new snow, next to the bed she found a dresser filled with clothing in her size. They were similar to what other Nerian's wore, thick fur-lined leathers, coats, jackets, pants, and gloves. The leather was supple and smooth, and the fur was plush under her hand. She dressed, the clothes sliding over her skin like a kiss.

The cottage was peaceful. A small bookshelf lined the entryway, and a duplicate was lined against the bedroom wall. Aza picked a book at random and plopped onto the couch in front of the fire, warming her weary bones and soul. She aimlessly skimmed the book, unable to focus, her foot bouncing energetically against the floor.

She eyed the door, weighing her options. The journey had been tough and was far from over, and she needed this rest, but like her private room in Kreeha, she felt restless and isolated, so unused to being alone. A strange energy at being in El'theren thrummed through her and even though the bath should have calmed her, a resolve to go out and explore was too persistent to ignore.

The nights came early in the mountains, and she peeked out of her glass panes seeing a fresh blanket of snow on the streets. Torches were lit throughout the city along the street and pathways. She was safe, she had come here willingly, she didn't have to hide who she was or wear a cloak obscuring her features. The following days would be spent in talks with Nivet and trying to figure out a plan to tackle Astaroth and what she would do next, but tonight—tonight was her one night to be free, free from the burden of her destiny and free to enjoy what this city had to offer, without the weight of the gods and goddesses on her mind.

She drummed her fingers against the windowsill and the faint sound of laughter traveled past her cottage, like the wind itself was teasing her, telling her to go, to experience. That decided it.

She raced back to the dresser and hastily pulled on a thick jacket with a fur-lined hood, mittens and warm socks. She shoved her feet into the boots at the door and swung open the door to experience El'theren.

This was the first time she had ever been truly alone since appearing from the Well. She had always been surrounded by people. Even if she loved them dearly, now was her time to discover who she was without them. For all the fierce stories about Nerians and their upbringing, the view of El'theren was just like a storybook, the winding pathways lined with snow and glistening lights. She didn't know where her feet were taking her, but she let the excitement guide her, following the distant sound of laughter and chatter.

People passed by as she wandered the streets, and she only received quick glances, a mere interest in seeing a stranger in their city which never hosted people from other provinces. But whether word had been spread from Nivet or otherwise, the people merely nodded their heads in respect or gave a small smile or greeting.

For so long Aza was taught to hide who she was, to shroud her identity, but this is what she truly wanted. To be part of the city and to feel its the pulse. She followed that call. It brought her to a building as beautiful as the rest of El'theren. She hesitated outside the wooden door.

A couple emerged and gave hearty goodbyes to the people inside. Music spilled out along with a vibrant warmth that Aza couldn't deny. She gave a smile to the departing couple and pushed into the building. It was many things: a tavern, a music hall, a ballroom. Aza struggled to find the exact wording. But it was crowded, filled with conversation and lovely music. The beat of the drums propelled her forward. She navigated the crowds, spotting people giving her a curious look, or a dazed expression. But no one hassled her.

A small pang of nervousness flooded her—an image of the inn where she killed the inhabitants. She shook her head; this was not the same. These people were not malicious. They were not looking to use her or sell her. She could let go and enjoy herself here.

Aza spotted a familiar set of long locs at a stool at the bar and made her way over.

"Hey, Reed!"

They turned and Aza chuckled. "I'm sorry."

Reed's twin sister let out a loud laugh, her eyes twinkling with mirth. "Do not be so concerned. I get it often enough up here." She gripped the handle of her glass and drained the remains of her drink. She gave a satisfied smack of her lips and turned with a hand extended to Aza.

"I'm River."

"Aza." She shook the woman's hand and arched a brow.

"I know." River shook her head sadly. "Reed and River, our parents had a fantastic sense of humor." She gestured to the wizened man behind the bar. "We need to show you some Nerian hospitality. I'm getting you a drink."

Aza sat on a stool next to River, glad for her first venture out into the city to be successful without any awkward encounters. Instead, she felt herself relax, her shoulders loosening, the tight knot in her back unwinding.

The barkeep slid two glasses over with an amber hue and Aza tentatively sipped it. It was vastly different from the Starwine she had partaken of when in El'en but no less pleasant, only different. Hearty and filling.

"So, tell me, Aza. Why are you out here tonight at the Bladed Beauty? From what I understand, you should be tired and fast asleep."

Aza shrugged and surveyed the room, the people dancing to the music, playing cards in the corner, partaking in a drinking game. It was a normalcy she craved. She settled on a simple answer. "I couldn't sleep."

"You came to the right place. Tonight is a pre-celebration. It is a relief that our top soldiers have returned."

"The community must be very tight, for even a few to be gone so long and for it to cause such distress." Aza sipped her drink. "It is nice."

River laughed into her glass. "If this is nice, you will really enjoy tomorrow. Prepare yourself." Her eyes widened and she grinned.

Aza gazed longingly at the dancing couples, the beat of the music impossible to ignore. She wanted to lose herself in the moment, to feel the strength she had developed over the months manifest in an entirely different way, not one of battle, but of surrender.

River drained her drink and clasped Aza on the shoulder encouraging her to do the same. "Come on, star girl. You have been staring at the musicians and dancers the entire time. Let's go dance."

The heat of the Bladed Beauty was cloying, sweat trickled down her skin. Her thick leathers and furs were too much with the crowded building. She stared at River's outfit, regretting her own. She was dressed in a loose purple dress with a delicate slit on the side and an open back organized in an artful pattern. Aza didn't know why she thought River was Reed in the first place, the only thing similar from the back was their locs.

"Next time, wear layers. Our buildings are well insulated and keep heat despite the frigid temperatures outside." River pulled off Aza's outer coat and tossed it on a nearby hook. "This will do for now."

River yanked Aza out onto the floor and danced. Aza hesitated at first, but eventually the rhythm took over and she relaxed, allowing her body to move of its own accord.

River smiled in appreciation and soon Aza was spun around by other participants. They cheered her on good-naturedly and soon the song melded into something new. Everyone took their place in a choreographed dance and Aza unaware of the steps prepared to slink away. River pulled her back. Aza laughed and held her hands up, claiming ignorance.

"Nonsense. You will pick it up easily enough. You are a natural," River chided.

Aza conceded and took a place next to her. Beads of sweat gathered on her forehead, and she felt breathless and light. Here she could forget her worries. These people did not view her with suspicion or even devotion. She was only another person, and Aza did not realize how much she craved to be viewed as such.

The music started and Aza clumsily tried her best to follow the steps; her partners encouraged her as she was spun from person to person. The faces were a blend of colors, their ages a mix. Aza only knew joy. Song after song, Aza found herself as one moving mass, tilting her head up with her eyes closed in bliss as she felt her body move as one, like waves in an ocean.

Breathless and thirsty, she reluctantly broke away from the music and returned to the bar in search of another ale or some water. River patted the stool next to her and Aza collapsed into it. "Tomorrow is supposed to be greater than this?"

River smiled, a smile so similar to Reed's. "Just you wait."

The night carried on with Aza alternating between drinks with River and losing herself to the music. As she grew more comfortable, she tried her hand at the card games and games of strength. There were no hard feelings. The winners and losers celebrated together with raised mugs of ales and raucous cheers with their comrades.

But soon enough, Aza couldn't ignore the weariness that settled over her like a warm blanket, so different from the constant checking over her shoulder for enemies, a weariness of contentment. The music was winding down and the barkeep was alerting everyone to get their final drinks now. It was time for her to leave.

"Thank you, River. Truly." Aza squeezed the woman's upper arm in thanks and turned to leave. River yanked her back into a fierce hug. "No, thank you, Aza. You brought my brother back alive and that is more than I can ever ask for." She pulled away, glanced over Aza's shoulder, and smirked. "I will find you tomorrow at the celebration."

River's departure was abrupt and strange, but Aza shrugged it off and turned. She smacked directly into a solid chest and scrambled back muttering apologies. She didn't think she was affected that much by the ales, but she shouldn't be running into random people at the Bladed Beauty. Her steps had been graceful while dancing, yet now they failed her.

The person offered her an arm and said, "Let me escort you home."

Aza rubbed a hand through her hair and finally looked at the person she ran in to, his voice familiar.

Nivet had a speculative stare. Something unknown hinged between them. She thought it was the familiar pulse and overwhelming pull of their magic in proximity to each other, but it was something else. Perhaps the alcohol had muddled her perception of him, but right now his magic energy seemed to surround her. She wanted to refuse on the principal of not falling into another god's thrall, but there was no harm in him escorting her back. In fact, there was something intriguing about the way he held himself, a solemness behind those eyes.

Aza found herself nodding and entwined her arm through his. He steered her through the crowded bar, the people looking for one last night cap before heading home.

The burst of cold night air steadied her and helped to clear the lovely fog inside her head. Besides the Bladed Beauty, the rest of the streets were quiet, peaceful. The snow still fell in soft spirals, the torches providing enough light to guide their path. Aza tilted her head back and loosened a great sigh in appreciation, a dazed smile growing on her face. Before she could stumble on the street, she straightened to look where she was going.

She could feel Nivet's curious and piercing gaze before he finally relented and asked his question. "What were you doing?"

"The stars. I have determined they look the best here."

Nivet tilted his head back in the same manner. "I would have to agree."

Her fingers brushed against his. "Or it could be this night that makes them better."

Their feet crunched in the snow, he was silent, considering. "Explain."

Aza took a deep breath, the cold brisk mountain air fueling her, steadying her. "I'm not really sure. It could be this place, or a feeling, but I feel...home. I feel safe. I think elsewhere there was always an underlying danger, and I understand Astaroth is still out there and the Hinterlands is still out of control, but here for this night, I feel free from such burdens. Does that make sense?"

He didn't answer, their pace slow and leisurely. When they came upon her small cottage he finally said, "Yes, it does make sense."

They paused outside her front door, staring at one another. Aza wanted to thank him for the courtesy, but the words caught in her throat.

He seemed uncomfortable as he assessed her cottage, then squinting at the stars. "I want you to hold onto the feeling you had tonight. There will be times when you might hate this city, hate everything. Remember the joy and freedom you felt tonight and do not let it go. Understand?" Dark brown eyes were engulfed with swirls of gold as he stared at her.

Many questions rose in her mind, eager to be asked. But Aza held back. This night should not be tainted by anything, this feeling she needed to cherish and remember if the moments to come were anything like he said. "I will. Thank you."

Nivet stiffly nodded, his eyebrows furrowed in concern before he left, leaving Aza to the comfort of her cottage.

She entered, her jaw cracking from her giant yawn, and collapsed onto her bed holding on to the feeling of tonight as if they would slip easily from her fingers.

Aza discovered the word she was searching for—belonging. She felt like she belonged here.

42

"I have not heard any news from Lorn in a month. I presume he is dead."
Cruvo's private journal

Day by day Lorn regained his sanity and tried to retain what little strength he could. Instead of spending his time cowering in fear of phantom shadows from his dreams, he plotted. His magic was still a shred of what it used to be before he had healed Pearl, but each day it grew and his ability to wield it became stronger. The biggest unknowns about his escape that plagued him: he had no idea where he was located, how long it would take him to escape, or where Lilit was located.

Down the cavern, the faint echoes of noises carried to him, potentially a voice muffled, an animal scurrying, a soft clink. Lorn ignored the sounds. It had driven him crazy to try and decipher the distance noises but decoding them was too difficult like he had dunked his head underwater.

Lorn's resolve hardened the day Lady Rasmina visited one last time.

The confident footsteps revealed who his visitor was; the servants did not walk with such authority. Feigning weakness, he remained sitting in the corner and raised his head to appraise her. She was always dressed like the high nobility, impractical for their current condition. The dress was form-fitting, long sleeved, and obsidian, like she was shadow given form flitting through the cavern.

The torches lining the wall gave him little light to decipher the intricacies of her fine-boned face, but he swore he saw a triumphant glitter in her eyes.

"The time is here, hunter. We have found what we are looking for and now your suffering will be over." She sniffed and turned her head to the side, peering down the hall. "I understand you won't care about my words, but I do regret giving you these poisons. *'The Tainted Reality'* is the name given for it. However, it was necessary so your magic and you would be confused." She paused, and steepled her fingers together, staring at Lorn like he was a long sought after prize. "You are necessary."

Lorn lolled his head to the side and tried his best to ignore her, an act to prevent her from seeing through his clear-headed state.

"Who would have thought such serendipitous timing? I viewed you and Lilit as such pests. Unnecessarily visiting our court, but upon further inspection, you are one of the missing pieces to my puzzle."

In a rare state of excitement, Lady Rasmina's voice grew hurried, and she loosened her tongue. "Light magic, like shadow magic, is extremely rare. However, how our magical properties transfer through from parent to child is fascinating. But your light magic is different, you are somehow stronger. The wall, the dam that blocks all of our true potential—yours has been lifted. I discovered this when you healed Pearl. Under any other circumstances, I would have executed you for her getting into danger. But no, right in front of me was the solution to my long-awaited problem. I had finally found what I have been searching for since that day in the forest." She grinned, the whiteness of her teeth shining like a ghost in the darkness. She gripped the iron bars of his cell and leaned her head against it. "You do not realize the gravity of this situation, but I thank you."

She pulled away and said with one departing sentence, "Be ready tomorrow. You will leave this cell."

Lorn placed his head in his hands and grinned. Tomorrow would be his escape.

He planned it perfectly. On the next rotation of servants, Lorn was going to escape. Confident in his abilities to wield magic, he could create enough of a break in the jail cell, find Lilit, and escape this underground jail cell.

~

The servant arrived, the dim torchlight and hood obscuring their features. Lorn's eyes widened when he realized the servant did not hold a tray of food this time. The servant nervously looked in either direction before fishing out a thick key from the inside of their robes and unlocked the iron door. It clanged noisily and before Lorn could scramble to his feet and thank the unknown person, they slipped the key inside their robes and sprinted away.

"Wait," Lorn uttered. He reached out a hand like it could capture them, but they were already too far.

It was unexpected, but at least this way Lorn wouldn't have to waste his strength and energy on summoning magic. He would need it later when he found Lilit.

Escaping his cell was the easiest step, the next challenge was trying to figure out where Lilit was and how to leave this prison.

Lorn swiveled his head in each direction and decided following the path of the servant would prove more fruitful than wandering aimlessly. They were at least headed somewhere.

His muscles screamed at him to run, to escape this desolate place, but he silenced the urge. Move quickly, but quietly.

The cave corridors twisted and turned. Errant noises spiked Lorn's fear of being caught as he clung to the walls in hope of being discreet. Luckily, there was only one path. He passed empty cells similar to his own. They were musty and cold, empty of the stink of people. He breathed a sigh of relief. Lilit wasn't here.

The deeper he went into the cave system, the more noises he heard. They were not clear, rather a disjointed cacophony that he couldn't interpret.

A fork in the path appeared. Lorn's head pounded with the sudden exertion after countless days spent in confinement. He leaned against the wall and caught his breath. This was barely the beginning. He needed to be strong enough to escape with Lilit without getting caught. Nausea rolled through his stomach. He was experiencing the consequences of days of meager food.

Lorn gritted his teeth and listened. The path to the left emitted more noise and the right was quiet. No, he strained further. On the right it seemed a single person was talking, mumbling, alone. It had to be Lilit.

With renewed determination, he pushed off the wall and veered right, his pace increasing. Empty cell by empty cell blurred past. His feet stumbled as he quickly padded down the hall, using the wall to steady himself when his vision grew blurry. Although he had dispelled the poison's effects, they still lingered and the sudden spike in activity exacerbated it.

The moaning and incoherent speech grew louder and Lorn threw caution away and sprinted as fast as he could to her cell. A crumpled figure lay away from the cell doors. Broken and defeated. He skidded to a halt and used the cell doors to steady himself from falling over.

"Lilit," he rasped.

She moved shakily from the floor, her head hung in defeat. Like his cell, it was shrouded in darkness, the weak light of the torch behind him only casting further shadows. She was hidden in the darkest corner like a beaten animal.

She still faced the wall muttering to herself. "Can't be. Can't be. Can't be him. It's fake, fake. Fake!" Lilit screamed and repeatedly hit her head over and over again. She must still be drugged, her brain addled like his was. Was he this bad? It was gruesome and cruel to witness. The once sharp mind of hers reduced to this squabbling mess.

"Lilit," he repeated calmly. He needed to maintain his composure. If anyone heard the commotion, all would be lost. "Lilit, I am here. You need to stop. Someone will hear and we need to escape. Now!"

Like the dead brought back to life, her motion was both disturbing and slow like she wasn't used to how her muscles and body moved. She turned to look at Lorn. The once lean and strong woman had waned, her eyes and cheeks sharpened like blades were gaunt and hollow. The gray eyes lacked any of the burning fury they once held. She hobbled to him. Bruises marred her skin. Dried blood was embedded into her clothing.

"What happened?" Lorn scanned her body. They had both been poisoned, but Lilit had been beaten.

She shrugged and with her voice devoid of emotion she said, "I fought back." Lilit staggered away from the iron bars clutching her head and screaming through clenched teeth. "He isn't real. Isn't real.

Steel your mind."

Lorn didn't want to create problems by arguing with her already troubled mind, but he needed her to leave with him willingly. He hadn't expected her to be this disoriented. He cleared his throat and ignored the pounding in his head. "I am real, Lilit. We don't have much time. We need to leave."

She faced him and cocked her head. On anyone else it might have been a sweet gesture, but with her lack of emotion it was the look of someone who had lost their mind. "Are you real, hunter?" She scoffed and pointed next to him. "Then Aza is real as well."

He looked to where she was pointing and shook his head. Her mind was a split of reality and fantasy. "No, Lilit. She isn't here. It is only me." They couldn't waste any time. Addled mind or not, he needed to escape with her. "Whether you are ready or not, I'm opening this door and we are leaving."

"Fucking hunter, are you so selfless? You should have left by yourself. Leave me here!" she raged. "Do you know what I have done? Why I was sent here as punishment?"

Lorn couldn't listen to her ravings anymore. "It doesn't matter." Summoning his magic, he clasped the iron lock, manipulating the metal just enough to break it open. "I don't care."

"She's lying there helpless. Pleading for me to do something. To help her. And I didn't. I left her there to rot." Lilit was staring beside Lorn, watching the phantom images play their sick masquerade of memories.

He froze, his hand clasping the cold iron bars. "Who?" he whispered.

A defeated, soft, laugh escaped her lips, her smile cruel and aimed to cut. "Aza, of course. I watched as the Nerians took her. They pinned her to the ground like some animal, completely helpless. In fact, she was begging me to help her. You know what I did? I left her there." With a cold, calculated movement she looked to Lorn. "Still want to save me now, hunter? Leave me! Let me rot!" She surged forward and pushed the iron door open into Lorn.

Everything clicked into place—her punishment, her banishment. She had let Cruvo's one desire be taken willingly.

Not too long ago, Lorn would have raged against Lilit's actions. At the injustice. At her selfishness. Their time spent together had taught him many things about her mannerisms. She was drowning in guilt, drowning in grief. If she did not care about her actions, she would not have admitted time and time again or withheld the truth from Lorn. She cared and that was enough.

He despised the fact that she let Aza be captured. The ugly picture she painted with her words was brutal. However, the broken, battered, and bruised person in front of him required mercy. They would discuss this another time.

The sharp rock wall bit into his back, shocking him into action. He straightened and in a strange moment of clarity, he wrapped his arms around her.

Lilit fought back, hitting him. But she never told him to let her go. She screamed again and again. "I deserve this. Leave me here. I deserve this."

The angry shouts morphed into giant sobs as Lorn embraced her and said again and again. "No, you do not." He was careful around her wounds, the deep purpling bruises.

The wet sobs began to subside and Lorn pulled himself away from her. Her eyes, which were only recently deadened, had a sharper awareness and clarity. "One day you will answer for what you did to Aza and only she can forgive you. But for now, we need to leave."

Lorn was surprised there weren't more people rushing down the hallway to stop them. Lilit's screams were loud, and the empty cavern would have carried the sound. But he dismissed those thoughts, his only concern was to escape.

Lilit heaved deep breaths and gave a faint nod. He scooped her arm over his shoulder and together, they limped out of the cavern. It was slow going, with frequent stumbles.

Each stop was excruciating. He strained, listening for guards, servants, anyone. But they were alone.

Each stumble caused Lilit's mind and body to regress. Fictional images and memories danced across her vision. Lorn knew this was happening when she would squeeze his arm tightly and hold her breath. At these moments he would pause, quietly reassuring her that he was real, and they were escaping. Her body grew heavier with each step. The weakness of their isolation and lack of food was taking a toll on her body. It didn't help that his own body was starting to falter. But he could not give up, not yet.

He followed the incline of the passages, their ascent giving him a small kindling of hope. He summoned any remaining strength and kept walking. The incline was steep, but that meant they were reaching the end. He couldn't see what was on the other side, but he had hope and that propelled him to trudge forward.

Lilit paused, her hand on the wall.

"Before I forget," Lorn whispered, "thank you for the message. It helped me in a dark time."

She tilted her chin up to look at him, her forehead lined with sweat, her eyes half open. "What message?"

"Never mind, let's get out of here first and then we can talk more." He slung her arm over his shoulder, and he heaved themselves up over the last few steps.

It wasn't the fresh scent of outdoors that greeted them. The cave plateaued, stretching out around them, the ceiling vast and wide. They were not alone.

"Lorn, thank you for joining us. Today you will change the world." Lady Rasmina smiled.

43

"Aza struggles to be close to me. The feel of our magics' proximity must be overwhelming. I must keep a respectful distance, only being around her when necessary."

Nivet's private journal.

The giant obsidian temple carved into the mountain was even more impressive up close. Aza closed her mouth, so she didn't look like a gaping fish. She was rarely nervous but meeting the Lord and Lady of the Nerian province seemed important, like a weighty judgment would be passed on whether she met expectations.

Before they reached the temple, Nivet reassured her that the Lord and Lady of Neria did not reside in the temple, it was merely for formal proceedings. The doors stretched high into the sky and were parted by the soldiers stationed on either side. Nivet led the group, with Aza trailing and Xira, Anwin, and Reed flanking her. Aza held her tongue but had so much to discuss with the three of them, from Anwin's pregnancy to Reed's twin sister and the fantastic night she had. It vanished as she walked to meet the Lord and Lady of Neria.

The temple expanded deep inwards. She wondered what could be stored within its vast depths. Polished obsidian walls gleamed their walls reflecting their torchlight. Giant, iron braziers were lit with enormous fires, the warmth sweltering. Chairs at the top of the dais were carved from the stone of the mountain, as rough and durable as the people of Neria.

Rune was an exact replica of his mother, except for the cutting stare, one that held little love for Aza. She raked it over Aza in disdain, her dark brown hair shaved short, but Aza caught the faint black whorls of tattoos on the side of her head, just like Rune. Age lines were etched around her eyes and mouth, but they did nothing to soften her. If anything, it only hardened her countenance. His father held a similar air, his head shorn, and mouth pinched in distaste as he took in their group. Even under the layers of leather furs, Aza could tell their bodies were honed and hardened.

"Aza, this is Rune's mother and father, Lady Sola and Lord Mika." Nivet gestured to them and then bowed his head in respect.

"It is a pleasure to meet you." Aza mimicked Nivet. Xira, Reed, and Anwin did the same. She kept her head bowed until either of them would speak, but the room remained silent except for the crackling of wood in the fire. The emptiness of the temple felt like a gaping maw threatening to swallow her.

"So, you were successful," Sola said, breaking the silence.

They raised their heads.

Sola's stare bored into Aza then Nivet, taking their measure. "Was it worth it? Taking my best soldiers, Nerian soldiers, and my son, the next in line to lead Neria, away from our protective borders to bring back someone, who from what I hear, didn't want to come here."

"Lady Sola-" Nivet attempted to chime in, but Mika cut him off.

"No, R-, Nivet. You will listen. We do not casually go into other provinces. We heard from our spies and first-hand accounts..." Mika turned to Xira, "of how risky this venture was. You nearly killed my son in the process."

"My Lord, we had already had this discussion when I returned. I would rather not rehash this now. I cannot change what has already happened. I can only plan for what will happen. War is coming. We must prepare and Aza is key." Nivet stepped forward, beseeching them to understand.

Sola left her stone-hewn chair and with grace and precision, descended the stairs one at a time. She faced Nivet, her chin held high. "So, *God,* you will use someone else for your purposes. My son wasn't enough, so now you must use her. Does she even know anything?"

Nivet grit his teeth and answered, "Not enough. That is why she is here."

Sola walked to Aza, inspecting her. "You truly don't know?"

Aza knew shreds of information from what she discovered in the Hall of Prophecies, yet it wasn't enough like Nivet said. She did not want to convey her abundant ignorance and responded, "I am here to learn, to understand."

Sola snorted with derision. "I'm sure you are. I'm sure that is what he told you." She cocked her head at Nivet. "I am warning you now, Aza. Run," she pronounced. "Run and do not look back. What you will learn will only haunt you. You will be destroyed by the knowledge."

"I will not run when all of Ithilia is in danger, and I can help. If I can destroy the Hinterlands then —"

Sola laughed. "Destroy the Hinterlands? What happens next, my dear? What is perhaps more devastating? What will wreak more havoc over Ithilia?"

Aza stiffened and didn't answer.

Sola ran an appraising eye over Aza. "Hmm, it seems you do know. The gods and goddesses from long before will run rampant. Inhabiting mortals is something they do for sport. What do you think they will do when they regain their full powers and bodies?"

"What would you have me do? I can't have the Hinterlands swallow the land."

Lady Sola laughed. "Maybe you should," she whispered.

Her husband, Mika, joined her at the base of the stairs. "Nivet, do what you must." Mika's eyes tightened as he gazed upon his son in the form of someone else.

Nivet clenched his jaw and gave a firm nod.

The Lord and Lady of Neria departed, leaving the group in the emptiness of the stone temple.

~

Once secluded in a private part of the city, Aza spun and asked, "What in the Darkness Below was that?"

"Lady Sola and Lord Mika are great leaders for Neria, but lately they have been bitter," Xira explained. "Their only son being taken over by a god was something they knew could happen, but they never expected it would."

"No one ever does," Reed added.

"Their anger is directed at the situation, not at you, Aza."

Nivet pinched the bridge of his nose. "They have every right to be angry; their son's mortal body almost died."

Aza whirled on Nivet. "Speaking of that incident, care to explain how you survived Eonas?"

"Another time. Right now, your learning will be split between myself and them. In the mornings, you will train with me. In the afternoons, you will join them as they train our Nerian soldiers. Xira, Reed, and Anwin will be preparing them for the upcoming war."

Aza's eyes bulged and her eyebrows shot up. She pointed a finger at Anwin and said, "She should be resting."

A relaxed smile crossed Anwin's face. "Aza, I'm not made of glass. I'm fine. Plus we aren't on the run anymore. I will be able to rest when I need to and the baby will be fine. The worst is over."

Aza held her tongue but doubted that the worst was over. The worst had barely begun. If war was going to break out, with the return of the gods and goddesses things would get much worse.

"Reed and I will be doing most of the training," Xira reassured. "Anwin will be working with our healers. The medicine we dosed you with required a great number of supplies and plants. So much, in fact, that our stores are empty. Anwin will be developing weapons that can be coated or imbued with that mixture, but just enough to dull their magic, not stop it like it did yours."

Aza gave a skeptical nod. "And these plant fumes won't harm you or the baby?"

Anwin laughed heartily while Xira and Reed chuckled. "She worries more than Kiasix."

Aza understood they were merely joking with her, but she couldn't shake the images of Anwin unconscious in the water after fighting the sea serpent or her nose bleeding from her magic use as they dragged her through the sewers, or from Lord Sune holding a dagger to her throat. So many times, Anwin was in danger, and Aza had already feared for her life, but now the life of her child was added in. Meeting her family did not abate the feeling of helplessness. All she could see was her husband and children's faces lit up with pure joy and love upon seeing her.

"Fine, I will stop worrying about your health."

The group's laughter died out. Anwin softened, reaching out to brace Aza's shoulder. "I appreciate the concern, my Lady. I do. It is very sweet, but I am a Nerian warrior. I agreed to this mission. I agreed to bring you home because it was the right thing to do. Xira and Reed risk their lives and their families understand the consequence. My family is the same. Kiasix knows who I am. I promised to return before the birth, and I have."

She understood they were each risking their lives, that their families would be equally devastated if one did not return, but Aza could not shake away the image of Anwin's young children, their faces filled with tears instead of joyous screams.

Aza's throat was tight, and tears swam behind her eyes. "Your children though..." She couldn't finish her sentence.

"They will understand their mom died in service to the Nerian province, died protecting them and Ithilia." Anwin's green eyes searched Aza's for a confirmation that she was okay. Aza gave a small nod, unsure of what was coming over her. A feeling she couldn't shake free from.

"We have a lot to get done before the celebration tonight. Aza, you will be with Nivet for the day." Xira beckoned Reed and Anwin to follow, leaving Aza with her flurry of emotions.

Nivet drew closer to her side but did not inquire further about her emotional state. He must have sensed a question would have her tears flow freely or result in a lash of anger. Instead, he gave her a moment to calm herself and walked to a looping path along the mountain. "Follow me."

Wanting to move and dispel the pent-up emotions, she gratefully followed. They wound through the snow-covered mountain leaving El'theren behind. By noon, Aza was breathing heavily, beads of sweat dripped down her back from the intense sun shining down. Blinding rays of light reflected off the snow. The trail narrowed with only one person able to traverse the slippery slope. Icicles lined the path and her foot slipped. She regained her footing and carried on.

Before she could ask where they were going, a giant roar split the sky. Nivet disappeared about the edge of the trail. Aza breathed a steadying breath and followed.

Dragons. He had taken her to the dragons. As she rounded a bend of the path, Aza recognized Isarr performing elegant spirals in the sky, lazily dipping and scooping into the air current. His beautiful wings opened and the span of them seemed to block out the sun before he pulled them in close and dove to the ground. At the last moment his wings flashed open, and he soared up into the air, instead of crashing on the snowy ground.

Nivet was seated on a ledge and beckoned her to join.

She was mindful to keep her distance. The lure of his magic was tempting, but she was trying her best to resist it. The prior night, her mind was muddled with alcohol, and she easily fell within his sway.

She was so preoccupied with Isarr, she didn't notice two other dragons hidden in the alcove of the mountain.

Whereas Isarr was a brilliant mix of white and blue like the snow and sky, an inky black dragon was tucked into the corner watching his movements. Its size was equal to Isarr, and it appeared mesmerized by Isarr's aerial dance.

"How are they here?"

Nivet leaned back on his hands, watching Isarr fly and maneuver through the skies. "With the creation of the Hinterlands, the gods and goddesses were banished and magic everywhere diminished. The average MagicBlessed's magic is minimal now. It had the same effect on magical creatures. They either died out or were forced into hiding, holding tight to whatever magic they could."

He took a sip of his water, offering it to Aza. She shook her head, declining. "The dragons were prized for their size and ferocity in battle. Before the Hinterlands, there were so few already. They were hunted. Isarr has been protected within Neria since before the creation of the Hinterlands. I hid him here and his mate, Druilinn." He tipped his head to the female dragon in the alcove.

Aza raised her eyebrows. "They are over one thousand years old?"

"Yes, dragons can be quite long-lived."

"What about that little one down there?" Aza pointed to a charcoal-gray dragon that was watching Isarr.

Nivet smiled. "Linor. It is their first hatchling."

"When did they have them?"

Nivet turned to Aza, his eyes swirling to gold. "When you appeared from the Well."

He brought his fingers up to his mouth and gave a sharp whistle. Isarr stopped his flying instruction to Linor and flew over to Nivet and Aza. He dug his sharp claws into the mountain, shards of stone falling to the ground below.

Nivet skillfully got to his feet and leapt onto Isarr's back. He gestured for her to follow.

Aza copied, her boots slipping along the slick ice. She rubbed her hands together and pushed off the ledge. She was weightless, wheeling her arms, before the dragon was beneath her.

Isarr did not wait and pushed off the cliff, falling to the ground. Aza's stomach dropped and she clung tightly to Nivet. He stiffened under her touch. Isarr attempted the same maneuver, waiting until the last minute and then yanking his wings open. Aza loosened a scream before it turned into one of exhilaration. Isarr gave a loud snort with a spew of ice. If she didn't realize any better, it appeared like he was chuckling at her expense.

Isarr gracefully halted and descended to the ground. Nivet slid from Isarr and Aza followed.

Druilinn slunk further into the shadows, examining Aza. She could barely discern the dragon's outline in the alcove of the mountain, her scales a beautiful obsidian that seemed to morph with the shadows and darkness. A faint glint from the sunlight bounced off the scales. Where Isarr was the snow and sky of Neria, Druilinn seemed to embody the night.

"I want you to meet Druilinn."

Aza eyed the dragon and shifted uneasily from one foot to the other. "Are you sure she wants to meet me?"

"Yes, she does." Nivet's voice was firm and decisive.

Aza knew nothing about dragons, but Druilinn appeared uncomfortable and unwilling, the exact opposite of what Nivet promised.

Before she could argue, Nivet left and climbed on the back of Isarr. He launched into the sky, the two of them flying above in a small circle. Despite his departure, she could feel his prying eyes, watching from a distance trying to give them some privacy.

Aza looked around, searching for little Linor. At the opposite end of the clearing, a cavern opened into the mountainside, and she spotted a glimpse of charcoal gray backed into the corner.

She didn't understand why she was here. Surely there were more important things for Aza to accomplish and learn, but Nivet deemed this important and so she would have to trust his judgment.

Druilinn swiveled her head and pierced her with one liquid silver eye. Aza faltered. It was like looking into a mirror, the eyes similar to her own.

When Aza watched earlier, Druilinn was comfortable watching her mate and hatchling fly and move about, but when she spotted Aza, she had slunk away. It reminded her of an abandoned dog, cowering in the corner for its owner. Except this dog was thousands of pounds, enormous, and could wield magic.

The only thing to do would be to try. Aza firmed her spine and stepped forward. Isarr's words echoed in her head, *Welcome home.*

Aza took another step forward and Druilinn stilled, the silver eye tracking her movements. "Nivet wants me to meet you. He deems this important," Aza said out loud. Talking to herself seemed to help her nerves. She squinted her eyes at Druilin. Something about the dragon seemed familiar, like a dream she couldn't quite remember. "You are quite stunning." She was only twenty feet away from the magnificent creature. "I will not force you to bear me as a rider. I only wish to meet you." Ten feet away now. Before Aza realized what she was doing, she kneeled down, bowing before this great creature. It was like an echo from a memory long ago. She didn't know how long she had been kneeling, the cold biting into her skin, but she did not use her magic to warm herself. She wanted to feel the elements, to show her submission.

Giant steps shook the ground, but Aza kept her head bowed. Black scales caught the edge of her vision. The scales were like black, sparkling diamonds and were as beautiful up close as they were far away. A giant huff of warm breath moved her hair and coasted along her back. The dragon rested her head next to Aza's shoulder.

A voice resonated in her mind. *He is right. There is a kernel of her in you, but you are something else. Something different.*

Aza finally lifted her head to look at Druilinn.

Rise, my Lady. I have missed you these long years.

Druilinn positioned her head next to Aza's, bringing her snout low to the ground. Like Anwin's husband did to her, Aza brought her forehead to Druilinn's and breathed in the scent of the dragon— the crackle of a fiery piece of wood, a faint hint of smoke, but something entirely different like the air of the Nerian mountains.

Let us ride together. It has been too long.

Aza broke from their embrace and used Druilinn's massive foreleg to climb onto her back. She positioned herself, and without warning, Druilinn launched into the air. Aza tilted her head back and loosed a freeing whoop into the air. Druilinn chuffed in response and spiraled up, twisting Aza's vision, the mountains going blurry.

It feels both new and old. Druilinn's voice felt ancient like the very stones of the mountains.

Aza agreed. This sensation so familiar, like a nagging feeling at the back of her mind, but she pushed it aside and focused on the beautiful flight.

I must introduce you to my hatchling. Her voice took on a note of pride. *Linor. My son.*

Her son.

The words scratched at her, raking through her mind. She couldn't shake free of them. Something was wrong. She didn't have control of her body. Aza loosened her grip on Druilinn, convulsions wracked her body. No. She couldn't hold on any longer. She tried weakly to reach for Druilinn, but she couldn't even bend her arm to grasp the scales. Her mind was scrambled, and she only had enough energy to weakly say, "Druilinn."

Aza fell through the sky, her body limp and useless. She had no control as she watched the snow-covered ground rush up to meet her. The pain and convulsions that tore through her body were so overwhelming, she didn't mind meeting her imminent demise. She just needed the pain to stop, so much pain. Maybe it was better to end this rather than endure this soul-crushing pain. Before she blacked out, she heard a faint scream.

44

"While a nuisance, Lilit was a advantageous person to keep close. Her supreme skills in battle and knowledge of weapons was helpful. Plus, she would do my bidding easily, for I only need to threaten her lover for her to act."

Cruvo's private journal

Lady Rasmina was not alone. The vultures that surrounded her at Lighthold accompanied her now. What Lorn thought would be his salvation, his escape, was only another place within the maze-like corridors in this gods-forsaken cave system. The room yawned open with strategic torches placed along the wall. The light played tricks on his eyes, morphing and changing on Lady Rasmina like she was a ghost from beyond, her pale visage floating in front of him, the sharp slice of a grin etched across her face in triumph.

His weakness and tiredness had finally caught up to him. Lorn stumbled, Lilit collapsing with him on their knees. The unforgiving rock sliced into him, but he could not give up.

"It was a valiant effort, hunter," Lilit coughed. Her eyes threatened to close, but he could not allow her the mercy of unconsciousness. He needed her awake if they were going to escape. Tears of frustration rimmed his eyes. He was so close, he had found her, they were going to leave. Lorn shook Lilit. "Stay awake," he barked.

She smirked. "Quite the time for you to grow a backbone." But her tone had no bite, no energy. Her body slackened. He tightened his grip, pinching her. The sharp pain jolted her awake momentarily.

Lady Rasmina stepped forward. Lorn's sight blurred. He tried to focus on who flanked her. The vague forms of her advisors, Maline and Flint were there and a retinue of soldiers. But there was someone else standing at the edge, he couldn't quite place. He knew them from somewhere, but his recently poisoned mind had trouble placing it.

Lady Rasmina crouched in front of him and placed a delicate finger under his chin, lifting it up to meet her gaze. The vaporous blue eyes fogged his mind. "You are too easy to manipulate. Do you think I would let our servants willingly swap out your water? Do you think my own advisor Flint would betray me and whisper a message to you from Lilit? Do you think this hasn't been meticulously planned. To give you hope, to see if you are strong enough, to get you here to this moment?

Lorn shuddered. This had all been carefully orchestrated and he had fallen for it. He couldn't stay here and subject himself to her mockery any longer. Summoning any remaining energy, he pulled forth his magic. He needed a distraction, a blast of energy, a bright light, something to distract.

Before he could release it, Lady Rasmina stepped back and *tsked.* Guards intervened restraining him. Lilit was yanked from his grasp, her head lolling on her shoulders. Lorn writhed against their grips, against the cold steel of their sword on his throat, as Lilit looked on blearily through cracked eyes.

"Do not waste what little strength and magic you have fighting," Lady Rasmina announced.

"You think I care what happens to my life anymore?" Lorn shouted and fought against the restraints of the guards. The sharp sword nicked his throat as he pulled and fought.

Lady Rasmina motioned, and the guard sheathed his sword. "No, I do not think you care about your own life. But you do care about hers." She pointed to Lilit. "You risked your life to pull her from her cell when at any point you could have fled and left her to rot." She interwove her fingers in front of her body, the very prim and proper lady she was raised to be. "Every time you fight back, you resist, she will be harmed. Whether by magic or force."

"Don't worry, hunter. I'm ready to die anyway. Don't let them force you to do anything," Lilit muttered under her breath, each word requiring such effort.

Lorn weighed his options and acted. Despite the pounding in his head, despite the lack of food and water, he reached deeply and summoned the magic that was bestowed to him.

With an expert touch, he set fire to the guards holding Lilit. A quick fire, merely to scare and cause them to scatter. She collapsed, her legs unable to support her body any longer. A bright light beamed from his body, blinding the guards around him as he sprinted to Lilit, desperately trying to lift her on to his shoulders and carry her out.

But his attempts were useless. They were too worn, too exhausted.

A fist slammed into his face, and he crumpled to the ground, Lilit's body landing on his own. He groaned and scrambled his legs to find some purchase.

Guards separated Lilit's ragged body from his, escorting her to Lady Rasmina's side.

"I hate that it must come to this, Lorn. If only you had listened, she would have been spared this pain."

Another guard jerked Lorn to his knees, their fingers digging into his scalp, pulling him by the hair to watch.

Lilit was held between the two guards with little awareness of her surroundings, her eyes glazed and unseeing. The guards' hands were burned, red, and raw. Their faces contorted by anger and thoughts of revenge.

Lady Rasmina nodded. With a suddenness Lorn didn't expect, one soldier held Lilit while the other yanked Lilit's arm backwards suddenly and smoothly. The bone popped, and her arm hung loosely at her side. Lilit loosed a feral scream.

Lorn writhed and raged on his knees. The guard's fingers dug into his scalp, holding him in place. "Stop! Stop it!"

"You chose to do this, Lorn. You chose to fight back. This is what happens to those who do not listen."

Lady Rasmina nodded again and while Lilit cried out, the guard held her forearm and set it on fire. The skin on the arm burned, blistered, and bubbled. Lilit kicked her legs and released a blood-curdling scream. Just as quickly, the flame vanished, leaving behind a mangled arm. The guards released her, and she collapsed to the floor like a marionette without strings. Without the use of her arms, she could not brace herself for impact and she smacked against the ground.

After a few seconds, she rolled to her side, teeth gritted, her face contorted with pain. She looked into his eyes. "Lorn..." She began, but spasmed in agony. "Don't you fucking yield!" she spat. The fierce declaration descended into mewling sounds of pain.

Lorn's stomach hollowed as he fought against his restraints. He wasn't sure of the words that spilled from his mouth, but they were a declaration, a promise of vengeance. The miserable whimpering from Lilit fueled his anger as he spewed his hostility. She who prided herself on her strength, resilience, will to fight was reduced to a broken, burned mess on the ground.

Lost to shouting and screaming, the pain in his body finally won and he stopped. The exertion was too much. His vision tunneled and the room darkened.

~

A splash of water woke him. Maline crouched before him with a glass of water and a bowl of stew. The smell alone was enough to revive him, but his mouth watered at the sight—warm, filled with rich meat and vegetables floating on the surface.

"Eat."

She shoved the bowl into his hands, and he shook his head.

"Would you like more harm to come to Lilit?" Lady Rasmina interjected. She motioned to her, and the guards began pulling her broken body off the ground. Her whimpering grew with each unwanted touch.

"Fine," he barked.

Lady Rasmina nodded, and the guards lowered her back to the ground.

The stew was rich and well-seasoned. His stomach roiled as the first bite dropped heavy into his stomach. He was not used to such decadent food, the meager scraps of bread and spoiled meat he had been fed had destroyed and degraded his body. He wanted to shove the whole bowl in his mouth and greedily swallow each bite, but he forced himself to go slowly. With each spoonful he eyed the cave, formulating a plan.

Lady Rasmina walked towards him. Her hand dipped into a pocket on her dress. Her guards clustered tightly to her when she approached Lorn, but she waved them off. They both knew he wouldn't attempt anything further after she had proven her point with Lilit.

"Do you know what this is?" The hand opened, revealing a tiny clump of rock—ore.

Lorn took a measured bite and shook his head.

"This is what we have been looking for. This is the key to our future." The ore seemed to be the very absence of light.

Everything he knew clicked into place. The reason why townspeople were being taken and forced to work in the caves. It was for this. They were working night and day to find this for Lady Rasmina.

"I studied every book, every journal, everything from when the gods and goddesses existed. It was quite difficult. Something happened, something was triggered that destroyed most of the information. But I was relentless. In an ancient book, I found a mere mention of an ore that when mined, folded into metal, and forged into a weapon, can mortally wound the gods and goddesses. It couldn't just be a story. So, I searched, relentlessly digging, pursuing, searching for this mysterious ore. It was described as the blackest of night, a black so dark you could not see your own hand in front of your face. We mined and found nothing. Of course, we found our typical gems and riches, the kind of wealth that keeps Gara prosperous, but not this one. Until recently. Hidden in the depths of this mountain, I found it. The Gloomstone." She held it gently between her thumb and index finger, the ore seeming to swallow up any light.

Lorn scoffed. "You found it? Or the people you have enslaved?"

Lady Rasmina looked down on him with disdain. "They will be free, once we mine enough. This is for their safety. It is for the good of us all to take down the gods and goddesses."

Lorn arched an eyebrow at her claim.

"You doubt me? The gods and goddesses will return, mark me. Your dear Aza is a sign of that. It will only be a matter of time, and when they do come, they will raze all of Ithilia to the ground. We must be prepared."

"Why do you need me? You already have your precious

Gloomstone."

"When the Gloom and Radiance are intertwined, only then will the balance be regained and the everlasting perish once more," she recited in a single breath.

"I studied this text again and again, understanding the gloom is referencing the Gloomstone, but I was stuck on the Radiance. Until you showed up and healed Pearl. I asked Lilit to explain what happened multiple times, unaware of what I had stumbled upon. You are the Radiance. Your power is the Radiance."

Finished with his stew, he placed the bowl aside and stared at Lady Rasmina. "So what will you have me do?"

The person Lorn had trouble placing, stepped forward. The broad, muscle-hardened woman seemed out of place, nervously running her fingers together, her grim eyes darting around the cave, finding it difficult to land on a specific spot.

"You must infuse your power, the Radiance, with the Gloomstone. Hidara, our skilled swordsmith, will forge the two powers together to create the ultimate sword that can kill every god and goddess. And that will not be all, Lorn of Verta." Lady Rasmina gripped his chin hard, her eyes alight with triumph. "After the sword is successfully created, we will banish the Well of our magic next."

45

"I do not fault Sola and Mika their anger. Every day I chastise myself, the very same anger burdening me. Sometimes I wish for the carelessness of the other gods and goddesses. They do not allow themselves to feel the trivial emotions of the MagicBlessed. It is an affliction in myself I cannot ignore."

Nivet's private journal.

Her mind was a jumble of images and sounds. A dragon roar and Nivet's steady voice murmuring soothing words as a comforting swell of magic eased the pain and convulsions. It did not last long. Her body was now relaxed on some soft surface, the cold of the mountain no longer biting into her skin.

A wood log crackled and splintered. The snap woke Aza.

She blearily opened her eyes and was greeted with wood beamed ceilings, rich fabrics, and a soft downy blanket tucked in around her body. She groaned. Her body felt like it had been beaten. She shifted slowly to her side and was greeted by Nivet lounging on her couch, his back bent in concentration, writing. His feathered quill furiously scribbled, his eyes narrowed in concentration. He sighed and closed the journal.

"This wasn't the first time," he stated.

Aza swallowed, her throat dry and scratchy. "No, it wasn't."

Nivet gathered a glass, poured water into it, and gave it to Aza. She murmured her thanks and took small sips, the soothing liquid easing her discomfort.

She was too weak and vulnerable to mentally block the feel of his magic and presence. "Do you mind returning to the couch?"

He merely arched an eyebrow at her request and followed her request. She pushed herself into a cross-legged position, closing her eyes to subside the pounding in her head.

She didn't need to ask what had happened. While riding Druilinn something triggered an episode and ended with her mind at war with itself.

He watched her with a discerning eye. "It will get better."

"Will it?" she scoffed, the reaction causing her head to pulse in pain. She brought up a hand to steady herself and sighed. "How can I learn, if every time something triggers me, and I collapse into a convulsing mess?"

"You have been to the Hall of Prophecies?"

Aza nodded.

"Then you have read the prophecy and the journal entries linked to you. It will take time for your mind to reconcile."

Aza remained silent, stewing in her frustration. She who was always so strong, felt so weak and untethered by mere words, stabs of supposed memories.

"Do you know what caused the reaction?" Nivet's words were soft, curious, not for Aza's sake, but almost for his own sanity. Like he was treading on delicate ground.

Aza ran her fingers over the rim of her glass, trying to remember what happened prior to her falling. "Druilinn was speaking to me. She mentioned her hatchling, her son. Linor." Her fingers tightened on the glass. "Then I fell," she finished lamely.

Nivet stiffly rose from the couch and walked over to the door. "You need your rest," he said tightly. "The celebration will be tonight." He turned to the door his hand hovering over the door handle. He kept his face turned to the door, his voice a low whisper. "It will get better. I promise." Without another word, he left. A piece of wood crackled and sparked in the hearth.

Aza worried her lip. She slid back onto the comforting bed to seek a small reprieve into oblivion.

~

A soft hand jostled her awake. Multiple soft hands poked and prodded her body. Little giggles sounded beside her.

"Fier, Enbre," a voice chided. "Enough, she does not need to be poked like a piece of meat." More giggles sounded. "Yanna, can you get the bath ready please."

"Yes, Mama." Small footsteps padded to the bathroom.

Aza cracked open an eye to find two pairs of deep blue eyes staring back at her, their fiery red hair haloing their heads in a chaotic mess. A boy and a girl. Twins. Aza didn't realize it earlier, but the resemblance went beyond siblings.

"Mama, look at her eyes," the little boy said.

The little girl reached out her tiny finger and poked Aza on her cheekbone. Aza winced.

"Enbre, Fier, I said you could come with me to wake up Lady Aza, but now you must go with your father."

"But Mama, we want to help you get her ready for the celebration tonight," Fier whined.

Anwin crouched low and looked at each of them. "Go find your father. You need to get your faces painted tonight just like Neria's fierce warriors."

The children's faces lit up with joy and they clapped their hands together. Without a second glance back, they raced out of Aza's cottage, the door slamming behind them.

"I'm sorry. They were excited to come help me wake you up."

Aza sat up and chuckled, rubbing a hand over her hair.

"It's fine. It's nice to see children, to see them so carefree and happy after...everything."

Anwin's eyes softened in understanding, and she clicked her tongue at Aza. "Come on now. You need to start getting ready. Yanna, is the bath ready?" she shouted over her shoulder.

Yanna emerged, her deep auburn hair beautifully braided into a coronet at the top of her head. "Yes, Mama."

Anwin clapped her hands together. "You go slip into the bath, relax, and we will handle your clothing and hair." She lifted her eyebrows mischievously.

Although Aza didn't want to make a fuss, it was nice for someone to care for her.

"It's a good thing you rested. The celebration will go long into the night." Anwin pulled Aza out of bed and firmly guided her to the bathroom where she shut the door. "Relax, but don't take too long, okay?"

Yanna smiled behind her hands at her mother's pushiness.

The bath eased any residual tension in her shoulders. The aroma of plants she wasn't familiar with wafted in the air. Something warming and cloying.

A soft fur-lined robe was hanging nearby, and Aza slipped into it.

When Aza emerged from the bath, both Anwin and Yanna were outfitted in their celebration attire. Aza had never seen Anwin in anything so delicate. Even at the castle of El'en, Anwin and Xira were constantly wearing black leathers. Rich, deep green fabric draped over her body and gathered over her chest and shoulders with the fabric crossed over her shoulders and down the back into a flowing gown. It was light and delicate, highlighting the sinewy strength of the Nerian warrior. Her daughter was in a similar dress but in a rich red that complimented the girl's pale skin and auburn hair.

Anwin's dress highlighted the soft bump of her stomach and Aza cursed herself for how clueless she was. It was something she just never took note of. Her red hair was loose, flowing down her back.

"You both are beautiful."

Yanna bashfully hid a smile and Anwin beamed back. "You always are, but we are going to get you absolutely shining tonight."

Aza was coaxed onto the couch in front of the fire and Anwin and Yanna expertly oiled Aza' silver coils, and ran their fingers through her hair, defining each strand. She closed her eyes and melted against the couch, letting them do their work.

Yanna tentatively brushed Aza's shoulder. "Lady Aza, we are finished."

Too soon, she thought.

She was reluctant to move from the couch and the warmth of the fireplace snapping before her, but she stretched her stiffened limbs and gently rose to her feet.

"Here is your dress, in your measurements." Anwin handed her a package. "We will leave you to finish up. See you at the celebration." With a small wave from Yanna they departed.

The dress was beautiful, but she expected no less. The fabric pooled at the floor and short sleeves capped her shoulders as the fabric split into a V down her chest. The fabric reminded her of the onyx temple carved into the mountain its black stone glittering in the light. The fabric seemed to do the same, shifting and changing color. It wasn't the only item, it was paired with a loose coat, the thick material instantly warming. She was careful donning the dress; she did not want to disturb the meticulous job Anwin and Yanna had performed on her hair.

Before leaving, she caught herself in the mirror. Anwin and Yanna were gifted, having spent much time on her hair. Aza usually ignored it, either loosely pulling the curly silver strands into a loose ponytail or letting it free, the coils falling into her face and blocking her vision. Now, her vibrant silver hair seemed to glow and shine with the oils rubbed in. Elegant twist outs lined her face with the rest of her hair loose and free, framing her face. While Anwin was busy with Aza's hair, Yanna had dedicated time to moisturizing Aza's wind-chapped skin and she appeared luminous and well cared for. So vastly different from how she looked departing with Nivet in the morning.

Shrugging on the rich and luscious coat, she gave one last look at her cottage and followed the hypnotic drumbeat of the celebration. People laughed in the streets. The tantalizing scent of cooked meats wafted in the air as Aza ambled to the main city square. The cold air was biting, but copious torches lined the streets giving off a blast of warmth. The close-knit bodies helped to provide more heat. Swirls of snow blanketed the streets, but people were still out enjoying the celebration. A stage was erected in the center of the city square. A crowd gathered in front of the stage, awaiting something. Aza merged with the crowd, holding her breath. People glanced at her curiously, but all left her alone, which was refreshing. The young children openly stared, which she found amusing, their innocence apparent on their slack-jawed faces.

A hand pulled at hers. She turned quickly expecting to reprimand some drunken reveler. Instead, River stood next to her with a wide smile.

"Hey, Aza. You look amazing. Let me guess, Anwin did your hair?"

Aza touched the strands and answered, "Yeah, how did you know?"

River nudged her in a friendly manner and said, "When she isn't busy being a badass warrior, we often flock to her to beg her to do our hair…when she isn't swarmed with her children, that is." River's own locs were threaded gold jewelry. The small coils complimented her light brown skin, the minuscule jewels smaller than Aza's freckles. They created a mystical view when caught in the torchlight.

The audience quieted as the Lord and Lady ascended the stage, both resplendent in sleek black robes. Although the people were relaxed, she could see the duality of their presence, both hardened warrior and content people.

Lady Sola spoke first. "We welcome each and every one of you here tonight. As you know, our god, the guardian Nivet and his retinue of our fiercest Nerian soldiers have returned at last." The crowd was silent, their respect for their leaders unmatched. Their gazes remained unwavering, rapt on Lady Sola and her fierce, resolute face.

Lord Mika stepped beside her and raised his voice to match hers. "Welcome your soldiers home," he roared. The Nerians roared with him. An all-consuming applause rippled out, with cheers, shouts, and whoops. Nivet climbed up the steps, followed in line with Xira, Reed, and Anwin, each equally outfitted in their finest clothes, wearing their hardened expressions.

Lady Sola added, "This celebration will be a time to not think of the troubles ahead. We pride ourselves on being a transparent province. Something is brewing like the cold winter wind that whips through the Nerian mountain range. A storm we cannot ignore. War will be coming, but for tonight, embrace each other and use these memories to bolster you for the tough times ahead." Her eyes roved the crowd and latched onto Aza. "But in times of war, we rise up. Nerians do not back down! We do not surrender!" she shouted, raising her fist in the air. Her husband echoed her movements, one fist raised in the air, and the other beating his chest. The crowd copied the pulsing beat.

"Tonight, we drink! Tonight, we love! Tonight, we celebrate!" she screamed, the sound booming across the thumping crowd.

Lord Mika released a guttural yell followed by Nivet, Xira, Reed, and Anwin. The cheers and exultations from the crowd were bolstered by the Lady's compelling words. The normally reserved River shouted fiercely beside her. Aza could only join as Lady Sola stared at her, the weight of what was to come held within.

~

The harsh morning sun slanted through the parted curtains. Aza cursed and turned over in bed, determined to ignore the sharp light that stabbed at her senses. She only needed a bit more sleep to regain her sanity and senses. Her night spent at the Bladed Beauty was nothing compared to the festival celebrating the return of the Nerian warriors. A carousel of drinks from Xira, Reed, Anwin and River flowed her way, along with merry cheering and encouragement to dance. A distant pain twinged in her legs, an echo and reminder of her unstoppable feet from last night. It had been such a relief, the same sort of relief as the Bladed Beauty when the citizens did not look at her differently, but reveled. She was able to match them drink for drink, rising to the bait of their good-natured challenges. Aza groaned and stuffed a pillow over her head, unable to ignore the steady call of the day.

The door hinge creaked in protest and Aza jolted upright, magic ready.

"It is late into the day. Come there is something we must do."

Aza blearily ran a hand over her face and shucked her pillow aside. "It must be done today? The softness of her bed did not want to let her go. With strong determination, she slipped her feet over the side of the bed, carefully avoiding Nivet's prying gaze.

"Give me a minute and I will be out." She stared at her lap until she heard his retreat. In the bathroom, she splashed cold water on her face in a vain hope to dispel her grogginess.

Last night replayed in her mind and she couldn't ignore it. She had already vowed to not entangle herself with another god and goddess, the proximity of their power too confusing to understand her true feelings, however she found herself inexplicably drawn to Nivet. He was always in her peripheral, or some other senses knew where he was and tracked him. She did not fail to notice when someone else was wrapped around the god's arms or trailing him with a friendly smile.

Reed noticed her expression falter and said, "That is Hakim. Rune and he were promised to each other." She remembered his hesitancy and how Reed's eyes welled with an unspoken compassion. "It is very murky."

Aza blinked away the fleeting emotion— jealousy —and loosed a cool laugh. "It is of no interest to me, I am simply trying to understand." She couldn't help but think of Lilit in love with Lord Aldrich, the situations eerily similar.

Aza let the icy cold water linger on her skin, hoping to wash away those confusing feelings. She wasn't going to be caught up in a situation like El'en again.

Nivet stood, waiting, looking intently at the crackling fire. He was composed and awake, showing no ill effects from last night's entertainment.

"Dress warm, it will be cold."

Aza grabbed her thick coat, smashed her feet into the thick fur lined boots, and nodded at Nivet. He reached an arm out to her. She froze and eyed it, looking back at him questioningly

"The day is already halfway over. We will be shadowing to our location."

She steadied her breath, braced herself, and reached her fingers over to his. With the barest touch, she gripped his gloved hand, but even through the layers of their clothes the contact was electric. It was overwhelming, comforting, and everything she had hoped it would be based on his magical signature.

She gritted her teeth and ignored the sensations bouncing inside of her. It had been the same with Cruvo.

Like being draped in a layer of the softest silk, the shadows enveloped her, and in the blink of an eye, they had been transported.

Isarr greeted them, his imposing shadow dwarfing them. Aza looked for Druilinn and found her far behind Isarr, pushed against the mountainside as if she was carved from it.

"She is embarrassed that you fell," Nivet answered. Forgetting where she was, Aza quickly released her grip and tried peeking behind Isarr to see Druilinn fully.

"It is not her fault. She can't predict how I will react."

"Nevertheless, she bears the responsibility." Nivet skillfully climbed up Isarr and looked at her expectantly.

Aza knew what she must do. She brushed past Isarr, the massive dragon eying her as she walked towards his mate. Druilinn did not break eye contact as Aza crossed the expanse, the snow crunching underfoot like the snapping of bones.

Druilinn huffed a warning breath, not at Aza but at herself. She blamed herself and Aza needed to assuage her guilt. She snapped her wings open and braced her legs to take flight, but Aza would not let such a thing happen.

Abandoning any sense of dignity, Aza sprinted at Druilinn and flung herself at the dragon's head. Her breathing ragged, she bowed her head to Druilinn's breathing in the smoky brimstone and earthen mountain scent.

"It is not your fault," Aza said through clenched teeth.

You could have died, Druilinn's voice wove inside her head.

"I am always in danger, but you cannot predict when I will have an episode." She gripped the dragon's hide, her gloves scraping over the rough and beautiful scales. "Do not abandon me for fear of my death."

It was so faint Aza almost didn't hear it, it was barely a whisper in her mind, like Druilinn did not mean to convey such information. *I cannot lose you again, my Lady.*

Aza ignored the plea and used a tactic familiar to her, Nerian strength. She stepped back from Druilinn and announced, "Bear me as your rider. But do not cower in your mistakes. It is not the Nerian way." Aza lifted her chin and stared down Druilinn. They both needed to be strong. Strength would harden them both like the finest gems.

Like dusting off a layer of snow, Druilin emerged from the shadow of the mountain and shook out her great wings. She turned her head and leveled Aza with a hard stare. If the dragon could smile, Aza imagined it to be so.

You have her spirit.

Aza smiled and with a sprint, climbed up the enormous dragon's back. When she gained her seat, Druilinn launched into the air in a beautiful spiral. Breath escaped Aza. The biting cold, the harsh and beautiful mountains of Neria. A single thought resonated loudly like the clang of a stone in a water well. This was home.

"Thank you," Aza murmured and bent her forehead to rest against

Druilinn's back. Since their ride through the sky and clouds, Druilinn had recovered her proud, unshakable demeanor and did not view Aza as some fragile piece of glass, easily broken. Instead, their bond was building, and Aza felt the tension in Druilinn relax, her focus no longer on Aza, but rather the experience of flying and having a rider again. There were no echoes of the pain and convulsions. Instead, the two strayed away from conversation and enjoyed the freedom of flight, how the crisp winter air embraced her and strengthened them.

Finished with their flying, Nivet silently appeared by Aza's side and shadowed her back to El'theren. Keeping contented silence, they walked back to Aza's cottage.

There were many questions Aza yearned to ask, but she was content to continue to her peaceful home in silence. The brutal descent of winter afforded her time. She would take every second she could, like a miser hoarding gold.

There would be no return.

46

"They have brainwashed her. She rejected me. Aza is clearly not in her right mind. The situation is more dire than I could have imagined."

Cruvo's private journal

Innumerable times throughout Lorn's life, he felt powerless to prevent the tragedies that unfolded in front of him. This time was no different. He watched helplessly as Lilit lay crumpled on the ground before him, her soft sobs of pain died down to distant mewling as her mind volleyed between consciousness.

Lady Rasmina had played him well. She had seen through him, revealed and capitalized on his many weaknesses. Too soft-hearted, too emotional, too easy to be manipulated.

Lilit had been correct with every remark about people's behaviors, trying to get Lorn to understand. Yet now she was battling demons both fictional and real. She had committed many mistakes, but Lorn had forgiven her already. When she returned to her right mind, they would have multiple discussions and arguments, lay her transgressions out like cards on the table. But now was not the time. Not when she lay distorted on the ground with a dislocated shoulder and her opposite arm sticky and raw, turned into some grotesque meat slab.

He vaguely remembered agreeing to Lady Rasmina's demands and being hauled to an adjacent chamber. It was compact and tight, with an obsidian table commanding the space. His head was fuzzy, but the table seemed familiar, like something he had witnessed before, in a life before. A life where he had a shred of his sanity. The table seemed oppressive, like a heavy presence weighed him down.

Hidara was pushed in behind him, releasing an irritated exclamation. The muscular, older woman's auburn hair was streaked with gray and pulled back into a tight braid, her countenance the same as when Lorn met her in Lighthold Proper. Her eyes darted around the room nervously and locked with Lorn's like she was silently trying to relay a message.

Lorn's sanity was threadbare, and strange laughter bubbled to the surface. His mind was distant from his body, like they were two forces that were always connected, but in this moment disjointed. A hollow, husk remained, a time reminiscent of when his wife had been violently taken from him.

"The sword, Hidara," Lady Rasmina ordered.

One of the soldiers stepped forward bearing a sheathed sword. Hidara gripped the sheath and reverently removed the sword. The Gloomstone sword. It had already been crafted—the ore melded within. The sword was a perfect match to the Gloomstone. It was the very absence of light. Even as Hidara moved it, it seemed to cleave the shadows apart. She nervously placed the sword on the dark table, the two blending together.

Lorn stared at the sword, sensed it calling to him like the faint buzzing of a fly near his ear. His vision narrowed on the sword, it seemed to call to him. His feet moved forward, reaching for the Gloomstone sword, his body, his magic called to it.

He was vaguely aware of soldiers reaching for him, but at a barked command they stopped. It was happening at a distance from him. His only focus was the sword. Like a moth to a flame, he could not back down from its tempting call.

The days of toil, of his body broken and worn were stripped away in the sword's presence. He was not Lorn of Verta any longer, but a higher being. The magic gifted to him, surged forth. What was exhaustion when you had the embodiment of the gods in your body? He could not be contained. His power could surpass everyone around him. He could break free from this meager cave, but only the sword called to him, and he could not resist. It needed him, craved his magic, craved the light like only the dark could. Like it was starving. Unfed.

A smile cut across his face as his fingertips caressed the sword, the Gloomstone within the sword feeding his frenzy. Following ancient instructions his body understood his magic and surged forth, a tidal wave he would never dream of stopping. The wave of magic built, growing, and like the dawn breaking, his light burst forth.

The cavern was luminous, each facet of darkness was banished. He only had eyes for the sword. Calling to something within he formed and molded the magic like clay, like when he fought the specter so long ago, the magic seeming to come forth without thought. With a fortitude he didn't know he possessed, he funneled the magic into the sword.

Time was a concept he was not aware of. He only knew his magic, his light. The sinews of his body glowed like he had swallowed the sun. It poured from his fingertips, from every inch of skin. It poured like an endless waterfall, pounding into the sword. An intricate balance was forming, the Gloomstone needed an anchor, and the light was its balance.

The Gloomstone sword greedily swallowed the light. He produced more. More and more until his body was shaking, his forehead lined in sweat, his eyes adjusted to the brilliant shine of his own light. When the sword could absorb no more, Lorn's light flickered, the only sign of his power faltering.

His senses returned. He gasped for breath, heaving. Every part of his body was alight, everything was on fire. His body a mere vessel to provide this magic. Like the sun finally resting below the horizon, his light dimmed until only darkness filled the room.

He looked to his hands in astonishment. The Gloomstone sword retained its darkness, yet a faint buzz of energy emitted from it—the light magic he had suffused.

The room tilted. The walls seemed to pulse. Lorn steadied himself against the table and breathed deeply as Lady Rasmina stepped forward, her delicate fingers wrapping around the hilt of the sword.

"It seems Hidara, your skills with swords was not needed." Soldiers gripped her by the shoulder and steered her out of the cave. Lorn caught her widened eyes locking onto him in warning.

A giant boom shook the cavern. Everyone staggered. Lady Rasmina's fingers loosened on the sword, almost dropping it. Angrily, she looked back and shouted. "Go check on the workers." A pair of soldiers nodded and left, sprinting towards the chaos.

Another boom shook the ground. Shards of rock broke from the ceiling and rained down on them.

Lady Rasmina sheathed the sword and clutched it tightly. Something so precious would not be willingly let go. "We need to leave," she announced.

"What about them?" one of the guards asked, gesturing to Lorn and Lilit.

"Bring them." Soldiers flanked both sides of her as the others propped Lilit between them. They had no care for her dislocated shoulder, or the mangled wreck of her arm and she screamed in pain. They betrayed no sign of irritation and stoically dragged her to the entrance.

Back in the main cave, the soldier sent to check on the disturbance raced back to them, breath huffing. "The workers have escaped."

Lady Rasmina's lips thinned in displeasure. "How?"

"I'm not sure, but we need to leave. This entire cave system could collapse at any moment. Everything is broken, there are fires, smoke. It is dangerous for us to stay. They are armed."

Lorn felt miles away from the conversation, his own focus on his body, on the struggle to stand and how welcoming it would be for him to lay down and never rise again. But his eyes fell upon Lilit. He could not give up.

Another great shake had the soldiers gripping their swords in fear, their knees bent to stabilize themselves.

When the ground stilled, they hurried to the exit, only a small incline. It was cruel how close Lorn and Lilit had been to escaping, their exit a mere sprint upwards to freedom. It was like a knife had been pushed between his ribs and turned sharply.

The dimly lit sky laden with gray clouds was too bright for his sensitive eyes. He shied away from the light and inhaled a deep breath. The smells of nature welcomed him back, the rich, wet earth, and fresh biting winds.

He knew this place. The roaring of water greeted him. The sensory deprivation he had experienced was torture. Was it weeks...or months? His mind could not fathom how much time had transpired. He fought the desire to collapse to the ground in thanks and bow his head into the rain softened ground.

Another violent shake dropped them to their knees. Hidara's

auburn hair caught the corner of his eye. Without the soldiers keeping a watchful eye, she turned her head, and mouthed, *"Run."*

But he could not, not without Lilit. He would not abandon her. She had not abandoned him. Despite her vicious words and her dubious actions, she had never left him to die.

After receiving their barked orders from Lady Rasmina, a group of soldiers ran out in to the woods, chasing the disturbance.

The spongy ground softened Lorn's thoughts, his actions. The heavy drops of rain plopped on his back. He closed his eyes and felt a pulse of magic nearby. Strong, powerful magic.

Had Aza somehow found her way to him?

Before he could think further, he was yanked up to his feet by a soldier. Only a handful remained, along with Maline, Flint, and Lady Rasmina.

"We need to return to Lighthold," Maline said.

"The horses have scattered in the panic. We would not make it back until deep into the night—even slower with Lorn and Lilit," Flint responded.

Lady Rasmina eyed them, considering. "We cannot stay here. Somehow the workers have escaped. We have the sword. That is what matters."

The soldier holding Lorn offered, "Shall I cut their throats?"

Lady Rasmina vaporous blue eyes flickered between them and said, "No, I may have use for them yet. Despite how slowly we will move. We need them. Let us go."

Lorn wished he could summon his magic and decimate the entire group, but he could barely lift a finger in protest. It was difficult enough to stand on his feet and walk down the slippery mountain path. Lilit fared even worse, the soldiers uncaring over her state. At points she would go limp, her body rolling over jagged rocks and slipping over exposed roots. Lorn shouted at them, screamed at them, but they didn't care.

Their location itched at his brain, the mountain, the river. It roared in fury. His mind thickly fogged, he couldn't place where they were.

A rare clearing formed in front of them, the trail wide and the trees felled. The group moved with a dogged focus, even without their horses. Their determination was strong. The rain fell in earnest, the pathway became muddy, and his vision worsened. But the strong, undercurrent of magic he felt before was here. They were walking right into it.

The group halted suddenly and a slim figure with curly hair slunk from the trees. Even with his vision obscured from rain, there was no mistaking who had come.

She marched to the center of the clearing and Lady Rasmina's guards closed around her.

"Mother!" Pearl shouted over the din and fury of the storm. Energy gathered to her body, the air crackling in anticipation. Trousers and a fitted shirt in black clung to her body. A cloak lay discarded on the forest floor.

The soldiers readied their swords, but with obvious hesitancy as they recognized Lady Rasmina's beloved daughter. "How could you? All of those people, *our people*, enslaved, underground, without their families."

"Stand down!" Rasmina shouted at her guards. They faltered and slowly disengaged, stepping away from her, lowering their weapons. "Pearl, we can talk about this. Let us go back to Lighthold. I can tell you everything."

"No! There is no time left to talk. Those families you stole from did not have more time. Why are we any different?"

Lady Rasmina inched towards her daughter. "We can talk about this. We have found the solution to our problem. I will release all of those people. They will be able to go back to their families," she reassured. The rain poured down even heavier, but Lady Rasmina only had eyes for her youngest daughter.

"No!" Pearl screamed. A single bolt of lightning careened down from the sky in between Lady Rasmina and Pearl. "Do not talk to me like I am some stubborn child." Pearl clutched her head and sobbed, muttering to herself.

Lady Rasmina shook her head slowly, in denial.

"Enough!" Pearl shouted, but it wasn't at Lady Rasmina, rather it was someone else. Someone not here. "I have saved them. I freed them to return to their families. You will enslave them no more!"

Lady Rasmina sank to her knees, the mud sullying bottom of her formal dress, still shaking her head in disbelief. "Where is your magic from?" she asked. Lorn could barely hear her voice over the roar of the storm.

"Pearl, where is your magic from?" Lady Rasmina moaned, a low sound, like an animal dying. "What have you done?"

Pearl twitched, her fingers curled into her palm. "We made a deal."

"Who, Pearl?" Rasmina whispered. She crawled forward on her knees, her black hair sodden and dripping down her back. "Don't tell me you made a deal with her. Anyone but her."

Pearl faltered, her eyes softening in pity. "I had to, Mama. I couldn't let you continue to enslave our people."

"Who? Tell me the goddess you made a deal with."

"Kerali." The switch in Pearl was immediate. Upon uttering the goddess's name, Pearl's eyes glowed and a flurry of lightning cracked on the ground behind Pearl. A backdrop of chaos. "Enough!" Pearl suppressed the goddess, her breathing ragged like she had slammed a heavy door closed. "She is not allowed to take over until I am finished. That is our deal."

Lady Rasmina paled further. Lorn held little love for her, but he saw how the air had left her body, and one small wind could shatter her. "Do you understand what you have done? She will destroy you like she destroyed your father."

Pearl furrowed her eyebrows and looked at her mother in disbelief. "She will not. I will not let her."

"My sweet Pearl." Lady Rasmina clambered to her feet, the Gloomstone sword still held tightly within her hand. She shakily reached forward, her free hand clasping her daughter's face. Pearl softened and they leaned forward, mother and daughter, their foreheads touching. "I cannot let her have you."

Lorn saw her intentions too late, his reactions too slow. If he hadn't been isolated for weeks, near starvation, he would have noticed the Gloomstone blade cleave upwards. If the situation were different, he would have been able to stop what was about to happen.

47

"Aza is something Other. I know this in theory, but every day I am exposed to its truth. She is not like Her. I cannot help but be enamored by her tenacity, her dedication. Every morning, I find myself holding my breath, if only to see her radiant smile directed at me."

Nivet's private journal.

Aza's life had changed to one filled with the fear of pursuit and capture, into pure freedom. The people of El'theren valued hard-work, rigor, and a slow-moving lifestyle that resonated to Aza, a peace she had never experienced. The only thoughts nagging at her, marring her contented life, were thoughts of Lorn. While riding Druilinn, her mind strayed. How easily she could fly to Gara and rescue him from whatever inane mission he was sent on. Yet, she did not know where he was or how to find him. She hoped wherever he was, he was finding peace.

They followed a predictable routine; visiting the dragons, practicing her magic with Nivet; and joining Xira's leadership amongst the soldiers. The deadly teeth of winter had sunk in, and Neria was a flurry of snow. Aza would trudge through the piles of snow, her clothes thick and cumbersome but necessary. Although her magic was available to use, her days on the road with the Nerians had left her with the discipline to only use it in the most extreme of times.

One morning she thought herself helpful and dissipated the snow on the road, so the citizens could move freely without it burdening them. They had thanked her through clenched teeth and wary eyes. With a feeling of unease, Aza admitted her mistake to Nivet, who explained that the Nerians valued their labor above everything else, even magic. The toils of nature were a part of their world's cycle and to disrupt it was a mistake. While Aza did not agree with every aspect of their perspective, she respected it. The following morning, she ignored the thick bank of snow that had accumulated and trudged through it, the same as everyone else.

Her mornings with Druilinn were her favorite. There was nothing like experiencing the beauty of the open sky on the back of a dragon. Most days they rarely spoke and only shared in the collective calm. However, there were times when they discussed life, Isarr, and how Linor came to be—the coincidental timing between Aza's appearance and the birth of Linor. Aza sensed Druilinn's hesitancy to discuss Linor, afraid of another seizure overtaking her body. But her hesitancy thawed, and Aza adored her conversations with Druilinn, like falling back into step with a familiar friend.

Although the Nerians had strict procedure when it came to magic and its use, there were no such rules when training with Nivet. It was the same freedom she felt when sparring with Cruvo in her dreams, even though she was loathe to make the comparison. But she felt alive, like the answer to a call deep within her soul. Her magic jumped and thrilled at its use. Like an instrument abandoned and covered with dust had been uncovered and played by a skilled musician. Her magic converged in perfect harmony with Nivet's, rising to meet his. It was a vault she could finally leave open without any reprimand. He viewed her the same, with or without her magic, and he did not shy away from her strength. She couldn't help but compare how Cruvo regarded her the same way, without reproach or fear. She was wary, careful to not let their training and experiences bewilder her feelings. Any heat that flooded her body at his presence, she shut down. Cruvo had manipulated her because of it, and she would not let such a thing happen again.

Nivet kept his distance, their sparring sessions respectful and knowledgeable. He taught her the intricacies of shadowing. With his instruction, she realized her magic had been akin to a battering ram, whereas he taught her to use precision like the finesse of swordplay.

Finished with their practice, Aza would be deposited back to her cottage and spent her lunch break wandering El'theren. It was an experience she longed to have back in El'en, but fear had kept her apart from the city. It was not the case here. She wandered unaccompanied among the people, and they welcomed her, granting her the same courtesies of any other Nerian. Most treated her like anyone else, only the slight widening of eyes and stuttering of speech betrayed any deference to her power. This behavior was more typical among the children. But to them she was more a rare creature, like the spotting of a butterfly on a leaf. They wanted to flock to her and bask in her beauty. It was sweet and innocent.

Through her wanderings, she became acquainted with the city, its people's mannerisms, her favorite shops to frequent, when food shops were ready for the day, their food piping hot for her to purchase. This time allowed her to observe the Nerian people and make her own judgments.

Although Aza forged her own path through the city, she could not help but gravitate towards Nivet. He was often mingling with his people, another man at his side. The man had the glow of youth, younger than Lorn, with a bright-eyed eagerness as he joined Nivet for lunch or other meetings around town. Aza's curiosity got the better of her, and she tailed the gentleman to his work. He was an artisan, crafting beautiful pots and vases. They were etched with delicate scenes from nature or animals from the mountainside. Despite his age, his artistry was unmatched. Aza found herself outside the shop window looking in, trying desperately to not draw attention to herself.

One day she gathered her bravery, drew a breath, and entered the shop. He looked up from behind the counter, his smile faltering at the sight of Aza. He recovered and said, "Welcome, Lady Aza." The shop suited him, his skin the color of a fawn, was dusted in the flakes of his artistry. His shoulder-length, charcoal hair was pulled away from his face, a few belligerent pieces breaking free of the binds. His bulkiness did not detract from his grace, but rather added to it, demonstrating how fluid his movements could be, how delicate amongst such finery. His light brown eyes, color like the budding of a tree sapling, traced over her, inspecting her like he would one of his pieces, checking for imperfections. Disappointed at finding none, he wiped dust from his hands and stood waiting.

"I admit, I have passed by your shop many times. You have such a way with your medium." Aza's fingers grazed a nearby vase, etched with a family of wolves. She studied it instead of meeting the man's gaze. She firmed her back and faced him. She saw his open, trusting face. "Hakim, I am here to apologize. I understand what your relationship with Rune is, and I want to reassure you, my relationship with Nivet will not tread on yours."

Hakim's body stiffened. "I appreciate your reassurances, but I fear you do not understand our relationship. Do you know what it is to watch your heart's flame abandon you? To take the mantle of some duty they did not want and take that burden upon themselves? To have their body shared with a god, albeit a kind one, but still shared, nonetheless. Rune must fight beneath that torrential surface. It is wretched to be next to the one you love, but they are not that same person. I am there to provide comfort for Rune. To show that I can always be there for him. This lordship, this duty to protect the five provinces took precedence over our relationship, and I will forever be thankful for his sacrifice, but do I think you understand it? No, I do not."

Aza curled her fingers into her hands. She could not imagine the torture Hakim went through, watching the man he loved every day *be* someone else, controlled by someone else, yet retain his purity of spirit. She was a necessary evil—something he tolerated, but like the splinter embedded in his skin, he wanted to forget that she was there, she would be gone eventually.

Aza nodded and walked to the door. She thought she could ease the burden Hakim was experiencing, but she was only making it worse. "I apologize, it was careless for me to come in." She pushed it open, hoping for one more reassurance. "I won't interfere in your relationship with Rune. I am not getting in the way, nor will I."

Hakim laughed, the sound grating to Aza. "Lady Aza," he sighed, placing his hands on his hips and leaning back to take in the ceiling of his building like it held answers. "If it were only Rune, his heart belongs to me and mine belongs to him. But we both know it isn't only Rune. Nivet is the one in control and I am not blind to how he reacts around you. You are two heavenly bodies caught in the inexorable pull of one another. There is not much I can do except stand by and watch."

Aza shook her head slowly. "I promise you, it is not like that, nor will it come to that."

Hakim raised an eyebrow, his expression shifting from disbelief to pity. "Then why are you here?" He turned his back to her and said over his shoulder, "Good day."

Aza bolted from the shop, the sharp cold outside bringing her senses to the forefront. Hakim was wrong. She was merely curious about the man who accompanied Nivet every day during their lunch hour. Any feelings were nonexistent—they had to be.

~

After her lunch break, Aza was able to visit Xira, Reed, and Anwin who were fastidiously training the Nerian warriors on the peak of the mountain. Nivet guided her the first time, winding around the back of the obsidian temple. The military training grounds could be considered its own city. It sprawled over the mountainside, with the main artillery located within a carved-out section of the mountain. Weapons glinted back at her, almost goading her into using them, the blades honed and sharpened.

She had grown accustomed to Xira, Reed, and Anwin—their habits and their mannerisms. However, seeing them in their element, training the Nerian soldiers, altered her perceptions. Oron's teachings from so long ago came clattering back to her. How revered and fearsome the Nerian warriors were regarded. The sentiment held true. Aza's smile at seeing her friends faded. Each of them stern, stoic, and relentless with the soldiers. Their actions were as quick and sharp as their tongues. Even Anwin, outfitted in her fighting leathers, the bump of her baby apparent, was fearsome as she scolded warriors training —picking apart their style, technique, and flaws. Droves of warriors filled the mountainside, each subjected to a different training regimen. Anwin oversaw ranged combat, Reed taught them tactics, strategy, and field work. Xira taught hand-to-hand combat and weaponry.

Perfection was the expectation. Aza understood now why scars lined the Nerians' bodies. Throughout their travels, she had witnessed them in various states of undress and always marveled at the scars on their bodies. She was curious about how each wound had been caused. The answer was now in front of her. If a warrior faltered and blood was spilled, they would not use magic to heal it. Anwin's lesson popped into her head. How they believed the soldiers would remember their errors and correct them in the future or find they had no place here.

Aza's combat skills, while developed immensely, still did not compare to her companions. Seeing them in their true glory without any weariness, or threat of pursuit was amazing. Each of them so clearly in their element.

Aza walked through the soldiers, careful not to disturb their training. Xira did not let her slip by so easily. The ghost of a smile crossed her face before she barked her name. Although Xira had a serious expression, Aza noticed the faint twinkling of mischief in her eyes.

"We have such a rare opportunity, warriors," Xira called to the sparring soldiers. "Lady Aza will be helping you train. Two versus one. In this session, each participant can use their magic to their fullest ability." Xira gave Aza a nod, indicating she step forward.

The soldiers she sparred with were skilled and efficient, but they were no match for the amount of magic she wielded. She burned the hilt of their swords, pulled the ground from underneath them, froze their feet to the ground, pelted their bodies with fierce winds, shadowed herself when they would get too close. But they persevered.

After the first match, her opponents were scratched, bruised, and bleeding but would not relent, their breathing heavy. Xira called for an break.

"Do you see what we are up against? The gods and goddesses will return, and their magic will be far worse because Lady Aza is holding back. Her magic knows no boundaries, no limits."

Xira growled, loud enough for all to hear, "Show them."

Aza took a breath, grinned, and crooked her fingers at the soldiers.

The soldiers yelled battle cries and began to move. Aza was quicker and unleashed her power. The ground shifted underfoot, the soldiers falling to their knees. Aza rose into the sky, the ground lifting her up. The warriors scrambled and tried outrunning the crumbling ground and shards of rock Aza hurtled towards them. She was not aiming to hurt them, merely scare. The sky rained down small rocks around the warriors. She created rings of raging infernos to encircle larger groups of warriors, the thick snow and ice melting into a wet sludge. She stopped others with walls of ice and raging winds. She disarmed her opponents with timely and precise shots of magic, just like Nivet had taught her.

As she corralled them like horses, some slowed, and others rose on shaky legs. They watched her with awe.

Xira nodded and Aza withdrew her magic, the ground reverting back to its original shape. She had tried to her best not to disturb the delicate ecosystem of the mountain, but she spotted animals fleeing in the distance. The earth's rumblings sent them quaking.

"What do we do when faced with such an opponent?" Xira yelled to the crowd.

A soldier with blonde hair plaited back and a serious expression answered, "You don't."

Xira narrowed in on the soldier and beckoned her to step forward. "Explain."

"If Lady Aza was aiming to kill, we would all be dead without a second thought. It is an insult and sheer stupidity to your fellow warriors and to yourself to face such a losing battle."

Another soldier with half a shaved head shouted with his chin held high, "But we as Nerians pride ourselves on never giving up. Never backing down. Answer the call of the fight within your blood."

Xira grinned. "Both your fellow warriors are correct. We are Nerians," she shouted and raised a fist in the air. The gathered soldiers responded in kind, with their fists in the air. "We have taught you to never back down, to do whatever it takes to conquer them. But Triss is correct. It would be an insult to yourself and your fellow Nerians to make such a foolish mistake. The gods and goddesses are unmatched. They will crush us and take what they think is theirs. But we will not let them! So, what do we do?"

The warriors stared at Xira, their minds collectively thinking of how best to triumph when they were the weaker opponent.

Reed emerged from the warriors, his hand grasping firmly on a staff. "You level the playing field."

The soldiers nodded their agreement and the blonde warrior, Triss, asked, "How?"

Anwin broke through the crowd, lifting a plain dagger. "With this."

The warriors broke into hushed whispers. They would never

openly mock Anwin, one of their feared leaders, but Aza could feel the hesitation.

A slash of a smile crested Anwin's face at their disbelief. "It is no ordinary dagger."

The whispers vanished, the crowd's attention on Anwin. She gestured to Reed and the two of them joined Xira and Aza at the front.

"Reed, demonstrate your magic," Xira ordered.

A ball of water formed in his hand, and he bounced it from one hand to the other. While he balanced the water in one hand, Anwin placed the edge of the dagger against his open palm and pulled. A thin, precise line of blood welled, and his magic stuttered. The ball of water broke apart, dripping down his hand.

"We have been studying the properties of a rare plant on our mountain. Using a precise alchemical process we can fuse it with our weapons. On a typical MagicBlessed it will stall their magic, like a boulder blocking a rushing river." Anwin walked over to Aza and whispered so only she would hear. "Will you allow me to demonstrate?"

Aza's heart stuttered and she hesitated.

"Your magic loss will last roughly thirty minutes. I promise it will not be long."

Aza forced herself to nod. She trusted them. How ironic that they had used this very alchemical process to wipe out her magic mere months ago and she was willingly allowing them to do it now.

Delicately, Anwin gripped Aza's hand and turned it over to show the palm. The slice was quick and smooth, Aza didn't even feel it until the blood began to well. Like the shutting of a valve, she felt her magic begin to stop. Not gone, but merely asleep. It tucked away into the corner of her mind, a slumbering beast. This was different than last time.

The Nerian crowd watched with wide eyes.

"Lady Aza, please demonstrate your magic again," Xira announced.

Aza knew what the result would be, but for the benefit of the crowd she attempted. The slumbering beast did not wake. She prodded and poked, but it merely shifted.

"I cannot," Aza said.

"Good." In a blur, Xira attacked.

If Aza had not spent the last several months training without her magic, she would have gone down easily. But Lorn, Lilit, and the Nerians had taught her well. Xira did not use weapons, merely her fists and body. The fighting stance came to her naturally. She dodged each attack. Her time with Xira had given her insight to Xira's fighting tendencies.

Anwin and Reed had tactfully retreated.

Xira did not relent, and this time Aza did not intend to lose. With or without her magic. Aza met her blow for blow. Xira feinted and jabbed at Aza's cheek. The hit landed, but Aza absorbed the blow, but was able to deflect most of the force. Her cheek smarted, but Aza did not falter.

Every time they sparred, Aza kept her civility. She played fair. But as she dodged Xira's attacks, she realized they were not fighting fair. They had quelled her magic. She had considerable size over Xira and without a second thought, Aza dove forward, tackling Xira to the ground. Before they tumbled, Aza savored the satisfaction of seeing Xira's eyes widen in surprise.

Powdered snow flew up around them as they grappled. Although Aza had the advantage of size, Xira was nimble and had years of experience. Xira expertly locked her legs around Aza and flipped their position. Xira twisted Aza's arm at an unnatural angle. Any further and the arm would dislocate.

"Yield," Xira said.

Aza panted. Everything around them blurred. Her only focus was on Xira. Stubbornness and sheer stupidity caused her to yell through clenched teeth, "No!"

A ghost of a smile flashed over Xira's face before Aza knew only pain. What seemed like a distance away she heard a pop from her arm. Aza swallowed a cry and shakily stood even with the pounding pain in her shoulder.

Xira stepped back and turned to the crowd. The warriors were silent. Then, like the spark of a flame, a pounding beat began. Beginning with Reed and Anwin, the fellow warriors picked up the beat, a closed fist beating in rhythm over and over on their chest. It rippled through the crowd, the warriors beating their fists. The sound carried over the mountain. Xira was the last to join as she made her way back to Aza's side. Staying on beat, she lifted Aza's unharmed arm into the sky.

"Nerian!" Xira shouted.

"Nerian!" the warriors responded.

"Nerian!" Xira, Reed, and Anwin screamed. A scream of welcoming, a scream of belonging, a scream of protection.

Aza could only look on as the battle-hardened soldiers screamed back in acceptance, their shouts and beats of defiant fists on their chests rang out over the snow-covered mountainside. "Nerian!" they called her.

48

"I do not particularly like the other gods and goddesses. They only will get in my way."

Cruvo's private journal

Lorn watched as Lady Rasmina, quick as a viper, pulled from Pearl and swung the Gloomstone sword upwards in a sickening arc. He screamed, his voice hoarse. Something, a warning, anything to incite action. But it was only Rasmina and her daughter in the center of the clearing. He watched as that blade seemed to move in slow motion towards her own daughter. Her daughter. Choosing the death of her daughter over that of a capricious goddess controlling her. Lorn's body was weak. Despite his pathetic attempts to get to his feet, they slipped out from under him, the muddy ground providing little support.

He couldn't look at this brilliant and beautiful light being doused, like so many others, like his wife. Lorn's stomach twisted, but he owed it to Pearl to watch. He did not deserve to look away from such horror. He must bear it, because someone must look at the brutality of this world and remember it.

The blade was a hand's breadth from Pearl before an abrupt force interceded. Rasmina was blasted away from Pearl, her small body collapsing in a heap.

Pearl's body swayed. From a distance, he finally understood the battle being waged. Pearl was fighting for dominance in a body with the goddess Kerali, but Kerali was winning.

Kerali looked dispassionately at Lady Rasmina. The Gloomstone blade had not left her grip though. Rasmina fought to gain footing, her limbs shaking, and feet clambering for a hold.

The guards moved at once, aiming to protect her. A casual flick of Kerali's fingers sent them flying backwards, crashing into the trees. Thunder cracked. The earth quaked.

Maline and Flint abandoned their position, running away amidst the giant trees.

"You will not have her!" Rasmina shouted over the din of the storm. Lightning arced down into the cleared and made her look like a banshee given form.

A mocking smile appeared on Pearl's face. It chilled Lorn.

"I already have her. I am so glad we were able to have this reunion. How many family members of yours have I destroyed?" Kerali took measured steps to Lady Rasmina, who was uncomposed. Mud drenched her body, her sleek black hair matted from the rain, a feral look in her eyes. Lorn did not understand how he had thought her an unfeeling creature. She was the face of someone who felt everything, but kept it carefully restrained. The carefully curated mask she donned slipped, and in its place was vengeful wrath.

"How does it feel to know the daughter you chose to protect from me, graciously accepted me into her body—to challenge you." Kerali eyed Lady Rasmina. "It would have been easier if you let me have her as a babe. She would have suffered less."

Rasmina screamed and sliced the Gloomstone blade at Kerali. It was uncoordinated, her weight clumsy and awkward. Kerali easily dodged. Rasmina was not a fighter, but a lady born and bred, who had not been taught to wield a sword. But Lorn saw by the clench of her jaw and the proud tilt of her chin. Rasmina would not give up that easily. She would fight for her daughter, to rid the world of this cruel, vindictive goddess.

Rasmina gave another hardy swing, but she was overbalanced and fell to the ground.

Kerali gave a cruel laugh. "You wish to hurt me? You made a Gloomstone blade, and you think I should be scared? I have endured all of eternity. I have been here since the beginning. You are a mere bug for me to toy with." Kerali's eyes glowed and the ground quaked. Rasmina slumped to the ground, her head hitting the dirt. Blood welled from a gouge in her forehead.

A hand guided Lorn to his feet and slung his arm over their neck. Lorn tried to pivot and see who was helping him up. Their slender build did not fully support Lorn's weight, but it helped. His mind was dulled, but with what felt like a lifetime ago, he was able to place who they were. Rye, the gem store owner from Lighthold Proper, was propping Lorn up.

"We need to leave. Now," they said.

Hibara lifted Lilit and cradled her like a large child, her body limp.

"What about Pearl?" Lorn croaked. He wasn't sure what he could do to help, but he couldn't leave her here alone, not with Kerali taking control over her body.

Rye cast a worried glance to Pearl and shook their head. "I'm afraid she's too far gone. It was our only way to free the prisoners."

"We cannot leave them here!" he cried.

Rye shifted Lorn's weight across their shoulders and heaved a sigh, guiding Lorn away from the clearing. "How could you possibly help in your state?"

He fought their hold, forcing them to stop. "I'm not sure, but I need to try."

"You will only be killed, and your life could be better used elsewhere."

Kerali had Rasmina pinned to the ground, shocks of electricity coursing through her body. She alternated the flow of electricity, aimed at increasing her torture in bearable amounts. The Gloomstone blade lay discarded mere feet from her.

Lorn tried to drown out her screams of anguish and walk with Rye, but he could not ignore them. The persistent cries. The screams caused by Rasmina's daughter under the thrall of a goddess. He could not abide by it any longer.

"I cannot let this continue. Both of them will die." Lorn pushed away from Rye and slumped to the ground.

Lorn had no clue of what he would be able to contribute, but he could not leave. When the Howler killed his wife, he had been too far away to prevent her death. But here, he was not. He only lacked the stamina. His body was shutting down after the immense energy he had transferred into the Gloomstone blade.

But Kerali was distracted, focused on prolonging Rasmina's torture, electricity pulsing through her body while Kerali taunted her about her past exploits, the death of her husband, her lover, and the soon to be death of her daughter.

Rasmina, the once proud woman, groveled between the courses of electricity, pleading again and again. "Not my daughter. Let her go. Do not do this to her," she cried. Again and again Rasmina pleaded, begging for the life of her daughter, fighting for her like she fought for her that fateful day in Holdsfast when Kerali killed her husband.

Lorn's strength was depleted, his energy nonexistent, but he could not let this go on.

"Help, Hibara. Take Lilit away. Do not turn back."

Rye was about to object but saw his unyielding resolve. They wordlessly hurried to Hibara, both shooting looks of pity at Lorn. It was clear they did not believe he would survive.

Lilit's words from their beginning foray in the Silent Stretch replayed in his mind. She believed he was always willing to sacrifice his life, because dying a noble death was better than pursuing a hollow life. But this time it was not a reckless sacrifice, this time it would be worth it.

His body protested his every movement. He had no idea what he could accomplish in this situation, but he had to try. He could not let Lady Rasmina be subjected to this torture at the hands of her own daughter. It was a cruel twist of Fate and he would not be an accomplice due to inaction.

Kerali did not care about the people around the perimeter, the unconscious guards, Hibara carrying Lilit, or Rye. They shook their heads at Lorn's decision, but his life had never been his own. Since the day his wife was killed, his life belonged to everyone else. He could serve and sacrifice himself for others.

Ignoring the pain lancing through his body and the blurriness of his vision he bolted forward. The muddy clearing, the torrential rain, dulled his vision, but he pushed onwards. His sight locked onto the Gloomstone blade. It was the only thing that could stop Kerali. He understood what Rasmina was trying to accomplish. When she wielded the blade against Pearl, it was not to kill her, but to wound Kerali, to force her to be mortal to create a separation between goddess and daughter. He would succeed where she failed. While

Kerali was obsessed with Lady Rasmina's pitiful screams and pleas, the blade was like a void against the muddy ground pulling Lorn toward it, beckoning him. the alluring call too great to ignore.

He was so close to reaching it when Kerali finally noticed him. She turned her head to look at him, her eyes glowing like the flash of lightning on the sea. He was singularly focused. He sprinted recklessly, aware that Kerali was preparing to strike him down.

A voice screamed, *Lorn slide!* He complied, the wet ground easily giving way underfoot so he could slide. Issi had not abandoned him, the echoes of her scream still jolted his body.

Where he was standing a second ago was smoking and cratered by a focused blast of lightning. Lying flat on the ground, he wrapped his fingers around the Gloomstone hilt, a ringing vibration shaking his arm at the connection. He rose to his knees and swung at Kerali, aiming at her legs. But he was too slow, his body too fatigued. Kerali was a goddess, her years of experience and magic superior.

She sent a a bolt of electricity into his body, and he convulsed on the ground, his grip slackening on the Gloomstone. The strange connection shattered, and he was consumed with wracking pain. Kerali cocked her head, staring at Lorn like he was a mere oddity.

Delicate in her torture, she stopped and Lorn's chest heaved. Kerali furrowed her eyebrows and crouched beside Lorn. He couldn't help but see Pearl's young and innocent face stare at him, like two discordant images fighting for dominance.

She forcefully gripped his chin and turned his head one way then another inspecting him like a piece of meat. "You are something else," she muttered. Pinching his chin with her fingers, she leaned closer. "What a mix you are. Who would even consider giving you their power?" She straightened, grabbed the Gloomstone blade by the hilt, keeping it far from her body, and tossed it further in the clearing. "Despite how interesting you are, you should know better than to interrupt my playtime."

Lorn could barely focus on Kerali. His body felt like it was failing. A door cracked open in his mind and Issi's voice frantically whispered instructions. *Lorn you will die. Use everything we have practiced. Use your light. Heal Pearl. Push the goddess out of her body. You have the means to do it. View them like a parasite. Rid her of it. Otherwise, you will die. Kerali will not die, only be displaced as we all are.*

"I cannot," he whispered, delirious. He was losing his mind. Issi was not here. He was near the end of his life and could not think straight.

"Who are you talking to?" Kerali asked. "The only reason you are still alive is because you are mildly interesting. Like a colorful flower amongst a backdrop of green." Her eyes brightened and a grin slashed across her face. She leaned her head back and shouted. "Whatever god or goddess is helping him, watch as I kill him."

Lorn you must do this now or you will die! Issi screamed.

Lorn tunneled into his magic and found the raw kernel of his power, the same he had used to imbue the Gloomstone blade, the light that never died, merely dimmed because of his fading lifeforce. He coaxed it forward and before Kerali could attack, he rolled, reaching out his hand to touch Kerali. Contact was necessary. The memory of healing Pearl came back to him. He channeled that same feeling, that same energy now.

Kerali tried to back away, her eyes widening, but their contact was like glue. Neither could break from the touch.

Lorn focused his entire being, his entire energy into this moment. He summoned all his reserves of strength and powered his magic into her.

Lorn vaguely heard Rasmina's grief as her cries rang out, "Save my daughter. Do not hurt her." Instead of being a distraction, the words were a buoy. He latched onto them, reminding himself of Pearl, her smile, her innocence, her stubbornness, her willingness to do good and save her fellow Garans.

He clung to those sentiments and imagined Kerali as the corruption. Instead of blackened, withered, foul decay clinging to her body, it was like twisted vines, wrapping around and suffocating the host. Kerali clung desperately to the lifeforce of Pearl and Lorn had to use the utmost care and caution to separate the goddess from her host. One wrong cut would sever Pearl's lifeforce. Instead of brute force, it required finesse, the artful skill of a sculptor, painstakingly removing pieces from their clay.

He was vaguely aware of his body. The pain that pulsed with every breath, how his body seemed to fracture with the effort he expended. Sweat dripped down his forehead, falling into his eyes, blurred together from the rain. Chills wracked his body, but he pushed on, screaming from exertion.

Among his own screams he heard Issi in a rare fit of emotion urge him on. *Lorn, do it now!* she yelled.

His light grew to encompass the entire clearing. Kerali, Rasmina, the rain, and all of his physical sensations melted away underneath the brilliant light. He was unfathomable light. The brightest rays of the sun. Piercing white. There was nothing else.

The vines of Kerali's hold loosened and faded. Pearl was free. Banished to the ether, Kerali was gone.

The unshakable contact between Lorn and Pearl released. He rolled on to his back on the muddy ground and rain soaked him. He was unable to feel pain, feel cold, feel anything.

Pearl's body thunked to the ground beside him. He struggled to gain his wits, but he had finally hit his limit. He closed his eyes and let the rain drown him.

49

"I do not hate Rune, but I hate being confined to this body. I want my own back. I want Aza to see me instead of seeing another man. I cannot hurt Hakim either. It would only cause more pain" Nivet's private journal.

When the cries and cheers had died down, Xira clapped Aza on the back. Reed and Anwin escorted her to the side, where they discreetly popped her shoulder back into its socket. Aza slumped against Reed, her cry muffled against his chest. Anwin gave her a reassuring squeeze on her arm before addressing the crowd.

Anwin informed the warriors that they were creating more weapons that could quell the gods' power. They were in production and each warrior would be outfitted with one. For years, they had been experimenting with daggers, swords, arrows. If a weapon could bear it, they were going to use it.

Aza regained her bearing and muttered a quick thanks to Reed. She did not know how long Nivet stood watch, but he sidled next to Reed, whispered a few words, and gently led Aza away from the proud warriors, who gave her nods and thumps on her back. She braced herself for the pain, her shoulder still tender. They parted through the crowd and the warriors swayed towards them like flowers to the sun.

Too tired to be overwhelmed by Nivet's presence, Aza was grateful to use his arm to lean on. Her strength had waned, and she was ready to rest.

At the edge of the training grounds, Nivet leaned in, and Aza fought the shiver that swept down her spine. Despite her exhaustion, her magic still called to his. She dismissed the feeling. It wasn't rare. It was a feeling that resonated with all of the gods and goddesses. She could not and would not pay it any heed.

"I would like to take you somewhere relaxing. Would that be alright?" Nivet asked.

Aza gave a tired nod and in the blink of an eye, Nivet's shadows cocooned her like a comforting blanket, and she was transported.

Pine trees laden with snow greeted them. The bone-deep chill that permeated El'theren was lessened. The valley of Kreeha sprawled below them. Aza crept to the edge, peering down. They were on a hidden mountain trail of Neria, on the border between the two provinces.

Their escape up the mountain left little time to appreciate the sights. With a heaviness, she plopped onto the ground, her legs dangling in the air. A thin pile of pine needles crushed under her fingers as she leaned back on her hands. Her body crumpled under the stillness. All of the day's work piled onto her shoulders and she was finally feeling the effects.

Dainty, red flowers popped around her body in an unexpected burst. The slumbering beast of her magic had awoken. She closed her eyes, letting herself soak in the peaceful moment. "Thank you for bringing me here." Her words spilled out slowly like the gentle pour of honey.

Nivet chuckled. "This is not the final stop."

"Regardless, I find it relaxing."

"I hate to move you from this spot, but where I am taking you will be more relaxing."

"Please, another minute." Aza lingered but was finally tempted by his offer. Slowly, she opened her eyes and brought herself away from the cliff's edge, gathering her legs underneath.

Nivet patiently waited and led her through a small trail that snaked upwards. Heat curled invitingly towards her, and she picked up her pace. The trees thinned to reveal an alcove of water, steam wafting from it. Sulfur assaulted her nose, and she tentatively placed a hand over it. The hot water was inviting. She crouched down and dipped her hand in. The hot water was bliss. Her body ached just from looking at it.

"The hot springs are rumored to have healing properties," Nivet said. He joined her at the edge. "I thought you would enjoy the privacy and a break from El'theren." He stared in earnest at Aza, his eyes flashed through with gold.

She looked away from his intense stare and focused instead on the tendrils of steam swirling in the air. "El'theren is beautiful. I do not need a break from it. Since appearing from the Well, I had never felt like I had time to truly exist, to breathe. Time is going by too quickly and I want to treasure every moment given."

Nivet straightened. "Then do not view this as a break, view it as a moment to ground yourself."

Aza rose. She was being silly avoiding his eye contact. She had her magic under control, and although his magical signature was overwhelming, she should be used to it by now.

Aza took a discreet breath and met his gaze. "Thank you. This was very thoughtful." She looked around. "Where will you be while I bathe?"

Nivet's eyes crinkled in amusement. "I will be out here."

Aza furrowed her brow.

"The best part of the hot springs is actually through here." Behind a tree, a cave cut into the mountain. He led her in, the darkness swallowing them. Nivet felt around a wall, found a torch, and lit it. He guided her through the cave formation. The smell of sulfur was overpowering but the temptation of the hot water soothing her aches was stronger. It was not only a physical weariness she could ease with magic, but also a mental one. She needed this time as Nivet had phrased it. A moment to ground herself.

"This will be yours for the evening. As long as you want." Nivet placed the torch on a bracket on the wall. The cave was small. Aza was able to see the back wall with the torch in place.

"I will be outside. You can call me if needed, but no harm will come to you here. Allow yourself to relax. You deserve this time." Nivet walked back up the small path to the outside hot springs.

Alone and with time to unwind, Aza stripped her sweat-encrusted clothing, discarding it in a messy pile. She eyed the water and without further restraint she entered. A moan of pleasure escaped. The hot spring water gently bubbled and unwound her tight muscles and eased her aches. Her feet skimmed the bottom of the pool but dropped off on the farther end. She swam a few laps and then found herself clinging to the edge, her face resting against the warm stones.

Due to her rigorous training, she had taken to protecting her natural hair into two braids. It helped when flying on Druilinn and sparring with Nivet and the Nerians. But with the tension on her head, she wanted to unwind them, yet her body was heavy, and she didn't want to waste the energy to attempt.

"Aza," Nivet called into the cave. "Can I come down to drop off spare clothes?"

It required great strength to give an audible response. The hot water caused her mind to melt.

She peered up from her forearms to see his shadow descend against the cave wall. The water covered her body, but her heart quickened as he approached.

"I figured fresh clothes would be better for you to change into when you are done. Is there anything else you need before I leave?" Nivet asked.

She paused. It would not be strange to ask Xira, Anwin, or Reed this question. It should not bother her to ask Nivet.

He turned to leave when Aza stopped him. "My hair is braided, difficult to unwind, and my body is tired. Would you mind undoing it for me?"

He cleared his throat and joined her. She watched as he rolled up his pant legs to the knee and dipped his calves in the water. He spread his legs and motioned for her to go between.

Careful to only keep her head exposed, she drifted over. She focused on keeping her breathing even as his deft fingers began on the binds holding her two braids.

The plink of water echoed throughout the cave, but Aza felt like they were both as tense as stringed instruments.

Nivet broke the silence first. "They would have always accepted you based purely on Xira, Anwin, and Reed accepting you. But you and Xira fighting like that, without your magic. Today you earned their respect, and they will all go into battle for you."

"I wish no one had to go to battle for me," she admitted. Her taut shoulders relaxed as he unwound her braids. She tensed, expecting him to reach a snag in her hair, but when he didn't, his fingers expertly both massaging and unwinding. He was methodical and did not rush.

He gave a long sigh before answering, "I understand, and I wish the same. But you are not blind. War is coming and we all have a part to play."

Aza did not want to follow this bleak line of thought and instead blurted out, "How did you escape Eonas?"

His fingers stilled. "I made a deal."

"And what was the deal?"

"I owe Eonas a favor whenever they regain their body."

She did not envy the deal he made with Eonas—the binding pact of their agreement. Nivet was only trying to save Rune.

"But I saw the wave, it crashed into your body. Rune's body. It should be crushed." She wanted to turn around and decipher his expression, but she could only rely on the touch of his fingers, or slight hitch in his movements. Her braids loosened, but Nivet did not stop. He massaged her scalp and worked free each coil of hair.

"I used my remaining energy to protect Rune's body and bargained with Eonas. They stilled their waves, and we talked. They left me to struggle and by the time I returned to shore, I had no idea where you were. So I headed to Neria. I needed to protect Rune. I couldn't..." Nivet paused. "Despite what Lady Sola and Lord Mika think, I do not envy taking over their son's body. I am trying to keep it intact."

Aza nodded. "One thing has been bothering me."

Nivet made a brief hum for her to continue.

"If you were able to shadow us to the Vertan shore, why didn't you do it earlier? Why face the serpent? Why waste this energy?"

Nivet had finished untangling her hair and the relief was palpable, but she kept her back to him, allowing him a small amount of privacy to gather his thoughts. "You understand you are part Goddess, correct?"

Aza muttered, "Yes."

"You are this divine creation, a beautiful melding of our magic, an essence of our divinity, and the Hinterlands. Your very being, your proximity, is kindling to our magic. It helps to awaken us. Our magic is magnified. In our current state, it's like a stimulant. It draws us to you and due to your proximity, we are able to expand and utilize your magic. It is subtle, but it allows us to tap into your amplifying powers the closer we are to you.

"Your magic belongs to you. It should never be tampered with, altered, or stolen. To bring you all to safety, I tapped into your amplifying powers and shadowed you away." His voice hardened, his words crisp and without emotion.

Aza turned, keeping her body below the water. She caught the gold of his eyes twinkle within the dim light. His head hung in defeat. She couldn't help herself. The thrum of her magic seemed to pound in time with her heart as she reached forward to console him. Her hand met his thigh, and he looked to meet her gaze.

"I would gladly let my magic be used multiple times again, if it was used to save my friends." Her throat locked up, the words difficult to say. She couldn't imagine coming to Neria without Xira, Anwin, or Reed, their families devastated, Xira's parents without a daughter, River missing the absence of her twin, Anwin's family, the children bawling, screams of despair at the loss of their mother. She had watched as Lorn struggled with his grief. It had swallowed him whole. If her proximity to Nivet allowed him to tap into a stronger power, then so be it.

His lithe, roughened fingers clasped her hand. A sad smile of denial moved slowly over his face. His fingers tightened on hers. "At what cost?"

Before Aza could respond, Nivet disentangled his hand from hers and stepped away. In a brisk voice he said, "I will be outside whenever you are ready. Take as long as you want."

Aza held her breath as he walked away, attempting to quell her rising emotion. There was more he was withholding. She needed to discover it. Holding her breath, she dove under the water, the heat and darkness a welcome reprieve.

~

Finished with the hot spring, Aza looked forlornly at the water before climbing out. She decided to lay on the warm stone and air-dry before putting clothes on her wet body. Relaxing against the warm ground, her eyes fluttered closed and a unbidden dream popped into her mind —of darkness and a voice whispering *my shadows*. It was a time when she was in Lord Aldrich's castle, the dream coming to her mind when in the bathtub. From what she could recall this was the same place. Her eyes flashed open, and she sat up using her hands to prop herself up. She looked around trying to piece the vague memory with her current reality. Although she couldn't say confidently this was the same as her dream, her instinct was blaring a different truth. It was.

Her state of relaxation vanished like tendrils of steam from the hot spring in the cold air. With her body now dry, she quickly shucked on her clothes and walked back to the entrance of the cave.

A rare, cloudless night greeted her. The full moon shone brilliantly at her, and she traced a path back to the outdoor hot springs. Nivet was not there, but she spotted tracks leading back to the cliff side. She took a steadying breath and ignored the pulse of magic that emanated from him. It bowed, submitting to her.

Nivet cut a strong silhouette against the night sky. He sat at the edge, his feet dangling in such a similar manner to hers, she couldn't help but give a smile and join him. He did not stir.

"Did you know I have a memory of this place?" Aza asked. She wanted to be direct. No more hidden secrets like she had with Cruvo.

He turned to her, and Aza could see it plain in his face. "No, I did not. I should have foreseen that. This is a common spot for Nerians to unwind. Secluded, relaxing, with natural hot water. I apologize. I hope it didn't upset you."

Aza believed him. "No, it didn't upset me. It was just jarring. The memories feel like a dream world I once experienced—I guess they are."

Nivet shifted and looked at her directly. "Aza, I cannot begin to fathom what you are experiencing, but please close your eyes."

Aza arched an eyebrow at the request and with dramatic flair, obeyed.

"You are not her, just as I am not Rune. I need you to remember that. Her memories, the pieces of her, are a part of you, but they are not *you*," he said fervently.

"Is it hard for you?" Aza whispered. "Feeling like two people?"

"It can be. Especially when I am around his family and friends. It is a constant reminder of who he is and who I am not."

"Like Hakim?" Aza tensed to hear his response.

"Yes." Nivet answered. The night around them seemed to still as if eavesdropping on their conversation.

Although she didn't want to admit his tactics worked, having her eyes closed allowed a certain vulnerability to their conversation, as if they could each admit their flaws, weaknesses, and fears.

"I met him today," Aza admitted.

Nivet released a long sigh and Aza heard him shift, the snow crunching underneath. "He is Rune's lover. They have been friends since childhood. It devastated Hakim, once he learned of Rune's choice to accept me into his body, even though it was necessary. But like cracking open a worn book I can view his memories, however vague. They can influence my mind and I feel myself becoming a alternate version of him. It is confusing, but I would rather have him there instead of squashing his being entirely."

"This is not an exercise for me though," he said. "I want you to think of every experience you have had since your birth from the Well. Every feeling, every interaction, every landscape that unfurled before you."

Aza let his words form a tapestry. Since the moment of her birth from the Well, she felt like shimmering starlight given form, a heady powerful feeling. And she saw a man kneeling before her, one she felt a kinship to almost immediately. She remembered their friendship, his steadfast and loyal presence, their escape from the Hinterlands, their success when they left, their echoing whoops in the still night. Exploring the province of Iyera, the radiant castle of El'en, the delicious food, the farmlands of Verta, the austere beauty of the Kreehan sand dunes, the majestic Hall of Prophecies, along with the beauty of the three rivers that split the palace of Cyran, and she couldn't forget the breathless feeling of riding Druilinn among the snow-capped mountains.

Those were her memories, her experiences.

He patiently sat beside her as she envisioned each and every moment. They belonged to her.

After what seemed an eternity, she opened her eyes, the night clearer, the moon brighter, the stars sparkling in answer to her. "Thank you," she breathed.

A faint electric shiver coursed through her body. She gazed fondly at the stars, their brightness searing into her eyes, a faint hum answering throughout her body.

Nivet was kind. He was forthcoming. He was nothing like Cruvo, yet she cursed her mind and her body and how it responded to him. She could not decipher what were her true feelings compared to that of the melding.

His face was held in rapture to the sky, and Aza did not want Rune's body next to her, but rather Nivet. The rare image she caught of him while riding Isarr had not left her. Tapping into that unbridled magic, she reached out and tentatively touched her hand to his.

He jolted, his eyes meeting hers. Like delicately playing an instrument, she plucked the strings of her magic and urged Nivet's true image to surge forth.

It was exactly how she imagined him. Rune's lithe, muscular shoulders blurred into a broader form, the dark skin, lightening to a taupe with a soft blur of sparkle like a gold sheen was added to his skin. His hair lengthened into a silky black curtain, tied back with a leather throng. Tendrils escaped framing a strong jaw and a prominent nose. He was beautiful, ethereal, and every bit of the celestial being she was claimed to be. His gold swirled eyes studied her.

Magic pulsed and rippled, and she felt herself drifting towards him, lost in the gravitational pull of his proximity. It clouded her senses. She leaned forward, entranced by the haze of his eyes, the strength of magic, an inevitable collision. They were a mere breath away from one another, when Aza removed her hand from his. Her magic faltered, returning Nivet's features to Rune's like the sudden wakefulness from a dream.

Nivet said nothing, only waiting for her. Sorrow flicked through his face. If she wasn't paying such close attention, she would have missed it.

Instead, she pulled away from the person she wanted, the person who sympathized with her, one of the few gods who had shown her true kindness and let the night sky, with its multitude of stars, wash over her.

The two of them sat, their legs hanging over the cliff, the cold snow piercing their skin, a strange mixture of both god and human considering their existence underneath the celestial heavens.

"The night belongs to you," Nivet said.

At first, Aza wanted to respond, confused over the statement, but she let the comment sink into her skin in the same manner of how the hot springs had cleansed her and she found the statement resonated. Aza merely smiled up at the sky, the stars shining back in agreement.

50

"I have demonstrated extreme patience up to this point. I have waited one thousand years. I can wait one thousand more."

Cruvo's private journal

"Lorn," a woman murmured.

He stirred, his fingertips brushing soft linen. He knew that voice, the homecoming of his soul. His eyes fluttered open.

A long curtain of raven-colored hair was braided away from her deep brown skin, loose fabric draped over her muscle-hardened body. Her concerned eyes light up at Lorn's wakefulness. She smiled and he could only smile back.

"Lakesh," he whispered reverently like a blind man who had regained his sight and was witnessing a sunrise for the first time.

Lorn achingly pushed himself up in bed. His throat was raw, his body stretched to the point of oblivion. However, Lorn would choose the same actions again and again, just to be here with her. He laced his fingers in hers, idly tracing small circles on the back of her hand. Ignoring the building ache in his body, he brought himself to the edge of the bed and placed his forehead against hers, eyes closed, inhaling the breath she breathed.

"Lorn, you cannot stay here. I'm sorry. You are not finished. Not yet."

He pulled away from the comfort and warmth his wife provided and looked around. The visage of his cottage on the edge of Verta greeted him. Returning to the comfort of his home was a particular

"

brand of torture he would endure time and time again if it allowed him to be reunited with his wife.

For once he wanted to be able to enjoy the comfort of his wife's touch, to bask in their reunion. Death was a mercy his soul craved, and he was so tired. His soul had been cracked and hastily repaired. He craved a final rest—a final reunion in the Meadows of the Undying with his wife by his side.

But Lakesh watched him, expectation heavy in her eyes. "You cannot fail them," she whispered encouragingly, and brought her forehead to rest against his. Aza, Pearl, even Lilit, he needed to return for, his time was not done.

He heaved a painful breath, pulled away, and nodded. "I understand."

Lorn studied Lakesh, cataloging every facet, every curve, every mannerism, and sealed it inside his heart—an image he would never forget. She was carved irrevocably on his heart.

Tentatively, Lakesh leaned forward and brushed feather-light kisses on each side of his temple, while his eyes brimmed with unshed tears of frustration, of want.

When her lips brushed his skin, the tears released, one drop at a time. She caught them on her fingertip. "Do not cry, Lorn. I am here." Her palm flattened against his heart. "You are never alone." Her voice thickened with emotion. "And I am so fucking proud of what you have accomplished."

She swooped forward, her lips clashed against his. Lorn forgot his sorrow, forgot his aches and pains, everything except for his wife's kiss. He felt it. Every piece of devotion, of love, of adoration. He was loath to break the connection, but it was not he that pulled away.

Lakesh drew back, her bronzed cheeks flushed with a faint current of pink. "You are not done."

The room swirled away in wisps of black, darkening, morphing.

~

Pain—endless pain coursed through his body. He moaned and

attempted to curl on his side when something wet touched his face. It was persistent. The wet on his cheek now moving.

He was cold, drenched, his body shivering.

But something kept nagging him, forcing him to open his eyes. With reluctance, he peeled open his eyes to find a giant dog looming over him, its pink tongue lolling out of its mouth.

If he had any energy remaining he would have been startled, scrambling away from the giant beast, but his body was made of the heaviest stone, and he could barely manage a groan.

Lorn struggled to latch onto a thought, his mind in disarray. His mind was scattered. There was only a dog hovering over him, the wiry hair standing out erratically. Wide, brown eyes considered him.

Lorn attempted to move his body. Only the fingers on his right hand obeyed, briefly curling.

The dog noticed the soft motion and furiously licked him as if that alone could give Lorn the strength to rise.

He groaned again, a stiff smile spreading. The dog was persistent. Controlling his muscles was an immense struggle. Like a baby learning how to manipulate their body, he forced his lips to form words, to call the dog. A soft clicking of his tongue brought the dog's attention from his hand back up to his face.

The dog grew worried, anxious over Lorn's lack of movement and barked at him. It nuzzled its head against Lorn's side in an attempt to move him. Lorn screamed. Each brush of movement felt like nails were being hammered into him.

The dog bounded away and Lorn missed its presence. He strained his eyes, desperately trying to discern his surroundings. Giant trees loomed in his periphery, their pine needles heavy and laden with water.

The dog barked frantically to the right of Lorn. With immense effort he twisted his head to look over where the dog was barking.

A body was crumpled on the ground—a young woman, her dark curly hair obscuring her face. The dog barked. Its huge, wiry, furred body jumped desperately around the woman. The dog's bark boomed like the pounding drums of war, or a crash of thunder.

Lorn's eyes widened with realization. "Thunder," he whispered. Upon hearing her name, the dog bounded back to Lorn, gratefully licking his face. He huffed a tired breath through his nose.

The recollection of what happened bled through him like a stain: Pearl overtaken by the goddess Kerali, how he had used his light magic to banish the goddess from Pearl's mortal body, how Lady Rasmina was tortured at the hands of her own daughter, the soldiers discarded like broken toys, and Hibara and Rye escaping with Lilit. Each memory assaulted him, and his body quaked with recognition.

With another heave of his head, he tilted it to the left and found Lady Rasmina. Thunder's excessive barking caused her to stir, muttering words about Pearl.

"Pearl," she rasped, her throat hoarse from her screaming.

Lorn watched as Lady Rasmina, caked in mud, her dress plastered to her skin from the rain, feebly pushed herself up to her forearms. Lorn could not fathom the fortitude and resilience required for such an action, her body depleted after the excruciating torture. His own body was useless. He was barely capable of swiveling his head from side to side.

Gritting her teeth, Lady Rasmina struggled to crawl forward and slipped on the muddy ground. But she gave no protest, despite the pain she must have endured. Again, she attempted. Painstakingly slow, arduous. She pushed herself up to her forearms, body shaking from exertion. One arm after the other she yanked herself forward, gaining inch by inch to her daughter.

Countless times she slipped, the muddy earth playing tricks on her weakened and deteriorating body. Mud and grass were embedded in her fingernails as she raked herself forward, dress tearing in the process, but her focus was undeterred. She spared no glance for Lorn, her eyes only for her youngest daughter, the daughter born from her union with a man of the sea.

Lorn could not look away. Despite the torture and weeks of solitude, his resentment softened like dried soil treated to much needed rain. Any hatred withered and Lorn only viewed her as a mother trying to reach her injured daughter.

Thunder ceased barking.

Within arm's reach of her daughter, Lady Rasmina surged forward with determined speed, and with a tenderness gripped Pearl's arm. She draped herself over her daughter and lamented. Anguished cries rang out through the clearing. Lady Rasmina repeated herself, in hopes of Pearl stirring, in hopes of seeing her bright, vivid tenacity rise back to the surface.

Rasmina was too weak, and she was unable to lift her daughter in to her arms. Instead, she ran her fingers through her hair, over her face and eyes. Lorn pictured Rasmina as a young mother, tenderly stroking her daughter's face as a babe. Age changed nothing to a parent—an adult transformed into merely a child before their eyes, a different sort of magic taking place.

Lorn attempted to move his body, but failed, only achieving the barest twitch of his fingers. Lying there while the rain washed over him, his body numb and unresponsive, he hoped Hibara and Rye had escaped with Lilit. He desperately hoped Pearl's plan of rescuing enslaved people was successful, he wished for many things, but his mind finally settled on Aza. He hoped she was happy and safe.

The sobs of Lady Rasmina transformed. The repeated cries of Pearl's name died out and was replaced by a frenetic silence.

Through his blurry vision, he spotted Lady Rasmina, eyes closed in concentration, her fingers held to Pearl's throat.

The cries of desperation changed into excitement, and impatience. "Pearl! Hang on!"

She lay next to her daughter, her eyes closed, humming. Even in Lorn's weakened state, he felt the release of powerful magic, the subtle change like ether in the air morphing and transforming.

Lady Rasmina remained next to Pearl, clutching her like she was a mere babe in her arms. She hummed, the melody sorrowful and haunting. The tendrils of healing magic spread over the land, seeping into the ground.

Lorn was helpless to change the course of action Lady Rasmina had decided.

He could do nothing as her voice softly trickled away, like whispers on the wind. Any warmth that remained in her visage leached away as she funneled her own lifeforce into her daughter's.

Rumors of this secret magic existed—accessing your own lifeforce to bolster another, but her lifeforce had already been greatly diminished. He watched as Lady Rasmina ignored her own suffering, pulling from the limited well of her magic and health. She clutched Pearl, her hands softly stroking her daughter's hair one last time before her eyes closed permanently—her last sacrifice for her children.

Thunder sat dutifully, observing as Rasmina passed. When her final act of generosity was done, Thunder whined, placing her nose on to her body, trying to nudge Rasmina awake again.

With a gasp, Pearl launched upward. She grasped at her chest, feeling the foreign motion of her chest heaving, of breath entering and leaving her body. She closed her eyes in disbelief and suddenly realized who lay next to her.

"Mama?" Her once proud, tenacious voice had gone soft. She reached a hand forward and placed it delicately on Lady Rasmina's face, such a similar motion to how her mother touched her. "Mama?" she asked again.

Thunder's low whines snapped Pearl out of her tender touch, and she began to frantically search her mother's body for signs of life. She checked her throat, wrist, eyes. "Mama!" she cried.

The sound broke Lorn.

He thought his emotions had long withered, but watching Pearl frantically call out to her mom, broke a part of his heart he didn't realize he still had.

"Mama! No, you cannot do this. You cannot leave me. I'm sorry. I'm so sorry, Mama, for everything. Come back! Come back. I love you." Pearl heaved Rasmina's body into her lap and cradled over it, sobbing violent tears. Thunder curled next to Pearl, resting his head on her thigh.

Lorn felt obligated to watch, to partake in this sorrow, for no one else was here to understand the complexities of their relationship, of what they had fought for and lost—but he would share this burden.

Pearl choked on tears, singing while restlessly rocking her dead mother back and forth.

In the meadow,
Down the way
I spotted a bird
And heard her say,
Come along, my love
It's time to go
There's more for you
Beyond the gate,

Beyond the gate.

In the forest,
With home behind
I spotted a deer
She let out a sigh,
Keep going, my love
The forest is wild
The end is worth it
Beyond the trees,
Beyond the trees.

In the ocean,
I did stand
I spotted a fish
They beckoned me in,
Swim on, my love
The ocean is endless
Beyond the shore,
Beyond the shore.

51

"Aza is nothing like I expected. I do not envy her burden, but I can help share it."
Nivet's private journal.

Months blurred by in a haze. The familiarity of Neria began to sink into the marrow of her bones. She yielded herself to the routine, to the lessons the people and the mountain could teach her. Aza soon found she knew every person who lived in El'theren and learned of the villages that chose to live secluded on the sides of the mountain. Their people would make pilgrimages to El'theren during major festivities, but often remained isolated.

The Nerian soldiers welcomed her eagerly into the fold, listening to her expertise on magic and trying to learn from it. They wanted to better themselves and to understand the intricacies of what she could accomplish with her magic. Willingly, she let them practice against her while they utilized the imbued weapons. Her magic was siphoned from her for those short moments, but she did not feel bereft. The confidence and trust between her and the Nerians were unmatched and there was no fear. She knew her magic would return.

Aza grew to understand her companions in a leisurely manner. Their friendship bloomed over nights drinking in the Bladed Beauty, in daytime hikes over precarious mountain trails that would lead to breathtaking vistas. There was an underlying, persistent edge to each outing, a feeling that this would be the last time to enjoy these moments together without the threat of war. It loomed on the horizon, on the cusp of every conversation, but the subject was not broached. They ignored it, not in ignorance, but in choice. It was a choice to savor each other's company, for it might be the last opportunity they would ever get.

Winter in Neria was not for the faint of heart. Most days the storms were too fierce to wander past her front door. On those days, her lessons with Nivet were moved indoors. Despite the storms the Nerian soldiers still trained, utilizing the weather to their advantage. Small scouting groups, led by Reed, traversed the mountain in hopes of ambushing the other warriors. They were expected to be able to withstand all types of weather and terrain. Snowstorms were no exception.

Yet sometimes when the weather grew too fierce they were dismissed early, and they would find solace in each other's homes. Those moments were Aza's favorite when she could find peace, their laughs at some benign joke filling the room. For those moments she could pretend she wasn't tasked with leaving Neria and banishing the Hinterlands—that she could stay here forever. It was an illusion she clung to in desperation at night when the reality of who she was and who she was destined to be became suffocating, chains of burden lashed across her back.

Each of her friends' houses bore a distinct energy that fit their personalities. Xira's house held a precision in each element, each decoration placed with intention. Although her house was sparse in decor, it was still inviting. Aza was surprised to discover Xira was the best cook. When she had time and wasn't busy training the regiments of soldiers for the upcoming war, she would compile a set of artful dishes that complimented each other perfectly.

In their free time they would find themselves in Reed's house whenever their conversation turned warm and slow like melted chocolate. Each person would lounge in the plush, decadent seating he had in his house. Luscious blankets would be piled nearby. Aza would grab a blanket and snuggle in while her friends would lounge nearby in similar states of repose, a raging fire crackling merrily in the hearth. Too many times, Aza found herself asleep on Reed's couch with too many blankets piled on top of her. River would let herself in the house without knocking and wake up Aza with a hot cup of tea. Falling asleep in Reed's house helped to quiet the nightmares that loomed threateningly on the edges.

Anwin's house was in a constant state of chaos with children running underfoot. At any moment, a child would run up to her and ask her to play or demonstrate a feat of magic. They would marvel as Aza sent lights dancing around the room, or when she played a wicked game of hide and seek dousing the entire house in darkness. The children's laughs were piercing and sharp, but Aza collected them like prized jewels. The children's comfort with Reed and Xira was apparent as they easily climbed over and on them, often wrestling on the floor or playing games of subterfuge. Fier and Enbre, Anwin's twins and the youngest often teamed up together to try and take down the Nerian warriors. Even sweet Yanna took on a fierce disposition modeled after her mother when playing. Aza wondered how often the children saw their mother in training.

Kiasix, Anwin's husband, bustled around the house, rounding up the children under both arms while they screamed their delight. Rich pastries and bread were available on every counter in the house. Kiasix was one of the town's bakers and kept his house in high supply of his goods.

Each house was a beacon of love and friendship. Aza drifted between the three houses soaking in every happy moment, every smile, every long night where she found herself asleep on their couch. When the winter winds rattled the houses, shaking the windows in protest, she did not mind. She was safe with her friends—this community she had built.

Nivet did not often frequent.

Aza had confronted him about it after the end of one of their lessons.

He responded, "I am only a reminder of who I am not. Their friend Rune is not the one in the room with them. I am only causing more pain."

Aza did confront him again.

The time of peace and comfort could not last. Winter was beginning to wane, and she needed to descend from the safety of the Nerian mountains and banish the Hinterlands. The other leaders would grow bold without the threat of winter looming.

The clash of memories persisted, but her mind's resilience had grown and the seizures that followed lessened. This was another sign that her body and mind were reconciling who she was, who she was made from and that she did not have further time to delay.

Acceptance began. She could not ignore who she was formed from, the parts of her as intertwined into her existence as magic itself. She was not only Aza formed from the Well, part goddess, she was part Her and she could not ignore it any longer.

~

Anwin's baby came three weeks early. Reed crashed into her cottage mid-discussion with Nivet, panting. "The baby's here."

The next few moments were a blur as Aza and Nivet scrambled to follow Reed. They sprinted on the trail passing by fellow Nerians as they looked on in bewilderment. Reed reassured them with a passing shout of, "Anwin's had her baby." The people would smile and nod in understanding, a few chuckling.

One woman shouted as they passed, "She has birthed three before, I'm sure the fourth was not a problem."

Anwin's two-story house appeared before them. They clambered over the threshold, screeching to a halt once they passed the doorway. A baby's faint cries carried through the empty hall.

Aza and Reed went upstairs where they found Xira in the hallway.

Rare tears shimmered in the captain's eyes. "She is healthy. The baby is healthy," she announced at sight of their worried faces. Xira peered inside the room, said a few muffled words, and popped back out. "We can go in."

The massive form of Kiasix sat on the edge of the bed, his arm slung protectively over Anwin, staring down at the baby in her grasp. Fier, Enbre, and Yanna each held delicate smiles, watching their parents welcome the new baby.

Upon their entry, Fier and Enbre exclaimed running up to Xira, Aza, and Reed hugging their legs, jumping up and down, in a mock whisper that was much too loud, "We have a sister!"

Anwin chuckled. "Xira, Reed, do you mind taking my children downstairs for a minute? I would like to talk with Aza."

They nodded, each holding one of the twins in their arms while Yanna trailed behind. She cast a concerned look at her mother, but she was gently guided out of the room by Reed who held a squirming Enbre.

Aza stood, uncertain. The babe was so small and fragile compared to the two massive parents she came from. She was hesitant to step closer.

Sweat drenched Anwin's body, her cheeks red from exertion, but Aza thought she had never looked more beautiful. "Aza, her name is Kia. Would you like to meet your goddaughter?"

Aza misstepped.

"During our journey, you have saved me multiple times. Saved *us* multiple times." She rubbed Kia affectionately. "I found a friendship in you, Aza, and you deserve the world."

Aza's throat was choked with emotion. She opened her mouth to speak but words failed to form. "I..."

"You would not have to do anything differently. You are already enough."

Tears flowed down Aza cheeks. Kiasix stood, his fist clenched over his heart, head bowed. "I would be honored for you to be godmother to my daughter."

Tremors of magic pulsed through her body. Aza nodded quickly and hastily left the room. *Not here,* she repeated.

The room seemed to melt away as Aza tumbled down the steps, her hand remembering vaguely to grip the banister.

The image of little baby Kia flashed through her mind, displaced as another image took over. A different babe with a different hand, thickened with baby fat reaching towards her.

Magic loosened from her like a tear in a seam. It trickled out and Aza's only thought was to leave this house, so she wouldn't put Anwin's family in danger.

Dizzy, she crashed into the front door and vaguely heard Reed call out from a distance, "Get Nivet."

Free from the confines of Anwin's house, Aza ran, racing away from the destructive tendencies of her magic, the loss of control. Too many images fought for dominance and her vision grew so blurry, she only knew the cold bite of snow as she sank to her knees in defeat. She clutched her head and gave an animalistic groan, fighting to keep her magic in check, to keep it restrained.

Strong hands gripped her arms and suddenly she was weightless, transported to an empty clearing on the mountain.

A faraway voice said, "Let go."

Aza obeyed.

Instead of her body seizing and shutting down, it erupted. Magic burst from her in an angry blast, the very earth quaking. Around her, ice morphed from different stages, hardening, softening, melting, turning into a tornado of water whipping around her form. Light meant to pierce, meant to blind, shined through the chaos. Darkness bled from her body, the soft, smoky form whipped into an elemental tornado. A cocoon.

Trauma bled from her body in each elemental form, wanting to lash out, wanting to hurt. She screamed, but it was fruitless, the scream falling into the whiplash of her magic.

Her throat was raw, her face wet from constant tears and still her body had not given enough. Still her endless magic obliterated her surroundings, where she was crouched, her head pounding in fury, in frustration, knowing that whatever she did, it would not change the past and would not change the memories that collided unbidden into her thoughts. She was a mere witness. The trauma that *She* experienced was embedded into her body, her soul. Aza wanted to shatter from the brutal duality of her nature.

Aza was both; herself and Her.

Time moved slowly, as every scraping breath of pain tore at her throat, as every tear carved a torturous path down her face.

The magic abated.

Nivet stood patiently across from her, his steadfast silhouette dusted with falling snow. She ignored the stiffness of her legs as she rose and sprinted towards him, to the only salvation around. Only he would truly understand.

She ignored the pulse of his magic and wrapped her arms around him, sobbing. "The child. There was a child. She had a child." A heart-rending cry ripped from her throat again, the emotions threatening to drown her, but the surety of his arm kept her in place.

"She did," Nivet said. It was his only response, his own voice thick with emotion.

Aza knew that Nivet understood. Aza was not referring to Anwin, she was referring to Her.

~

The cliff ledge jutted daringly over the expanse of empty sky overlooking the giant trees of Gara. Aza kicked snow off the edge, watching it fall to the ground far below. She asked to be brought here. She remembered this vision when she was still sequestered in the El'en palace. Sitting across from a man, their legs dangling preciously over the ledge looking upon these giant trees. The world seemed both extremely large and extremely small.

Upon her explanation, Nivet shadowed her to this place—the Ocean of Trees, it was named because of the current of trees blurred together like an endless wave, undulating on hills.

Yesterday, during their lessons Aza caught herself staring at Nivet and her lips moved of her own accord. "It's time, isn't it?"

Nivet lips thinned, and he nodded. "It is."

Any longer would be toying with the time that was already given to her. She was able to experience El'theren, she was allowed extra time with her friends to fall asleep in their houses, to hear the far-off chatter of Anwin's children squealing, or River aimlessly braiding her hair. These small moments amounted to extra time, and she could not steal more, not now.

"My spies have told me; Astaroth is on the move and the Hinterlands are growing increasingly unstable. You have learned enough. You will be able to banish the Hinterlands." Nivet stood and offered his hand. Aza had grown used to the feel of his magic, the comfort it provided. She clasped her hand in his and they went to say good-bye.

They met Xira, Reed, and Anwin at the Bladed Beauty. At their gathering her friends already knew what they were going to announce. No tears marred their faces. But Aza heard the hitch in their breath as they each hugged her, whispering good-bye and good luck. She saw the tightness at the corners of their eyes, the rigid way they moved their bodies. They were trying to not make this more difficult than necessary.

Aza memorized each of their faces, carving their mannerism onto her heart. Even without their presence, they would be with her.

"Nivet," Xira, Reed, and Anwin announced. They each encircled Aza, staring across at Nivet. "I entrust you with, Lady Aza of the Well. She is yours to protect, cherish, and honor is our absence. Do you promise this vow as long as our hearts beat in our chests?"

Nivet pulled his fist up to his heart and bowed, reciting, "I vow to protect, cherish, and honor Lady Aza of the Well in your absence."

Tears welled in Aza's eyes, but she did not let them fall. This was not a permanent goodbye. She would be able to return to this place, to this time. This was not the end.

They departed, and Aza did not let herself forget the image of her Nerian friends, standing firm and waving goodbye.

~

As they were exiting, a voice cut through Aza's clouded haze of thoughts. A voice she had not heard in months.

"Nivet, I wish to speak to Aza alone." Lady Sola cut a striking figure amongst the crowded streets of El'theren, her back straightened, gaze piercing like a sharpened sword.

Nivet looked between the two women and nodded, gesturing Aza follow Lady Sola.

Lady Sola watched Aza walk to her. Each step felt like a judgment, the proud curve of her cheek, the jut of her chin, her shorn hair, the short curls revealing the swirled tattoo, an exact replica of the tattoo on her son's head.

Aza matched her pace as they walked in silence away from the heart of El'theren. People bowed their head in deference as Lady Sola passed. Although stern, she clearly held a love for her people as she gratefully acknowledged each person with equal respect.

They emerged on a secluded outcropping of the mountain away from the bustle of the city and the clustered buildings.

Lady Sola turned and interlaced her fingers together holding them in front of her body. "So, it is time."

"It is," Aza replied.

Lady Sola's features wavered with her inner turmoil, her stern demeanor softening slightly on the edges, with what Aza construed as regret.

"The citizens of Neria are taught the true history of Ithilia, history the rest of the five provinces have decided to ignore. Long ago, the other provinces collectively agreed to ignore the tragedies of the past and live in ignorance. Neria stood alone. They did not want to forget the sacrifice and the tragedy that occurred. It is easy to turn a blind eye to discomfort, but our Nerian ancestors were not weak like the other provinces, and they meet their pain head on." Lady Sola looked out over the expanse of the mountains, in deep consideration of the snow that coated the mountains and the dense clouds overhead.

"Nivet, while an unfortunate necessity, has kept the knowledge of what happened one thousand years ago alive. He does not let us forget and he urges us to remember our history."

While Aza listened, she forced herself to keep a neutral expression, to not reveal her inner thoughts. However, her eyes widened at the subtle praise of Nivet.

"I can see your shock. You believe I hate Nivet." Lady Sola sighed and placed a hand against her brow. It shook, and soon was wiped away. "Some days I do. He has erased any semblance of my son and all I see is a walking shell of the boy I had birthed and raised. My radiant boy, now a man, doomed to inhabit a god. It is not fair. But I am conflicted. Nivet is aiming for the good of Neria, and even I am not blind enough in my rage to see that clearly." She turned sharply away from Aza and planted her hands on the wooden railing. Aza joined her.

"I fear no matter what you have learned and experienced here in Neria will not matter in the face of what you will confront. I have heard reports of your 'episodes', but nothing will compare to the devastation of what you are about to do. As rulers we are told the story, the sacrifice." She quieted and stared at the sky, her stiff spine melting against the railing, her gaze grew contemplative.

"I am ready," Aza answered.

The softness of Lady Sola hardened once more as her head whipped to look at Aza. "I don't think anyone will be ready for such a thing."

Her tone softened, and her hand snaked out to grip Aza's in solidarity. "However, I do not envy your task. All of Neria, all of Ithilia will be in your debt." Quick like the swipe of a tiger's paw, she removed her hand like it was never there, straightened her spine and left.

Aza remained on the outcropping, savoring the last few picturesque views of Neria, storing them like a vault of precious jewels, sealing these feelings, these images away for when she would need them most.

After delaying, Aza walked down the mountain, found Nivet, and they shadowed to their dragons for one last ride.

~

The dragons sensed what was happening before Aza told Druilinn. The ancient dragon stiffened at the news and then swept her elegant, leathery wing around Aza, protectively wrapping. She would not cry. This was not the end. This was merely the start of another beginning. This would not be the last time she embraced Druilinn, the silent companionship they provided each other. The breathtaking views she had experienced, the feeling of freedom was first achieved upon Isarr and Druilinn's spiky back.

Linor, Druilinn and Isarr's son, crept away from the safety of their cave. Whenever they met the dragons for their morning ritual of riding and practicing, she would leave Linor to his privacy, shooting him shy waves as his mother pushed off the ground and flew away. Aza caught the fascination in his face as he watched them spin and dive freely through the sky. He was still too young to attempt flying, his wings underdeveloped for the size of his body, but he watched, and his skittish behavior softened day by day.

Aza relaxed her head against Druilinn's neck, embracing the warmth, her familiar smell like burnt hickory wood, and the crisp mountain air. Her breath bobbed in and out and too soon Aza pulled away. She could not stay here like this forever. Nivet stood patiently next to Isarr, his brilliant color glistening. Although her connection to Druilinn was stronger, Isarr had still been here for her, supported her, and displayed tremendous patience. She gave a faint smile as she walked over to him. He lowered his head in permission, and she dropped her forehead to his, eyes closed.

"Thank you, Isarr."

You are brave, my Lady.

Aza snorted. "I am nothing of the sort."

Flashes of images were planted into her mind. Her spars with Nivet, her plummet off Druilinn's back. Small moments captured through Isarr's eyes, with Aza fierce, holding her own against Nivet, grim determination set in the line of her jaw and the firm set of her mouth.

The dragon did not view her as weak or feeble. Isarr saw the strength and resolve that dwelled within, hardened like a jewel under pressure and found it to be brilliant. A radiant light for others to bask in.

You are something new, made from parts of Her, yes but also parts of yourself. Unique and wholly your own. Do not diminish your fire. Isarr pulled back and pierced her with a sapphire eye.

Aza gave a slight nod and looked over her shoulder at Druilinn. Linor was positioned in between his mother's massive forelegs, his head cocked in curiosity.

His innocent, slate gray eyes swirled like shifting fog over the mountains. He took a tentative step forward and Aza matched his movement. They had never interacted before, besides the stray waves she sent his way, but he marched with dogged determination towards her. She would not fear an episode in his presence.

They carved two paths through the snow. Meeting in the middle, Aza crouched before the offspring of Druilinn and Isarr, his small, gangly body still growing, but Aza saw the strong lines of muscle developing, the leathery wings underdeveloped, but soon with time would be as graceful as either his mother or father.

"You take care of your mom and dad. I will be back."

Linor nodded, a serious expression on his face. His soft, young voice sprang into her mind in a chaotic manner. *Silver lady, silver lady. Do not leave us. We will miss you. Silver lady. Silver lady. You look like me and your skin looks like my Mama's.*

Aza laughed, the sound ringing out among the mountains. The pure chaos of his ramblings was so reminiscent of Anwin's young children and despite being different species, their young were the same.

"Sweet Linor, I will be back." Aza reached out a hand, waiting. Linor closed the gap and pushed his face into her hand, releasing a huff of sparks from his mouth.

Silver lady, he whispered.

She could not let this one dismantle her emotions.

Breaking the connection, she stood, and strode back to Druilinn. She lowered herself to the ground so Aza could easily climb up to seat herself between the spiky ridges of her back.

Nivet made to copy on Isarr when Aza shouted out, "No leave Isarr. Someone must stay to protect Linor. Ride with me, Nivet."

Aza whispered to Druillinn, "As long as it is okay with you."

The dragon snorted and responded *I have no issues with him.*

Nivet spoke in low tones to Isarr, Aza was too far away to decipher what was said, but soon Nivet jogged over to Druilinn and effortlessly climbed onto her back seated behind Aza.

"Fly, Druilinn."

The lift off from the ground was one of Aza's favorite parts of flying. It was the beginning, the anticipation of soaring to great heights, with her stomach in her throat. Druilinn bent her strong legs and pushed off from the snow-covered mountain, white flecks of snow bursting from her force.

Isarr and Linor narrowed to little specks on the ground, but Aza would not forget Linor's eager voice repeating, *Silver lady.*

She hoped her promise was true, that it was not a lie. She would return. Banishing the Hinterlands would not break her.

52

"I can feel it in the wind. Something is changing, shifting, and I am ready."
Cruvo's private journal

Lorn's body was left to the ground. The rain, the mud swallowing him. He was returning to the earth. His mind should have registered the cold, the needle raindrops that seared his skin, the tenderness of his body, sapped of its strength, his magic dissipated.

He was both present and not, his mind trying to salvage what meager scraps of energy were left. There was only cold, only darkness, only the savage, mourning cries that echoed throughout his soul. How he craved to end it. He had saved the young woman, the woman who now cried with a rending heartache no one else could cure. Was saving her worth it, if she was thrust into the savage throes of grief? Why was he still alive?

Vaguely through a thick fog, he remembered promising someone to try, to persevere. But that seemed a silly promise when he could not even move his body, his mind fractured like shards of glass. There were brilliant pieces, but to reassemble the glass into something beautiful and working would take time and effort—too much effort.

~

A strange stillness settled, and birds flocked overhead. Their black silhouettes seemed never-ending as they fled.

The ground quaked. Lorn's body was unresponsive as he attempted to sit upright. His muscles, the very sinew of his body declined his attempt. His body was thrown with the rough movements, each jolt causing acute pain. Trees trembled, the screech of distressed animals filled his ears. The earth rumbled, and Lorn endured.

The violent vibrations grew and grew until Lorn feared his body would break. Finally, it ceased and a giant boom cleaved the air.

The tiny kindling of lifeforce that remained in his body was snuffed out. The rumbling of the earth was too much to endure, and he closed his eyes in resignation and acceptance. He had held on longer than he thought was possible.

Lorn wished to see Aza one final time, to say goodbye to his friend.

53

"There is no room for doubt. I do not doubt the appearance of the sun over the horizon. I do not doubt the blanket of night covering El'theren in darkness, nor the brilliant stars to emerge. I do not doubt Aza and her ability to banish the Hinterlands. I am not allowed doubt, but I am allowed fear."
Nivet's private journal.

Druilinn landed on the outskirts of the Hinterlands, clear of any towns. It was abandoned, most unwilling to live in such close proximity. Oppressive energy, the reek of death and despair, weighed heavily on her shoulders. She had forgotten the suffocating feeling of the Hinterlands, how the very land seemed poisoned, the flora and fauna twisted into grotesque shapes, the moss choking the trees, the leaves blocking any light.

But despite the despair, a thread pulled her forward, insistently yanking her towards a destiny she must fulfill.

Words were not required as Aza clasped Druilinn one final time. The tears that threatened to drop lingered, but Aza forced them back. She had not cried yet. She would not yield now.

Nivet, ever stoic, peered nervously beyond Aza's shoulder at the Hinterlands. Its existence caused him to be on edge. He steadied his breath and winced. Was the proximity to the Hinterlands causing him pain? His magic vibrated, the pulse resonating in Aza's head.

She ignored the growing pain and stood awkwardly unsure of how to say goodbye. Their own Fates were interwoven in strange ways. The initial kidnapping and frustration she felt towards him, the devastation of his loss, paired with the reunion, the patience he demonstrated with her training, the respectful distance he maintained. She ignored the ever-pulling lure of his magical signature and focused on who he was as a god. Solemn, kind, well-meaning.

He closed the distance between them and embraced her.

She was stiff, surprised at his sudden display of emotion, and like ice thawing, her arms moved of their own accord as she wrapped her arms around him. The tension between them had drawn taut, another thread pulled tight, but she squashed the desire and only embraced him as a friend.

He was her friend. He could never be anything more.

Slowly, she let her head fall onto his sturdy shoulder, breathing in the intoxicating scent of worn leather, the crisp mountain air, and the faint scent of Druilinn.

"You are strong, powerful, kind. I won't even begin to fathom what you will face in there, but you can do it. You have learned. You understand *who* you came from, *what* you are. But you are more than that. You are Aza of the Well. You are Aza of Neria. You are more than the small pieces that make up your creation." Nivet whispered the words fiercely into her ear, feeding her soul, dismissing her doubts. He held her closely, like he would lose her permanently if he let go.

There was no more time to delay, and they both pulled away from each other. Nivet gripped her upper arms tightly. "You will transcend, all of us. You are more than everything in this world."

The nerves in her belly finally loosened, the snakes writhing. Nivet, everyone, had such faith in her—she could not let them down.

The edges of their magic danced around each other, chasing one another like playful dogs bounding after one another. She had resisted this long, but with his powerful words and his golden eyes looking at her like she was the only thing that mattered in this world and the next, she could not combat it any longer.

Aza reached a hand to his cheek, wishing she did not see the face of Rune. She did not want to be reminded of this harsh reality that Nivet had forced someone to be his host.

"I would like to see you. One last time."

Understanding what she was asking, he nodded, and Aza used the amplification of her magic to strip away Rune's handsome face and in its place was Nivet. The skin softened to its taupe color, the nose becoming more prominent, his black hair flowed loosely down his back. Golden eyes swirled at her, captivating, entrancing.

The bow of his lips was too tempting to ignore.

She kept the connection of her hand on his cheek. An irresistible force pulled them closer, her face so close to his she could see flecks of gold woven into his skin. Their breath flowed between each other's, the distance between them inconsequential. All it would take would be a gentle sway and their lips would brush.

The swell of their combined magic was overwhelming and Aza wanted to lean forward, to find comfort with the other god who understood her and understood her plight.

His eyes held a question and she felt herself moving until she remembered Hakim. She placed her hand on his chest as a barrier and pushed away, gently but firmly.

"It would be a betrayal to Hakim. You are not in your own body. Rune belongs to him."

The illusion of Nivet melted away. He looked away sharply and nodded.

"We will wait for you. Always."

Aza allowed herself one last indulgence, another minute with Nivet. He met her gaze and held it, words unnecessary any longer. With a firm nod, she turned on her heels, leaving Druilinn and Nivet behind, leaving her new life behind.

She entered the unknown.

~

The boundaries of the Hinterlands swallowed light and noise. She walked far enough into its depths that the images of Druilinn and Nivet were gone. She moved soundlessly through the forest, unsure of what should happen next. She needed to find Her, but how to reach Her?

Aza cleared her mind and focused on her intention. *Banish the Hinterlands.* She repeated it again and again, forcing the other memories away.

She startled, stifling a scream. Along the rugged path, deformed creatures sat on each side.

She readied her magic, but the beasts did not move. They warily eyed her as if they were patiently waiting. Aza took a tentative step. The beasts remained. Every form of creature waited, their bodies preternaturally still. She stepped again. Still nothing. Multitudes of creatures were sitting and watching her—distorted forms of bats, wolves, mountain lions, bears, birds, and more. They gathered on either side of the path like they were attending a funeral procession.

Aza quelled her magic, firmed her back, and walked through the hordes of creatures. They remained unmoving. At the end of the path, there she was—the woman of the Hinterlands. Even from Aza's distance, she could make out the shadows that licked at her feet, ever-shifting, restless.

Luminescent eyes of yellow and red tracked Aza as she made her way to the woman of the Hinterlands. Aza firmed her back and took deliberate step after step, never letting her gaze drift.

The silence was profound. Aza's heartbeat pounded. She kept her intention pure. Her mind wanted to dart in different directions, but she cleared it, a still lake, with no ripples marring the surface. There was only Aza and Her. The forest melted away as Aza's sight narrowed on the woman.

There you are, she thought. *Do not be afraid.* It was a sentiment for both of them.

Closer and closer Aza stepped until she was within reach.

The woman's sharp, angular face appraised Aza. Geometric tattoos graced her face. Tattoos for a Nerian.

In a dream-like state, Aza's hand reached forward of its own volition, cupped the woman's face, and brought their foreheads together, like Nerians greeting after a time apart. It felt natural.

The woman was stiff, but she still let Aza move her willingly.

Aza spoke. "I am here to help you. You do not have to suffer any longer." She repeated Nivet's words to her, the simple command. "Let go."

The woman shivered and loosened a long breath. "As you wish."

The shadows that swirled about her feet grew, engulfing them in darkness. The creatures screeched, howled, and raged as their mistress unleashed her power.

Aza tightened her grip, holding onto the woman who had created the Hinterlands, the woman whose unending chasm of trauma had ruptured, creating this monstrosity. A piece of her was in Aza and Aza would not relent. She was here to heal. She was here to succumb.

Pain radiated through her body, through every muscle, sinew, and bone. Into the very essence of her soul. She did not let go. She did not yield. The Nerians had taught her endurance, pain, resilience. She utilized all three of those tenets as she held tightly to the woman, their foreheads locked in concentration.

She would not relent.

Shadows and suffering devoured her.

Aza shattered.

54

I should not exist, but here I am. I am not granted rest in the Meadows of the Undying. I am not graced to be with my family, their souls departed, waiting for me. Instead, this damned forest is my home, my prison. These ideas are fleeting. Thoughts, rationale, everything that used to make up my mind has vanished. All I know is unending rage. My twisted creations, the creatures of the Hinterlands are my only company.

Time carves itself violently into my flesh and my mind. Memories and moments vanish entirely. Days and months disappear like they never existed.

I am a specter forced to haunt this land. I do not require sustenance, warmth. I am now relieved of everything from my past life that I considered a burden, however it is not relief. It is torture. But I do not dwell on it long, because my mind forgets. During times of clarity, when I recall who I am and what I have done, I cling to it desperately like a person embedding their nails into a cliff face afraid to fall into fathomless depths.

People enter my borders, but they die, either from my creatures or from the madness—madness I am forced to endure.

Until I encounter a man. He seems…familiar. I cannot place him, but his sorrow resonates with my own. Intrigued, I follow him as he traverses my boundaries. I cannot find it within me to hurt him like I have the others, his very presence, his magical signature like the call of a long-lost friend.

Save me! A voice inside me wants to scream. I stay my hand from the violence I so desperately crave. It takes immense effort, but a blinding clarity pierces through me when he is near. So I wait. And I watch.

~

The strange man has killed one of my creatures. My hand shakes with fury as I clutch the sword. This creature of my creation did not deserve such a brutal death. Red overtakes my vision. The familiar call to hurt, to kill, pulses through me in a vicious drumbeat. It takes everything within me to stay my hand from stabbing the sword through his throat, letting the blood coat the earth. But as I near, the clarity of my mind returns.

He is important.

I shadow away.

~

The man is in danger. I do not know why I came to rescue him, but he requires it. I cannot stand to see him in pain, blood dripping down his face, his resigned expression ready to die. He cannot die yet. I will not allow it. I call back the creatures; they are only trying to protect my borders. They are bound to me.

I do not help him beyond this. If he is as strong of mind and body as I believe, he will survive. If not, then it matters not to me.

~

I feel...different. Like I am not wholly myself anymore. I miss the man who was here in the Hinterlands. He and the woman left. Curiosity got the better of me and I wanted to see her. She was so intriguing. But our proximity felt poisonous, off. Like a discordant string being plucked in a haunted ballad. I could not stand our nearness—of how I began to feel. I left and so did they.

I miss them.

~

I cannot control my borders. My forest is ravenous, devouring neighboring towns. I hear the cries of the people as my beasts merely follow their orders. I try to hold it together, to maintain my magic, but it does not listen to me anymore. I am fractured. The forest knows of my growing weakness and capitalizes.

~

From a vast distance, someone calls to me. But I am drowning. In despair, in hopelessness. She resonates. She is familiar too. I try to greet her, but the sorrow is too much and pulls me back. Like a knife through flesh, she cuts the burdensome darkness, freeing me momentarily. She greets me softly, calling to me, and I obey.

I have overtaken her body. And He is there. The small semblance of control cracks and fractures. He should be thrown to a void, where not even the wind can caress his face. Wishing a fiery pit of death is too good for him, because he would still be able to feel the heat on his face as he is burned alive. He deserves to be nothing, feel nothing, to be absent from this world. He deserves to not feel at all, just as I have. How could she do something like this? Align herself with Him? I care not. All I care about is vengeance.

~

Although I would argue my mind has been cleaved, my psyche absent, now I truly feel it. Days have little meaning. My forest and creatures do not obey me. A sickness pervades and I am helpless. I wish to be gone. My family waits for me in the Meadows of the Undying and I cannot join. Their faces are difficult to discern, their images blurred. My mind is finally broken where I cannot imagine the warmth of their embrace, the slash of their smiles, the pealing ring of their laughter.

~

Her familiar presence rings on the outside of my forest, like a siren's call. It is a splash of water over my confusion, providing the clarity that I so desperately crave. She is the sun—her power radiating, warming, consoling.

Even my beasts eagerly await her return in two lines formed along the path she walks, like they are greeting royalty.

But in her presence, comes a wash of emotions, feelings, memories. They are too much. My body freezes and I can only watch as she navigates my forest. Can she feel it? How the creatures, the trees, the magic bows to her as it bows to me.

My shadows underfoot are restless like I am. She is gentle, far gentler than anyone should be with me and what I have done.

Her touch is kindling to the fire of my soul and a spark ignites between us.

I understand it now. My soul has been split. A part of me resides in her. She is merely returning it. I relax in her sure grip, our foreheads meeting together. I have not been greeted like this in so long and my memories surge forth. I cannot let her be overwhelmed by my magic. If I do, it will kill her. So I withhold.

But she has other plans. She commands, "Let go."

Those two simple words are my undoing. I obey.

The shadows, the suffering, the pain, the agony, every feeling that has been my companion during these dark days is unleashed upon me and upon her.

I fracture.

55

"It is with my own hand I write this. I did not think the day would come."
Cruvo's private journal

Piercing blue eyes stare at him. Tendrils of white-blonde hair blow in the wind. "Lorn of Verta. You will not succumb to death. You are still needed. Rise."

Lorn blinked repeatedly. This was just another dream. Issi stood over him, her pale skin carved from marble, glinting in the light of dawn.

He flexed his hands, his fingers obeying the simple command. The unending pain and agony were gone, wiped clean as if it had never happened. He stood expecting shaky legs, expecting resistance. But the pain was truly gone. He examined his fingers, turning them over back and forth. This was a well-crafted dream.

"This is real, hunter," Issi said.

"Then—," Lorn began and paused. His mind was whirring, with reasons, conclusions. "Aza has banished the Hinterlands," he whispered reverently. "She did it."

"There will be time to explain later, but now we need to get to safety."

Lorn searched the vast clearing. Pearl and Lady Rasmina were not there.

"Come, hunter. There can be no delay." Issi beckoned him forward.

Only now, with his senses returned, did he realize Issi's magic surged from her body in erratic pulses, the force crushing.

With no other direction to go, no understanding of what would come next, Lorn joined the goddess.

The clearing trembled, in anticipation of war.

56

Hall of Prophecies Record Entry by Roan of Kreeha

I have diligently spent my life researching this topic. This topic has plagued my existence. However, the research is sparse. I have traveled far and wide, compiled decades of prophecies to come to this conclusion.

Please see my annotations located at the bottom of the article for specific references to texts and prophecies.

I have been told countless times by many scholars to abandon my research. It was viewed as folly and a pointless venture. I disagree.

How Ithilia operates, our knowledge of magic, is like that of an acorn compared to the entirety of the trees. What I want are the roots. I want to know what secrets lie beneath that rich soil, the ecosystem that operates below.

From what I have gathered, roughly one thousand years ago, a cataclysmic event happened—the formation of the Hinterlands. But what caused the Hinterlands? What was life like before that formidable forest appeared?

The records from before that time are unclear, almost like all information had been wiped out, removed, burned from existence. How I wish I could access the secluded mountains of Neria! I believe the knowledge held there could unlock the secrets that hound me day and night. But for now, I will lay my speculations on this paper and see if the truth rings clear, like the purest tone of a bell.

The gods and goddesses ruled Ithilia before the creation of the Well.

Why are they not present today? What happened? The Hinterlands was created and they were banished from their physical forms, doomed to existence amongst the ether.

But what caused the Hinterlands? Why did it form and why did it banish the gods and goddesses as a result of its formation?

I searched endlessly for a whisper of information. Finally, I discovered the name, Saiha. She was the foretold, from long ago, destined to bring about darkness, and destruction. I think the prophecy remnants I found were mistranslated. Oftentimes, the prophecies are transcribed in a fantastical format, utilizing prose, and delicate words and the meanings can be deciphered in a variety of ways.

With the name Saiha, I researched diligently, praying for a scrap of information like a wolf on the prowl for scraps. I think her prophesied entrance only led to disaster and she has a tragic story. Somehow, her power manifested into the Hinterlands. I am unclear as to what transpired in history, but this is my best assumption.

However, what I want to focus on is not the creation of the Hinterlands, rather the coming of something new. Due to the prophecy given by Ulmina of Iyera, I believe a new being will be formed from the Well. She will be part Goddess, but part something else. Since Saiha was a cornerstone for creating the Hinterlands, I believe a part of her essence, her spirit will reside in this new being. This new creation, will be a manifestation of both Goddess and Saiha. Her powers will be unlike anything we have ever witnessed.

My further conclusion is that with this newly created person, the Hinterlands will begin to destabilize. The absence of whatever part of Saiha is imbued into this new creation will cause a disruption and the Hinterlands will either collapse or expand into its surroundings.

To provide stability, the new Goddess/Saiha hybrid will need to meet Saiha within the Hinterlands and be a solid foundation for Saiha to finally let go.

What will this mean for the new Goddess/Saiha hybrid? I'm unsure. I hope for all of Ithilia's sake she survives.

The seismic energy involved for such a release could devastate Ithilia. On top of that, with the Hinterlands banished, I predict the gods and goddesses will return to their physical forms.

These long-winded ramblings will be kept hidden within the Hall of

Prophecies. I do not know who will believe them or if people will use them for their own ill-gain. I would pray to the gods and goddesses for mercy, but if my prior records indicate correctly, they will not grant me any.

Instead, I pray to myself.

Acknowledgements

This story would never have been possible without the support and help of my family and friends. I deeply appreciate each and every one of you who have supported me during this journey. Whether from discussing potential plot lines, pronunciation of character names, or just listening to me ramble, you are the reason I am able to create.

A special shout-out to my husband, who is constantly talking me off a creative ledge and is able to ground me when I get too caught up in the daily minutia of balancing my day job with my creative pursuits.

Also, to my daughter, who I hope one day sees a true representation of what it means to a strong woman. It is not only a physical strength, it is the ability to form friendships, to be silly, to be able to cry, to rely on others. Surrounding yourself with family and friends who uplift you is not a weakness; it is your greatest strength.

And finally, thank you to my parents. This may not be your preferred genre to read, but your endless support and love allows me to unleash my creativity into this fantasy world.

To all readers, we have precious free time and a never-ending TBR. I am especially humbled and grateful for you taking the time to read my book. Thank you!

Author portrait by cloudycitrus
@cloudy.citrus

A.N. Fox is a schoolteacher who writes fantasy in her spare time. She lives in California with her husband, daughter, dog, and her three cats. For fun you can find her playing board games, reading fantasy novels, or binge-watching anime. Transcend is her second novel.